THE JA
CHRONICLES

ACROSS THE UNIVERSE

BY CAELI ENNIS
Illustrations by Claire McDonald

Printed in the United States of America

ISBN: 978-1-956019-50-6 (hardcover)
ISBN: 978-1-956019-51-3 (paperback)
ISBN: 978-1-956019-52-0 (ebook)

Canoe Tree Press

4697 Main Street
Manchester Center, VT 05255
Canoe Tree Press is a division of DartFrog Books

For Grandma Peg and Grandpa Al, the original writers of the McDonald family. Also for Mrs. Marable, who always viewed one's differences as their greatest strengths.

In whichever dimension of the space-time continuum you all reside, I wish you everlasting peace and joy.

"Differences of habit and language are nothing at all if our aims are identical and our hearts are open."
—*Albus Dumbledore*, Harry Potter and the Goblet of Fire *by J.K. Rowling*

THE JALOPY CHRONICLES

Book 1: Across the Universe

Contents

THE UNIVERSAL UNION

The horrifying visions of fiery volcanoes and the sounds of explosions quickly transformed into the greyness of a ceiling and complete silence. Every time the president opened his eyes after a night's sleep, the nightmares shifted into his terrifying reality.

His mind started to race once he realised he was officially awake, as it always did. This wasn't part of the job description. He couldn't be in charge of a decision of this magnitude and come out of it successfully. There was too much weight on his shoulders, and he could feel his breath amplifying into hyperventilating gasps. Within a few minutes, his breathing regulated back to the normal inhale, exhale pattern. This was the usual schedule of morning events. The panic usually lasted for a few minutes, and then he'd manage to regain feeling in his body and work his way out of bed.

This morning, the president opened his bedroom door. There in the hall, a delicious breakfast, a pot of black coffee with an empty mug, a clear glass filled with an orange goo, and a printed-out agenda awaited him on a silvery tray. He noticed his reflection in the tray as he picked it up with his shaking hands and froze to analyse the view in front of him. His green eyes were sullen and bloodshot. A patch of grey hair even caught his attention. Bony features protruded. He was not the same man who had entered the office eight years ago—the handsome one with vibrantly glowing, dark skin, thick black locks of curly hair, and somewhat thicker features. He shook himself out of the nightmarish trance, carried the tray inside the room, and shut the door behind him. He placed the contents on the tray in their usual position on his desk: agenda off to the left, breakfast and coffee pot pushed to the far-right corner, and coffee cup placed directly in front of him, which he filled half with coffee and half with the orange goo. He didn't exactly know what the orange goo was, or even who was regularly equipping him with it. He only knew that it calmed him down and happily digested without question. Its only drawback was its pungency, which caused him to wrinkle his nose as he stirred the drink with his pinky finger until it completely dissolved. After taking a few gulps, he peered in the direction of his agenda:

Saturday 22 April 2220
6:00 a.m. Breakfast served in dormitory
8:00 a.m. Daily United States of America press conference in the Flag Lounge
11:30 a.m. Lunch with Universal Union in Danforth Commons
3:00 p.m. Earth Day celebration press conference with the United Nations and the Earth Rehabilitation Association in the Green House
5:00 p.m. Dinner served in dormitory

The president chuckled to himself at the Earth Day celebration to be taking place at three p.m. It was such a lie. Why celebrate a planet that would soon be uninhabitable? But that wasn't public knowledge yet. He wondered if the Universal Union would come to a decision today—any decision, something that would make him feel less of a conductor driving the public to their impending deaths. A feeling inside him hoped the Universal Union would help him, much to the dismay of everyone in his circle.

A knock at the door startled him. He rushed to open it after taking one last gulp of his morning beverage and found an empty hallway, save for another tray waiting for him with an earth-coloured suit folded gently on top.

Once dressed in his predetermined suit for Earth Day, the president made his way to the Flag Lounge, where only a podium with a microphone and a backdrop with the seal of the United States of America awaited his arrival. The rest of the room was dimly lit and dusty. Flags of the world were all strewn about the room, having fallen from their mounts on the ceiling. No one except the president ever came in here anymore, so it was not well maintained.

The president stood lifelessly behind the podium while glancing at his watch. It was nearly time. He knew the drill: Read the speech, smile, and walk off.

A screen turned on in front of him and displayed a digital countdown. *2:00 . . . 1:59 . . . 1:58 . . .* He stepped off the podium and paced around the musty room. *0:48 . . . 0:47 . . . 0:46 . . .* The president grumbled as he noticed that he had accidentally spilled a bit of hybrid coffee on his white shirt. He pulled the lapel of his suit tighter over the exposed area. *0:19 . . . 0:18 . . . 0:17 . . .* He walked to the podium, stretched his neck, and took a few deep breaths. *0:02 . . . 0:01 . . . 0:00.* A small light appeared above the *"0:00,"* signifying his camera to which thousands of pairs of eyes and ears were now affixed. His heart started to hammer. The usual triumphant trumpet melody started, and a monotonous deep voice introduced him.

"And now, the daily update from the President of the United States of America."

He cleared his throat and put on the smile that won him the election nearly eight years ago. His eyes met the pre-written speech displaying on the screen.

"Good morning, my beautiful country. Happy twenty-second of April, better known as Earth Day." He clasped his hands in front of him. "Even though the current climate does not allow for life to be exposed to the outside, this does not mean we cannot love our planet for the safe"—he emphasised the word—"and reliable home that it provides to many thousands of inhabitants. I encourage each of you to open an old book and bask in the beauty that the Earth once offered to its previous residents.

"Earth is rebuilding its foundations piece by piece. Soon enough, we will be able to go outside again. Humanity can begin to repopulate and prosper. We have lost too many lives—over ten billion—because of accidental breaches of the environment. Once we regain control, we will be able to grow plants, fruits, and vegetables in gardens. Nutrients can come from more than the artificial food reserved in our pantries. We will re-engineer oceans to restore marine life. The air will be safe to breathe. We are almost there.

"In order to accomplish and streamline these exciting rehabilitation efforts, we will introduce revenue enhancements for all United States citizens to support the ERA, the Earth Rehabilitation Association, in hopes that those extra dollars will lead us to the success we've all been waiting for. The wait is almost over. Please tune in to the United Nations press conference later today at three o'clock Eastern Standard Time. Leaders around this beautiful planet will be celebrating their favourite extinct species of plants and wildlife. Have a wonderful day, and I look forward to seeing you all basking in the sunshine very soon."

The president's smile flashed confidently. He continued to stand firmly on the podium, smiling broadly, until the camera light and teleprompter switched off. He suddenly felt very alone again. The silence was overwhelmingly loud as he coursed back to his dormitory.

After another nightmare-filled nap and the remainder of the coffee and orange goo combo, the president changed his white shirt to a less coffee-stained one and re-slicked his hair back so the greys weren't as freely flowing. He headed back out of his dormitory around quarter past eleven a.m. and found his way to the nearest staircase. As he descended one floor, his stomach began tying itself in knots. He needed more orange goo to comfort himself for what was about to come. The Universal Union was a difficult bunch of beings to compromise with. Composed of representatives from across the universe, the Universal Union convened on one of the delegates' home planets once every 19.438 Earth days to discuss the universal issues. Time had different meanings for every planet in the group, and the equivalent of 19.438 Earth days was the frequency chosen that made most sense for the delegates' schedules. The main topic as of late was the state of Earth and whether action ought to be taken. The president himself nobly accepted his nomination as Earth's delegate, but he'd heard rumours about his predecessor having unfortunately been squashed by another, much larger delegate—on accident, of course—which made him slightly concerned for his wellbeing.

The president approached the door to Danforth Commons, his heart beating so quickly that he began to feel lightheaded. He knew he had to defy the wishes of the Earth Rehabilitation Association. There was just . . . something inside of him telling him it was the right decision. He couldn't place the feeling; it was almost as if his body were making the decision for him. He knew there would be repercussions, but he was willing to make the sacrifice. He was more terrified of asking for intergalactic help from the Universal Union. They petrified him to his very core.

Ahead of him were two doors with D-shaped brass handles. He grabbed both handles firmly and pulled them open in one smooth movement. Walking in, he wore his famous flashy smile amid his fluttering heartbeats.

"Welcome to the White House, fellow delegates. I hope your travels were uneventful."

The room was filled with the most diverse set of beasts that anyone could imagine laying eyes on. There were many thousands of delegates in the Universal Union, but only about one hundred could cram into the largest room in the White House. The number of delegates in the group fluctuated quite a bit, primarily because of common incidents such as the squashed Earth delegate, and also because of many populations' unwillingness to participate, extinctions, new communities forming, and inability to communicate, among other reasons. These delegates were from all populations across the universe. They ranged from the size of an electron all the way up to the size of a skyscraper (the largest beings couldn't be accommodated in the White House, for obvious reasons). Some beings could float, unaffected by gravity, while others would disintegrate from too high a gravitational force (again, obvious reasons for not attending). Some beings were all colours of the rainbow, and others were invisible. Some beings had mass, and others didn't. They were all sorts of shapes, and they occupied a variety of dimensions: first, second, third, and even those undiscovered by humans.

There were still delegates arriving through large, clear, cylindrical travel tubes on the left side of the room. These travel tubes, referred to as Jalopy Cabins, allowed the delegates to travel between their home planets and to those of each Universal Union meeting host at very quick speeds, regardless of where in the universe they resided.

The president looked around at the crowd in disbelief. Some were gorging on the light snacks that had been set on each table, stuffing the food into their mouths (or features that looked like mouths). But once the president made his entrance, everyone froze and turned toward him. He sincerely hoped none of them could notice the pounding of his heart through his clean shirt.

A mousy-looking, purple-skinned individual popped up from its seat in the far-right corner of the room and ran over to the president on its three sticklike legs. It pointed to the president's mouth and then ran back to its seat in silence. All the remainder of the delegates stared at him blankly, even those without eyes.

"Oh, right," said the president, forgetting that no one in the room could understand him. He tapped his left wrist three times and walked to an empty seat at one of the neatly set white tables in the room. He stood behind the chair and said once more, "Welcome to the White House, fellow delegates. I hope your travels were uneventful." His smile flashed brightly as if he hadn't missed a beat.

There were various grunts from around the room, all in different tongues. One of the delegates started to bounce around in its seat, since movement was its form of communication. The responses streamed inside his head in English.

"That blasted Jalopy closed on my wing again!" squirmed the bouncing delegate from Antympanica.

"It always smells a bit funny on Earth," grumbled the delegate from Olfinder.

"It's so dark on Earth," squeaked the delegate from Vignet, whom the president couldn't even see with his naked eye.

Tough crowd.

"I apologise for the inconveniences," the president said, "but I certainly am glad our delegate from Kilo-209 is enjoying our delicacies!" He gestured toward a hairy, monstrous-looking being that had just shovelled a whole cake into its mouth.

"Let's get to business, shall we?" started the delegate from Rhothgo—a rather angry-looking, rock type of being who towered above the president threefold and served as the leader of the group. The Rhothgan angrily glared at the delegates around the room with its one large eye that was directly in the middle of its spherical exterior. "We've already wasted a year's worth of time on Rhothgo. I can't afford to waste more erosion time," it grunted deeply.

"Yes, you are correct. Let's cut the small talk!" exclaimed the president, sitting on the edge of his seat. "Pomber delegate, have you taken attendance and allowed those who can't be here in person to listen in?"

The purple-skinned being anxiously squeaked a weak, "Yes!" and sank into its seat. It was delicately but quickly typing on a handheld device that was most likely the communication device for the delegates who couldn't attend in person.

"Excellent," said the president. "What's the first order of business, then?" He'd hoped they could start with anything but the state of the Earth.

"Urgent order of business is to start with the state of the Earth's climate, sir," whispered the dainty Pomberian.

The president's heart hadn't yet calmed from its fast-paced rhythm. The Rhothgan turned to him.

"Please provide a status report since the previous meeting," it announced angrily.

The president cleared his throat and slowly rose from his chair with false confidence. He puffed out his chest and took a deep inhalation before speaking.

"Universal Union, I say this to you with complete and utter honesty: Earth cannot survive much longer. We need your help for the survival of our planet."

The entirety of the Universal Union's eyes, or alternative structures to eyes, were completely fixated on the president. It gave him a feeling of vulnerability that was paired with a sense of safety he hadn't felt since he had entered the office eight years ago. After clearing his throat once again and gradually turning around to speak to the rest of the room, he continued.

"GeoLapse terrorism has left us with only fifty thousand humans. The GeoLapse cannot be controlled. They are responsible for eradicating our atmosphere and killing innocent humans. The atmosphere is so poor that if any human is exposed to it for even a split second, they are completely carbonised."

The Tortoine delegate piped up from the back corner of the room. It was a small, blueish and greenish creature with a shell that resembled that of a turtle, except the shell was spiral shaped around its midsection. "What is the GeoLapse? Where are they? Do they pose any threat to us?"

"Thank you for the questions, Tortoine delegate!" exclaimed the president, extending his arms out in praise. "The GeoLapse are a murderous group of humans who want control of the planet. They cause breaches to the environment, like blowing up buildings, and end up murdering innocent humans in the process. I don't know their whereabouts, just that they have secret headquarters on every Earth continent. They may pose a threat universally. I have heard rumours that they seek total universal control. Their present numbers do not allow them to do that just yet, but they will easily kill the remainder of our population—if they don't recruit them all first."

"Why would anyone join this horrible group?" piped the Pomberian. Some delegates, including the president, were shocked to hear the Pomberian freely speak at all. It was quickly embarrassed upon realisation of its outburst and sank lower in its seat.

"Excellent question, Pomber delegate. The truth is, I'm not sure. Perhaps for a second chance at life; that is my guess. The promise of posterity and universal control may also be attractive. Humans are living with next to nothing at this point. I'm sure some would do anything for a glimmer of hope."

There were many nods of approval and agreement from the diverse crowd. The president's heartbeat was returning to normal.

"Why isn't the Earth Rehabilitation Association doing anything about this catastrophe?" boomed the Rhothgan, who slammed a fist onto the table, nearly cracking it in half. This caught the Kilo-209 delegate, sitting across from it, off guard, as the pie it had his eye on was thrown to the floor.

The president gulped audibly. "My suspicions are that the ERA is collapsing. I have no evidence of this, but it's my gut feeling. The GeoLapse might be bribing them or even holding them hostage."

"So, how do we help you?" asked the Epiton delegate in a smooth but menacing tone. This delegate was extremely muscular with a dark-skinned exterior. It had many similarities to a human, but it had two horns on top of its head instead of ears and one sharp claw extending from each hand, and it was considerably taller. "It's obvious that the Earthlings must be sent elsewhere within the next Earth year in order to avoid an extinction; however, the issue is where can they safely be relocated? Unfortunately, their kind requires very specific living conditions."

"Tell me again why you all can't just go underground?" said the Cipto delegate, who was facing the opposite direction of the president as the being did not have any eyes. It was a translucent, jelly-like blob, with its blobby body hanging over each side of its chair.

"Ah yes, a great question," the president started. "Unfortunately, the Earth's surface has hardened to the point of stone. The water has been drained because of the atmospheric emissions. And no moisture is able to fertilise the ground to keep everyone cool enough, even if we were to get everyone down there. The lack of lighting doesn't suit us well, either."

"Oh. Forgot about the 'light' concept," responded the Cipton. "What a strange way to live." It flattened in its chair with a sad sigh.

"It's settled, Earth," boomed the Rhothgan. "All in favour of relocating the Earthlings to another home to avoid extinction?" asked the Rhothgan in an annoyed tone, looking around the room with its menacing eye.

To the president's surprise, many delegates had their hand (or equivalent body part) raised. His hand even slowly rose with caution. The ERA wouldn't know his vote.

The Pomberian rose out of its chair to begin the count.

"Ninety-seven in favour and twelve opposed," said the Casper delegate, already having counted the votes within a millisecond. They were the math geniuses of the universe, with heads the size of a large watermelon.

The Rhothgan huffed at the overwhelming response.

"Then it's settled," the Rhothgan groaned. "At the next gathering we will devise an agreement for where the Earthlings will be sent. Earth, please come prepared with a list of needs required by your people, and we will choose adequate living environments. You're lucky I'm granting you this nicety. Next order of business?"

The president couldn't even focus attention on the remainder of the meeting. Relief poured through his body like the fresh water he'd never seen. He didn't even care what the ERA would do to him. Think of the people he would save! For the rest of the meeting, he didn't have to worry about the next meeting agenda items. One of them concerned sending extra security to Pomber for fear that a large asteroid would collide with their planet in the next week or so. The other was about transportation to Minag's annual music festival (and by annual, it was essentially every week on Earth with their concept of time). There would be no easy mode of transport for humans, but the president wasn't even paying attention by that point.

The meeting adjourned, and the Rhothgan threw his fist on the podium to dismiss the delegates. Creatures and beasts of all sizes started to hop, squirm, hobble, and float toward the Jalopy Cabins. Some of the delegates lingered to offer the president supportive groans, moans, and various movements to let him know that Earth would be taken care of. The Cipton even grasped his hands tightly with its jelly-like body to show its support. The president politely avoided getting too close to well-wishers who looked as if they could crush him with the flick of a tail.

"Anything our community can do for you, we will be there for your Earth," squirmed the Cipton, kindly.

The president had tears welling up. Luckily the Cipton didn't have eyes to see this vulnerable moment.

The last of the delegates had exited through the Jalopy Cabins, and the room was finally empty. The silence filled his body chillingly once again. What had just happened? Did he just agree to move Earth's entire population to different planets across the universe? Was that safe? Ethical? He wasn't even sure which of the planets would agree to a population of humans joining them. How would the cultures interact? He didn't even know where to begin with basic necessities. Food? Water? Air?

It was all too much to comprehend for the moment. He wasn't even sure how long he was standing behind his seat, staring at the blank, windowless walls. The president suddenly snapped out of his trance and noticed that his watch was nearing three p.m. He hopped out of his seat and ran to the Green House for the Earth Day celebration with the United Nations and the ERA. It was hardly a greenhouse, just a pseudo-glass room inside a large meeting room one floor below Danforth Commons. There were obviously no windows even to look outside.

He snuck into the room right on time as members of the UN and the ERA were arriving through a tunnel in the main terminal of the room. A bus would have driven them all from across the Earth to be at the White House today. The buses attached to the tunnels, which was similar to what old-time airports used to transport passengers from the airport to the airplane. The president wondered for a moment why the humans didn't travel with Jalopy Cabins, but he remembered that there were only a few on Earth. And they were all located in Danforth Commons.

The president was normally happy to see the UN members in person, as he and a mysterious tray-bearing crew he never caught a glimpse of were the only current inhabitants of the White House of whom he was aware. But today he wasn't particularly interested in discussing current affairs with anyone. The ERA were all relying on him to stand up to the Universal Union and keep universal collaboration at bay. The "aliens" would only "destroy the Earth faster," "kill us all as soon as they had the chance," and "interfere with the laws of natural selection." That was just a small portion of the danger surrounding the Universal Union, from the ERA's perspective. But the president believed in the Universal Union's values of universal cooperation. It was important to stray from a geocentric mindset and expand Earth's horizons now that technology was skyrocketing into new frontiers. But he was nearly the only leader on Earth who believed in this concept. Luckily, the UN wasn't aware of the ERA's commands to get him to cooperate with their views. They were merely peacemakers for each country that promoted the welfare and wellbeing of humans. The UN was full of naivete with the current situation of the Earth residing solely with the president and the ERA.

"Happy Earth Day, Mr. President," said the UN member from England, the prime minister, who caused the president to hop yet again out of another trance.

"Oh, hello, Ms. Prime Minister!" said the president anxiously, reaching out his hand to greet her. "How are you doing on this great holiday?" He tried to sound chipper and divert any such subject regarding the prior Universal Union meeting.

"Just lovely, thank you," she replied sweetly. The president pretended to notice something in the corner of the room, and he slowly stepped in that direction.

"How did the Universal Union meeting go today?" she interrupted as the president was mid-step.

He winced, out of her field of view, then turned to her with his famous smile.

"It went very well. I was able to relay everything I believed would be of value." His stomach gurgled with his omission of the full truth.

"Brilliant," the prime minister said with a toothy smile.

Throughout the remainder of that meeting, he relayed the same message to every UN member who came up to him. The UN and ERA members in attendance aired an annoyingly happy message to everyone on Earth about celebrating the planet, exploring old texts on nature, and sharing pictures of favourite extinct flowers and animal species with their families back at home. Each UN member broadcasted a small message to their respective nations, and old videos of nature were presented by the ERA. It all felt so fake to the president: the smiles, the rejoicing, the promises of a brighter future. He fell into an autopilot state for most of the celebration.

"Bonjour, monsieur."

The president snapped yet again out of his trance and whirled around on his heels to see a young, pretty woman with a green ERA lab coat, only this time when his brain registered the face speaking to him, he didn't emit his famous, flashy smile. He blushed. He recognised her as Dr. Blair Watson, one of the chief scientists within the ERA. She had long, straight brown hair pulled tightly into a ponytail. She had a severe sort of beauty. Her thin stature emphasised her cheekbones and gaunt eyes. Her gaze pierced into his soul with such ease. He found her rather beautiful, but also extremely intimidating. He quickly tapped his wrist three times so that her French could translate into English.

"H—Hello, Dr. Watson. How are you today?" The president held out a trembling hand for her.

"Fine, thank you." She gripped his hand firmly with her long, bony fingers.

The president cleared his throat. "It's very nice that the ERA sent representatives to the celebration today. It's important that Earth's people—"

"When are the humans being moved?" she asked, her eyes gripping his with great intensity.

The president was caught off guard. He tried to play dumb. "I—I'm not sure what you mean, Dr. Watson."

Her voice fell silent to a barely audible whisper. "This is between you and me. The humans need to be moved *now*." Her fingernails dug further into his palm. "Forget what the rest of them are telling you. We need help. There is no chance of survival." Tears welled up in her eyes, but she shook her head and they disappeared as quickly as they had appeared.

"The ERA is lying to you. They have been overtaken. Your suspicions are correct." The begging in her voice was heartbreaking. He wanted to hug her, but he was still afraid of her. He also knew it might raise suspicions if the two of them were seen sharing an intimate moment.

"Dr. Watson," he said quietly, pulling her out of view of the remainder of the smiling and laughing crowd. "They know. They are movii., There isn't a timeline yet, but—"

"It has to be now," she repeated firmly.

The president was confused. "Exactly how much time do we have left?" he said under his breath, his eyes piercing into hers.

She swallowed loudly. "Three months. They need to start moving everyone immediately." She let go of his hand, patted down her slightly ruffled lab coat, and walked away as if their conversation had never occurred. The president watched her perfectly elegant brown ponytail swish as she walked toward a group of her fellow ERA members. He felt a smidgeon of confidence in himself now that someone in the ERA was on his side, but terror filled him as he recognised what it meant. The ERA had fallen. There was no more reigning body of government since the UN was completely useless. He was alone.

Back in his room, the president neglected to eat his dinner that had again been left outside his bedroom door. He instead focused on another glass of orange goo and mixed it with the lemonade that was provided. He felt the calmness wash over him as he finished his beverage, even though the smell of the goo stained his nostrils with a disgusting stench. He fell into bed, hoping tonight's nightmares would be bearable.

* * *

"How did 19.438 Earth days go by so quickly?" thought the president, with his face completely engulfed in his hands. He was sitting alone in Danforth Commons at one of the white tables. This meeting was to be held on Pangica, so the president was mentally preparing for his trip through intergalactic space via the Jalopy Cabin closest to him. This was the meeting where the fate of the Earth was to be decided. And Dr. Blair Watson had reassured him that it was the right thing to do, even though the remainder of the UN and the ERA

ression that the president was just having casual
meetings.

d up slowly from his seat and took a few seconds
He caught a glimpse of his reflection on the out-
...... of the glass entrance of the Jalopy Cabin. He stared for a second in awe of how much skinnier he looked compared to just a few weeks prior. As he stood in front of the Jalopy Cabin, the door immediately opened before him, and he stepped inside. The curved back wall and floor of the Jalopy Cabin was plush, just in case of turbulence, while the curved front wall remained glassy.

The door closed behind him and the inside of the Jalopy Cabin illuminated in a neon green colour. As he turned to glimpse at Danforth Commons through the glass door, a touch screen with many differently coloured buttons popped up in front of his eyes. A slowly spinning map of the universe also appeared.

"Hello, Mr. President," said a soft voice that filled the Jalopy Cabin. "The Jalopy is ready to depart. Please state your destination."

The president cleared his throat before articulating, "Pangica Fields."

"Enjoy your trip," said the Jalopy Cabin's intercom voice.

The neon green colour faded and the Jalopy Cabin started smoothly accelerating upward without hesitation. The glassy front of the Jalopy Cabin tinted itself with a star map before his eyes. There was a blinking dot that showed his location and the current path that was to be taken to Pangica.

The ride to Pangica wasn't taking too terribly long. Even though it was 2.537 million light years away in the Andromeda Galaxy, it was still one of the nearest locations of communities to Earth that was also in the Universal Union. The blinking dot of the president's current location was showing eighteen percent journey completion. A rerouting bumped down the completion to fifteen percent. The travelling conditions were slightly unpredictable since the technology was still being perfected and the route had to be continuously adjusted because there were innumerable supernovas, black holes, asteroids, and many more obstacles in outer space that could enter the flight path at any given instant. The Jalopy Cabin also had technology to mimic the Earth's gravitational force so when the path had to be suddenly rerouted, the passenger wouldn't even feel it, but since the technology was still being worked on, it had its faults. The plush wall of the Jalopy Cabin proved to be useful for this particular rerouting.

The president touched a small flashing yellow button above the spinning universe model, and it dissipated like a breath of smoke. The entire interior and exterior of the Jalopy Cabin turned completely transparent, including the plush walls and tinted glass. Looking down, stars were jetting beneath his feet. He was just flying through space completely on his own. There was no sense of up, down, left, or right, besides the gravitational pull from the Jalopy Cabin.

Outer space was a beautiful sight, something he never really remembered to stop and watch to soak in all of its glory. He crouched to the ground and folded his arms tightly around his knees, pressing them to his chest. His head was held back against the still plush yet transparent wall of the Jalopy Cabin. It was hard to look anywhere in particular; it was just one big open space that inspired incredulity. He felt so small, surrounded by the vastest landscape of stars that resembled Christmas lights strung in every direction, near, far, and farther. The breathtaking starlight warmed his skin. It was the first time in a while that he had felt as if the pressure of the world were lifted from his shoulders—perhaps because he had been physically lifted out of the world. The president fell asleep in that position, comfortable and warm in his bubble of solitude, whizzing through outer space surrounded by the most enchanting and ominous views.

"One Earth minute until entering Pangica Fields," said the soft voice in the Jalopy Cabin.

The president awoke with his head on the floor and his body slumped to one side. The Jalopy Cabin tinted the glass, and the view of the stars disappeared. The walls and floor returned to their plush-looking material. The multicoloured buttons reappeared on the tinted glass in front of his eyes.

"Prepare for landing," continued the voice.

The president took three deep breaths as the anxiety started to wash back into his system. In. Out. In. Out. In. Out . . .

The Jalopy Cabin came to a halt and opened the tinted glass door, revealing him to the delegates who had already arrived in Pangica Fields. As he stepped down to touch the dusty ground with his black shoes, his famous smile flashed on. He tapped his left wrist three times.

The delegates of the Universal Union eyed the president intensely, as if he were the sole reason they had been required to get up and leave their home planets for this meeting. Their stares seemed angry, although he couldn't be sure because emotions were shown in various ways among this bunch.

He made his way to what looked like a fallen log and sat down to wait for the meeting to start. He was immediately propelled off it, and he faceplanted into the sandy ground.

"Watch it!" shouted the log, who was, in fact, a delegate in the unfortunate shape of a seating area.

"So sorry, won't happen again," said the president, horribly embarrassed for himself. He stood up and dusted the sand from his trousers. The Pomberian was standing close by, and the president walked up to greet it. The Pomberian was once again typing feverishly on a handheld device.

"Hello, Pomber delegate," said the president sweetly, with his teeth shining through.

The delegate jumped up and dropped the device it was typing on.

"Oh," started the president, "I didn't mean to scare you. I'm so sorry—"

The awkward greeting was then interrupted by the Rhothgan, who was banging on a hollowed-out log nearby to get everyone's attention for the meeting to start. The log completely broke in half, and the Pomberian squeaked under its breath in response to the loud noise. The president was hoping it wasn't another delegate whom the Rhothgan had just shattered, but the log-like delegate he had just sat upon appeared unfazed, so he regained some of his composure.

"Let's get this meeting started," boomed the Rhothgan, unperturbed by the shards of wood that had flown into the nearby delegates' faces, tails, and other various body parts.

The president looked around and noticed that this crowd was slightly different from the one at the previous meeting held in the White House. There were many larger-sized delegates at this meeting, some nearing the size of a skyscraper. He kept a mental note to stay clear of the skyscraper delegate since he didn't want the same fate as the previous Earth delegate.

It was also very strange for the president to be in an outside environment, if this could technically be considered "outside." The sand under his shoes felt surprisingly nice compared to the usual dirty, marbled floor of the White House. The wind in his hair felt freeing. Seeing land along a horizon felt foreign. There was greenery in the distance. Pangica was so beautiful, just as Earth once had been, hundreds of years in the past.

"Earth?"

The president snapped out of his trance while sifting sand from the ground through his fingers. All eyes, or other strange body parts, were pinned on him. The delegates were completely silent.

The president blushed in embarrassment. "Please excuse my lack of focus," he announced with a smile. "I was just admiring your beautiful scenery, Pangica delegate," he blabbed, peering toward the Pangican with his sandy hands held up in the air, gesturing toward the horizon.

There wasn't even a flinch of movement.

"Please restate the question?" inquired the president, dropping his hands and turning his body toward the Rhothgan.

The Rhothgan's fists shook in fury. "I said, have you come prepared with your list of needs for your people? We need to ensure that we can match them with the appropriate hosts so they can be effectively and safely moved."

"Yes!" exclaimed the president, jumping to his feet and reaching in his inner jacket pocket. He pulled out a piece of crumpled paper with a few notes scribbled on it. He cleared his throat and began summarising his notes.

"There are approximately fifty thousand humans remaining on Earth, and that number is decreasing by the day—"

"AND APPROXIMATELY HOW BIG ARE THE EARTH DWELLERS?" rumbled one of the skyscraper-sized delegates. The president thought his ears were going to start bleeding right then and there. He waited for the ringing to stop before he answered.

"They are all around my height, give or take a few feet," answered the president, holding up his hands one above the other to denote the approximation of a foot.

"THANK YOU FOR ANSWERING MY QUESTION," thundered the skyscraper again, nearly knocking the president off his heels this time; however, he managed to maintain his balance.

"Anytime," he smiled sweetly, feeling silly smiling up toward the likes of a skyscraper. He continued, looking back down toward his list.

"Basic necessities include water, vegetation, shelter, a heat and light source, and a breathable atmosphere made up of twenty or so percent oxygen, seventy-five percent nitrogen, toss in a minimal amount of carbon dioxide, and the like." He glanced up from his sheet of paper to get a quick idea of how this information was being perceived. The delegates were looking and facing in all directions. He heard murmurs translating inside his head:

"Is this guy nuts?"

"What in Entropon's name is 'water'?"

"Isn't oxygen toxic on our planet?"

So far, so good; there was no one directly fighting him yet. He continued on with his list.

"There are a few lesser things that aren't absolute requirements, but would be nice-to-haves. For instance, music!" He gestured toward the

Minag delegate, who looked rather excited and bouncy. "And perhaps a community that is technology-driven. And one that isn't particularly harsh with punishment, and maybe one that is capable of love."

It was as if he had asked each delegate to sacrifice a family member. The group instantly fired back comments.

"Are you suggesting that you want us to *mate* with your people?" spat the Sinx delegate, a two-dimensional creature who resembled a wiggly line.

"Oh, not necessarily!" reassured the president quickly. "More so I meant love in the way of a sense of community," he elaborated. This seemed to ease the crowd's concerns.

The Rhothgan spoke up. "Earth, you must realise that each civilisation in the Universal Union is remarkably different. The origins and makeup of our societies have been built from very specific conditions." His voice rumbled, but not nearly as loud as the skyscraper; the Rhothgan's voice almost sounded like a whisper in comparison. "There needs to be some sacrifice if this is going to work. I realise that will be difficult for your people; however, the choice is either to stay behind on a quickly dying and dangerous planet or learn to integrate into a new society." The Rhothgan looked out into the crowd. The president was thankful that the delegate's threatening eye was no longer glued to him.

"This is a great opportunity for us all," continued the Rhothgan. Everyone looked shocked, as the delegate wasn't known for a soft side. "This group was founded on morals of intergalactic peacemaking. We drop everything and help our communities in need. Earth has been an active member of this union, and I'd like every delegate to consider these needs and present yourself forward if you believe that your planet would be a good match to host the Earthlings." The Rhothgan's words were enunciated sternly. The crowd remained silent for a few moments.

The president stood still with his scribbled list of needs tightly gripped in his hands. Then, the Cipto delegate hopped forward from the crowd and slithered its way up to the centre of the circle, directly in front of the Rhothgan. The Cipton wasn't focusing its attention anywhere in particular, considering it didn't have eyes to focus with. The president remembered the Cipton as having been very friendly to him at the end of the last meeting. The Cipton squawked its response.

"The Cipto community would be honoured to host as many of the Earthlings as we can."

The president beamed, his anxiety lowering slightly.

The delegate continued: "We can house approximately ten thousand Earthlings, but it may be a squeeze. We have everything Earth mentioned on the list except for a light source. I believe it is still a livable temperature for them, but we live in complete darkness."

The president's heart dropped a little. That might be a problem.

"That sounds adequate," started the Rhothgan. "Pomber delegate, are you getting this?"

The Pomberian squealed and jumped at the typing device so that it could record the meeting minutes.

The Cipton happily hopped away back to its seat.

Another delegate must've been directly behind the Cipton because the Rhothgan started addressing it.

"Yes, Vignet delegate, how would your planet be a good fit?" he questioned.

"We are a very energetic bunch! We would make sure the Earthlings are always entertained, and we have plenty of light sources!" said a high-pitched and very fast-paced voice. The president cocked his head and squinted his eyes in search of some sort of beast that could be making such a high-pitched noise but didn't see a thing. He guessed it was either extremely tiny or invisible, but he didn't dare say a word for fear these kind beings would retract their offers, however outrageous they were.

The Rhothgan shook his head. "Your offer is generous, Vignet delegate. But I don't believe that a community of photons that live on a star is compatible with Earthling life. It will be too hot, and they surely would all be carbonised even coming within one light year's distance of your home."

The president assumed the Vignet delegate was flying away, or whatever photons do, but he made sure to step forward and shout a hearty "Thank you for the offer!" in the general direction of where the voice had come from.

One by one, hundreds of delegates stepped forward. The president was in awe of their willingness to help. The Rhothgan listened to everyone's offers intently and wholly until every last one had spoken. Most of the delegates' civilisations were completely unlivable for humans. The skyscraper delegates even offered their neighbouring planet that was completely empty, but it was in the flight path of a planet-shattering asteroid in exactly 5.125 Earth years, according to the math-genius Casper delegate.

Unfortunately, many other delegates' offers fell under similar scenarios. The Pangica delegate even stepped forward to offer their planet as a host since it was probably the most closely comparable planet, having vegetation, three suns collectively equivalent to Earth's current sun, plenty of fresh water, and a structured society. But the Casper delegate piped up again that their entire galaxy was projected to be engulfed by a massive black hole in about 11.894 Earth months. The Pangican nearly fainted at this news.

"Not to fret, Pangica delegate," said the Rhothgan, noticing the fear on the delegate's face. "Your civilisation will be handled appropriately after we sort out the Earthlings." The Pangican still managed to pass out right on the spot.

In the end, a total of five planets were deemed adequate hosts, and it was decided that the humans would be split among them: Cipto, Epiton, Antympanica, Olfinder, and Harvinth. Each came with its own environmental and societal challenges, but these five were the least problematic when compared to the remainder of the proposals.

"That's settled then, Earth," announced the Rhothgan loudly, banging his fist on the smashed hollow log. "Your people will be moved whenever it is most suitable for the hosts—"

"We need to go now!" shouted the president, who looked surprised at his own outburst.

The Rhothgan glared at him as if he couldn't possibly be asking for more. "What do you mean?"

The president gulped and then stepped forward in front of the crowd. "I have inside information that our planet won't survive three more Earth months. This is coming from a reliable source within the ERA."

The Rhothgan fell quiet. The president half expected to be lifted off his feet and bashed to his death. He shut his eyes in anticipation. The Rhothgan then eyed up the host delegates of Cipto, Epiton, Olfinder, Antympanica, and Harvinth.

"Prepare your planets for the Earthlings immediately. We will separate the humans based on how they will best acclimate to your various host planets to ensure longevity of their population. We will conduct the testing as soon as you can alert the Earthlings." The Rhothgan spoke calmly but sternly.

"Thank you," the president croaked in gratitude. "For everything." That was all he could muster without starting to cry.

"Meeting adjourned. We will discuss other items at our next meeting," shouted the Rhothgan. "And, Pomber delegate?" he added, halting everyone who had started getting up to leave.

The Pomberian looked as if it were about to turn to jelly and melt, even though its body form was already fairly gelatinous.

"Y—yes?" it stammered, shaking violently.

"Please add the fate of Pangica to the next meeting's agenda," said the Rhothgan with a sigh. The president caught a distant sight of the Pangican, who was still passed out despite the Minag delegate's attempts to revive it. The Pomberian also seemed as if it was nearly on the edge of passing out from the sheer speed with which it was trying to type the Rhothgan's request into its device.

The trip back to Earth was much faster than the trip to the meeting, partly because there were fewer reroutings to avoid obstacles in the flightpath. The president tried to think of all the ways he could break the news to the UN and the ERA that the entirety of Earth's population was to be distributed among five different planets to live completely different lives. Fear of putting his people's lives in danger grew in his head as he processed the meeting. He lay on the floor of the Jalopy Cabin while Dr. Watson's words of warning from the ERA jolted through his brain. "Three months." And that was nearly one month ago. He was going to save as many people as he could. But how could he save anyone with the ERA being taken over by the GeoLapse?

* * *

A little over one month later, the president sat at his desk, having just finished his morning coffee and orange goo mixture. He sat so still that he could feel his body moving only slightly with each beat of his heart. Weird flashes of memories flooded in his brain, and they were surprisingly calming. A woman with blonde hair holding his hand. A boat soaring through space. What did it all mean?

After a few moments, he managed to snap out of his trance. Today was possibly one of the most pivotal days he would have in his life. He was going to announce to the UN and the ERA that the humans had to be moved to new planets. There was no telling what would happen. He just hoped he'd live to see tomorrow—although, if he didn't, maybe it wouldn't be so bad.

He stood and dressed in the midnight-black suit that was left at his door on a silvery tray earlier in the morning.

On his way out of the dormitory room, he meditatively walked directly to the entrance to Danforth Commons. He closed his eyes and took three deep breaths, lifting his chin as the cold air sharply entered his nostrils and seemingly surrounded his brain, then bowing his head as warm air flushed back out.

"The smile. Don't forget the smile," he told himself under his breath. He flashed his famous smile, opened his eyes, and pulled the doors open.

Inside, the UN and ERA members were casually dotted around the room. Small conversations became a blurred noise, overwhelming the president's acute senses. Teacups and coffee mugs clinked, crumbs fell from muffins being eaten, and the sound of quiet laughter among random conversations filled the surroundings.

The president's hands started to sweat. He wiped them on the soft, velvety fabric of his suitcoat and began walking toward one of the elegantly set white tables where he might be able to sit away from the bustle of the guests. As he sat down and shakily poured himself a cup of coffee, a group of European representatives from the UN surrounded him in a looming semicircle. He turned his head mid-pour.

"Oh," he said, startled but with a quick recovery of a flashy smile. "Good morning, everyone." He was sitting and they were standing, which was causing an extreme power imbalance. He felt small but remembered the UN's naivete regarding the state of the Earth.

"Good marnin', Mr. President. How are ye?" chimed the Irish prime minister, a skinny but tall man with a cheery voice. The rest of the semicircle followed suit with a collective "Hello."

"We just wanted to stop by and tell ye that we appreciate all the tough work ye've been puttin' in wit' the Universal Union. It can't be easy dealin' wit dem scary beasts," continued the prime minister in his jolly tone.

The president collected his thoughts for a moment. This is exactly what he had been hoping to avoid. They all thought that he had told the Universal Union to leave Earth to meet its own demise. However, he replied with nothing. He just emitted a larger smile than the one already on his face. The looming representatives all nodded and walked back to their seats.

Dr. Blair Watson walked to the podium at the focal point of the room. The president watched as her green lab coat and high ponytail swished with each footstep. Even through his anxiety over having to present after her, he still managed to watch her with an intense attraction paired with an equally intense intimidation. As she began to speak with her French flair, there was something about her that he couldn't quite place, almost as if her face was familiar to him from his past. She presented a speech on ERA updates, eyeing him up as she spoke.

Her monologue contained all her usual lines. "Working toward a brighter future" . . . "using taxpayer money to restore water sources" . . . "animal genetic restoration therapy" . . . "greenhouse centres to be established worldwide." His trust in her quickly turned into anger. How dare she put up a front when there was less than one month of survival left? Was she that selfish? Was she in the GeoLapse? The president looked around the room while the remainder of the green-lab-coated individuals of the ERA nodded along with her updates. The members of the UN were also buying this false information. Did no one realise this was the same speech they had heard over and over, with no progress on any of the points? It was infuriating, and a little bout of confidence bubbled up inside him that he had done the right thing by agreeing to move Earth's people off the planet. He glared at Dr. Watson, surprised that she was allowing this sort of nonsensical information to come out of her mouth when she had been the one telling him that the ERA were a bunch of liars. His brow furrowed even deeper when she neared the end of the speech and encouraged everyone to "remain optimistic and be ready to enjoy the fresh air in a few short months." As the crowd clapped, her gaze into his eyes was one of remorse, almost as if she had been reading his mind through the whole speech.

"And now, a word from our Universal Union Earth delegate, the president of the United States of America," she finished, nodding her head and walking away from the podium. As the president and Dr. Watson passed each other en route to their respective destinations, Dr. Watson reached out a bony hand to him for a handshake, but the president was so enraged and full of adrenaline that he continued past her to the podium. Most of the audience didn't see him reject her handshake because of the many cheers following the president's introduction.

He reached the podium, trembling with fear and anger. He raised his right hand and moved it in a sweeping motion to silence the cheers. There was no smile on his face, and the crowd dimmed its noise in a hush. Words popped up in front of his eyes, just as they did when he presented his daily speeches. He had no idea what the words said—and he knew he would never find out because he had mentally scripted his own monologue.

"My colleagues of the United Nations and the Earth Rehabilitation Association, I come to you today for your listening ears, your understanding, and your willingness to live." The room remained quiet, and all eyes were on him.

"As you know, I have been in constant contact with the Universal Union, which represents beings across the universe that live in harmony with one another. The Union identifies the needs of the communities on member planets and addresses them as needed. Each society's needs are considered fully in exchange for full support and the promotion of peace in the Union. I am honoured by the rapport I have developed with these diverse delegates. As different and sometimes scary as they appear, they have reached out with open arms to ensure that Earth's continuation in the Union is guaranteed, because we are an important part of the universal community."

One group of ERA members, who had moved their table closer to the entrance just before the meeting began, started whispering to each other. They appeared to notice the deviation from the prepared speech. Could they have been the ones writing his speeches all along, using him as their puppet after they were overtaken by the GeoLapse? He decided he needed to speak more quickly instead of prattling on. A bad feeling was bubbling inside him.

"That being said"—he took his eyes off the table of ERA members as his trembling was becoming noticeably violent—"I decided to let them help us."

"You had no right!" shouted a small, rotund woman at the ERA table, who immediately shot up from her seat. She had wild, curly grey hair that bounced as she angrily pointed a stubby finger at him. "You don't have the facts to back anything!"

The president was caught off guard. He looked at Dr. Watson, who was seated at the same table, but she had averted her gaze to the wall with the doors. He was shocked at her continued cowardice.

"I—I—" he stammered for a second. "I just had a gut feeling that not everything being relayed to me was truthful."

"You should be arrested!" continued the screaming, pudgy ERA woman.

"Can I jump in here?" asked the Irish prime minister, pushing his chair back and standing up at his table. All eyes locked on him. "Pardon me, but what is going on here?"

"To put it quickly," said the president, spreading his gaze across the room, "the Earth is no longer livable and has no chance of surviving the next couple months from the environmental atrocities and GeoLapse terrorism. We are going to be moved to different planets in the Universal Union."

Gasps echoed loudly. The king of Spain audibly choked on the muffin he had just taken a bite of. The prime minister of Canada clapped him on the back a few times.

"But I don't understand," said the president of China rather calmly as she stood up. She was another member of the UN, a thin woman who stood with unflappable confidence. She turned to look around toward the ERA members. She began to address them firmly.

"Please explain yourselves. Is it correct to say that you have been feeding us lies?" she demanded, stoically remaining still in her stance. "I have been telling my people daily that things were on the mend. Now my people will lose trust in me and are in harm's way? Do you take ownership of this?"

It was as if everyone's heads were remote-controlled. All focus went from the president of China to the ERA tables, robotically. The ERA woman, at a loss for words, lowered her finger to her side. Dr. Watson slouched further into her seat as a middle-aged South Korean man stood up beside her and addressed the crowd in a smooth tone.

"As an Earth Rehabilitation Association Senior Scientist, I can assure you that what we have relayed to you is far from propaganda. Our team is dedicated to serving the global community—"

"Can ye tell a single truth?" said the Irish prime minister, causing all focus to turn to him.

The ERA scientist smiled what looked, from the president's perspective, like an evil grin. "Let me ask you one question. Are you going to believe our whole team, who have conducted hundreds of scientific studies, or a lone man who hasn't left the comfort of his bedroom in nearly eight years?"

Murmurs rippled through the crowd. It was a valid point. Even the president had to think about the answer to that question for an extra second.

The president of China spoke valiantly above the murmurs. "Mr. President, sir! Please finish what you came to tell us. When will we be moved?"

The room fell silent again.

"As soon as possible. Our new homes are awaiting our arrival."

The air in the room was heavy. A few people started crying.

"Well, I'm alerting my people as soon as I return to China. Please send over the details as soon as—"

But she never finished her sentence. A deafening bang issued from the back wall of Danforth Commons, the one farthest from the doors. As the wall was blasted open, exposing those inside to the outside, the UN members sitting closest to the window were immediately charred. This included the president of China, whose lifeless body carbonised upon contact with the floor.

About a dozen dark-clothed individuals ran into the room in a disorganised group. Their faces were covered, but their golden GL badges glinted in the light. They began picking up members of the UN and throwing them toward the hole in the wall that led to the outside.

Time felt like it was suddenly in slow motion for the president. He watched in horror as many of the world's most powerful and peaceful leaders were instantly killed and those still alive didn't know where to run. The entrance to the room had been blocked off by the GeoLapse, ruining any chance there might have been to escape to another location within the White House. Some of the UN ducked under tables, some cowered in the corners of the room, and others grabbed one another and held on for dear life. The GeoLapse had just carried the Irish and Canadian prime ministers to the dangerous outside. He had to escape. No one knew the plan to move the humans except him, so he had to run if he was going to be of any use.

He ran to the nearest Jalopy Cabin with adrenaline dictating every move. He saw a member of the GeoLapse in his peripheral vision, running toward him.

"Come on come on come on!" he shrieked, slamming against the door of the Jalopy Cabin with his right arm. Tears were streaming down his face. The door opened, his feet catapulted him inside, and the door closed just in time. His GeoLapse pursuer smashed into the closed door of the Jalopy Cabin, missing him by milliseconds. The neon green light illuminated the inside of the Jalopy Cabin.

When the president regained footing, he looked out through the glass. The bloodbath was filling by the second. The GeoLapse began crowding around the Jalopy Cabin, pounding their fists on the glass, but they couldn't make even the smallest crack.

He then noticed a swarm of green toward the Danforth Commons doors. To his horror, all the members of the ERA were untouched by the GeoLapse. Dr. Watson had been telling the truth. Yet she was also standing amongst them, so even though she looked terrified, he hated her. The entirety of the ERA were calmly leaving out of the entrance doors single file, paying no attention to the terrorist activity happening behind them. Some looked as if they were in a state of boredom, checking their watches for the time. The senior scientist and the grey-haired woman walked out of the room together, in deep discussion.

It finally occurred to the president that the ERA must be entirely composed of the GeoLapse. They had set everyone up for failure, baiting humanity toward its demise. Anger boiled in his body, his muscles twitched, and his pupils shrunk to pinholes. Everyone else in the room was dead in piles of ashes. He was the only member of the UN remaining.

"Hello, Mr. President," said the soft and familiar Jalopy Cabin voice. "The Jalopy is ready to depart. Please state your destination."

He didn't know where to go. He wanted to go anywhere but here. He cried, wailing at the top of his lungs. His fists banged on the door, mirroring those of the GeoLapse members who were still trying to penetrate the glass. "My wife!" he cried. "I just want my wife!" The president didn't even know what he was saying; words just spewed out of his mouth. He sank to the floor, hopeless, confused, and saddened. But then the Jalopy Cabin started to rumble.

"Enjoy your trip," said the voice. The Jalopy Cabin accelerated upward and away from the horrifying visions of the GeoLapse and his fallen comrades.

CHAPTER 1

THE MCHUBBARD FAMILY

The McHubbard family gathered for dinner, as they did every evening. The family lived in a cramped, two-storey home in Portsmouth, a city in the south of England. Tonight they crowded around a rickety circular table in the kitchen, which was covered with a variety of colourful, aromatic foods. Henrietta and her daughter, Elbina, carried the last plates of the brown bread to the table.

Henrietta was a rotund woman with wild, curly grey hair. Her cheeks were rosy against her pale skin, matching her sweet nature. She bore an apron that she rarely took off, as there was always something to cook in the kitchen for her family, even though their food rations were limited to pantry items and frozen foods.

"You can all thank Elbina for this delicious food tonight. I barely lifted a finger!" said Henrietta proudly, a big smile on her face. Everyone at the table was starving and didn't care to acknowledge who had made it, as long as it would soon be in their stomachs.

Henrietta started placing multiple slices of bread onto the plate of her oldest daughter, Luna.

"Mum, I can do it myself. I can still see what's in front of me," said a grumpy Luna as she pulled the plate from her mother's hand. Luna reserved one piece of bread for herself, matching her thin frame, and passed the remainder of the plate into the already extended hand of her younger brother, Griffin.

"Elbina, darling, here's your bottle," said Henrietta, passing a litre-sized bottle filled with a murky liquid substance to her second-youngest daughter. Elbina sat down to the right of Luna, took the bottle without a word, and lifted her shirt to stuff it into a contraption affixed around her waist. She connected a piece of tubing to the top of the bottle, then roped a flexible plastic tube around her ears and into her nostrils. The contraption began to make a soft buzzing noise, which no one cared to acknowledge. Elbina shut her eyes while her feeding treatment began. Her straight brown hair fell off her ears and in front of her face as the contraption buzzed.

"Riff, can you please slow down your eating?" sparked Knitsy, the kids' grandmother and Henrietta's mother. Knitsy was a slender older woman with silvery, wispy hair that curled perfectly behind her ears. Her pale complexion matched Henrietta's. "With the state of things, the best thing to do is keep healthy!" Knitsy stabbed her potatoes with her cutlery in frustration and started into a coughing fit. Henrietta patted her back until the coughs ceased.

"Nan, leave him alone, it's not worth it," said Luna in a monotone, not looking up from her brown bread. Griffin, more commonly called Riff by those close to him, didn't seem to care, or notice, that his eating habits were up for debate as he gleefully stuffed three pieces of buttered bread into his mouth.

Knitsy rolled her eyes. "I'm just saying this is not the time to be risking our health. You all are aware of the news."

Henrietta shot Knitsy a fierce glare.

"Fine, I'll say no more. Now where is Ann Lou, for heaven's sake? The food's nearly gone!" barked Knitsy, eyeing up Riff sternly.

Henrietta put down her cup of tea as she said, "She'll be along. Her roller hockey team had their championship game this afternoon, remember? The bus should be dropping her off any minute now." She picked up her tea and took a few big gulps.

Seemingly annoyed by the family conversation this evening, Knitsy held her tongue and continued cutting her potatoes, small coughs poking through her bites.

"Riff, pass the bread this way," Knitsy demanded.

Riff didn't seem to notice the request and continued working his way through the dinner in front of him. Luna anticipated her grandmother's frustration and handed the bread over in her direction.

Knitsy grabbed the bread and dropped it purposefully on the table, which got Riff's attention at last. His head shot up from his dinner, causing his cap to fall off his head. He scrambled to pick it up to cover his wavy red hair that desperately needed a trim.

"For the love of all that is holy, what is wrong with you all? Getting angry at your mother? Not speaking? Ignoring me? Allowing your child to not even come to dinner?" Knitsy said as she stood up and looked at Luna, Elbina, Riff, and Henrietta respectively with each accusation.

Just then, a small, young girl opened the tunnel door at the front of the house and peered in the kitchen. She had pin-straight, light blonde hair that nearly touched her elbows, piercingly light blue eyes, and an extremely muscular build. Where her left forearm would normally be, it was replaced with a metallic prosthetic.

"Ann Lou! You're just in time. I made you up a plate. Come sit and tell us about your game," said Henrietta with a relieved tone in her voice. Henrietta stood up to let Ann Lou reach her usual seat in the corner of the kitchen, between her and Luna. Ann Lou tossed her hockey bag and stick in front of the stairs and made her way to her seat.

"It was fun. I scored the most goals of anyone again," was all Ann Lou said before she sat down and dug into her food as if she hadn't eaten in days.

Knitsy rolled her eyes once more and continued eating without a word for the remainder of their dinner.

The next morning started like every other morning. All but Riff were settled in the kitchen, some watching the news and the rest preparing their breakfasts. All but Elbina had a cup of tea in front of them.

Luna started rummaging through the cupboards for her breakfast, causing her mother to bounce out of her seat.

"Don't mind me, just getting some toast," said Luna in an annoyed tone as she felt for the correct cupboard, the one with the plates. Luna had essentially memorised the spatial properties of the house and had little to no trouble doing everything an emmetropic person could. Henrietta started to walk toward her.

"Let me help you, dear—" started Henrietta.

"No, Mum. Please, just let me do it," begged Luna, frustrated but understanding the intention. Henrietta sat back down and quietly pushed Luna's untouched cup of tea closer to the centre of Luna's table setting.

"Can you believe what the government is trying to do?" snapped Knitsy as she kept her eyes on the news. Updates displayed on a small television attached to the kitchen wall. "Acting as if everything is fine, as if we aren't out here in a dangerous world putting our lives at risk while they do nothing. Nothing!" She slammed her cup of tea to the table and started a coughing fit.

"Mum, let me get your breathing patch," said Henrietta, starting to get up.

"No, you sit down now," demanded Knitsy firmly, reaching under the table to grab her oxygen mask and patch. Henrietta slumped into her seat.

Luna brought her prepared toast to her seat, sat down, and pushed her glasses closer to her nose. She buttered the toast and took a small bite while the rest of the family watched as the prime minister prepared for her daily speech on the news.

"Good morning, England. We remain hopeful as our Earth continues to suffer. Temperatures are at an all-time high. We live inside, quarantined, longing for the fresh air that used to bring life into our souls. Our healthcare workers are working overtime to fill the need for mental health rejuvenation. Our industrial and civil engineers continue to innovate, planning new ways for humans to survive and *thrive* indoors."

Luna chuckled at the prime minister's emphasis.

"Our community is stronger than ever before, and I am certain that we will come out of this crisis new and improved. Keep in mind the beautiful worldwide celebration of Earth Day we held several weeks ago, as we continue moving forward to bring the Earth back to its green history. Have a lovely day."

The prime minister waved to the camera, and the broadcast ended. Ann Lou turned from the now-blank television screen to Knitsy. "Didn't that speech sound familiar to you?"

Knitsy shook her head with disgust toward the television. "She's a lying, cheating Tory, that one is." Ann Lou giggled under her breath.

"And for crying out loud, they never even mention the GeoLapse!" belted Knitsy.

"Do you think it's intentional? Maybe it would scare people," suggested Ann Lou.

As Knitsy shook her head and cleared her throat to respond, Henrietta sprang from her seat.

"Oh dear, would you look at the time! The bus is nearly here! You kids cannot be late for your exams! I need to get Riff downstairs immediately. Elbina, get the tunnel dock ready!" She dashed up the stairs toward Riff's room.

Elbina slowly rose from her seat and walked toward the front door, then started pushing a series of buttons with her thin, bony fingers. Out of the front door frame, a tunnel accordioned out, similar to those that used to bring passengers from the inside of an airport to an airplane. There was no view of the outside as the tunnel extended outward to the road. The tunnel was lined with indicator lights flashing red, meaning that it wasn't safe to exit yet. Elbina pressed another set of buttons, initiating a cleaning and sterilisation of the tunnel.

A hefty aluminum bus with no windows rolled up to the end of the tunnel dock. The bus began the process of attaching the entrance to the farthest point of the tunnel dock, which opened up like an old garage door once the attachment process was completed. The tunnel's red indicator lights were replaced with green ones, signaling that it was safe to enter the tunnel to reach the bus.

Riff came running down the stairs, papers nearly flying out of his rucksack. Elbina opened the front door to the tunnel, and they all started running out of the house toward the bus.

"Have a great day, my loves!" shouted Henrietta, waving to her children. "Be safe," she added, under her breath, unable to look away until the bus entrance shut and they were out of sight.

Once the school bus was gone and Knitsy was ready for her nap, Henrietta grabbed her own bag and was waiting for the next bus to pull up to collect her. She heard Knitsy call from the living room.

"There's something about to fall out of your bag."

Henrietta squealed, nearly dropping a green piece of fabric that was sticking out of her bag. She proceeded to shove it to the bottom. She wished her mother a restful nap and hurried into the tunnel.

The kids' bus rolled up to Houndwell School, which was a campus separated by a series of above-ground tunnels to divide the primary, secondary, and sixth form students. It was a rather boring-looking campus. Supposedly it had once been a very scenic location since a series of rivers that featured daily cruise ships used to surround it. But the sea had dried up about one hundred years ago, making the periphery of the campus quite desert-like, similar to the remainder of the Earth. The McHubbard kids were unfazed by this deadened land since they had never experienced it firsthand. In fact, they had never even seen a glimpse of the outside world. All they knew was that it was too dangerous to be exposed to.

Once the bus came to a complete stop and docked to the school's tunnel, Ann Lou jostled past everyone, including her siblings, off the bus and into the accordion tunnel so that she could be the first one to try out the cleaned hardwood floor of the roller rink at school.

Twelve-year-old Ann Lou was almost done with her first year of secondary school and loved everything about it. Even as one of the youngest students, she was already known as the popular girl. Her roller hockey career was also taking off as she was already the best player on campus.

Ann Lou had a rather egocentric personality. The students at school admired her but were quite intimidated by her strong presence. She always had people following her, offering some of their lunches or homework answers, just to be in the in-crowd with her. Everyone swooned for Ann Lou, even some of Riff's mates in year eleven. Ann Lou didn't particularly care about having friends at all but did nothing to discourage her constant posse. She really only cared for her roller hockey team and her best friend, Hayden.

She bolted through the tunnel and was first in line at the check-in area. There were added restrictions now that terrorist forces were becoming a major issue on school campuses.

"Start scanning," droned a teacher who had her abnormally large nose stuffed in a book titled *Effective Communication*. She gestured to a small circular cuff beside her that scanned microchips.

Every newborn human had a microchip embedded under the skin of their left wrist. This was the only method to keep track of the human population because the GeoLapse terrorism rate was so high in recent years. Each microchip had an abundance of capabilities, but it primarily recorded one's basic identification information and previous locations. Anytime there was an act of terrorism, theoretically a scanned microchip could tell you who was in that location at the time of the attack and therefore might have been involved. The concept was highly flawed since the GeoLapse members ended up removing their microchips, quite painfully, so that their locations couldn't be tracked and they could live undercover. But at schools, each student still had to scan in and out to keep track of who was in the buildings at all times.

When Ann Lou was at primary school at the end of last year, her microchip had disintegrated, along with her left forearm, in a horrible accident. A member of the GeoLapse had targeted the primary school building and tried to expose the children to the outside. The general objective of the GeoLapse was to keep the Earth uninhabitable so that they could reign as the leaders of the human race. They had developed their own bodysuits that allowed them to sneak around in the outside environment and cause havoc freely.

The GeoLapse had placed a bomb on the outside of Ann Lou's classroom wall, and it blasted a hole in the side of the room, causing outside exposure. One of the GeoLapse snatched up a little boy and tried to run off with him but was stunned when a huge thwack to the back of the head made him drop the child. Ann Lou had hit him with her hockey stick. The GeoLapse member escaped but left the child behind. Ann Lou had been standing near the exposed hole for too long, which ultimately caused the left arm from the elbow downward to disintegrate.

She decided to opt for the prosthetic option when she arrived at the hospital, which allowed her to perform basic functions of opening, closing, and gripping using the muscles in her upper arm, but all sensory function had been lost, as well as the microchip that had identified her. The prosthetic was made of chromium metal—"in case you ever have another exposure of that arm," they had explained. "This way the extreme environmental conditions won't erode the arm." She always thought it would be quite a coincidence to have another exposure on the exact same area, but she never questioned the doctors' reasoning. She had applied for a new microchip from the government, but since they were all so focused on the affairs of the environment and dealing with near-constant GeoLapse terrorism, she never received a response.

"Mrs. Doyle, it's me, I can't scan. Remember?" said a hurried Ann Lou as she waved her prosthetic arm in front of her oblivious teacher's book.

Mrs. Doyle finished the sentence she was reading, slowly raised her eyes to meet Ann Lou's, and then shooed her with a flick of her hand. Ann Lou catapulted past the security area and through the doors, headed straight for the roller rink.

Ann Lou bounded into the locker room and carelessly threw her rucksack on one of the benches, then started rummaging through her designated locker. She had a free period every morning and used that time to practice her skating and shooting techniques while no one else was using the rink.

Once her skates and pads were on, she hobbled out of the locker room and onto the rink with her stick and a few pucks. She pushed off the ledge into the cool rush. It was completely smooth, as if she were skating through the stars in her own little world. Her body felt so powerful as she dug her blades into the floor. She raced herself, pushed herself faster and faster with each digging motion. Her prosthetic arm felt weighty and unnatural on her movements, but that didn't dampen her spirits.

She was about to take a slap shot when she heard the rink doors close and quiet footsteps echoing. She whirled around in one graceful turn on her heel.

"Hey, you," said the approacher.

"Hayden!" she screamed. She tossed her stick to the floor and leaped toward the rink wall closest to her best friend.

A boy her age with dark skin, wavy, jet-black hair, and piercing green eyes greeted her with a hug over the rink wall and a shining smile. He brushed his fingers through his hair multiple times while talking to Ann Lou.

"Annie Lou, your technique is killer today," he said.

Hayden was the boy that Ann Lou had saved in the GeoLapse attack last year. Since that day, the two had become best friends. They went everywhere together in school—in the hallways, at lunch, and next to each other in class, whispering and passing notes while the teachers droned on. The two were inseparable.

"Thank you! I'm finally starting to get some control of this thing," she said with a laugh as she wiggled her prosthetic arm limply.

Hayden high-fived her, his smile widening. "That's totally rad, dudette!" Hayden changed his accent to sound American and held his hands up in a peace sign. He often spoke with an American accent when he joked around, mostly because it made Ann Lou laugh hysterically.

They both laughed as she broke into a fit of giggles and then pretended her arm weighed a ton, leaning to the left side. "Help! It's taking over!" she joked along.

"Well, should I tell Mrs. Doyle you'd prefer to spend the day on the ground and skip the history exam, or do you wanna walk to class?" he asked her.

Ann Lou leaned back upward, quickly skated toward the centre of the rink, picked up her stick, and raised it as she rapidly approached a puck. She swung with such force that the puck collided against the wall with a loud *BANG*.

"Let's go!" she shouted, skating back toward the rink exit.

Hayden and Ann Lou strolled the hallways to their second-period class, talking nonstop. They discussed the tricks Ann Lou had been practicing with her stick and puck, and how Hayden was planning on joining a band.

"You can't join the GeoLads!" whined Ann Lou, drooping her head as they walked. "Riff is my brother! You can't associate with him; he's literally the most annoying person in our house." Ann Lou was actually quite fond of Riff; he always agreed to play goalie when Ann Lou wanted to play hockey in the small hallway just outside their bedrooms on the upstairs level. Her sisters would never dream of roughhousing. But Ann Lou felt weird sharing Hayden with him since Riff had his own friends in the band, and people just generally liked Riff.

Hayden side-eyed Ann Lou with a smile. "He's my brother's best friend, Annie Lou. They needed a singer. You know their friend Joe who plays bass? Apparently, he was dating the lead singer and they had a nasty breakup last night. Well, that's what Matt told me. Anyways, she totally quit the band. So he asked me."

Ann Lou looked confused. "Why you?"

Hayden dropped his head in embarrassment. "Matt said I was the closest sounding to a girl he could find on short notice. I swear once I hit puberty, I'll get him back."

"You're too nice," said Ann Lou, shaking her head and rolling her eyes. "You need to toughen up!" She thwacked her hockey stick at a set of lockers to her right and caused Hayden to jump and fall into a fit of giggles.

Hayden caught a glimpse of someone behind them a little way down the hall, and he whispered to Ann Lou. "Uh, heads up. Elbina is giving you a death glare."

Ann Lou whipped her head around to see Elbina standing almost exactly where she had struck the lockers just moments ago. Her face was crimson with anger, and her fists were shaking with fury, holding the textbooks she had dropped from Ann Lou's scare.

"Sorry, Elbs," said Ann Lou halfheartedly, still walking away. Hayden continued looking back at Elbina, feeling sorry for her.

"Annie Lou, go apologise to her. Don't give her a harder time than she already has here."

Ann Lou stopped dead in her tracks and groaned out loud. She did have to be nicer to Elbina. She turned around and walked straight up to Elbina, donning a fake smile. Hayden followed behind her.

"Sorry, Elbs," Ann Lou repeated, bending down to pick up the remainder of the notebooks Elbina had dropped. As she knelt, she noticed red blots on the floor. She looked up to see that Elbina wasn't angry at all—she was crying. Ann Lou had accidentally struck her with her stick and drawn blood from her already thin and weak arm.

Hayden noticed it at the same moment and grabbed Elbina's shoulders to direct her down the hallway. "Let's get you to the nurse!"

Elbina didn't dare say anything for fear of letting out an audible cry. Ann Lou jogged behind Hayden and Elbina, watching them weave their way through the oncoming students.

Fourteen-year-old Elbina had a skeletal frame and short stature that helped hide her in a crowd. She hung her head, envious of her younger sister's popularity, which Ann Lou didn't even seem to know she possessed. Elbina was also in secondary school with her sister Ann Lou, except she was two years ahead in year nine. She was quite the opposite of Ann Lou. No one really knew who she was, other than "that girl who can't eat her lunch." At lunch time, she'd usually hide in the bathroom stall in the teacher's wing because they were all busy chaperoning lunch for the remainder of the students.

Elbina had no friends at all in school—not even the students in the culinary and French clubs, both of which she had been an active member of throughout secondary school so far. None of the students talked to her, because why would someone who can't even digest food be in the culinary club? It was a little too bizarre for their tiny brains to fathom. Elbina's one and only true friend was her oldest sister, Luna. She desperately wished the two were the same age so that she could have at least one friend in school, but Luna was already nearly done with her A-levels in sixth form and would be off to a university in the fall. Luna was the only person who didn't see Elbina for her disability. Everyone else at school seemed to think she was a waste of life.

Ann Lou watched as Elbina's bottle of murky liquid fell from beneath her large jumper, which Ann Lou caught before it could shatter on the ground. Riff had dubbed Elbina's feeding contraption "the Gasser." Using the Gasser made Elbina feel very self-conscious and embarrassed. The worst part was that it wasn't completely silent, so the students at school always knew when she was feeding.

Elbina needed the Gasser because her digestive system couldn't handle any liquids or solids. She would immediately get sick if anything, even water, entered her digestive tract. The only solution was for her to get nutrients in the gaseous state. The Gasser held a liquid mixture of basic nutritive elements. When turned on, it heated the liquid until the elements became gases. The gases entered her nasal passages and made their way into her lungs, where her blood collected and distributed the nutrients to the correct places in her body.

Hayden rushed Elbina into the nurse's office and sat her down in a chair, then ran and grabbed gauze from a first aid kit to wrap around her arm. Ann Lou raced to the school nurse and ordered her to tend to her sister.

The nurse, clearly bothered that she needed to get up and work, reluctantly walked toward Elbina and eyed her up and down. Elbina's face was hanging low, covered by her wispy brown hair. It was easy to see her blue veins popping out from her bony features. Her eyes had dark circles around them, and her lips were extremely chapped.

The nurse just said a measly "You'll be fine" and took the gauze from Hayden, who didn't have a clue what he was doing but had still managed to wrap the entirety of her bleeding arm. The nurse secured the gauze, then walked back to her desk and shut her eyes, leaving the three of them sitting in the chairs, awkwardly. Ann Lou figured she should say something supportive.

"If worse comes to worst, we could be twins!" she stated enthusiastically, waving her prosthetic in front of her face.

Elbina continued to look at her feet without a word, whimpering softly to herself. Hayden shot Ann Lou a stern look and gently placed his hand on Elbina's shoulder.

"Are you hungry, Elbina? Ann Lou, give me the bottle," he said gently, reaching his hand out to Ann Lou for her to pass the bottle for the Gasser.

Elbina took it graciously, slipping a small smile toward Hayden. She lifted her jumpers (she needed a few on at a time since she was always so cold), placed the bottle in its holder, looped the plastic tubing around her ears and into her nostrils, and switched on the Gasser. The low rumblings shook the seat she was sitting in, but Ann Lou and Hayden could tell that Elbina had instantly felt comfort from her Gasser treatment. After a few moments of silence, Elbina looked at Hayden again.

"Did you see my journal?"

Ann Lou passed Elbina her beat-up journal that she always carried with her everywhere they went. Elbina quite liked having a journal since Luna also kept a journal with various writings. She thought it was rather odd how much Elbina idolised their oldest sister since Luna never really socialised with anyone else, but it made sense to her that the two most antisocial people in the family would band together as a unit. Elbina shakily took the journal and opened up to a page with small handwriting. It looked like a recipe of sorts, but Ann Lou couldn't read a word of it.

This was her recipe journal. Elbina had never tasted anything, not even the cakes and stews that usually filled her home with delicious aromas. But that didn't stop her from using the process of cooking food for her other senses. Her last entry was for a red lentil daal, which everyone had enjoyed the taste of just a few days prior. For someone who had no idea what food tasted like, she was an excellent cook. It put her in a temporary happy place.

"Hayden, what's your favourite thing to eat?" asked Elbina sweetly. She had a pen ready to write.

As Hayden spewed out his answer—some stew his mother always made—Ann Lou sank in her chair with a groan. She thought Elbina's crush on Hayden was pathetic. Another person she didn't want to share Hayden with! She figured she didn't need to worry since Ann Lou was certain that Hayden had had a crush on her since last year, when they became friends. Ann Lou didn't really care whether or not she personally liked him back. She just wanted him to herself.

"What language is that?" Hayden laughed, watching Elbina write his answers.

"French," she replied, still writing feverishly. "I practice writing in French to perfect my skills in both areas. Plus, I think I can make the stew better than your mum makes. I have a few ideas for ingredients to add."

Ann Lou rolled her eyes. "Okay, Elbs, I think we should get you back to class before we all get detention for being late to our exams."

The three walked together to see Elbina off to class. Elbina was reciting her recipe in French to Hayden.

"*Jus de cornichon.* That's what this stew needs," she said under her breath as she scribbled down the missing ingredient.

Elbina waved as she approached her classroom, and Ann Lou smirked and walked off. Hayden called back to her, "I look forward to that stew." Elbina blushed and rushed into the classroom so he couldn't see her red face.

Ann Lou walked with Hayden to the basement of the school for his band practice after classes had finished for the day. They made their way into the practice room, where Riff, Hayden's brother Matt, and Joe were already setting up. Joe was tuning his bass. Matt plugged in his electric guitar, and Riff started unpacking his drum set.

"There's our newest GeoLad!" exclaimed Matt, tossing his hands up upon sight of Hayden. Matt resembled Hayden to a tee, except he was four years older: sixteen, just like Riff. The rock band thought titling themselves the GeoLads was a funny spin on GeoLapse, but most other people found it not so funny. Matt tossed Hayden a microphone from across the room, and Hayden caught it, barely, with the tips of his fingers.

"Ann Lou, please tell me you're joining, too?" Matt asked hopefully. "We were looking for a girl all along! Maybe you guys could duet. That would make some killer harmonies."

"One singer is enough," sighed Joe from behind them, clearly bothered by all the changes going on.

Ann Lou walked over to Riff and waved her hands in front of his eyes to get his attention. Riff's hearing was nearly gone, so the family had to use visual methods to get his attention. The family had spent the past few years learning sign language to communicate with him more effectively, although Knitsy generally resorted to just shouting at him.

Music was the only thing that kept Riff feeling alive most days. It was also the thing most detrimental to him. He'd grown up listening to music nonstop. He couldn't get enough of it and blared it in his head every chance he could get, causing the rapid decline of his hearing at a young age. But he couldn't stay away from the music. He'd gladly accept total deafness if it meant he could just play in this exact moment. Riff could feel vibrations easily, which is why he loved the drums.

Riff caught Ann Lou's attention and smiled as he pushed his moppy red hair back from his face. He was very tall, yet he still had a bit of weight on him. He appeared more like a friendly giant than anything.

"Hello," he signed to her. "Are you going to stay and listen?"

"I wouldn't miss it," Ann Lou signed back, smiling at her brother.

Matt started tuning his guitar and nodded his head once he was happy with the tuning.

"Your low E string is flat," said Riff out loud. He started drumming a basic beat.

Matt was astonished. "How can you hear that, but you don't hear when Mr. Rutherford tells you to wake up in class?"

Riff didn't respond, either because he hadn't heard or because he was starting a more complex beat.

"Let's quit the chat and start," snarled Joe. He started finger-picking a smooth, bouncy bass line.

Ann Lou took a seat by the door and watched the band perform some of their original songs. She enjoyed watching Riff completely lost in his music. His energy ramped up as they got farther into the song. His red hair bounced with the beat. His eyes were closed, and he improvised a drum solo when they all took their instrumental solos.

He was sweating from the energy release and smiling more than he had all week. They spent the next several hours jamming, singing, dancing, composing, and vibing to their creations.

Ann Lou felt Hayden's eyes on her for most of the practice. She'd pretend to be looking at something else in the room, but she could see him in her peripheral vision, staring at her. She liked the feeling of having him close.

After practice, she waited for Riff to pack up for the bus ride home. As they left the room, she could hear Joe talking to Hayden in the background.

"Mate, by the way, your vocals suck."

That evening, seventeen-year-old Luna was the first one home from school. Without missing a beat, she walked straight up the creaky, wooden stairs and felt with her fingertips along the right-hand wall until she reached her room. She tossed her rucksack down and sat at her desk, ready to study for her last A-level in English. She just needed one more A in her class to have the qualifications to get into the University of Oxford, where she had always wanted to study English Language and Literature. She often wore a University of Oxford t-shirt underneath her flannel shirt. Luna was the bookworm of the family and always the go-to when there was a problem to be solved. She put a hairband on her wrist, then pulled her long wavy red hair up into a high ponytail and grabbed a large book out of her rucksack to continue reading. It was a braille book, filled with a series of raised bumps that she could read with her fingers.

Ann Lou appeared at her door once she, Riff, and Elbina arrived home later. She carried a small tray with a cup of tea on it.

"Hey, Luna. Mum wanted me to bring you a cuppa." She walked in with the tray and placed it on the desk in front of Luna.

Luna was annoyed at their mother's clingy nature. She was nearly eighteen years old, the oldest child, yet she was by far the most doted on by her mother. But Luna bottled the frustration as best as she could most days.

"Mum knows I can get my own tea," said Luna stubbornly.

Ann Lou wasn't one to take stubbornness from her siblings easily. "Then tell her you want her to leave you alone. I'll drink the tea myself, then, if you want to be all grumpy about it."

Luna shot Ann Lou a look that basically just said, "Leave it."

"That's what I thought," sighed Ann Lou. "So, how did your English A-level go?" she asked, trying to be nice.

"It's tomorrow," replied Luna curtly, her finger still grazing the pages of her book.

Ann Lou groaned and slowly backed away from the desk as Luna took off her glasses and rubbed her eyes. Ann Lou couldn't help but notice her older sister's hazy corneas. She wondered if her sister could even see her at all.

Luna's vision had been deteriorating slowly throughout her life. Both of her eyes had developed cataracts at a young age, which hadn't been tended to because, unfortunately, healthcare in the current global crisis was essentially nonexistent. The population was dying out; humans weren't receiving the natural vitamins needed for survival anymore. Anyone with a disease who wasn't immediately dying had no hope for treatment. Ann Lou had been lucky to get a prosthetic arm after her accident; if she hadn't been at death's door, she wouldn't have been allowed into the hospital at all. Luna, on the other hand, had not received even the courtesy of being seen by a doctor for her cataract problems. So she lived with deteriorating vision.

Luna hardly noticed her disability, and she plainly hated being labelled as disabled. Even though her vision degradation was noticeable and required adaptations, she'd had nearly eighteen years of learning how to adapt to her surroundings. Yet she still was treated like a child at home.

As Ann Lou was about to leave the room, she noticed Luna pull out her journal, just like Elbina's. Ann Lou was curious about its contents.

"What do you write in there?"

Luna looked over to Ann Lou's general direction, confused as to why she was making small talk.

"Ideas," she responded curtly.

"Ideas about what?" pestered Ann Lou, annoyed at her reluctance to share more.

Luna groaned. "Like, story ideas. But nothing ever comes of it."

"I think you could write one of those books you read all the time," said Ann Lou.

Luna perked up for a moment but quickly sank down in her chair. "No way."

"You won't get into Oxford with that attitude."

As Ann Lou walked out, Elbina rushed into Luna's room. She felt a twinge of guilt upon seeing Elbina's patched-up arm. Ann Lou peered in from the hallway and watched them for a few minutes. Elbina was zealously writing down recipes and was reciting them aloud in French, and Luna flipped between writing in her journal and reading her book. Ann Lou was happy her two sisters had one another to be their weird selves with.

"Psst! Girls!"

Ann Lou whipped her head around to see their mother lingering by Luna's door. Ann Lou's spying had been discovered.

"I need your help. Nan is napping, and I want to make her birthday dinner special tonight."

Ann Lou felt bad that she had forgotten that Knitsy's seventy-fifth birthday was today.

Henrietta eyed Elbina. "Darling, I need your expertise in the kitchen. We're running low on ingredients for the sponge. Do you think you could help me improvise a cake?"

Elbina flipped to a page halfway through her journal. "*Recette de gâteau d'anniversaire!*" She dashed downstairs and into the kitchen.

Henrietta then eyed the other two girls. "I need you two to stall Nan while we prep the meal."

"What about Riff?" whined Ann Lou.

Henrietta tossed Ann Lou a comical look as she started down the stairs toward the kitchen. "We want her to be in a good mood tonight."

Luna and Ann Lou found Knitsy in the living room just as she was waking up from a nap. The living room doubled as Knitsy's bedroom since walking up the stairs was no longer within her capability. The couch was a pullout bed that she slept on quite happily. The best part was that it was extremely close to the kitchen, convenient for whenever she needed to sneak a midnight snack.

"How was your day, Nan?" Ann Lou ran over to Knitsy's bedside and jumped on the bed, startling her grandmother.

Knitsy started in a fit of coughs but still managed to pat Ann Lou on the shoulder to greet her. She then scrunched her face in disgust and pinched her nose closed.

"Ann Lou," she spat in a nasally voice, "you march straight to the loo and clean yourself before dinner! I will not have that hockey smell stinking up the living room again!"

"I'll shower after dinner, Nan," replied Ann Lou, trying to stall for time, as her mother had requested.

"Tell me about school," Knitsy demanded of the girls.

Neither Luna nor Ann Lou knew what to say. The kids typically shied away from their grandmother, and she desperately wanted to be a part of their lives, even if she was much older and less agile than they were. Ann Lou decided to take one for the team and tell her about Riff's band practice.

"Oh, you and that Hayden," Knitsy winked.

"Ew, Nan! He's my best mate. That's gross," smiled Ann Lou, playfully sticking her tongue out.

"Don't say I didn't warn ya! Your mother and father were the same way when they met—"

"Dinner's ready!" shouted Henrietta from the kitchen. Henrietta never spoke of their father, and she planned on keeping it that way. The kids were all too used to not asking about him. He had left just before Ann Lou was born. Luna had been only five years old at the time, and she didn't have many memories of him. They knew nothing about their father, which was fine with them since their mother somehow managed to support all six of them on her own.

"I'm starved," said a happy Knitsy, trembling as she stood up from the support of her cane. Luna and Ann Lou followed her to the kitchen table in the room adjacent.

Once Riff came downstairs, they ate a marvelous dinner of carrot soup and Yorkshire puddings. They sang "Happy Birthday" to Knitsy while she blew out candles on a magnificent sponge cake. She bounced with glee in her seat, sneakily poking her fork into the cake before it had been cut.

"Mmm, delicious, Elbina. I may not leave any for the rest of you," she joked, slapping Riff's hand away as he reached over to cut a slice.

As Henrietta cut the cake, Knitsy caught sight of Elbina's injured arm.

"My goodness, Elbina! Did you get any blood in the cake?"

Elbina gasped and covered her arm with her jumper. "Erm, no. I just fell in the hallway at school." She hung her head low.

Knitsy could sniff out a lie in an instant. "Bollocks," she swore. "Absolute bollocks."

Henrietta looked concerned but said, "Mum, if she doesn't want to tell you, then allow her to keep her privacy."

Knitsy shot her daughter a look of dismay. "You're fine with this? Your daughter is nearly six feet under as it is, and you don't even want to know why her arm is bleeding?"

"Nan, I'm okay, really!" urged Elbina, sitting a little bit straighter in her chair.

"You need to toughen up like your sister over here." Knitsy pointed to Ann Lou. "Get yourself a frying pan from the culinary club and whack a bully over the head with it. That's how the McHubbards do business."

Ann Lou poked at her puddings, pretending she wasn't hearing any of this. Elbina didn't say a word in response either.

Knitsy started brandishing her fork like a sword, then began to cough. Henrietta ran to her and reached underneath her mother's chair for her breathing patch, but Knitsy waved her away. Her coughing fits were such a frequent occurrence that no one seemed too concerned except for Henrietta. Knitsy reached underneath her own chair and pulled out a little box containing a small patch and some clear tubing with a breathing mask in the middle.

Knitsy slapped the patch onto her arm and covered her nose and mouth with the mask. Each time she exhaled, the device captured the unused oxygen, stored it in the patch, and recycled it into her respiratory system. It was quite an innovative product. It was a closed-loop system that was entirely self-sufficient and didn't require a motor, any bulky accessories, or even the Earth's atmosphere—yet it still unnerved Henrietta that her mother was relying more and more on this device for her breathing. After a few deep breaths, Knitsy's normal breathing was restored.

"Don't worry, everyone," said Knitsy to a barely attentive crowd. "I'm not going anywhere."

Henrietta let out a sigh of relief.

CHAPTER 2

THE PLANETARY DIAGNOSTIC TEST

The next morning, Ann Lou and Elbina, who shared a bedroom, woke up to the usual deafening sounds coming from Riff's room. Riff was blaring heavy metal in the room adjacent. Ann Lou was not fully ready to seize the day with The Death Brigade, or whoever was screaming in her ears that morning. Without sitting up, she grabbed a puck off her nightstand and hurled it at the wall between her and Riff's rooms.

Ann Lou groaned, then slowly rose from her top bunk. Elbina had already left the room without a word. Ann Lou secured her prosthetic, collected her rucksack, hockey stick, and a few pucks, then sluggishly made her way to the hallway and descended the stairs in slow, sleepy strides.

Everyone was already in the kitchen as usual, except for Riff, who was still blaring cacophonous music in his room. The usual argument between Luna and her mother over whether Luna could get her own breakfast had ensued. Knitsy was talking to herself, deliberating today's train wreck of a talk given by the prime minister. Elbina was helping to finish washing up since she had already done her Gasser treatment earlier in the morning.

"That no-good, rotten woman," growled Knitsy, referring to the prime minister. "When will she ever fit it into her tiny brain that this planet is dead?" Knitsy continued, visibly fuming. "And she has the bollocks to tell us to have a good day?"

Ann Lou snorted as her grandmother uttered the term *bollocks*. "I still feel like the speeches are all sounding recycled," said Ann Lou through a mouthful of toast.

"Don't speak with your mouth full, girl," said Knitsy, pointing a shaky finger at Ann Lou. "It was probably familiar because the woman has gnats in her brain. Doesn't realise that there are other words in the English vocabulary."

Ann Lou chuckled again, forgetting about the eerily familiar speech.

"Can we please have a more upbeat conversation since it's the last day of school? And can someone get Riff?" asked Henrietta, who was washing the dirty pots and pans. She looked worried that Riff's breakfast was getting cold.

"I'll get him!" announced Ann Lou, flouncing out of her chair. She rushed over to the living room area that was directly below Riff's room, lifted up her hockey stick with her prosthetic arm, and started banging the top of it on the ceiling, knowing he'd feel the vibrations coming through the floor.

"Quit that racket! You'll put a hole in the ceiling again!" spat Knitsy, tossing her hands up in the air, including the hand that was holding her teacup, causing some tea to spill on Luna, who had just sat down next to her. She started into a fit of coughs once she noticed that her tea was strewn about.

"Nan, that's hot tea!" growled Luna, frustrated that she'd have to get up again and change clothes.

"Oh, it's just a bit of dirty water, that's all," said Knitsy, rolling her eyes and covering her mouth as she coughed.

"I'll get you a fresh shirt, Luna," said Elbina, racing up the stairs.

"Get your brother while you're at it, please!" called Henrietta in her usual sweet but worried tone.

Once Elbina returned with a fresh shirt for Luna and a hungry Riff, Henrietta gestured for everyone to gather around the table. She looked extremely pleased about something.

"I think we have some good news to celebrate, everyone," said Henrietta cryptically, bouncing around in her seat. She pulled a large white envelope from under her chair.

"What's that?" asked Luna, squinting through her glasses from across the table, still fitting her arm through the sleeve of her flannel shirt.

Henrietta handed the envelope across the table to Luna, who gingerly took it and held it up close to her nose. She saw a blurry blue crest in the top left-hand corner and instantly knew what it was.

"It's Oxford!" exclaimed Elbina, sitting up so quickly that the Gasser bottle fell out from under her jumper. She quickly readjusted it and added, "Open it!"

Luna stared at the envelope and lightly touched the crest with her finger. After more shouts and prods from her family, she opened it. She could see only a haze where the words were, so Ann Lou hopped up and looked over her shoulder to read aloud to the family.

"Dear Miss Luna McHubbard, we are pleased to inform you that you have been accepted into the English Literature and Language degree programme at the University of Oxford—"

Henrietta shot up out of her chair with an excited shout and ran over to kiss the top of Luna's head and hug her. Luna winced, uncomfortable at being kissed, but the rest of the family did the same as Henrietta—except for Riff, who looked up from his breakfast in utter confusion.

"What's happened?" exclaimed Riff in all the excitement. He pointed to his ear.

Ann Lou signed "Oxford" to him, and he gave her a thumbs up. He added, "Oi Luna, since you've officially proven that you're smarter than all of us combined, I'll let you have the last spoonful of Elbina's delicious oatmeal."

"You're so kind, Riff," she joked as he passed her his nearly empty bowl.

"What do you think, dear?" Henrietta asked Luna, clapping her hands together.

"I haven't even finished my exams yet. I'm confused, honestly," Luna confessed.

"It's because you're overqualified," Elbina smiled. Henrietta nodded in agreement.

Suddenly, the television in the kitchen flashed on. Henrietta sighed in frustration. "Let's not watch anything, my dears—you know the rules at mealtime."

"Mum, the remote is over there," said Ann Lou nervously, pointing her prosthetic arm toward the kitchen counter that none of them were in close proximity to.

A dark screen with a dim light appeared before their eyes.

"What's happening?" asked Luna, squinting at her screen to no avail, unable to pick out anything that was happening. She still clutched her acceptance letter in her hands.

"I can't hear anything," said Riff, entranced by the screen, oatmeal dripping from his mouth.

"Shhh!" said Elbina, her hand forming a "hush" gesture near her mouth.

Someone on the screen was positioning a video camera in a dimly lit room. They looked quite familiar.

"Isn't that . . ." said Elbina.

"The U.S. president, yeah," answered Knitsy, in complete awe.

The family listened to the first few words of the unexpected news-flash. The camera had finally been positioned according to the president's liking. He looked completely ragged, almost dirty. The dim lighting contoured his face in an eerie shadow, making him appear ghastly.

"Bloody hell, what has the government done to the poor bloke?" said Knitsy under her breath.

"Hello, everyone. I'm so sorry to have woken you up if you live in North America, or interrupted your workday if you live in East Asia. Wherever you are, I can assure you that this message is essential to your survival." The president spoke calmly but with urgency. The McHubbards were fixated on the screen as he continued with his monologue.

"The Earth Rehabilitation Association has been lying to all of you. The Earth is beyond the point of mending. They are associated with the GeoLapse terrorists, who haunt our world with cruelty. Our atmosphere will completely evaporate within the next month. Stores of fresh water are quickly being depleted. There were never any plans to restore extinct animal and plant life. I fell for this lie, and I apologise that your leaders did, too. Earth will be unlivable by the end of the month. No one will be able to leave their homes, and the essential elements in the air will no longer be able to circulate through homes, causing everyone to suffocate to death."

"What in the actual bloody hell?" whispered Luna.

"Those no-good, rotten pieces of—" Knitsy started to bellow, knocking her teacup to the floor and breaking it into many pieces with a loud crash. Ann Lou grabbed her mother's hand. No one else could formulate words.

"I am very sorry to say that the peaceful leaders of the United Nations have fallen. The GeoLapse has killed every last member by exposing them to the outside world. I am in hiding so that I can relay this message to you while maintaining an inkling of hope for my survival. Please take a brief moment of silence with me to remember your fearless leaders, no matter what beliefs and views they had on life. They were sons, daughters, siblings, mothers, fathers, grandparents, spouses, and leaders who had hoped to help all of you, and they were lied to. I send my sincerest thanks and love to each of them as they go to a much more peaceful and loving place to rest in eternity."

The president bowed his head for a few seconds. The McHubbards did as well, only just beginning to grasp the horrendous situation.

"One secret that I must reveal to you is that Earth is an integral part of what's called the Universal Union. It is made up of other communities across our known universe. I was chosen to be the Earth delegate to deal with issues to keep peace and harmony amongst our intergalactic friends. I know this may sound absolutely crazy, but they've come up with a possible solution to save humanity." He took a deep breath before continuing.

"Five planetary communities have voluntarily offered to host humans. These communities have been selected based on specifications essential to human life. None of the communities is exactly like Earth. Each would come with its own set of challenges; however, each would allow you to continue to live much longer than what your remaining lifespan would be on Earth. The planets chosen for humans to be moved to are Cipto, Harvinth, Olfinder, Antympanica, and Epiton.

"Each household will shortly receive a test to determine which planet will be best suited for your individual lifestyle. I want to make it clear that you will be chosen for the planet where your chances of survival are the highest. You might not be able to move to the same host planet as your family and friends. The purpose of this transfer is for your longevity. Complete your tests immediately after this briefing to ensure placement in one of the five communities. If you refuse to complete the testing, it will be assumed that you choose death over life, and therefore you will be forced to stay on Earth. The communities have graciously agreed to be at peace with Earth as long as we respect their homes. Please take this opportunity to collaborate with your new communities to promote universal welfare. All the information you need to know will be on your screen. For now, this is goodbye. I wish you all a long life. You all deserve a second chance."

The screen went blank, and the McHubbards stared at it in silence. No one knew exactly what to say. Henrietta especially looked as if she were about to cry.

"Wait a second!" exclaimed Ann Lou, who had just started piecing together the president's words in the announcement. "So, there's a chance we can't all live together?"

"Well, why don't we just all put the same answers for the test?" suggested Luna. "That way we'll probably get assigned to the same location."

They all nodded in agreement and started to look hopeful.

"That's a fab idea, Luna. Someone call out their answers," piped Elbina, placing a gentle hand on Luna's arm.

"So, when's the test then?" asked Ann Lou.

"Should be any second, I suppose," said Luna.

Knitsy sat in her chair, eyes widened, still surrounded by shards of her teacup. She took a deep breath, which forced her into a coughing fit. Henrietta passed her breathing patch over and situated it for her on her body.

"I'd rather just stay here," she said through coughs. "What good am I to anyone?"

"Nan, you're taking the test. No one will be left behind," said Ann Lou with a stern voice.

The television screen displayed words in white block letters as a soft, droning voice read along. "Welcome to the Planetary Diagnostic Test. McHubbard Family, if you wish to take the test, please scan your microchips." A beam of light appeared just above the kitchen table and a countdown started.

"Thirty . . . twenty-nine . . ."

"Put your arms in!" exclaimed Henrietta, reaching her left arm into the beam of light, palm up. The family thrust all their arms in simultaneously, except for Ann Lou. The countdown continued.

"Fifteen . . . fourteen . . ."

"But . . ." Ann Lou trailed off. Her heart was pounding. The remainder of the family didn't seem to notice at first.

"Ann Lou!" shouted Henrietta, gripping her daughter's prosthetic wrist with her right hand.

"Three . . . two . . . one. Now entering the Planetary Diagnostic Test."

The family disappeared before Ann Lou's eyes. Henrietta's grip on her wrist vanished into nothingness. Ann Lou started screaming and bawling. She ran to her and Elbina's room, jumped onto the bed and clutched the nearest pillow to her chest. Where had her family gone? Were they gone forever?

She needed to speak to someone who could comfort her, so she decided to message Hayden. She only had to think of the message in her brain and it automatically sent to him. Their message conversation popped up in words before her eyes since texting with thumbs on phones was completely outdated.

Ann Lou McHubbard: Hayden, are you there?

Hayden Murphy: Annie Lou! I'm just about to take the test.

Ann Lou McHubbard: I am so scared. We just heard the announcement and I don't know what to do.

Hayden Murphy: I don't want you to worry, Annie Lou. I'm here for you.

Ann Lou McHubbard: I don't even know if I'll be able to go because I don't have a chip. I can't even take the test!

Hayden Murphy: You're gonna get out of here. I'm sure of it.

Ann Lou McHubbard: Thanks, mate.

Hayden Murphy: I gotta go now. Just take some deep breaths. You're not alone. Understood?

Ann Lou McHubbard: Thanks so much, Hayden. Good luck.

Hayden Murphy: We'll speak soon.

Ann Lou didn't know what to think anymore. Should she just accept the fact that she'd be left behind? Was there any hope for her to leave Earth? She felt silly. Just minutes ago, these scenarios would have never seemed plausible. Her blonde hair spilled out across the pillow as she dug her face into it, continuing to cry. The thought of not being able to play hockey on her team anymore ripped her heart even farther apart. It was the one thing that made her truly feel like she lived a normal life. She loved her family and friends, but hockey gave her a sense of passion and determination. She felt incredibly alone in that moment, a feeling she had never quite experienced before. She didn't want to die.

* * *

The rest of the McHubbards couldn't tell whether anything had happened at all. As far as they knew, they were still in the kitchen standing over the table with their arms extended.

"Did . . . anything happen?" said Luna.

"Ann Lou's gone!" said Elbina in a terrified voice. She looked around to see if the kitchen was still, in fact, the kitchen.

"This is all wrong!" shouted Henrietta, trembling where she stood.

"Ann Lou doesn't have a chip to scan," started Luna. "I'm sure she's all right." Luna's reassurances didn't seem to stop Henrietta from violently shaking.

They all stood there for a few seconds. Then the narrating voice continued.

"Round One."

"Round One?" inquired Knitsy, her voice coupling fear with anger. "I'll go bloody mad if something comes at me."

"Look!" shouted Riff, pointing to their home's front entrance, the one that used to lead to the tunnel.

They all looked in the direction he was pointing in and gasped. There was an opening, as if a door was opened, except there was no door; there was just white light and nothing to see beyond that. They all ran toward it simultaneously and without thought, but then stopped dead in their tracks just before completely stepping into it.

"Guys, look at your microchips!" said Elbina. Each of their microchips was lighting up under their skin in a pulsating, soft green light.

"That's weird," said Riff, examining his wrist. He gently grazed the light with a finger and immediately hopped backward. Within the periphery of his field of view, a bunch of numbers popped up in a soft green colour. They were changing ever so slightly, almost like informational displays in a video game.

"Touch the light on your chips," he said.

They all followed suit.

Riff looked around in circles to see if the numbers would go away, but they stayed within his visual periphery. Everyone else did the same circular head movements, trying to get rid of their numbers but failing in the process. Luna was the most in awe of any of them: the numbers in the periphery of her field of vision were completely legible, even as the rest of the visual field was the usual hazy blur.

"What do these numbers mean?" asked Riff.

"They look like . . . vitals," said Luna.

Knitsy looked at her granddaughter in shock. "You can see them?"

"What do they mean, though?" asked Elbina, who was trying to focus on the numbers but instead moved her whole visual field in the process.

"Yeah, they are vitals," vocalized Luna, more confidently. "Like, the one at the top right looks like a breathing rate. Uhh . . . the one in the top left is your heart rate. Bottom right is your body temperature. Bottom left looks like . . . some sort of glucose level? The other ones, I have no idea."

They silently agreed with her, still trying to get used to the constantly changing numbers.

"Well, shall we?" said Riff, gesturing to the opening.

"I'll go first. My life is much less precious than all of yours," declared Knitsy. She pushed Riff aside with her cane and stepped through the opening before anyone could stop her.

Knitsy found herself outside in a new world. She'd never been outside before in her whole existence. She didn't understand the wind blowing through her hair, or the rustling of trees, which she had only seen in books and pictures. These trees looked quite different, more exotic. The ground beneath her feet felt foreign but freeing. The sky was a pale grey and it was quite foggy in the distance. But she stood there in the open air, closed her eyes, and breathed in. Her breathing patch and mask were still on from her previous coughing fit, but it was a nice feeling not being locked up in a four-walled area. She dropped her cane and extended her arms like a bird. Her grey hair blew backward in the wind. Knitsy looked angelic and at peace. She took a few steps forward and noticed that the ground had a springy feeling to it. She put more effort into a bounce and started giddily hopping around the foreign world. Soon, the rest of the family were outside along with Knitsy, extending their arms and hopping like bouncy balls on the spongy ground.

Then strangely, Henrietta began to cough. After a few moments, Luna started coughing also. The cough cascaded to Riff next, then Elbina. Knitsy, who wasn't coughing at all, opened her eyes and lowered her arms, confused.

"You're all turning into me," she chuckled, making light of the situation. But their coughs only escalated.

"What's happening?" she asked them, not sure who to comfort first.

"I . . . can't breathe," choked Elbina, falling to the ground but bouncing as she made contact with the springy surface.

As they coughed, they all noticed that the numbers in their peripheral vision were pulsating red. Their breathing and heart rates were drastically decreasing. Luna fell in a bounce to the ground next to Elbina, clutching her chest.

"I don't understand," cried Knitsy, panicking. It seemed her whole family was losing consciousness, or maybe even their lives, right before her eyes. She ran to Henrietta and tried to pick her up and give her the Heimlich manoeuvre, but Henrietta's eyes rolled back and she was no longer breathing. Knitsy held her in her arms and watched her three grandchildren stop breathing within minutes.

"No! My grandchildren! Please, stop this! Stop!" Her heart rate started to increase, causing the vital to pulsate in red within her periphery. Knitsy was curled over in shock. Why was she the only one who could breathe in that moment?

"Take me! Not them! Please!" Tears streamed down her face as she covered her eyes with her hands.

"Round Two."

Knitsy looked up, and the five McHubbards were around the table again, left arms extended. They all looked incredibly confused.

"Oh my goodness," said Knitsy, grabbing Henrietta and hugging her tightly. She then ran to the other side of the table and grabbed Riff, Luna, and Elbina in one swoop and hugged them. Knitsy rarely showed any affection, so they winced at her embrace.

"Ann Lou?" Henrietta ran toward the stairs, thinking Ann Lou might be upstairs. She made it halfway up and was knocked backward to the bottom of the stairs by a hidden forcefield. Riff ran and helped her to her feet.

"I don't think we're done yet," muttered Riff.

Henrietta grudgingly walked back to the table with Riff.

"What now?" asked Knitsy, in a childlike voice. The family all looked toward Luna with an air of innocence, as if surely the bookworm would know all the answers.

"We're not actually in our kitchen. This is just a simulation," Luna started. Knitsy slumped into her chair.

Luna continued. "My assumption is that there will be five rounds, one for each planet. Each round will test our natural reactions to the different environments, hence the vitals being displayed. Did anyone else notice blinking red numbers as we were losing consciousness?"

"I was more concerned with the fact that I couldn't breathe," said Riff, smartly.

"Well, if you'd have paid more attention," she signed and spoke, shooting Riff a look, "you'd have noticed. So . . . right, we just have to act naturally. They're probably recording our vitals to determine which planet will be the most suitable for our longevity."

"Guess there's no sharing answers in this test," said Elbina, sounding a bit saddened.

"That makes sense," started Knitsy. "But why could I breathe if none of you could?"

"I'm not sure, Nan. I'm sure this will all make more sense once we get our results," replied Luna.

Knitsy looked defeated. There was no way she could bear to see her family suffer like that again.

"Do we have to go outside again?" asked Elbina, looking sternly at the open hole near the front of the house.

"I'll go first," announced Riff, puffing out his chest and starting to march toward the opening.

"Let's just all go at the same time," suggested Luna. "It might speed up the process."

They all locked arms and prepared to walk outside together in a row. As soon as they were exposed to the outside, they were immediately washed over with extreme heat. The temperature had to be hundreds of degrees Celsius. This time, the outside was like a barren desert, with large, active volcanoes on the horizon. Everything looked as if it had a colour palette of reds, yellows, and oranges.

Henrietta immediately fell over, pulling down Riff and Elbina, who were on either side of her.

"Argh!" she exclaimed as she fell. The ground felt like hot coals. She rolled over to avoid touching them, but she couldn't escape the burning feeling. Her skin was being visibly burned by the second.

"Riff, grab Mum, and let's get back inside!" shouted Elbina, feeling the heat burn through her skin. She watched redness spread across her skin from the point where her arm had impacted the ground. She was sweating so much, yet it was drying immediately on her face, causing even more heat to be trapped in her body. Elbina saw her body temperature indicator increasing until it was red and pulsating.

Riff picked up his mother, but he was starting to breathe with more difficulty from the excessive heat. They raced toward the opening to the house, but just as when Henrietta had tried to go up the stairs, the two were bounced backward by a forcefield.

"We're stuck out here!" he cried, catching his footing as they bounced.

The pain from the heat of the environment was quickly becoming overwhelming. Each of them was being burned to death as they collapsed to the ground. Everything was red: the flashing numbers, the erupting volcanoes, the rubble on the ground. The smell of burnt flesh surrounded the five McHubbards. All of them quickly saw their body temperatures rising, their heart rates slowing, and the other vitals that they couldn't identify pulsating in red numbers.

Riff could barely stand, but he held his mother in his arms while he stood, trembling, on the heels of his feet, which were beginning to burn as the heat penetrated the soles of his trainers. He was crying to himself, trying not to look at his family around him suffering. Within minutes, nearly all of them had been burnt over most of their bodies, and their vitals were abnormally out of range. Riff fell to his knees, still holding his mother. He felt himself starting to fade.

"Mum, I'm sorry!" he cried out.

"Round Three."

Again, the McHubbards were rehomed at their kitchen table, left arms extended. Not one of them had a burn in sight.

"Well, that one was bollocks," said Riff softly, covering his face with his hands to wipe away the exhaustion.

"What was the one vital that was on the middle of the right side? It was going up quite quickly," said Elbina, directing her question at Luna.

"I was trying to figure that one out myself," said Luna, thoughtfully putting her thumb and index finger to her chin. "I'm guessing it was some sort of pain scale. I noticed mine reach the high eighties before I passed out from the pain."

"This is inhumane!" shouted a fearful Knitsy. "We have to report this! They're going to kill us!"

"Report it to who, Nan? Our dead prime minister?" said Riff sarcastically. "We have no burns to report, so whoever is running this test is technically not doing anything wrong."

Knitsy hushed up. Her grandchildren seemed to have more sense in them than she did by a long shot. She watched Elbina walk to the light and was surprised to hear her say, "Well, three to go!"

The remainder of the family slowly walked over to the opening with the bright light.

"I'll go first," said Luna bravely. She walked out of the opening, the others hesitating for a few moments to stall the next round.

Luna walked out into the new world. It was a little chilly but nothing extreme. This world was pitch-black from her perspective, except for the illuminated vitals in her periphery, but the lack of identifiable features didn't really bother her since her usual eyesight was rubbish anyway. Her hands naturally glided out in front of her to feel around in case she bumped into something. Her right hand brushed something solid, and she pulled it back to her side in fright. But nothing grabbed her or made a noise, so she brushed her hand again on the mystery object, which in fact felt like a big stone wall. She reached out to her left side and felt another wall.

"Hmm," she thought out loud. Her brain imagined a straight path, so she began walking forward, not feeling particularly frightened. She moved her arms above her head to see if she'd bump into something, and, sure enough, the stony wall eventually reached arm's length above her head as she continued forward.

She felt a corner with her left hand and turned in that direction. Her footsteps were light and careful in case any obstacles, such as a hole or a rock, were to come across her path. It was a lot like walking through the upstairs hall at home, avoiding Riff's things that always crowded the hallway because he was too lazy to clean up after himself.

Luna felt a sense of empowerment as she walked along the stony maze. There were many twists and turns, steps, and a few bumps in the road, but Luna easily manoeuvred the environment and pictured the entire path in her head as her fingertips grazed each surface. At one point she noticed the ground sloping upward, the stone ceiling sloping downward, and the stone walls sloping inward. It was as if she was reaching the apex of a pyramid. Where she anticipated the point to be, there was a small hole instead, just large enough for her to fit into. She crouched down, just about to crawl in the hole, when she heard a scream from way behind. She hopped around, orienting her body to where the scream was coming from, still in complete darkness.

"Elbina!" she yelled, recognising her sister's cry for help. She could hear the rest of them start to call out. They must have just gone through the opening of light.

Luna started to run toward their cries. Having mostly memorised the route, she needed only one hand to aid her around the twists and turns. But before she could reach the others, she was bounced backward to the hard, stony ground. The forcefield wouldn't allow her to go back and help them.

She was worried about them but figured it would be best for her to finish whatever this round entailed. "Feel your way through the maze!" Luna shouted to them.

Luna made her way back to the apex and wriggled her tall, lanky body through the hole and into a narrow passage. She squirmed through the hole, her arms close to her chest, completely surrounded by cold stone. It felt like the passage would go on forever.

After a few minutes of crawling, Luna finally reached an opening where she could take her arms out from her chest. She reached down and felt the ground about a foot down. The ground felt like a bunch of small rocks. Screams trailed behind her. Her breathing rate was increasing, the indicator pulsating in red, just because she was so worried about her family. But she at least knew there was nothing harmful that would meet them along the way.

Luna used her hands to walk herself forward until her feet were free from the hole. Standing up, she reached out her arms again and walked a few steps, looking for a wall. But there was nothing within reach except for the one she had just come out of, which felt as if it had a slight curve to it, suggesting she might be in a giant circular room. She walked away from the wall for about twenty paces and the sounds of her footsteps were echoing more than they had before. Confusion settled in as she lost track of the path.

"Where . . . ?" She turned her body around a few times, thinking she might see a speck of light, but nothing popped into her visual field except for extreme darkness. The rocks crunched under her boots. She bent down and grabbed one in her hand. It felt smooth, with no bumps or cracks. Standing up, she tossed the rock ahead of her. It hit a wall not too far ahead.

"That must be where I just came from," she figured logically. She turned 180 degrees and tossed another rock. It sounded as if it fell to the ground without hitting anything. She repeated this activity, throwing a rock and following the sound it made, until she threw one that seemed to clang against something metal—except the sound went in the downward direction, as if the rock had fallen down some sort of pipe. Luna carefully treaded to that area. Sure enough, there was a slightly curved wall with a hole in front of where she stood. This time, however, the hole was going downward, just as the sound of the thrown rock had indicated.

Crouching down again, she grazed the circumference of the hole with her fingertips. It was metallic and rusty. She knocked on it gently and the sound echoed several times, indicating that the bottom of the hole was a long way down. There was no other choice. She had to jump. She could tell from the distant screams from behind her that her family hadn't gotten much farther from where they had started.

She jumped.

"Round Four."

Luna shuddered, thinking she was still falling, but quickly came to her senses when she saw the soft haze of the kitchen and her family surrounding her. They all made fearful cries but quickly calmed down when they, too, realised that the round was complete.

"That . . . was so . . . scary," said Elbina breathlessly.

"These planets don't have great marketing schemes, do they?" said Riff, slumping into a chair and hiding his face in his hands. "If I were them," he continued, "I would promote the fun parts of living there— not the absolute worst things about the damned place."

"Language!" shouted Knitsy.

"These aren't tribulations to the creatures that live on these planets, though," said Luna matter-of-factly. "They're only making sure we can survive."

"Well, I don't know about you," said Riff, "but I'd rather die a slow, painful death on Earth, where I can at least lie in the comfort of my own bed. These aliens can burn or suffocate themselves for all I care."

Henrietta looked sick, as if she couldn't keep going. She went and hugged Riff. "I never thanked you for helping me in the second round. You're such a good boy."

It was rare that Henrietta praised Riff, since he so frequently used foul language in front of his grandmother. But it was nice to have his mother comfort him. He hugged her back tightly.

"Well, we've all nearly suffocated, burned, and been blinded, so what could possibly be worse this time around?" said Knitsy.

"Please don't jinx it, Nan," said Elbina, eyeing her grandmother cautiously. "Let's just go."

They decided on walking out of the opening together again, locking arms. The McHubbards were glad to find that, this time, they could see a world around them. They had entered a sort of desert-like place, but it was not nearly as hot as the world in the second round had been. This one was barren, with sandy ground. The sky was bright and the air was dense, with overwhelmingly high humidity. In the distance, they saw something that looked like a tiny oasis with greenery surrounding it.

"It's so humid," panted Riff, wiping away the sweat that was already forming on his forehead.

"I'm thirsty," mumbled Knitsy, licking her lips.

"And hungry," added Luna.

They all agreed out loud that they were all getting thirstier and hungrier by the minute.

"Shall we walk to that little pond over there?" suggested Henrietta, attempting to take the lead.

"Yeah, lead the way," said Luna. Elbina gripped her arm tighter. They all slowly approached the oasis. It looked very out of place, with nothing but desert land for miles around.

They were all panting and gasping for something, anything, to quench their thirst. Riff went up to the small pond, got down on all fours, and stuck his face directly into the water, and started gulping. Meanwhile, Elbina, Luna, Knitsy, and Henrietta inspected the greenery around the oasis. There were strange looking plants that seemed like they might be flowers. Purple stems came up from the ground with leaves sprouting off the sides in all different shapes. There were yellow leaves that were square-shaped, blue leaves that were triangles, and even some pentagonal green leaves that emitted a pink glow. Luna, Knitsy, and Henrietta, without uttering a word to one another, quickly picked the strange plants and began to eat them. Wherever they broke off a piece, new growth instantly sprouted, allowing the three to continue picking and eating them uncontrollably. Realising that their thirst was still unattended, they ran and knelt beside Riff at the small pond. They stuck their heads in just as he had. They were all drinking excessively, taking many gulps at a time before coming up for air.

Elbina stood and watched them in horror as they ate and drank ravenously. She, too, needed satiation, but she knew she couldn't eat or drink anything besides what was in her Gasser treatments or else she would get extremely sick.

"Aha!" she exclaimed. The Gasser was still around her waist. She pulled up her jumper and noticed that she had finished only about half of her meal from breakfast. She turned on the Gasser as quickly as possible and closed her eyes as she felt the relief flowing into her body. One red, pulsing number then went back to green within the periphery of her vision. It must have been her hunger level.

Riff came up from the pond and ran to the plants that his family had just been eating. He, too, picked and ate them and was thrilled when they instantly regrew. However, after several mouthfuls, Riff suddenly threw up all the water he had drunk and all the flowers he had eaten, mixed with a lot of blood. Luna, Knitsy, and Henrietta followed suit after a few more gulps of the water. Each of them watched their displays as their hunger and thirst levels plummeted into complete starvation and their pain levels skyrocketed. Even though they had all lost a lot of blood, they continued to drink the pond water and eat the flowers as if they couldn't stop themselves. Henrietta jumped into the pond and Riff followed her.

Elbina stood just feet away as they kept vomiting water, flowers, and blood yet continued to drink and eat from the poisonous oasis. To Elbina's horror, their bodies slumped over and they began to drown. She fell to her knees in tears, knowing it was almost over but terrorised by the sight of her suffering family when she was feeling completely fine.

"Round Five."

Back in the kitchen surrounding the table, the McHubbards all sighed in relief.

"What was that about?" inquired Luna, gasping for air.

"It almost felt like I was getting thirstier and hungrier the more I drank and ate," replied Riff, eyes widened. "But my stomach couldn't hold any more. And my thirst and hunger levels were way stronger than the pain in my stomach."

They all agreed. Elbina stayed quiet.

"Last one, kiddos," said Knitsy. "We're almost done."

"Yeah, until we have a lifetime of this," said Luna aggressively toward her grandmother.

Without another word, they crossed the kitchen toward the opening with the beaming, bright light. They locked arms, afraid to move into the last round. Their bodies were all trembling with fear.

"Let's do this one for Ann Lou," said Henrietta, still staring straight in front of her toward the opening.

"For Ann Lou," repeated Knitsy. They walked out in one synchronised stride.

Riff immediately felt himself leaning a little too far to the right, but he caught himself and maintained his balance. He looked around, hoping to catch a glimpse of his siblings, mother, and grandmother, but none of them were there. He was in the middle of what looked like a dense forest, with lots of strange trees and shrubs.

The trees' trunks were massive at the base, so large that Riff would not have been able to wrap his arms all the way around their circumference. As he looked up, he noticed that the trunks were conical in shape, like a dunce hat. Strings of light shone through the forest canopy; however, there was something strange about this place. It was completely silent. He noticed some fallen leaves on the ground were tumbling ever so slightly in the wind, yet they made no sound. He could hear no sounds of life at all, not even the sound of his own heart beating.

"Where did everyone go?" he thought to himself. He looked around for some sign of his family.

"Mum?" he tried saying, but nothing came out. He tried articulating a little louder, but still, nothing came out. He screamed at the top of his lungs, but there was nothing but complete silence and a strange feeling of terror.

Riff's heart rate started pulsating in red. "Calm down," he thought to himself. Almost instantly, after a few deep breaths, his vitals returned to their normal green colour.

He picked a random direction and started walking. As he thought about it, he realised the absence of sound was a somewhat familiar feeling. His hearing loss had formed him into a fairly introspective thinker, so talking to himself within his own mind was almost louder than the real world on Earth. This was no different.

He felt as if he had been walking for miles when he noticed a small muddy spot in front of him with footprints perpendicular to the direction he was walking. The footprints were smaller than his, and he realised they could have been made by any of his family. Excited, he turned in the direction of the footprints and walked faster. He could feel the blood rushing through his veins as he clutched his heart. He so desperately wanted to see any of the women in his family, but the mud trail stopped at a dead end. He crouched down, expecting the usual crunch of leaves, but there was only an overwhelming silence.

There was a small pile of leaves pushed to one side, as if someone had turned in that direction. He picked this new direction to follow and continued for a few hundred feet or so. He sang one of his favourite tunes, "Take Flight" by The Death Brigade. It was one of the songs he liked to play on blast in his bedroom every morning, mostly so he could hear it. He decided to take a stride with every beat of the song that played in his head.

"You don't wanna be with me, you see," he sang in his mind. "So put me out of my misery, and step away into the night, so my dear you can take flight." The chorus rang in his head, and soon enough he was skipping down the path, forgetting the task at hand. He tripped over a rock, and the fall, though silent, jolted him back into reality. He lifted his head quickly and pushed his moppy red hair behind his ears. He sensed something strangely familiar.

"What's that smell?" he thought.

He thought he could smell perfume, a familiar scent that Elbina wore every day. He hated the smell of it, and the two of them always bickered about whose perfume or cologne smelled worse.

Now, sniffing for Elbina's perfume, he felt like a dog. It was the last smell he'd ever thought he'd be seeking out, but it also engendered a feeling of hope inside him—a bright, warm feeling of relief that maybe he would be able to locate one of his family members. Then the smell grew fainter. He retreated to where it had been the strongest: beside the trunk of a tree with many protruding branches. He looked up and saw his answer. Elbina was above him, climbing the tree. Riff realised that she could have been ahead of him the whole time in the forest, just out of sight, and he wouldn't have heard her running. She was now climbing the tree rapidly while holding her jumper in her teeth.

"Elbina!" he tried screaming. He was jumping and waving his arms above his head. He just felt invisible. She, of course, couldn't hear a thing. He watched her in silence as she made her way over to a branch that was parallel with the ground. Riff was out of her field of view, but he saw her crying. His heart sank seeing his younger sister so sad.

"What is she doing?" he thought as he watched her tying her jumper around the branch in a tight knot. She then began to tie one of the arms of the jumper around her neck.

"Oh, no!" he mouthed, and he instantly hopped onto the tree, scaling it as quickly as his burly body could climb, which was far slower than Elbina had. This tree was relatively easy to climb, as it sloped toward the top of the cone. Still, it presented issues. The wood left splinters in his large hands, causing painful and bloody wounds.

Elbina still couldn't see him climbing just behind her. She inched her way along the branch to position herself where she wouldn't hit the tree on the way down.

"No no no no no!" mouthed Riff. He gripped a branch and tried to pull himself up, but it broke off in his hand. Elbina had stood upon that same branch with no problem; her bony body weighed nothing compared to his tall, bearlike frame. Riff planted his feet against the tree's trunk and tried to launch himself up to push against the branch Elbina was situated on with his free hand, so that maybe she would feel the movement he made. He missed. He dipped deeper into his squat and exploded upward, managing to grab the branch, which started to wobble. Riff's heart rate vital was uncontrollably pulsating in red.

Elbina looked back. She had felt the movement. Her eyes bugged when she saw Riff. Tears of relief streamed down her cheeks. A sense of warmth washed over him again as their eyes connected. He took a deep breath and reached his hand out to her to help her to safety, but she couldn't quite reach it. She started to inch her way back toward the middle of the tree. She had forgotten to untie her jumper from the branch, and when she was nearly close enough to grab Riff's bloody hand, she lost her balance. Riff's heart sank as she fell off the tree. Their voiceless screams echoed in his mind.

Still in a state of horror, the family was again situated in the kitchen around the table. The opening where the light had been was replaced by the usual tunnel where no light could penetrate through. The five of them couldn't utter any words.

"You have now completed the Planetary Diagnostic Test. Your results will be with you momentarily."

CHAPTER 3

A SECOND CHANCE FOR ANN LOU

"Ann Lou!" shouted Henrietta as she bounded up the stairs, forgetting that the last time she had tried this, she had been catapulted backward. Luckily, this time, she was able to reach the top.

Henrietta vaulted into Ann Lou's room and pulled her youngest daughter from her bed and into her arms.

"Ann Lou, get your arse down here!" shouted Knitsy from downstairs.

Ann Lou followed her mother down the stairs, looking incredibly confused, tears still streaming down her face.

"You'll never believe what that was like," said Riff, making his way to the couch and slumping into the fetal position with a whimper. The image of Elbina falling to her death was permanently etched into his brain, and he couldn't shake it.

"Did you guys even take the tests yet?" asked Ann Lou, raising an eyebrow.

The rest of the family looked at her as if she had a third eye growing on her forehead.

"We've been gone for ages," answered Luna, confused. "Have you been asleep or something?"

"No . . ." trailed Ann Lou. "I went upstairs less than five minutes ago, after you disappeared."

"Could you hear anything?" asked Knitsy with her arm around Ann Lou's shoulders.

"No."

"These aliens are stuck in some weird space-time continuum bollock show, and I'm not here for it," said Riff, now completely horizontal on the couch.

"Riff, don't get me started on the language," said Knitsy sternly.

"Nan," started Riff, looking directly at her, "we literally just lived a nightmare five times in a row. Let me say a damn swear word so I can release these dark memories that will probably be living in my brain for the rest of my life, which I hope is extremely short from this point onward."

No one answered. They all silently agreed with him.

"Damn," said Elbina. The family laughed at the sound of Elbina swearing, which was completely out of character.

"Alien bollocks," said Knitsy, chuckling along.

It was the first time in a while that the family was laughing together. Despite the situation, the lighthearted moment was more than welcome.

"The results are in," said a woman's voice.

The family all turned toward the kitchen television once again, where a woman was speaking. She was probably in her late twenties at the oldest, with blonde hair past her shoulders, but it was hard to tell much more about her because, like the president, she was broadcasting from a dimly lit and unidentifiable location. The family piled into the kitchen in their usual spots, all turned toward the television screen. Their breakfast settings were still in the same place on the table just as they had left them. The woman continued.

"McHubbard Family, congratulations on completing your Planetary Diagnostic Testing. The results of your test have been analysed by the Casper panel of the Universal Union, who reviewed your natural bodily reactions to simulations of life on the five host planets. Each of you has been placed for rehoming into the host planet that will be most suitable for your survival and longevity. But before I present your family's individual results, I will first introduce the host planets in the order in which you visited them during your recent testing activity!"

She was trying a bit too hard to sound cheery, as if the McHubbards had just gone on a tropical vacation and not endured the greatest horrors of their lives. The family didn't remark on it, as they were keen to see how else she could possibly try to sell the idea of living on these not-so-enticing host planets.

"Introducing host number one . . . Olfinder."

The view on the screen warped into a cluster of stars that appeared to be some other galaxy's map. It resembled the Milky Way Galaxy as far as they knew. Maybe their new homes wouldn't be as far away as they'd imagined.

"Located in the Triangulum Galaxy, two point seven three million light years away from Earth—"

"How far?" shouted Riff at the screen, his eyes bulging. Elbina shushed him.

"—it is home to a community of curious little beings! The Olfinderians share many societal similarities to humans on Earth. For example, they are very creative in the arts—particularly through song!"

The galaxy zoomed in on Olfinder, which was tucked in one of the spiral arms of the foreign galaxy. The planet looked fairly small in comparison to the ones surrounding it, but the McHubbards had no indication of how they compared to the planets in Earth's solar system.

Olfinder itself was enveloped in a foggy grey atmosphere. A second picture, of a representative Olfinderian, popped up on the television. It was completely covered in fur. With its forward-facing eyes and pointed ears, it resembled a dog, but it had no snout, at least not in the place an Earth dog would have had one. Its mouth was conical, like the end of a foghorn. Its four legs and tail were coiled like springs.

The narrator continued. "The weather on Olfinder is temperate, damp, and always foggy. We don't want too much sun, now do we?"

"Nice selling point," said Knitsy in a huff.

"One main difference between life on Earth and life on Olfinder is quality of the atmosphere. The air on Olfinder is slightly different in composition to that on Earth. But not to worry—those selected for Olfinder will get adjusted!"

"Enticing," added Knitsy in a monotone.

"Introducing host number two . . . Epiton." The view of Olfinder zoomed out to a wide view of hundreds of galaxies. Then it zoomed in on a different galaxy. After a pause, it zoomed in on a planet. This planet seemed to glow orange from the illumination of nearby stars. The entire planet looked red hot at first glance.

"This host planet is located in the Messier eighty-two galaxy, eleven point four two million light years away from Earth."

The McHubbards' mouths dropped. Not one of them was blinking.

"If you think you'd like the old summertime on Earth, then you'll love the weather on Epiton! Home of supervolcanic activity and many bright suns, this place is likely to feel like a sunny paradise all year round."

"I'd rather scratch my eyes out than go on a bloody holiday there," said Knitsy, feeling riled up.

"Epitonians enjoy activities similar to sport on Earth. They are very competitive in nature, and if you're lucky and up for the challenge, you'll get to join in an exciting game of Pyroll, the planet's favourite sport."

The screen showed an example of an Epitonian. It looked quite muscular and had arms and legs similar to those of humans, except its hands had one large, sharp claw each. It also had two small but sharp horns poking out from the top of its head. It stood very tall and had a charcoal-coloured exterior. The eyes were red-hot and menacing.

"Introducing host number three . . . Cipto." Again, the view zoomed out and back in to another galaxy and planet. This time, there was so little light that it was difficult to see the planet at all.

"Cipto lies in the Dragonfly forty-four galaxy, approximately three hundred twenty-six million light years away from Earth."

"I'll never complain about the bus ride to school ever again," said Riff, pushing his hair back with his fingers.

"There aren't many suns in the area to supply Cipto with light," the narrator continued, "but Ciptons are known to have the brightest personalities in the universe! They also are very enthusiastic story-tellers." The picture of the Cipton showed a creature that was basically a protoplasmic, invertebrate blob. It had no eyes, and it surely did not need any since the planet was completely dark anyway.

"Introducing host number four . . . Harvinth." The view zoomed out for a considerably longer time before it finally began to zoom in on a rather small galaxy. This galaxy was shaped like a spoon, and Harvinth was one of the planets on the tip of the handle of the spoon.

"Harvinth is located in the dwarf galaxy called MACS0647-JD."

"Rolls right off the tongue," said Riff, elbowing Knitsy playfully.

"This galaxy is located approximately thirteen point two six billion light years from Earth."

"You know, that last point two six is what really makes it a little too far, in my opinion," said Knitsy in Riff's direction. The two of them laughed.

Henrietta was seething with anger. Her face turned more and more purple until, finally, she popped. "How can you bloody two be laughing at a time like this? This is not funny! You should be ashamed of your-selves! Show some bloody respect toward your family!"

Ann Lou thought her mother was going to squeeze her right hand completely off her wrist. "Um, Mum, lighten the grip," she whispered, "or I'll need another new arm."

Riff snapped back at his mother. "Do you actually think I'm ready to go on holiday to one of these places? It's a damn defence mechanism," said Riff sternly to his mother. Knitsy immediately elbowed him in the side for his cursing.

The blonde woman continued speaking. "Harvinthians are a little different from humans in that they absorb their food through the atmosphere."

The next picture, showing a typical Harvinthian, was nothing like they expected. The video zoomed in to what looked like a single-celled organism.

"So, wait, what is that thing?" asked Riff, this time looking around at his family.

Luna said, "I guess since Harvinth is in a dwarf galaxy, life there hasn't existed for very long. That cell would only need basic nutrients from its atmosphere to survive and reproduce at this point."

The narrator continued. "Since Harvinth is located so far into the depths of the universe, time works a little differently there." She elaborated no further.

"So far, I'm not too impressed with the choices," said Knitsy, elbowing Riff with a chuckle. "Which ones like to drink?"

"And lastly, introducing host number five . . . Antympanica!"

Henrietta, speechless now, gripped Ann Lou's hand even tighter. The view zoomed out and in again to a new galaxy. "Antympanica is located in the Tadpole Galaxy, four hundred million light years away from Earth."

From space, Antympanica looked just as it had in the test: full of greenery and forests. The Antympanican being was small and round with short hair all over its body, which was ringed around its entire circumference by a web of skin that looked like a wing. The wing extended into the shape of a small parachute when it was not tucked into the body, giving it the resemblance of a sunny-side-up egg. It had three extremely large eyes on the top of its head, all looking in different directions.

"Antympanica is home to many exotic plants, lakes, and amazingly beautiful forest trails. The air is very dense, making it difficult to hear much of anything, but that doesn't stop the Antympanicans from enjoying a nice pint and gossip! Movement is key, since that is how they communicate with one another."

"There are my drunks," sighed Knitsy in relief.

The picture of the Antympanican disappeared, and the mysterious narrator warped back into view.

"And now, I will recite your placement results."

"Here we go," said Henrietta, grabbing the hands of Knitsy and Ann Lou, who sat on either side of her.

"Knitsy McHubbard," started the woman.

Knitsy audibly gulped.

"You have been selected for placement on . . . Olfinder."

"That's good, Nan!" exclaimed Elbina. "You were the only one who did well in that round!"

"But why?" asked Knitsy.

"I think it's because you have your breathing device that recycles oxygen and carbon dioxide molecules," said Luna, proudly reciting the connection she had made. "It doesn't require elements directly from the atmosphere, it just recycles your current breaths. You'll be able to breathe just fine on Olfinder as long as you keep your device on all the time."

Knitsy sighed, not with frustration but with relief. Maybe she did have a chance to survive on Olfinder.

"Henrietta McHubbard, you have been selected for placement on . . . Epiton."

Henrietta's face did not change at all. It was almost as if she had expected this result. Her trembling hands were still holding onto Ann Lou's and Riff's. She didn't inquire about the reasoning for her placement, but Luna announced her opinion anyway.

"Probably because Riff was holding you, so your burns weren't spreading as quickly as ours."

Riff felt entirely responsible for his mother's placement on a terrifying planet. The guilt grew on his face as he curled over and put his head between his knees. Henrietta looked ashamed for causing her son to feel so much guilt.

"It's all right, Mum. There probably are loads of other reasons you were chosen, too," Elbina reassured her.

"Luna McHubbard, you have been selected for placement on . . . Cipto."

"There's a no-brainer. Luna, that's perfect for you," said Elbina, now projecting her kind energy toward her oldest sister.

Luna shot her a smile in response but still couldn't shake the feeling that she might end up alone on Cipto.

"Griffin McHubbard, you have been selected for placement on . . . Antympanica."

"Riff, sit up! You just got placed!" announced Knitsy, grabbing his shoulders and trying to pick his head up off the table.

"Huh, where'd I go?" inquired Riff, slowly sitting up. Dried tears were stuck to his cheeks.

"Antympanica. The quiet one," signed Elbina, still looking forward. She was afraid to meet her brother's eyes.

Riff watched Elbina's response, and his stomach dropped. Even though Antympanica was probably the best fit for him, it held the worst memory of his life up to this point. And it involved Elbina. He dropped his head back to the table.

"Elbina McHubbard, you have been selected for placement on . . . Harvinth."

"Elbs, that makes the most sense," said Luna, nodding her head. "The Gasser is the answer to that one. No need to worry about the food and drink problem."

Elbina nodded back. She felt a lump in her throat and was absolutely devastated that she and Luna would not be on the same planet. She wouldn't have minded going to Cipto as long as Luna was there. But now she'd be all alone.

"And, lastly, Ann Lou McHubbard."

Everyone gasped and fell silent. Were they going to place Ann Lou after all? Ann Lou's eyes were glued to the screen.

The woman's jolly expression turned to one of fear, which she quickly changed to disappointment in order to cover her emotions.

"You have neglected to take the Planetary Diagnostic Test. You have been disqualified for selection and must remain on Earth."

Everyone's heart sank. The youngest in the family was being forced to stay behind and die with the Earth.

"No!" shouted Henrietta in a piercing scream that vibrated everyone's core. Ann Lou's heart was shattered.

"Thank you for your participation in the Planetary Diagnostic Test, McHubbard Family," said the woman, back to her expression of faux cheer. "Transportation will be sent on July second for relocation. I wish you all the best as you move and adapt to your new homes. Goodbye!"

The woman vanished. They were all alone in the room again, speechless.

Over the next few days leading up to July 2, the rehoming process was explained. On July 2, buses would collect the eligible humans from each remaining populated region of Earth, then deliver everyone to a central location. From there, they would be transported to their new homes. They were also instructed on how to pack in preparation for their new lives. They could only bring the bare essentials that would fit in a rucksack. On the evening of July 1, each of the McHubbards was silently packing in their room, except for Ann Lou, who was in the kitchen dribbling her hockey puck with her stick so that Elbina could have all the space she needed to pack for Harvinth. Ann Lou was taking her aggression out on one cupboard in particular, doing a slapshot every so often. Every time the puck made contact with the wooden cupboard, Knitsy would gasp and fall into a fit of coughs.

"Ann Lou, for the love of Queen Elizabeth the Second, may she rest in peace, stop that! You've nearly given me a heart attack again."

"Sorry, Nan," Ann Lou said, gently putting her stick down. Words popped up before her eyes, indicating that she had a message from Hayden.

Her heart sank as she read it and slumped in her usual chair. She had been avoiding talking to him since everyone had taken their tests yesterday. She was heartbroken that she had to stay behind and would never see her best friend again.

> Hayden Murphy: Annie Lou! Where are you going to? I'm assigned to Epiton!

Ann Lou exhaled loudly. She couldn't bear to talk to him. Words popped up again.

> Hayden Murphy: I just want you to know how much I'll miss you if we don't end up on the same planet. This won't be the last time you see me. I promise! I will find a way.

A tear rolled down her face and landed on the back of her left hand. Even though it was her prosthetic hand, she imagined the feeling of the tear as if it were on her skin. She stared at the spot. The softness of the small tear managed to hold so much pain. She ignored the messages and picked up her stick again, dribbling the puck but avoiding any cupboards.

Upstairs, the rest of the family was packing in their respective rooms. Elbina had packed her journal of recipes and a few jumpers to hide the Gasser under, even though she figured the Harvinthians, of all beasts, wouldn't really care about her appearance since she was hundreds of thousands of times their size.

Riff blared his music louder than usual and was singing along to The Death Brigade as he rummaged through his drawers. He had managed to fit all his Death Brigade posters and t-shirts into his small rucksack. He also packed his drumsticks in case he'd ever be able to play, though it seemed unlikely on a soundless planet. The only ounce of happiness that Riff had since the Planetary Diagnostic Test was finding out that both Matt and Joe, his GeoLads bandmates, were assigned to Antympanica as well. The three of them were so well attuned with their musical abilities that most of the time they all heard it in their heads anyway, making Antympanica a good fit for all three of them.

Ann Lou trudged upstairs and was about to challenge Riff to one more game of hallway hockey when she heard a groan from Luna's room. She stopped dribbling her puck in front of a goalie-ready Riff and signed "Luna" to him, and they went to her room, followed shortly after by Elbina. They found Luna sitting in the middle of her room, surrounded by a circle of books. She couldn't seem to decide which ones to bring in her rucksack.

"Having trouble choosing, there?" asked Elbina sweetly.

Luna looked up toward Elbina's direction and smiled. "There's too many good ones. I'll run out of stuff to read within days if I bring only the ones that'll fit in my rucksack. I want to bring my Oxford textbooks because they cost a fortune and I took a chance on buying them before I even got in!" Luna dramatically whipped her hands back and fell into the pile of books behind her. The three other siblings went to sit down around her.

"I see you're not a fan of the digital books then?" Riff joked.

Luna glared at him. "Kinda need my fingertips." She wiggled her fingers in the air.

"Why don't we all bring something that belongs to the rest of us? Something to hold on to for the difficult moments," suggested Elbina with a small glint of cheer in her voice.

The remainder of them nodded in agreement.

Riff held out his left wrist. "I am going to bestow upon all of you the greatest sounds of the universe. Each of you gets a different Death Brigade album. Listen to them. They're life-changing."

His sisters laughed under their breaths. They already knew every song on the albums, having been involuntarily exposed to them every day of their lives. Luna and Elbina held their left wrists up to Riff's so he could transfer the music into their microchips. All music was played using the ChipMusic feature of the microchips, and the actual songs were played inside the listeners' heads. In Riff's case, he played the music so loudly that his family could hear the music blaring through his ears.

"Sorry, Ann Lou, but you have to live with just a t-shirt. I'll give Mum an album in your honour," he said winking at her.

Elbina passed around a few of her jumpers. "Just in case it gets cold," she said softly.

Luna grudgingly passed around some of her Oxford textbooks even though her siblings couldn't read the braille. Riff wasn't particularly enthused as he didn't care much for reading unless it was musical notes. "I'm sorry to say that you might need a new hobby, little brother," said Luna.

Ann Lou gave them each a hockey puck. "I probably won't be on Earth much longer, so, I'd better give these away."

Her siblings took the pucks gingerly and were at a loss for words. They couldn't bear knowing their smallest sister would soon die while they were receiving a second chance. There was nothing they could do but take them graciously. The four McHubbard siblings met for a group embrace for a few tender moments. There had never been many such moments within the McHubbard household, and they had to take advantage of their final hours together.

"Let's check on Mum," said Elbina, looking around at her siblings. They agreed and followed Elbina out of Luna's bedroom and into their mother's.

Henrietta was sitting on her bed, looking intensely at her left wrist.

"Mum, you all right?" piped Elbina from the doorway. Henrietta jumped, not knowing they were watching her.

"Oh! Yes, darling. Sorry, you gave me a good fright there!" she said as she hopped up and walked to her closet, rummaging around for something.

"Mum, your rucksack is totally empty," noted Elbina, eyeing up the bag in the corner of the room. "Do you need help?"

"No," she said quickly. "Thank you, darlings. I just have been putting it off. Tough to decide which clothes to bring and which ones not to!"

"Well, don't worry, Mum," said Luna, peering in on the other side of the door frame from Elbina. "Epiton is going to give you new clothes. It'll be much too hot for anything you've got."

"Right, darling," Henrietta said, her sparkling eyes directed toward Luna. "Listen, Elbina, can you put the kettle on? Maybe start making a roast for our last meal as a family—" Henrietta burst into tears and fell onto the floor. Her four children ran in to sit with her.

"My children, my beautiful children!" sobbed Henrietta, burying her head in Luna's flannel shirt.

"Mum, it's okay!" urged Elbina. "We will see you again at some point."

It took Henrietta a few minutes to stop hyperventilating. Riff held her shoulder, and Ann Lou sat across from her, having a difficult time making eye contact. Riff helped Henrietta to her feet and sat her on the bed.

"I'm sorry, dears," Henrietta said, wiping tears from her eyes. "Can you please go sit with your grandmother downstairs? Keep her company. She needs it most of all."

The siblings obeyed.

"Be down in a few?" called Elbina, looking back into the bedroom as she and Luna began to exit. Henrietta nodded and wiped her cheek on her sleeve. Elbina smiled at her and led her siblings downstairs.

In the kitchen, Knitsy was already sitting at the kitchen table with a cup of tea and a leftover piece of sweet bread Elbina had made the night before. Luna went to sit in her usual spot at the table, and Elbina started pulling pots and pans out to make the roast.

"So, Nan, the Olfinderians seem really cute and sweet," said Luna, attempting to make conversation. "The woman from the results video said they like to sing."

"They look like bouncing little menaces," said Knitsy, slamming her cup of tea on the table and pursing her lips in anger.

Riff, behind Knitsy, quietly uttered, "But they're *singing* bouncing menaces," causing Elbina to stifle a laugh.

"So, Ann Lou, where is Hayden going?" asked Luna.

Elbina turned down the heat of the stove so that she would be able to hear Ann Lou's answer over the sizzling of the food.

Ann Lou rolled her eyes upon noticing Elbina's reaction. "He's going to Epiton. At least Mum might see him. I haven't spoken to him, though. It's easier to not draw out any goodbyes."

Elbina let out a quiet sigh.

"Ann Lou," said Luna solemnly, "that's like you not saying goodbye to us."

Ann Lou gulped and pushed herself up with her prosthetic arm. "It's just too hard, okay?" She walked off to the couch and lay down, tossing a puck into the air and catching it with her prosthetic.

Knitsy sniffed the air. "A roast, is it, Elbina? At least throw some chips in the oven for my last fat meal!"

The next morning, July 2, was the most difficult morning any of them had ever experienced. They managed to make it down to the kitchen bright and early. Riff hadn't even blasted his music, and he came downstairs without being reminded. But no one made a dent in the breakfast that Elbina had prepared for them. Elbina couldn't even stomach her Gasser treatment that morning. They sat in silence for some time, sipping their tea.

"What's the collection schedule?" asked Henrietta, quietly. She was holding Ann Lou's hand under the table.

Elbina peered at the television screen. "Erm, it looks like the first collection is Antympanica at half eight, Cipto at quarter to nine, Harvinth at nine, Olfinder at quarter after nine, and the last is Epiton at half nine."

Riff's eyes bugged out as he realised he would be the first to leave his family. He checked the time: eight fifteen a.m. "Bollocks," he muttered under his breath. Henrietta tearfully looked into her son's eyes.

"Ti—time to say your goodbyes, Riff." Henrietta stood up and sniffled. They all made their way into the living room and wordlessly hugged each other in one big circle, Riff in the middle.

"We love you so much, my sweet Griffin," sobbed Henrietta. "You'll make us proud."

Riff couldn't utter any words. He didn't understand how he could make anyone proud of him for being sent away to a foreign planet. He couldn't bear this. He hugged each of his sisters and his mother tightly. Last was Knitsy. He grabbed his grandmother and held her for the longest.

She whispered into his ear, "I give you full permission to tell off those aliens." He allowed himself to let out a solemn laugh, just as squeaking brakes sounded outside.

Riff wiped away a loose tear and slung his rucksack over his shoulder. He took a deep breath and pushed his fiery hair away from his face. He waved and walked away without a word, the family watching him walk through the tunnel. He stopped midway and turned around to face them one last time. "I love you," he signed. The rest of the family signed the phrase back to him. He took that as his cue to continue to the entrance to the bus. Once he was out of sight and the bus pulled away, each of their hearts broke a little in that moment. They had to still make it through four more goodbyes.

Next up was Luna. When the Cipto bus was about to arrive, she said her individual goodbyes to everyone. To Elbina, she whispered, "You're braver than you know." The two embraced tightly. Before they all knew it, Luna was walking down the tunnel, her fingers trailing along the wall. Henrietta was visibly shaking watching her oldest daughter leave, knowing she could no longer care for her. But Luna exuded a beautiful air of confidence as she walked, and she held her head up high.

Elbina said her goodbyes next. Ann Lou didn't know what to say to her. Was "sorry" appropriate at a time like this? She and Elbina had never seen eye to eye, but she was going to miss having her siblings around, no matter how quirky they were. Ann Lou said, simply, "Good luck." Elbina smiled in response. As she walked down the tunnel, the rest of her family watched as her head hung low and she clutched the Oxford textbook that Luna had given her close to her chest. And just like her older siblings before her, she was off.

"That girl is going to be fine," said Knitsy, putting a hand on Henrietta's shoulder. Knitsy picked up her rucksack, which contained only a few pieces of clothing and pictures of the family.

"Mum!" Henrietta fell into her mother's arms. Ann Lou tearfully watched the mother-and-daughter pair embrace for possibly the last time.

"Be brave, my dear," said Knitsy, pushing Henrietta's hair behind her ear. "You're an excellent mother. Way better than me, for heaven's sake," she chuckled. Knitsy then turned to Ann Lou and held her shoulders with her hands. "And you," she started, "are the bravest and most deter-mined little woman I know." She pulled her in for a hug. "Hit as many cupboards as you want, my love," she croaked, holding in a cry as she picked up her cane and put on her breathing patch.

Knitsy started down the tunnel slowly and courageously. Once she disappeared, there were only two McHubbards left in the family home.

Ann Lou turned to Henrietta. "Mum, I—"

It was then that she noticed Henrietta's left wrist was wrapped in gauze that was rapidly becoming soaked with blood. "What happened to your arm?"

Henrietta reached her right hand into her pocket and pulled out a tiny silver chip. "Take off your prosthetic," she said curtly.

"But why?"

"Take it off." Henrietta's glare sharply dug into Ann Lou's eyes.

Ann Lou slipped off her prosthetic arm, and Henrietta took it to the couch. She opened a metal panel and nestled the chip between two compartments within the structure of the wrist, then closed the panel and passed the arm back to Ann Lou.

"Put it back on now," commanded Henrietta.

"What did you do?"

"I gave you my chip. From now on, you're Henrietta McHubbard. Don't tell anyone your real name. You'll get in trouble."

"Mum, no!" wailed Ann Lou, realising what her mother had just done for her. "You're not staying behind! Please! I don't want you to!"

"Ann Lou," said Henrietta, calmly, "I am not leaving my child behind, no matter what. Epiton will give you a much better chance at life than this place will. I only got picked for Epiton because Riff saved me. You are much stronger than I am. You will be fine."

"No! I can't leave you!" screamed Ann Lou, grasping her mother around the waist.

"Ann Lou, the bus is here. You have to go. I've even packed your things." Henrietta handed her a rucksack and her hockey stick. Ann Lou slowly let go of her mother and took the bag and the stick. Clearly Henrietta had made up her mind.

Henrietta pushed her down the tunnel and onto the bus and said her last goodbye. "I love you, Ann Lou. You're safe now."

Ann Lou's departure felt as if it were in slow motion. Now the entirety of her heart was broken. She clung to the final tactile memories of her mother: her lips on her cheek, her soft hands pushing her through the tunnel, and the fabric of her clothing as it slipped out of her fingers. Ann Lou stood at the bus entrance and watched as her mother retreated down the tunnel and back into the house. That was her last glimpse of home and of her mother, with whom she now shared a name.

CHAPTER 4

THE FLYING BOAT

Ann Lou stood still as the bus started to roll. Her hockey stick held her balance as the bus accelerated forward.

"Sit!" grumbled the bus driver. Ann Lou's feet were like concrete blocks, her eyes fixated on the closed metal door in front of her.

"Ann Lou?" She jerked her head to the side. It was Hayden, running up to her. She hadn't yet connected the dots that she would be with him on this horrifying journey.

He grabbed her for an embrace. "See?" he said proudly. "I knew I'd see you again!"

"Can you both bloody sit?" spat the bus driver.

"Come on!" Hayden grabbed Ann Lou's stick, her hand still attached. All the seats had been removed so that about fifty people could cram into every bit of free space on the bus. Ann Lou followed him through the packed crowd, looking for a spot on the floor of the bus where they could sit together. Some of the passengers were praying, some were meditating, and some were crying on a stranger's shoulder. All Ann Lou wanted was to hold her mother's hand.

They found a spot in the back corner and sat down. Ann Lou slid down the wall in complete disbelief.

"Ann Lou, I—"

"It's Henrietta."

Hayden's brow furrowed. "What are you talking about?"

"You have to call me Henrietta. No more Ann Lou." She couldn't even look at him. Tears flowed down her face. Hayden started to put his arm around her, but she pushed it off.

"Why are you using your mum's name?" Hayden prodded. Ann Lou just looked away from him. They spent the rest of the ride in silence.

The bus came to a squeaky stop after only a few minutes. Everyone started shifting around, unsure if they should get up or not. The bus doors opened, and in walked an Epitonian carrying a large trunk. Ann Lou was surprised at how much scarier it looked in person than it had in the video. Even though many of its features were similar to a human's, the height difference, horns, sharp claw, menacing eyes, and charcoaled skin added up to a frightening sight. The Epitonian looked around at everyone on the bus, eyeing them up in disgust. Ann Lou crouched her head lower behind the person sitting in front of her so that she wouldn't meet its gaze. After a few moments of intense stares, it tapped its left wrist three times with its right claw. The Epitonian was met with confused looks and it began to hiss at the humans. Eventually everyone was able to get up to speed by understanding that they were expected to tap their own wrists, where their microchips were, three times. Ann Lou tapped her metallic wrist, unsure if whatever she was meant to be doing would still work for her; however, the Epitonian's hisses were replaced by an English translation in Ann Lou's head.

"Come get your suits, you moronic Earthlings," it was saying in a hiss.

Everyone timidly lined up and walked to the trunk, where each received a neatly folded suit. Ann Lou and Hayden were the last to grab theirs. The Epitonian sized up Ann Lou. Their eyes met intensely. It was difficult for her to break the gaze, but Hayden lightly touched her arm to head back to their seats.

"Hello, England-to-Epiton transfers. My name is Fintan, and I will be your transfer mentor for your journey to Epiton." Fintan's voice was deep, with a slight hiss. He swaggered to the centre of the bus. "We have arrived at the Epiton transfer dock. In a moment, you will be loaded onto a Jalopy." One brave boy in the crowd raised his hand. Fintan lifted an eyebrow. "Yesss?" he hissed.

The boy gulped. "What's a Jalopy?"

Fintan huffed. "A Jalopy is an intergalactic vehicle overseen by the Universal Union for the sole purpose of transporting beings. This Jalopy is disguised as an ordinary Earth object, quite like the one you are about to enter, which I am told is a *boat*, to reduce the chances of an act of terrorism during loading."

The boy squeaked, "Thank you," and lowered his hand.

"As I was saying," continued Fintan, pacing around the middle of the bus, "I'd like everyone to move quickly and quietly. GeoLapse activity has triggered a state of high alert today and we do not want to attract any attention to ourselves." Fintan spoke as if he had to recite a boring script.

"The last of the Epiton buses covering transfer for Europe have just arrived at our loading dock. We will shortly begin boarding one bus at a time. Your bus will load first. Tapping your microchips will allow you to communicate with other Epitonians and vice versa. We expect you to activate these whenever you are in the presence of an Epitonian as it is a pledge of respect." Fintan stared at Hayden for a few seconds. Ann Lou could hear Hayden slump farther down the wall next to her.

"You have suits that you must wear at all times when you are on mainland Epiton. Temperatures reach an average of approximately one thousand degrees Celsius, which I'm told is very hot for you Earthlings. I expect each of you to put these on over the dreadful clothing you are already wearing once you are loaded onto the Jalopy."

Passengers gasped. "A thousand degrees Celsius?" Ann Lou thought. "Are they mad?"

"You will live in the homes of volunteer Epitonians." Fintan turned around and gradually walked back toward the door of the bus. "If you disrespect our community or our planet, your time on Epiton will be cut short."

No one dared say a word or even blink.

"Understood?" hissed Fintan.

Everyone in the crowd piped up with "Yessir" or an "Understood."

"Good. And now, it is time to load the Jalopy. Everyone up and prepare for scanning."

The humans on the bus scrambled to their feet and quickly formed a single-file line toward the bus's doors.

"QUIETLY!" shouted Fintan, rolling his eyes. He pushed the humans at the doors out of the way so he could go first.

When Ann Lou finally made it out of the bus, she noticed that they were in a tunnel. There were two more Epitonians at the end of the tunnel by the entrance of the Jalopy. They appeared to be just as fierce as Fintan, with scowls on their faces.

"Whaddaya reckon they're gonna do?" whispered Hayden in Ann Lou's ear from behind.

Ann Lou shrugged, still feeling a knot in the pit of her stomach from the incident with her mother that morning. The line moved forward very slowly.

She heard a commotion up ahead as one of the humans in line was shoved into the tunnel wall with great force. Ann Lou peered through the crowd and saw the Epitonians with anger spread across their faces.

"You were supposed to go to Cipto, you idiotic Earthling!" shouted one of the Epitonian guards. "Away with you!"

The human didn't know which way to go, so he ran past the line of humans and back onto the bus. Ann Lou felt bad for him, but her nerves were frayed and she was mostly concerned for her own fate. She gripped her left wrist, hoping that her mother's microchip would get her past these menacing beasts.

"Quiet extends to you morons as well!" belted Fintan at the guards, as if he were ready to fight his fellow Epitonians on the spot.

As Ann Lou approached the two Epitonians guarding the entrance to the Jalopy, she looked straight upward, astonished by their height, mouth agape. One of them huffed at her, his hot breath steaming over her face. Ann Lou coughed as the scent of smoke met her nose. The Epitonian forcefully reached out his clawed hand. She reached out her right hand to shake his, but he instead reached for her prosthetic arm and forced it underneath a scanning cuff, similar to the one she used to pass by every day upon entering school. She could barely breathe as she waited for the scanner to read the microchip.

"Name?" the other Epitonian said darkly.

"H—Henrietta McHubbard," she stammered, unable to stop looking at the claw that was grasping her arm.

"Date of birth?"

"M—March twelfth, twenty-one seventy?"

The Epitonians didn't seem to understand the connection between human age and physical appearance, so her arm was released. She felt a huge relief in that moment, but she was also horrendously sad that it wasn't her mother that was about to board a Jalopy to safety.

"What's that?" asked the Epitonian who had grabbed her arm, just as she had almost stepped on the Jalopy.

She whirled around, unsure what he was referring to.

"Erm, sorry, what's what?"

The Epitonian pointed his sharp claw at her hockey stick, which was tightly held under her armpit.

"Oh!" she gasped, afraid they might take it away. "It's a hockey stick, for sport. I—I didn't mean to—"

"You should join our Pyroll team," the Epitonian said. His brow was furrowed, and he crossed his arms. He placed his body squarely in front of hers, about an inch from her nose. It was going to take a while, Ann Lou thought, to figure out Epitonian body language.

"Egan!" shouted Fintan as he was pacing along the line behind Ann Lou. "Can we get a move-on before we all get blown to bits?"

Egan huffed again and let Ann Lou pass. She wanted to get away from them so badly that she didn't even bother waiting for Hayden to get through.

She set foot aboard the Jalopy. It was nothing like she expected an intergalactic spaceship would be.

The first thing she noticed was the amount of light shining through the windows of the boat Jalopy. The only other time she had seen natural light in her life was when she had the incident with the GeoLapse the previous year at school. But this time there were no screams, no burning. She looked upward in awe. There was the sun, a round circle of light beaming its rays down on her face. The sunlight matched her blonde hair that she was running her fingers through, soaking in the warmth.

Next, she started to observe the shape of the Jalopy. She was in a wide space between two curved sides. Each end of the space, to her left and her right, narrowed to a point. Looking around, she saw rows of seats facing toward what she assumed was the front. This boat, this Jalopy, wasn't particularly well-kept; it was as if it had been abandoned when Earth's rivers had drained out one hundred years ago. There were cobwebs and a substantial layer of dust on every surface. She had obviously never been on a boat before and only knew about them from history books at school—long ago, boats used to carry people back and forth over the river between the Isle of Wight and her very own city of Portsmouth. Imagining rivers and boats intrigued Ann Lou, and she wished she could have seen the Earth when it was still suitable for survival.

Ann Lou walked over to the edge of the Jalopy, which was up to her chest, and she reached her left hand out to touch the window. The prosthetic's material clanged against the glass surface. There was a thick layer of glass separating her from the outside world.

"Wanna grab a seat by the front?" Hayden had found her wandering. He had a sad look in his eyes. He didn't take her silence very well.

Ann Lou took a deep breath. "Sure, let's go."

The two of them found a pair of seats toward the bow of the Jalopy and watched as the rest of the passengers quietly entered the boat. They heard whispers of many different accents that ranged from all over Europe: some sounded French, others Scottish, and there were more accents she didn't recognise. When the boat was packed full, it looked like there were about five hundred people on board. Hayden and Ann Lou stood up to let an old woman lie down across both of their seats. Rather than trying to find other seats, they went to stand at the bow, where they had a perfect, panoramic view of the outside. Ann Lou could feel Hayden looking at her, hoping she would talk to him, but she couldn't bring herself to even look at him at this point. She was too engrossed in observing the outside and preoccupied with the overwhelming feeling of missing her family.

Just then, screams of terror came from the port side of the boat, near the entrance—followed by an incredibly loud *BANG*. Everyone on the Jalopy stampeded toward the bow, trying to get away from whatever the danger was, scrambling over those who lost their footing. Ann Lou and Hayden got squished up onto the ledge by the crush of people filling the bow. Through the crowd, it was difficult to see exactly what was happening, but Ann Lou and Hayden saw flashes of horrid images of people near the entrance being burned to a crisp, screaming as they quickly carbonised in the air.

Ann Lou turned and pressed her face on the glass, trying to get a better view of what was happening outside. She saw no less than fifty of the GeoLapse, all dressed in their dark suits, their golden badges glinting in the sunlight. The tunnel to the Jalopy had burst open, and bits of it were strewn within a radius of ten metres. Ann Lou watched as people were torn off the unloading buses by the GeoLapse and immediately burned to ashes upon exposure to the outside. There had to be hundreds of them, being pulled out and flying away in the wind as dust particles.

Ann Lou suddenly remembered the image of her arm burning into a bed of ashes. It was all too fresh in her mind. She started to cry. Hayden, too, was feeling overwhelmed from the trauma of almost being kidnapped by the GeoLapse. He embraced Ann Lou, holding her head down with his so they didn't have to watch more of the terror unfolding in front of their eyes.

"Abort! Abort!" shouted Fintan. He bolted toward the tunnel entrance and pulled down what looked like a glass door from the ceiling. Egan and the other Epitonian guard dashed in just before the glass door closed. Within seconds, the inside of the Jalopy flashed a neon green colour and promptly accelerated into the sky. Everyone on board fell to the floor, individually or in piles, their bodies held down by the force of acceleration.

Screams were still ringing in Ann Lou's ears as she lay on the floor of the Jalopy, looking at the sky as she got closer and closer to it. Her body felt numb. How many humans had just been killed? They all had just been ripped apart from their families earlier in the day, hoping they'd have a second chance at life.

Within minutes, the Jalopy was outside of the Earth's dying atmosphere and in the vast, sparkling universe of space. Once the Jalopy had accelerated to its final velocity, the humans were able to stand and walk around freely, thanks to artificial gravity that mimicked the gravitational pull on Earth.

Ann Lou stared at the zooming stars, imagining she were in a movie. She wished she were actually in a movie, because none of this would be real. But the stars quieted her anxious brain for a moment. It was surreal: today, for the first time, she had seen not only the outside world on

Earth, but an infinite world beyond it that she had never known existed. She closed her eyes and imagined what Knitsy and her other siblings were feeling as they also zoomed through space. She smiled.

"Beautiful, isn't it?" remarked Hayden, lying down next to her, watching the passing stars. "Just the other day we thought we needed to worry about our maths exam. Now that all doesn't matter so much."

Ann Lou just said, "I'm going to stretch my legs."

As she walked through the centre of the Jalopy, she saw Egan slouched down next to the glass door that Fintan had pulled down during the incident. He was holding one of his horns with one of his claw hands, clearly in pain. Ann Lou approached him slowly.

"Are you all right?" she asked.

He looked up at her. Even seated on the floor, he was nearly her height. He huffed and lowered his hand, and a strange black gas puffed out of the side of his horn.

"Oh, let me help you!" She looked in her rucksack for anything that she could use as a bandage. Ann Lou took out Elbina's jumper, ripped off one of the sleeves, and tied it securely around Egan's horn. "It should help stop the . . . bleeding," she said.

He looked at her, then gently touched the wrapping. The entropic discharge of gas had stopped.

"Thank you, Henrietta."

Ann Lou felt incredibly out of place being called by her mother's name. But she had to pretend that it didn't faze her in the slightest.

"You're welcome, Egan. So, what happened out there?" she continued, putting the remainder of Elbina's jumper back into her bag. "What gave the Jalopy's location away?"

"The GeoLapse knew it was transfer day. The EPO, or whatever it's called, probably figured out the location and leaked the information."

Ann Lou was puzzled. "You mean the ERA?"

Egan nodded his head in defeat. "The chaos started when one of the Earthlings in line didn't have a microchip. We were told that they were the bad guys. Had to leave behind about half of the European transfers. A big shame. Most of them died anyway, but the rest on the buses won't be able to come along." His hand slid down to the floor.

"Can't we come back and get them later?" Ann Lou said, somehow thinking the idea had not already been considered.

"Well, Henrietta, it may seem easy, but transferring thousands of Earthlings over eleven million light years is risky business," he said in a very sarcastic and haughty tone. "Besides, each day the environmental and political situations on Earth are getting exponentially more dangerous. There can only be one transfer. That was the order from the Universal Union."

"Wait," she continued. "Why didn't you and the other Epitonian get burned to a crisp like the humans?" Her comment sounded rather blunt as it came out of her mouth, but she figured Egan wouldn't see it that way.

"Henrietta, do you know where we live?" he asked, with one eyebrow raised.

He stood up, now towering many feet above her, and started to walk away in a slow swagger.

"I'm sorry," piped up Ann Lou.

Egan stopped and looked back at her with confused but menacing eyes.

"I'm—I'm sorry that the humans hurt you," she elaborated.

He huffed again, puffing his chest out. "I hope you do consider joining Pyroll." Those were his last words as he continued walking away. Ann Lou watched him in disbelief. She had just had a conversation with an alien. But the word *alien* felt so . . . wrong. He was a being, just like her. Just like her family.

Alone again, Ann Lou sat down by the glass door. Beside her, there was a small pile of ashes, wind-blown remnants of a human who never made it on board. She bowed her head in silence for a few seconds and watched as they traveled through asteroid belts, past rocky planets, gaseous planets, bright stars, and lots of open space. She felt so small and so far away from home.

CHAPTER 5

EPITON

Ann Lou woke up lying on the floor in front of the glass door. The Jalopy was flying quite close to a circle of stars that had a small dot in the centre. As the dot became a distinguishable piece of rock, it appeared reddish in colour. Ann Lou had seen it before, on the television during the results. This red rock that was surrounded by the colossal ring of stars was going to be her new home. This was Epiton.

She looked around the Jalopy. There was no more screaming. Everyone was sitting on the floor of the boat with their knees tucked into their chests. A few people here and there were chatting. She glanced to her right, toward the bow, and saw Hayden having a conversation with the old woman. She felt bad for ignoring him; after all, he had just been ripped apart from his family, too.

"Prepare for landing, Earthlings!" announced Fintan, causing everyone to stir. Ann Lou looked outside to find that they were gliding downward toward volcanic terrain. Lava spewed from some of the volcanoes. She rose to her knees as her jaw slowly dropped open at the fiery sight.

"Why is no one dressed?" bellowed Fintan, waving his arms in fury. "Would you like to be turned to dust upon landing?" Everyone immediately started suiting up.

"That's what I thought. Stupid Earthlings," he muttered. He assisted an old man who had just put his leg through the arm hole.

Ann Lou pulled her suit out of her rucksack. It was silver and rubbery to the touch. She stood up and held the bottom half of the suit open so she could step into it. It was quite snug, so she had to shimmy and coax the legs up until she was able to reach the arm holes. She got her right arm in without much trouble, but the rubbery material simply would not slide along the metal of her prosthetic left arm. There was too much friction. "Argh, no!" she cursed. Her only choice was to take off her arm and put it on over the arm of the suit. A small girl stared, eyes bulging, as Ann Lou effortlessly detached and reattached her prosthetic arm.

The mask component was tougher to fit on. It was a clear, form-fitting mask that covered her whole face. There were bulges for the eyes, nose, and mouth, which allowed for a little bit of breathing room. The suit was smart enough to register when the mask was fitted on one's head and it promptly stitched itself together up the back within seconds.

The Jalopy descended over a flat and sandy terrain where volcanoes could still be seen far in the distance. Small holes dotted the surface. Epitonians gathered outside to see the flying boat approach their land. The Epitonians didn't look particularly thrilled, but Ann Lou wondered if they ever looked or felt thrilled at all.

The Jalopy hovered above the ground for a few seconds, then dropped what felt like ten feet in free-fall, touching ground with a small bounce. All the human passengers fell to the floor with a unanimous "Ugh!" upon impact.

"Sorry, we're still working out how to drive this thing," said Egan, who stood firmly on his feet, along with Fintan and the other Epitonian who looked disgustedly at the humans.

All the humans scrambled to their feet, nearly all of them suited up. The old woman was looking for a zipper in the back before she had applied her face mask. Ann Lou saw Hayden help her apply the mask and the old woman looked stunned when the suit knitted itself together once the mask was on.

"Come meet your new hutmates," hissed Fintan, clearly underwhelmed at the humans in front of him.

"Four to a hut," he added, pointing to the Epitonians who had gathered around just outside the glass door.

Fintan opened the glass door so the humans could exit the Jalopy, but no one moved.

"Well, come on, then!" shouted Fintan, pushing the young girl who had been staring at Ann Lou's arm earlier. The girl tumbled out of the Jalopy, which no longer had a tunnel connected to it, only a ramp down to the ground. No one else followed her.

The small girl looked to her left and then to her right as bits of dust rolled past her small suit. After a few seconds, she turned around and beckoned for everyone to follow her. Then she took off running into the crowd of beasts. The girl's mother scurried after her daughter, clearly in distress.

Ann Lou watched as the humans began to debark. When she reached the door, she was immediately overwhelmed by the heat. She could tell the suit was preventing most of the outside heat from reaching her body, yet she instantly began to sweat. Reflexively, she went to wipe her face with her hand, but the rubbery suit met the rubbery mask on her face, causing an uncomfortable friction. Her face felt pulled and stretched by the mask, quite like the celebrities that she and Knitsy always made fun of on television.

Ann Lou had no idea where to even begin finding a hut. She couldn't see any huts, only holes that the Epitonians were standing around. As she walked up to the periphery of one of the holes, she saw that there was a hut inside the hole, its roof approximately five feet from the surface. The roof of the hut appeared to be made of a material similar to the metal of her prosthetic. The hut wasn't much smaller in diameter than the hole, which made Ann Lou wonder if the only way in and out was through the roof.

She turned to see how her fellow humans were approaching the task in front of them. Some timidly approached random Epitonians but ran away when the Epitonians huffed in their faces. Other, braver ones sought refuge from the terrifying beasts by jumping straight into a hole, which was successful in a way. Ann Lou walked up to a hole that didn't have any Epitonians standing around it. There was a sign in front of it bearing a strange inscription. She focused on it, trying to see if it was written upside down or perhaps in a different language. The words rearranged themselves into the English translation upon her focus.

Be back later. Four welcome. Help yourself to the Polskin. Don't eat the Fava cakes.

She was quite impressed that her microchip also allowed for visual translation of text. Ann Lou knelt down by the edge of the hole and reached her hockey stick down to see if she could touch the top of the roof. With a large stretch, her stick grazed the surface of the roof.

"I can do this," she thought to herself. She stood, bent her knees, and hopped down into the hole.

She stumbled a bit as she landed on the roof's slanted surface but managed to stay upright. She looked around to find an entrance into the hut. There was a small opening in the centre of the roof at its apex, so she clambered toward it. Ann Lou heaved herself into the hole and fell into the middle of a circular room. There were two sets of bunk beds with grey metallic frames. Each bed was nicely made up with blankets, a pillow, and a personal trunk.

As she continued to search around the small hut to get a feel for what

Epitonians lived like, she noticed that there weren't any tables or chairs or other household items lying around. The only decoration sort of thing that Ann Lou noticed was a bowl with something glowing in it. The rest of the walls and floor of the hut were covered with coarse slabs of some sort of overly cooked meat, making the hut look like a crime scene. She gulped, hoping that she wouldn't become part of the meat collection.

The inside walls of the hut were made of hard clay, which seemed to make the inside of the hut cooler in temperature, although it might also have been the fact that the hut was below ground. Either way, it felt safe to remove the suit, so Ann Lou tugged lightly at the mask from her face. It peeled off easily, and the back of the suit unstitched itself. She contorted her face with a few stretches once the mask was off.

Ann Lou heaved her prosthetic, stick, and rucksack on one of the top bunks and started climbing the ladder to her new bed. She placed the small pillow and blanket on one side of the bed and dumped out her rucksack. She sifted through the contents that her mother had secretly packed for her. She knew of Elbina's jumper, Luna's textbook, and Riff's t-shirt but there were also a few practice pucks, a toothbrush, a hairbrush, a handful of now melted and slightly evaporated chocolates, a few teabags, and a neatly folded piece of paper. Slowly she unfolded the paper. It bore a message in her mother's handwriting.

Henrietta,
Don't be afraid to show Epiton how lovely you are. They are going to adore you. Surely it's hot enough there that the water is always ready for tea? Don't worry about me. I am going to be okay. Thinking of you and your siblings at every moment possible. I love you with all my heart.
Love, Mum

Tears streamed down Ann Lou's face before she had even stopped reading. Her mother was probably sitting in her usual spot at the kitchen table right now, alone, sipping on a cup of tea. The thought of that broke Ann Lou's heart. She slipped off the rest of her suit and put on Riff's t-shirt, which hung down past her knees, and she lay down amongst the contents of her rucksack and nodded off.

"This bunk taken?" asked a familiar voice, causing Ann Lou to wake up from her brief slumber. She propped her head up and looked down to find Hayden holding his things, staring at her.

She sighed. "No, go ahead, then." She watched him put his stuff down on the bottom bunk. There was silence between them for a few minutes as he unpacked his rucksack and put his things into his trunk, sliding it under the bed once he was finished.

All of a sudden, there was another thud on the roof. Ann Lou and Hayden could hear two humans dropping onto the roof and clambering toward the middle hole.

"Hello, neighbours!" said the cheery woman who was peering in. "Would you mind taking my daughter for me?"

"Of course," said Hayden as he hopped up from his bunk. He reached up on his tiptoes to collect a toddler from the mother, the same girl who was the first to leave the Jalopy.

The woman jumped down bravely and took the child back from Hayden. "Not the easiest entrance, but it'll sure help with my daily stretches," joked the mother.

"You all right?" asked Hayden once the mother had settled herself and her child into the other bunk.

"Well, of course. I'm fine," she said, looking taken aback. The woman had an American accent.

"Oh, sorry, it's just how we greet each other in the U.K.," said Hayden, chuckling. "I do a mean American accent, though, so I can make sure I don't confuse you dudettes anymore," he added in his classic American accent impression.

"Oh dear," giggled the woman. "No one says 'dudettes'!" She had honey brown skin, as did her daughter.

"I'm Jamie," she said, "and this is my daughter Teddi." She pulled off her daughter's rubber suit and began changing Teddi into her pajamas.

"I'm Hayden, and that's Ann—"

"Henrietta," interrupted Ann Lou.

"Right, Henrietta," he corrected himself.

"Nice to meet you both. Where in the U.K. are you from?" inquired Jamie.

"We're both from Portsmouth, England. Basically, it's the furthest south in England you can go," Hayden answered. "How about yourselves?"

"We're from Rochester, New York. You wouldn't have heard of it. It's the middle of Nowheresville," Jamie laughed. "We had a bit of a journey to our Jalopy in Washington, D.C. But we got to ride in the dome of the United States Capitol! Isn't that right, Teddi?"

Teddi squealed with laughter, completely unaware that flying in a Jalopy was out of the ordinary.

Ann Lou lay back down and let Hayden and Jamie continue talking. Her face was wet with tears again, but she managed to fall asleep, still surrounded by all the belongings spread out around her.

The next morning, she awoke to the sound of light chatter between Hayden, Jamie, and some mysterious voices. She sat up and peered toward the opposite side of the hut, where she saw Jamie cradling Teddi as Hayden spoke with two familiar-looking beasts. It was Fintan and Egan. The Epitonians looked at her and hissed and clicked. She gasped, gripping her blanket. Hayden pointed to his wrist, reminding Ann Lou that she wouldn't understand them if she didn't wear her prosthetic and activate the microchip.

Ann Lou quickly slipped on the prosthetic and tapped the wrist three times. Egan stepped forward and repeated, "Hungry?"

"Uh, not at the moment," answered Ann Lou, unsure if she would be left to eat the meat lying around the hut.

In her sleep, Ann Lou had rolled over the note from her mother, wrinkling it. She smoothed it out with her hand a few times and folded it the way it originally was. Then she gathered up her things and tucked them into her trunk.

"Need a hand?" asked Hayden, kindly. Jamie and Teddi were suiting up at their bunk.

"No, thanks," Ann Lou responded curtly.

"Want to come to the mainland?" he continued. "Jamie and Teddi are ready if we are."

Ann Lou was getting annoyed with his questions and his constant checking up on her. "No," she said, again in a snippy tone. She looked away and started fiddling with her hockey stick.

"Ann Lou, if I did something—"

"Don't call me that!" she said in a hoarse whisper, now glaring at him. "It's Henrietta!" A vein protruded from her forehead.

Hayden held up his hands in surrender. "Sorry," he said. He went to assist Jamie and Teddi in getting out of the hole in the ceiling of the hut.

Ann Lou was trembling. She couldn't explain the fury pulsating through her veins. There was no one in the world she loved more than her family and Hayden. But she felt responsible for her mother being left behind on Earth. She had taken her mother's only chance at life. The guilt reverberated through every inch of her body. She fell back onto her pillow, clutching her heart with one hand and her mouth with the other, trying to muffle her cries.

After she had calmed down to a point where she could focus on her breathing, she sat up, dried her tears, and climbed down from her bunk. She brushed her teeth and combed her hair and started feeling a little more like herself. She walked toward the middle of the hut and noticed Egan leaning back against the wall, inspecting the meat. His arms were crossed, and one leg was crossed over the other. He and Ann Lou were the only ones left in the hut. Ann Lou cleared her throat, trying to summon forth some of the courage her mother believed she possessed.

"Egan?" she asked with fake confidence. He looked at her with a menacing glare. She gulped and tried again.

"So . . . you live here?"

He huffed, and it almost sounded like a chuckle.

"Yes. Fintan and I live here."

"That's sweet. Are you good friends?" Ann Lou was hoping to establish some sort of rapport with her new landlords.

"We're married."

Ann Lou's jaw dropped. "You two? But . . . really?"

"What's wrong with that?" he asked, his charcoal brow furrowing into an acute angle.

"N—nothing at all." Ann Lou desperately needed to change the subject. "C—can you tell me about the food?"

Egan pushed himself off the wall and swaggered over to her.

"Right there you've got yourself Polskin meat. Polskin are really stupid creatures that only come out at night, when we venture to the ice cave of Epiton." He pointed to the blackened meat all around the room.

"Why do you go to the ice cave at night?" asked Ann Lou, who was becoming more puzzled with each question. "Don't you sleep?"

Egan laughed out loud from this question. "Sleep. Such an Earthling flaw. We don't need sleep. We search for food at night." Egan walked over to the bowl with a fiery glow that Ann Lou had discovered the day before.

"These are Fava cakes. Basically, they're freeze-dried lava desserts. My personal favourite," he added in a whisper, but still with a slightly dark tone.

"Oh. So you eat Polskin and lava?"

"Freeze-dried lava," Egan corrected her. "Try one."

Ann Lou looked at him, perplexed. "I thought the sign outside said not to eat them."

"I said 'one,'" he clarified.

Ann Lou grabbed a Fava cake and rolled it in her palm.

"Want to come to Pyroll?" asked Egan.

"Erm . . ." she responded.

"I'm taking a few other Earthlings, too. Once you finish your Fava cake, meet us at the top of the hole outside." He hopped up and caught the edge of the hole with his claw, then pulled himself up and out without the slightest hint of strain.

Ann Lou stood and stared at her Fava cake. She most certainly didn't have an appetite, but she knew she'd have to digest something at some point during her time here, so she decided to pluck up the courage to taste the Epitonian delicacy. It looked like a sphere of ice encapsulating a smaller sphere of something red. She figured the red part must be the lava. The cake was chilly to the touch but not as uncomfortable as holding an ice cube. Biting off a small piece of the sphere, she was surprised at how soft it was in comparison to how it felt on the outside. Her teeth weren't even sensitive from the chill of the cake. The outer shell was almost tangy, like Elbina's lemon pies. Once she reached the lava in the middle, she tossed the remainder of the cake in her mouth. Almost immediately, her tongue felt like it was on fire. She yelped, spitting out the flaming hot lava.

"You're not supposed to eat that part," laughed Egan, poking his head through the roof hole.

Ann Lou wasn't sure if he pitied her ignorance or actually found her to be amusing. She'd hoped he was starting to like her.

Ann Lou opened her trunk and pulled out her suit. Remembering the earlier debacle with her prosthetic arm, Ann Lou tied the left sleeve into a knot where her upper arm would end. She then suited up and fitted the prosthetic arm over the knot and her upper arm, which now allowed her to comfortably use both arms. She then stood up and applied her mask, prompting the back of the suit to close. All geared up, she hoisted herself up to the hole and pushed herself through with the help of her hockey stick.

As she clambered up to ground level to meet Egan, she noticed something out of the corner of her eye. A peculiar-looking animal was stuck in the small gap between the hut and the hole. It was completely blackened, with two hooves and a very round belly. It squirmed, looking frightened and slightly disappointed in itself. Ann Lou shot a look at Egan, imploring him to save the poor creature.

"I told you Polskin were stupid. That's how we catch them," Egan said, smiling darkly.

Once Ann Lou peeled her eyes off the poor Polskin that was most likely going to be their dinner, she sized up the humans in the group that had assembled to play Pyroll. There were about a dozen men, all older than her, the tallest of whom barely reached Egan's shoulder height.

"We're all here," said Egan. "Let's head out."

CHAPTER 6

Pyroll

Egan and the Pyroll-interested humans strolled through mainland Epiton. The men were all puffing their chests out and talking big talk.

"I played football as a quarterback in college."

"I think my arms are too big for this suit."

"Should've skipped arm day the past few years."

Ann Lou had heard plenty of such boy talk from Riff and his friends growing up. The men were clearly trying to impress Egan, who ignored each one of them. He even tossed an eyeroll in Ann Lou's direction, which made her giggle.

Around them were mountainous ranges of active volcanoes. The sky, ground, and all surrounding areas emitted a reddish glow. Ann Lou was sweating more and more under her suit but still very impressed at how comfortable she was considering the nearly one thousand degrees Celsius temperature.

Epitonians ran past them like bolts of lightning. Even at their lightest jog, they were faster than the quickest Olympian. Every time one ran by, Ann Lou would jump. Even Egan's walk was so fast-paced that it forced the humans to jog beside him. They walked for a while longer, all of them starting to get tired from the extreme heat and the jogging. Finally they reached the base of one of the volcanoes, which was the beginning of a steep incline leading to the top of the crater of the volcano.

"Why have you all stopped?" questioned Egan, who noticed no one was following him up the base.

"Isn't this kind of . . . dangerous?" asked the football player.

"It's Pyroll," replied Egan, matter-of-factly. "Of course it's dangerous."

"Then I'm out," said the football player. He started walking away without another word, and all but two of the other men in the group followed him. Those who remained weren't sure if they were more scared of Pyroll or what Egan would say if they left with the others.

"Well, come on, then," grunted Egan, continuing up the volcano. They climbed for an hour without saying a word. Ann Lou and the two men were panting and trembling, trying to grapple sturdy rocks. Egan climbed with ease, seemingly having memorised the best rocks to use as jumping-off points and handholds. The incline was only getting steeper, and by the end of their climb, they were all hanging by the tips of their fingers.

One of the men tried heaving himself up to the final plateau of the crater. He braced one foot on a protruding rock, which promptly snapped off. His hands could not support his weight, and he fell straight down the rock face. His screams echoed as he hit the slope and bounced and rolled toward the base of the volcano. Ann Lou screamed, terrified she might be next. The grip strength of her left hand was considerably less than that of her right, and she could feel herself slipping. Egan was strolling along the plateau of the crater.

"Help us!" shouted the dangling man. Egan sighed and crouched down, reaching one arm out to him and the other to Ann Lou. They grabbed on, and Egan lifted them to solid ground, where they lay and gasped for air.

Egan turned and walked toward the crater, calling back over his shoulder, "What's the holdup?" Ann Lou and the man glared at him and looked fearfully at one another.

"D—do you think he's okay?" Ann Lou motioned with her head toward the sheer drop.

"I hope so."

The man stood up and held out a hand to help Ann Lou to her feet. She noticed he was speaking a different language, but her microchip was able to still translate his words into English. The man towered over her, but he still was nearly a foot shorter than Egan. "I don't think this is going to be a light tennis match," he added.

The two trailed behind Egan, making small conversation. The man looked to be in his fifties, judging from the wrinkles that were visible through his mask. He appeared to be of Asian descent and had black hair with sprinkles of grey mixed in. His voice was hoarse from the strenuous climbing.

"What's your name?" asked Ann Lou.

"Jung-hoon," replied the man. "I'm from South Korea. What's your name?"

Ann Lou had to bite her tongue not to reply with her birth name. It pained her to utter the four consonants of her mother's name. She almost felt as though she had stolen it. Ann Lou had to beat down aggressively the overwhelming emotions that bubbled to the surface every time she had to answer that question.

"Henrietta," she answered softly. "I'm from the south of England."

Jung-hoon mysteriously looked Ann Lou up and down quickly and then averted his gaze back forward. "The south of England. Must have been nice in its prime."

The two continued walking together for a few moments in silence as they tried to catch up with Egan.

"Did any of your family come here with you?" asked Jung-hoon. He sounded genuinely interested in her answer.

Ann Lou swallowed hard, hoping the subject would change soon. "My best friend did, but none of my family is here. How about you?"

Jung-hoon looked down at the ground, which was losing its red tint and becoming grey. "All of my friends went to Cipto. Most of us are craftsmen, so we're good at working with our hands. Sensitive to touch, you know? I specifically worked with the recycling and reuse of materials."

Jung-hoon and Ann Lou walked over igneous rock as they reached the centre of the crater's circumference, where it was getting noticeably hotter. They walked up and stood next to Egan, who was now standing in a group of Epitonians. Ann Lou and Jung-hoon looked down and saw a drop of about one thousand feet that led straight into a lava pool. The lava sloshed around as if in slow motion, forming magnificent, fiery waves. Bits of ash rose up to their eye level. Ann Lou felt terribly uncomfortable from the amount of sweat she was producing, and she could hear Jung-hoon's breathing intensify.

There was a metallic arch spanning across the entire crater and extending about one hundred feet above their heads. At its peak was an unlit torch. A rope hung downward, holding a ball of fire at the end.

"Ready?" asked Egan abruptly, still staring across the other side of the crater. A clownish smile was spread across his face, revealing a full set of sharp fangs.

"For what, exactly?" Ann Lou said croakily, cocking her head.

"For Pyroll." Egan smiled.

"How do you play?" asked Jung-hoon.

"There are no rules," Egan whispered.

The ball of fire dropped from the rope, and Egan promptly jumped into the crater. Ann Lou and Jung-hoon gasped in unison. The

Epitonians followed suit and jumped in after Egan. Ann Lou and Jung-hoon spotted Egan as he landed part-way down the drop of the crater wall. The two went down on their stomachs and looked over the edge in complete awe and fear. The rope above them was burning at the end where the ball of fire had been released.

They could see a precarious ledge spiraling down the crater wall to the lava pool. The Epitonians quickly turned into moving specks speeding around the downward-spiraling ledge. The Epitonians chased Egan down toward the level of the lava pool. The orange glow of the lava shone brighter and brighter on their dark exteriors the farther down they went.

Egan reached the lava pool before the others. Ann Lou and Jung-hoon made little binoculars with their hands to get a closer view of the bottom of the drop. It looked like he was holding a small ball of light. It almost looked like the Fava cake Ann Lou had choked down that morning except it was all fire and not encapsulated by a sphere of ice.

Egan tucked the ball of light under his arm and started running back up the coiled path, barreling through his opponents on his way up. He pushed one so hard that it fell off the thin ledge of the coil and directly into the lava pool.

"Egan, up!" shouted a female's voice. Ann Lou and Jung-hoon looked to the source of the sound: it was another Epitonian, directly above Egan on the slope. Just as two Epitonians were about to tackle Egan head on, he extended his right arm out and tossed the ball of light upward, and the female Epitonian caught it as she continued up the spiral slope. Everyone immediately redirected their chase toward her direction. She was quick and versatile, somersaulting under opponents' legs as they attempted to grab the ball of light. She even managed to hop onto the shoulders of one Epitonian and launch herself up to the next level of the spiral ledge, landing with both feet planted firmly.

She seemed to have a clear path ahead of her, since most of the other players were behind her trying to catch up. But one Epitonian pounced from a ledge above her, landing directly on top of her and knocking her down to the ground, hard. The fireball slipped from her hands, and the attacking Epitonian scooped it up and started running up the slope. Ann Lou recognised him as Fintan.

Ann Lou and Jung-hoon laid still, watching Fintan sprinting toward them at full speed. The rope above their heads was nearly burned completely away. Fintan leaped onto the crater rim where Ann Lou and Jung-hoon were lying, and he threw the ball of light toward the torch at the centre of the arch. The ball flew like a meteor out of his hand, hitting the torch on the downward arc. The torch lit ablaze so all below could see.

"Victory!" shouted Fintan, jabbing his sharp fists in the air in triumph.

The remainder of the Epitonians came running up the coiled slope. Once at the top, about half of them went to embrace him, cheering some sort of Epiton chant. The rest of them looked at each other dejectedly. Egan and the female who had caught his pass walked up to Ann Lou and Jung-hoon.

"Why didn't you two join in? We could have won that game."

"You didn't really give us much to go on," replied Ann Lou in an exasperated tone, still traumatised about the poor Epitonian who had fallen into the lava pool.

Egan sighed in annoyance.

"Hush, Egan, they're just Earthlings," said the female Epitonian. Ann Lou and Jung-hoon weren't sure if they should be grateful for her snapback or offended. She looked back at them.

"I'm Aithne. I can teach you both how to play and get you started in the league." She was thin but muscular, and as tall as Egan. She, too, had a menacing look on her face but sounded sincere in wanting to help them learn.

"We can start you out in the youth league. The children learn at a young age and practice around a much smaller volcano," Aithne said. Ann Lou was hoping the youth league would start around a bonfire instead of a volcano.

"It's quite easy to play," she continued. "There are two teams playing against one another. The aim is to light the torch in the middle of the arch with the Pyroll that falls from the rope without the rope burning the torch first. If the rope burns the torch first, both teams lose. If one team lights the torch with the Pyroll first, they win!" she exclaimed, as if the game were as easy as a game of checkers.

"B—but, what if you—" Jung-hoon started, unable to find his words.

"What if you fall in the lava?" Ann Lou finished his sentence.

"Oh, don't do that," she assured. "Stay on the slopes leading away from the lava pool, and you'll be fine. Pass the Pyroll to a team member who is free so they can run up with no opposing defence or offence around them. It's really as simple as that. There are no rules about how your team lights the torch."

Ann Lou and Jung-hoon were not reassured in the least. Egan and Aithne were oblivious to the humans' concerns.

"Ready to put it into practice?" asked Aithne with an evil look on her face. "The children are set to play over there." She pointed down toward a smaller volcano nearby, where Ann Lou could see smaller Epitonians gathered around the crater rim, warming up by tossing the Pyroll around.

The children's volcano was much smaller, but Ann Lou and Jung-hoon would still have to scale down the current slope before climbing up the other one. Ann Lou sighed. "Sure. Why not?"

"Excellent," rumbled Egan. "Well, I'm going to get another game started here, Aithne. Why don't you get Henrietta and Jung-hoon acquainted with the kids?"

"Gladly," she said, wrapping her arms around Ann Lou and Jung-hoon, forcing them to follow her.

Aithne jogged down the volcano in flawless acrobatic lopes. Ann Lou and Jung-hoon decided to slide down, which ended up becoming more of a tumble but at least they were able to catch up to Aithne without wearing themselves out. They started scaling the second, smaller volcano, having just about as much trouble as they'd had with the first one. Aithne hopped, lunged, and swung up the steeper parts of the volcano and reached the top within a few minutes. Ann Lou and Jung-hoon were again out of breath once they reached the top but knew they had to hold it together in front of the children, who were looking at them as if they were aliens. Which they were.

The children were much smaller than the fully grown Epitonians, but they were as tall as most adult humans and just as muscular as the adult Epitonians. They stopped throwing the Pyroll around when the trio drew near, and they watched in silence as Ann Lou and Jung-hoon stood in front of them, gasping loudly.

"Henrietta and Jung-hoon, you'll be on my son's team. This is Apollo." Aithne turned to Apollo, a relatively slender Epitonian child who cautiously looked up at his mother.

"But, Mom, we want to win," Apollo whined, stomping his foot.

"Play nice, Apollo. These are our guests, and you will treat them with the same respect they show us," Aithne scolded. Apollo nodded, obeying his mother at once.

"Is there a plan?" asked Ann Lou, hoping some enthusiasm on her part would cheer him up.

"No rules or plans in Pyroll, my dear," said Aithne, answering for Apollo. "Just look out for your team. Don't let them down."

Ann Lou found the advice not at all helpful. When she used to play roller hockey, there was always a plan. She wasn't used to just playing without a cohesive team structure.

"Ready, children?" called Aithne. All the small Epitonians gathered around the circumference of the crater, which had a drop and a spiral ledge like the larger volcano. A similar arch structure with an unlit torch and rope with the Pyroll attached hung overhead.

"Pyyyyrooooolllll!" she shouted. The Pyroll dropped into the depths of the crater. Several of the children immediately jumped to lower levels of the drop and others started speeding down the spiral to the bottom. Ann Lou and Jung-hoon carefully started pacing down the spiral after the Epitonians had all entered the volcano, keeping their backs to the crater wall.

"Maybe we should play defence to their offence?" offered Ann Lou, trying her hardest to devise a plan. Every Epitonian was now at the bottom on the lava pool level, fighting over the Pyroll that had fallen from the rope.

"Honestly, I'm more concerned just making it out alive at this point!" Jung-hoon was trembling.

They looked down to the bottom, trying to see who was in possession of the Pyroll. One of the smaller Epitonians was dodging other children left and right. Ann Lou hadn't even figured out who was on their team besides Apollo, which made things even more difficult.

She gestured to Jung-hoon to crouch down where he was standing. She was going to sneak around toward the opposite side of the crater to launch a sneak attack against whoever came running up the coil. Jung-hoon would be the last defensive player before the level with the torch.

The small Epitonian was rounding the circle nearing Ann Lou. As he ran closer, unaware she was crouched low, he huffed, thinking he had a clear path to the torch. The Pyroll was clutched in the curl of his left claw as he pumped both arms harder to gain speed on the final round of the spiral slope.

Ann Lou leapt from the ground and into his chest, forcing him backward, and with an "Argh!" he dropped the Pyroll. Enraged, he shoved Ann Lou off the ledge. It happened so fast that she didn't even have time to scream. Her outstretched arms caught a ledge a few levels down, and she was holding on by the fingertips of her right hand. Miraculously she was still holding her stick in her left hand, but soon it started to slip out of her grip. She watched it plummet into the depths of the crater. The stick caught fire before it even landed in the deadly pool below. She was saddened and scared that she would be next.

"Henrietta!" shouted Jung-hoon from above, completely wrecking Ann Lou's idea for a final attack.

"Here!" Apollo was nearby and helped her up. He was now in possession of the Pyroll.

"Thanks," said Ann Lou, breathlessly getting to her feet.

"Next time, don't attack someone on your team," said Apollo, playfully. "Here, go fast."

He handed her the Pyroll. Before she knew it, she was darting up the spiral slope. Epitonians on upper levels began racing down the slope at her. She continued running forward, knowing that she was hopelessly slower than they. She didn't have much time to decide what the best offensive move would be. She crouched as one Epitonian lunged at her and swiftly ducked under his legs. A second Epitonian raced at her, growling, and swatted at Ann Lou, who twirled out of the way of her slow attack. More Epitonians raced toward her from all directions.

"Henrietta!" shouted an Epitonian across the crater from her. Ann Lou quickly threw the Pyroll as hard as she could in that direction, but her throw fell far short, and the Pyroll landed down near the bottom of the spiral ledge.

Several Epitonians collided with Ann Lou, squashing her body between theirs. Once they noticed that the Pyroll was at the bottom level, they quit attacking Ann Lou and all raced back to the bottom.

Ann Lou was completely embarrassed. How was she supposed to play a sport that she didn't have the strength for? She started running to the bottom level to get into the action with the other players, but as she neared the lava pool, the temperature was nearly unbearable. She couldn't get any closer or she'd pass out. The feeling of defeat filled her body. She wasn't one for giving up in a sport. An Epitonian raced past her with the Pyroll, followed by a stampede of Epitonians headed up the spiral slope after the Pyroll. A wall of them collided with her as she tried to turn around. Ann Lou was knocked headfirst into the wall. The world went fuzzy. She tried taking a step backward but fell off the ledge. The sky above her narrowed to a small beam of light as flames rippled around her periphery until her vision slowly faded into darkness.

When Ann Lou's eyes opened, she was no longer in the crater. She was in her bed in the hut, lying face up, with Riff's t-shirt on. Her body ached all over. When she tried to sit up, burning pain took her breath away.

"Sit still," demanded Aithne.

Ann Lou looked to the edge of the bed to find Aithne, Apollo, Egan, Fintan, Jung-hoon, and Hayden staring at her.

"W—what happened?" she asked.

"Pyroll," replied Egan, grinning like a little child.

"You did great out there for your first time, dear," said Aithne. Apollo nodded in agreement. Aithne was applying some sort of goopy Epitonian medicine on Ann Lou's forehead. She told Hayden how to apply the medicine to the burns on her legs.

"Thought you'd use your stick more?" questioned Egan.

"Did you not see it catch fire? Besides, no one else uses anything like a stick in the game," croaked Ann Lou. She didn't care how stern she was at this point. He'd have to learn to live with her, too.

"There's no rules in Pyroll," he added quietly, his smile broadening. "I think you have the potential to be really good. Your friend, on the other hand . . ." He looked at Jung-hoon, who hung his head in embarrassment.

Once the medicine was applied, the Epitonians said their good-byes and swaggered away to play more Pyroll. Apollo stopped just before jumping up to the roof hole and looked back at her.

"We practice every morning, same time! See you then!" he said in a sweet, youthful voice. Ann Lou chuckled and waved to him. He was quite adorable in her eyes.

"Here's a cup of tea for you, and a Fava cake," said Hayden, handing her a mug and the sweet.

"Thanks." She pushed herself up, withstanding the pain for a cup of tea, which she so dearly missed. She reached with her right arm and took a long sip, feeling the warmth of the tea rush down her throat and into her stomach.

"Want to talk?" asked Hayden sweetly.

"No," she said, taking a long sip and averting his gaze.

"I know it's been really hard for you. I miss my brother Matt more than anything, so I understand how you're feeling."

Ann Lou shot him a look of disgust and tossed the rest of the tea onto the floor so that it spilled just next to his feet. She couldn't hold in the anger any longer.

"You have no idea what I'm going through! You didn't have to literally watch your mother give up her life for you! I have to live with this pain forever!" Ann Lou's face was completely purple now with anger. Hayden stood there, speechless. Ann Lou's entire body was trembling as she fought the urge to throw her prosthetic arm at his face. She cried herself to sleep for a second night in a row.

The next morning, Jung-hoon raced to her bedside excitedly after a few hard bashes to the face on his way inside the hut. Ann Lou hadn't moved since falling asleep. Her face was covered with dried tears.

"I have something for you!" he exclaimed when she wouldn't turn to look at him.

He held up a long, thin object over his head so she could get a closer look at it from her bunk. In her periphery, Ann Lou almost instantly knew what it was. She rose slowly and reached for it, feeling the metal gingerly in her right hand. It was a handmade metal hockey stick.

"How did you do this?" she asked.

"I told you, all my friends are craftsmen. They taught me a thing or two about metals and welding." He held up his hands, which were wrinkled with age and callused from years of working with various materials. "This will at least let you stand a chance in Pyroll." His eyes twinkled as she stared at his creation in amazement.

"This is too much, Jung-hoon." She took the stick in her hand and tilting it both ways to feel the weight of it.

"No, it's not. Gave me time to explore something I'm good at. There's a mine near that first volcano we were at yesterday. These metals can withstand high temperatures, so you shouldn't have any issues with this down in the depths of the crater by the lava pool like you would with a wooden stick."

She lunged forward and hugged him hard from the top bunk, even though the movement awakened the pain from her aches and burns.

"I'll come to the next match with you. But I won't play," he laughed. "I'll keep my eye out for any wild Epitonians coming from your back!"

"Thank you," she said, laying her Pyroll stick beside her.

It took a week or so for Ann Lou to heal from her wounds. She barely left her bunk, only sitting up when Hayden or Jamie brought her food and tea. She hadn't really spoken to anyone during the week, only re-reading her mother's note and cuddling up to her siblings' belongings every once in a while to remind her of home. Once she felt strong enough to sit up without too much pain, she decided it was time to play Pyroll again.

Jung-hoon, Hayden, and Ann Lou ate a few scraps of Polskin, then suited up and walked together to the youth league's volcano. Ann Lou still wasn't ready to talk to Hayden, but the boys acquainted themselves with one another and became fast friends on their walk.

Ann Lou struggled at the start with gripping the rock holds in order to climb up the volcano. She tripped a few times, feeling frustrated that she had lost so much dexterity during her recuperation. Carrying the new Pyroll stick wasn't helping matters, either. The sweat was building up in her suit and her body still ached from the burns. She threw the stick down, unable to climb and ready to head back to her bunk. She abruptly sat down and buried her head in her arms. Jung-hoon and Hayden climbed down from where they were and comforted her.

"I'll carry your stick," said Hayden. "Just take it one step at a time."

Once at the top, the three of them spotted the youth league warming up ahead toward the middle of the crater. Aithne waved, and Apollo ran over to greet them.

"You're back! And you have your secret weapon, I see," Apollo said, pointing to her stick.

"I'm ready to try again," said Ann Lou, exhaling heavily.

"We're just about to start. You can be on my team again!" But his excitement turned sour once he saw Jung-hoon.

"Are . . . you going to play?" Apollo asked.

"Oh no, we're just watching, don't worry," said Jung-hoon, pointing at himself and Hayden.

"Good," snapped Apollo, pulling Ann Lou along as he ran back to the Epitonians.

Jung-hoon and Hayden chose a seat at the rim of the crater while Aithne prepared the Pyroll on the rope between the arch. She slid back down the arch effortlessly and faced the young Epitonians and Ann Lou.

"Ready?" she asked, looking fiercely at each player in turn.

They all clumped together by the spiral ledge that led down to the lava pool.

"Well, spread out a bit. You'll all be on top of each other." Aithne waved her arms in a circular motion so they'd all fill around the crater's circumference.

Ann Lou stayed near the start of the spiral slope, knowing that she would not be jumping. She held her Pyroll stick firmly in her right hand. It felt familiar, and she was instantly at ease.

"Pyyyrooolll!" shouted Aithne. As she finished saying the word, the Pyroll fell, leaving the rope to burn at its end. All the Epitonians jumped in the crater and started barreling down the slope. Ann Lou jumped to the crater wall to let all the Epitonians through before she continued. She didn't want another stampede incident.

She ran down the spiral ledge until she was about halfway down the crater. It appeared the players were still down by the lava pool fighting over the Pyroll. She looked up to see Hayden's and Jung-hoon's heads silhouetted in the light.

Looking back down toward the lava pool, she saw an Epitonian speeding up the spiral, Pyroll in hand. She tossed it to the opposite side of the crater, where another Epitonian caught it mid-run. He continued upward, fighting through the opposing team, knocking one of them off the edge. Luckily, the fallen Epitonian caught the ledge with its sharp claw, preventing a fall into the lava pool.

Some Epitonians, including Apollo, started positioning themselves higher up, near Ann Lou. When an Epitonian with the Pyroll came around, Apollo leapt on him, knocking him off his feet. Apollo rolled off him and grabbed the Pyroll, holding it close to his chest. Seeing Epitonians racing toward him, he cried, "Henrietta!" and threw the Pyroll up several levels of the spiral slope.

The Pyroll raced directly at her. Instinctively, she caught it in the curved blade of her stick and brought it down to the ground. She dribbled the Pyroll with her stick, just as if it were a puck, and started forward. An Epitonian ran at her, anger in his menacing eyes. She tapped the Pyroll gently with her stick right under his legs as she swiveled herself out of his way. He crashed into the wall, and she sped upward.

"Over here!" shouted a teammate from across the crater. Ann Lou took a swing with both arms and blasted the Pyroll across the bowl of the crater with ease. Her swing was far more powerful than her throwing arm. Her teammate caught the Pyroll perfectly in her claw and continued upward.

Ann Lou ran up the spiral still in pain, passing a throng of opponents who were heading down the slope to help their team attack. Ann Lou's teammates continued a steady pace of passing the Pyroll back and forth as the opposing team was playing a heavy defence. A teammate was finally approaching the level just below Ann Lou.

"Henrietta, go long!" The teammate threw the Pyroll as far as she could, just before attackers smashed her against the crater wall. Ann Lou extended her stick out at the flying Pyroll, catching it once again in the stick's blade. A final opposing Epitonian was the last thing standing between her and the open level of the crater. As she dribbled as fast as she could, he lunged for her feet, thinking she'd keep the Pyroll low to the ground. But she bounced the Pyroll on her stick upward and around his head in an arc, landing it perfectly on solid ground outside the depths of the crater. He fell face first onto the ground, and she skirted him to the outside, dangerously close to the edge. To her astonishment, she had a clear path.

"Go, Henrietta!" shouted Apollo from below. Coming out of her trance, she darted toward the Pyroll, then dribbled it toward a spot on the rim where she had a clear shot at the torch. She eyed the target, then brought both arms backward in preparation for a powerful slap shot. She could hear Epitonians racing toward her, only feet away at this point. She swung as hard as she could, pretending the torch was the opposing team's net. The Pyroll flew through the air like a comet. The arc of its flight ended with a perfect clang, and the torch lit ablaze. A toothy smile broadened on Ann Lou's face. Everyone cheered, even the opposing team. Jung-hoon and Hayden stood up to clap from the other side of the crater. All the young Epitonians gathered around her and embraced her, excited about their newest star player.

At that moment, the burden of guilt was temporarily relieved. She had finally found her place on Epiton, just as her mother had assured her she would. She was being cheered on by beings she had no idea existed only a few weeks ago. The sense of community was overwhelming, and she basked in the welcoming embraces of her new friends.

CHAPTER 7

IN THE DEPTHS OF MOUNT FAVA

O ver the next few weeks, Ann Lou played Pyroll every day. Her
prosthetic arm made it challenging to gain strength on her left
side. There were times she'd completely miss the Pyroll as it was
being thrown to her or stumble on the narrow ledge of the coiled slope,
but she enjoyed playing. Most of all, she enjoyed her new friend Apollo.

Ann Lou woke up this morning to a graceful thud on the roof, followed by another thump to the floor of the hut. It was Apollo, ready
for Pyroll and another day of adventure. Ann Lou could hear Hayden
groan in the bunk beneath her and stuff his head under the covers.

Teddi started to cry, prompting Jamie to tend to her distress. Ann
Lou caught sight of Egan and Fintan checking their nightly load of
Fava cakes. Egan shoved five in his mouth at once, setting Fintan off
like a bomb.

"How many times have I told you to not eat them all at once?" Fintan's charcoal skin took on an angry reddish pallor. He flung a claw under Egan's chin, which was now dripping in Fava cake.

As if on cue, Egan spat five Fava cake fireball pits from his mouth such that they landed in a neat pentagon on the floor in front of him. Fintan stomped out the resulting flames, even more enraged with Egan.

Apollo hopped up to Ann Lou's bunk with an easy push of his legs. The two huddled close, gossiping and laughing at the humorous scene unfolding in front of them.

"This happens *every* morning," Ann Lou bragged. "This hut is mad. They are absolute bonkers."

"One time Fintan nearly caused all of Egan's eelich to diffuse because he dropped the Pyroll in practice!" Apollo said in a hushed whisper. Ann Lou's mouth dropped. She had recently learned that eelich was the Epitonian version of blood—the black gas that was flowing out of Egan's head on the Jalopy journey after the GeoLapse attack.

"Do they actually like each other?" Ann Lou asked.

Apollo giggled. "Epitonians are serious when they pair up. It's tradition to have a wedding ceremony designed to test your limits. Those who make it out alive are basically confirmed soulmates. This is nothing for these two." He smiled at her brightly.

"What's the wedding ceremony like?" Ann Lou pestered him by nudging him in the shoulder.

Ann Lou suddenly felt a kick from below.

"What?" she barked. She poked her head out over the side of the bunk.

"Stop gossiping! It's rude."

"I was asking about their culture. Relax," she groaned, rolling her eyes at Apollo. Apollo laughed.

"No," said Hayden. "The stuff before that. Stop talking poorly about our hosts."

Ann Lou threw a pillow at Hayden, which caused Teddi to cry harder.

Hayden wasn't amused and began to put his suit on. Once he was geared up, he piled their trunks one on top of the other and climbed out of the hole in the roof with much effort. Jamie glared at Ann Lou and followed Hayden out with Teddi cradled carefully in her arms.

Throughout the day, Ann Lou and Apollo played their usual games of Pyroll, participated in other games with the Epitonian children around the mainland, and indulged in Polskin at Apollo and Aithne's hut. Their stomachs were full by the time Ann Lou was ready to head home to sleep.

"I don't want to go back to the hut tonight," she moaned, tossing her head back.

Aithne overheard the conversation and stepped toward them. "Why don't you come with us to the ice cave tonight? You can sleep tomorrow morning when you return. Egan and Fintan will be joining." She added the last sentence with a tone of bribery. The proposal sounded enticing and exciting. "We're heading out soon if you're up for the challenge."

Apollo, Aithne, and Ann Lou met a large group of Epitonians just outside the huts at nightfall— although it still looked like daytime, because "night" on Epiton just meant there were fewer suns in the sky.

Ann Lou and Apollo nudged their way into the dense crowd and found a small pocket of space to stand in. Shouts, hisses, and bellowing voices cascaded around the crowd, causing Ann Lou some alarm until Apollo joined in. The crowd started to shift forward slowly, then accelerated within a few paces. The density of the group was maintained, even with speed.

Soon Ann Lou could not keep up. Epitonians were pushing her out of the way, yet the mass of the crowd continued to propel her forward, causing her to bounce around like a pinball.

At once, she was scooped up and tossed onto someone's shoulders. Now riding smoothly with the crowd, she peered down at her saviour. It was Fintan.

Egan, sprinting beside them, waved to her. "Isn't this fun?" he bellowed over the loud rumble of the chaos around them.

She had no idea what this expedition even entailed. Would they have to fight someone? Or perhaps something?

Ann Lou shook her head of the scary possibilities brewing in her brain and focused her attention on the crowd of lightning-fast Epitonians now decelerating in front of her. They all came to a synchronised, screeching halt in front of what looked like a wall. Ann Lou squinted up at it and realised that it was a gigantic volcano, much larger than any of those she had played Pyroll on so far. She couldn't even see the top of it as she cupped her hand around her eyes into a pinhole. There was no way . . .

As Ann Lou scrunched her face in confusion, the Epitonians at the front of the group began to climb. Their claws dug into the surface, and they rose up the rock face as easily as if gravity had been working in the opposing direction. Now Fintan, still carrying Ann Lou on his shoulders, was inching his way to the wall, and Ann Lou gasped.

Fintan sensed her anguish. "This is Mount Fava. Hang tight," he grunted. Fintan's right claw dug into the rock, and he instantly began to propel himself and Ann Lou upward. Both of his claws were working rapidly and effortlessly. Occasionally he even used his horns to maintain his momentum, giving Ann Lou a fright every time he unexpectedly thrust his head forward.

As the pair climbed as one unit, Ann Lou felt Fintan's grunts, groans, huffs, and puffs. She felt bad about causing him extra strain on his climb and hoped that he could hold on for a little bit longer.

"Henrietta!" shouted Apollo from below. Ann Lou caught his eye, and he waved a claw at her. He was smiling, almost as if he were having fun.

The climb went on for hours, and Ann Lou got so accustomed to the rhythmic jostling that she fell asleep on Fintan's shoulders. He shook her awake once they reached the top, and she watched as the Epitonians formed a circle around a lake-like geyser of bubbling liquid. She looked behind them as Fintan slid her off his back, and she saw that they weren't in the depths of a volcanic crater; they were on a peak. She couldn't see anything recognisable in the distance. Looking downward only raised her anxiety, so she rested her eyes on the strange liquid contents of the geyser in front of her.

She quickly realised that the ambient temperature wasn't boiling hot. It was actually slightly chilly. The bubbling liquid also wasn't fiery red like lava in a lava pool; it was azure blue. Sparkling light shone from deep within the geyser, perhaps a thousand metres or more down. Bubbles rose out of the geyser, crystallised, and then shattered into ice-like crystals. Ann Lou stood there for a few moments in awe, watching the cyclic motion as the crystal shards fell back into the geyser and more bubbles rose. It was only when Apollo stood next to her and wrapped his claw gently around her right arm that she came back to awareness of her surroundings.

"Stay with me and I'll show you how it's done," he smiled.

Ann Lou watched as the Epitonians began to dive in one by one around the periphery of the geyser. They performed perfect swan dives, barely making a splash even with their oversized frames. Together, their graceful bodies looked like a charcoal waterfall.

"Ready?" whispered Apollo, moving his claw down to her hand, pulling it close to his tall, thin body.

Ann Lou smiled, and Apollo hopped forward, pulling her down limply with him into the geyser.

The azure liquid was a cool, refreshing change from the usual Epitonian climate. She held her breath for as long as she could but quickly realised that, thanks to her suit and mask, she could in fact breathe under the surface.

Apollo, still clutching her right hand, used his powerful legs to propel them into the depths of the liquid.

The glinting light from the depths of the liquid grew brighter as they descended. Epitonians sailed around them, waving their legs swiftly back and forth to propel them further into the geyser's depths. Bubbles trailed from the tips of their horns as they swam. As Ann Lou took in a panoramic view, it looked as if she was part of a school of fish, each of them following one another toward a single point of interest.

As they descended, the liquid around them grew colder, to the point where Ann Lou was shivering. She was glad that her suit was also cold-resistant to a certain degree, or she would have surely frozen into a statue. The colour of the liquid turned from azure to navy, rapidly nearing black. As her eyes adjusted to the shift in contrast, the glinting lights at the bottom shimmered, and she recognised them as bits of fire shooting from a layer of ice that lined the bottom of the cave.

Once they reached the bottom, Apollo let go of Ann Lou's hand and swam toward the shooting sparks of flame. They were just the right size for the small fires inside of a Fava cake. But where were the icy casings of the cakes?

Apollo came back with a handful of fires clutched in one claw and mumbled, "Grab a bubble!" More bubbles flowed out of his horns as he spoke.

How was she supposed to grab a bubble? On Earth, she had never been able to touch a bubble without popping it, let alone grab one. She looked around and through the glinting, sweeping light of the fires and saw Fintan and Egan easily grabbing bubbles in their sharp claws without a single pop. There were plenty of bubbles around, but Ann Lou wasn't sure if she would look awkward for popping them. She looked back at Apollo with even more confusion.

"Just try it," he urged. "I'll put in the lava."

Ann Lou watched intently as bubbles rose past her eyes. She reached up and put her right palm out to catch one as gently as possible. A bubble the size of her head glided right into her palm and settled there. Apollo grinned from behind the group of fires.

"That's a big one! I think it deserves two lavas."

He swam back to her, and she watched as he put one fire inside the bubble with his claw. All he had to do was let the fire come into contact with the side of the bubble, and it rolled perfectly into the centre, making a completed Fava cake. He put the second fire in, and they both held the beautiful bubble between them, with two identical flames glistening in the dark, icy depths of Mount Fava.

They returned to the huts in the morning as the suns rose. Ann Lou noticed that more humans were outside of the huts than usual. There was an air of sadness and fear about them that was overwhelming. Fintan dropped Ann Lou off his shoulders outside their hut. As he went inside the hut to deliver the Fava cakes, Ann Lou walked up to where Hayden, Jamie, Teddi, and Jung-hoon were standing.

"What's going on?" She could see many of the humans crying and holding one another. Hayden was stone-faced. Jamie and Jung-hoon were hanging their heads low, not speaking. Teddi sensed her mother's despair and had a look of woe on her face, as if she might start wailing at any moment.

Hayden looked up at Ann Lou with puffy eyes. "Earth's gone under."

Ann Lou froze. "What do you mean, 'gone under'?"

Hayden gulped. "It's been taken over by the GeoLapse. Everyone else is dead. It's all over."

Ann Lou didn't know whether to believe him. How could the GeoLapse just kill off everyone? Did she even want to know? Images of her mother flashed in her brain. The thought of her mother losing her life to the GeoLapse immediately dug up the feelings of guilt she had compartmentalised over the past few weeks. She felt tears forming, unsure of how to control her thoughts at that moment.

Hayden looked pleadingly at Ann Lou. "Please," he begged. "Please talk to me."

Ann Lou's body began to shake with grief. Something didn't feel right about breaking down in front of Hayden. It had been so long since they had talked like friends that the friendship already felt ruined. She couldn't show him vulnerability anymore. It was over.

Ann Lou walked away from him and made her way into the hut. She felt Hayden, Jamie, and Jung-hoon's eyes on her, all disappointed in her actions. Perhaps even Teddi was watching her with disgust as well. She couldn't face them. She was ashamed but much too stubborn for her own good. Ann Lou had Epitonian friends now anyway; she didn't need the humans anymore.

Once she was in the hut, she felt comfortable enough to speak to Egan and Fintan. They were bickering over Egan's having eaten half the night's stash of Fava cakes already.

"You must have heard the news by now," said Ann Lou, tears now rolling down her cheeks as she took off her mask.

Fintan and Egan looked at one another uncomfortably. She had never seen them in an uncomfortable or awkward situation. Their ferocity usually dominated whatever else they were feeling.

"We've heard rumours," said Fintan, stepping forward gingerly. He seemed to have developed a fatherly instinct since Ann Lou moved in, which she greatly appreciated even though it wasn't near the comfort her mother's presence would have provided.

"I'm sorry, Henrietta," said Egan, tucking another Fava cake in his mouth. Fintan let it slide.

"What's going to happen?" she asked. She was trying to sound strong, but her voice was cracking.

Fintan and Egan looked at one another, again at a loss for words. Fintan rested a claw on Ann Lou's shoulder.

"We don't know. We've been warned about the GeoLapse's plans about taking over the universe. I guess we really didn't understand how strong they were. I certainly didn't until that day on the Jalopy."

Egan cringed. Ann Lou remembered the eelich spewing from his horn and how traumatising the attack had been, both physically and mentally.

Fintan continued. "All that's important is that you're safe now, Henrietta. I will make sure no one hurts you. You have my word."

"And mine!" piped Egan from behind him, his mouth still full of cakes.

Ann Lou felt incredibly grateful for Fintan and Egan. She was safe, but the unfortunate fact was that the real Henrietta was not. It was difficult for Ann Lou to comprehend that she no longer had her mother alive. There would be no more hugs, no more tea brought to her room, no more delicious roasts made by her and Elbina. Life on Earth was now solely in her past.

CHAPTER 8

CIPTO

Over seven Earth years had gone by since the transfer to Epiton, and Ann Lou had found her niche, just as she always had back at school on Earth. She was a star Pyroll player and had made a large circle of friends, most of them Epitonians. She far preferred them over humans since Pyroll had become her new passion in place of hockey.

Her friendship with Hayden these days consisted of the occasional "hey" or "bye" as each of them came and went from the hut. The two hadn't properly spoken since before the move to Epiton, and they felt more like strangers with each day that passed. Hayden spent most of his time with Jamie, Teddi, and Jung-hoon. They ate each meal together and played games inside the comforting walls of Egan and Fintan's hut, rarely venturing out into mainland Epiton. They were like their own little family unit, which Ann Lou was jealous of, though she was too stubborn to admit it. Deep down, she missed that feeling of being in a family, but it was safer to push those emotions down rather than risk thinking of the family she had lost. Besides, she had her Pyroll team as her family now.

Ann Lou was out every morning playing Pyroll with her team and perfecting her dribbling with the stick Jung-hoon had crafted for her. Every evening, she roamed the volcanoes with Apollo and explored new Pyroll arenas. She'd almost forgotten about the life, now demolished, that she had left behind on Earth.

One evening, the top Epiton Pyroll team were discussing their championship game, to be held on Cipto. They met just before practice at their usual volcano, sitting on the edge of the crater above the lava pool.

"I hate travelling to other planets for Pyroll. The volcanoes are never the same. Plus, how does anybody see anything on Cipto?" huffed Egan.

"Well, we're chasing a ball of fire, so I think you'll manage," answered Fintan, who seemed ready to push Egan off the ledge. "But that's the fun of Pyroll. Each arena is different."

"Yeah, but it's not fiery and dangerous," whined Aithne. Egan nodded his head in agreement. Fintan rolled his eyes.

Apollo and Ann Lou were excited to have been recently recruited to Epiton's top Pyroll team, meaning that they were invited to play universally, including in the upcoming Pyroll Championship.

"Are Cipto any good?" asked Apollo, excitedly bouncing on the ledge.

"In theory, they're terrible. But we always have such a hard time in the complete darkness of Cipto that those annoying little jelly blobs give us quite the challenge. This year, though, I think we have a much better chance at clobbering them with the new additions to our team," he said in a more upbeat tone, looking at both Ann Lou and Apollo.

Ann Lou smiled and sat in silence. She was excited about the championship, but she was nervous that she might see Luna while on her visit. Just the thought of being reunited with one of her family members made a hole in her stomach. Ann Lou's siblings didn't even know that she was on Epiton. Luna probably thought their mother was alive and well. Would she be disappointed to learn that their mother had stayed on Earth and given Ann Lou her place on Epiton? She also wondered if Luna had felt the way she felt all these years: as if her anger and sadness had been held in for so long that it would feel unnatural to resurrect any portion of Earth life. Ann Lou knew she was the sole reason for her falling out with Hayden, but it was the only coping mechanism that worked—or, rather, the only coping mechanism she had dared to try all these years.

"It's getting late. Let's get one more good practice in now before we leave for Cipto tomorrow. Everyone put on your blindfolds. We can't practice on Cipto, so practicing blindfolded is the next best thing. Now, everyone get up and get ready," ordered Fintan, grunting as he began to prepare the Pyroll on the rope.

After practice, Ann Lou made her way back to the hut. As she helped herself to some Polskin and Fava cakes, she overheard Hayden and Jung-hoon having a conversation with Jamie at her and Teddi's bunk.

"I'm excited to see it. Maybe I'll see my old friends there," said Jung-hoon, sounding cheery.

"Me too, it'll be nice to get out of here. But, dude," said Hayden, putting on his American accent, "you won't be seeing anything on Cipto!" Jung-hoon laughed. "I only wish you two were coming," Hayden continued, gesturing to Jamie and Teddi, who were reading a book together in the top bunk.

"Teddi's afraid of the dark. There's no way we would make it five minutes without a screaming match," giggled Jamie, patting Teddi on the leg.

Ann Lou had just put the pieces of their conversation together.

"You guys are going to Cipto?" she asked from across the hut in a harsh tone.

Hayden and Jung-hoon looked at her with their brows furrowed. "Yeah," said Hayden. "And?" He crossed his arms.

"Well, why?" she snapped back. "It's not like you guys are on the Pyroll team."

"Oh, we know that, genius," snarled Hayden. "You know, people can come to the event and support their planet."

"Well, I don't understand why you'd want to go to Cipto. It's not like you can see what's going on. Plus, you don't even like Pyroll!"

"Says who?" Hayden's vocal amplitude was increasing with each word he spoke. Jung-hoon took a step back toward Jamie. "Just because you and I don't get along anymore doesn't mean I can't enjoy myself," Hayden continued.

Ann Lou scoffed and turned away from him, lying down on her bunk. "You're such a git."

The next morning, Ann Lou sat alone in the far corner of the hut and munched on her Polskin in peace. She felt a tap on her shoulder. It was Teddi.

"Hi, Henrietta," she said in her sweet tone. "Can I have your autograph?"

Ann Lou noticed some other younger humans and Epitonians poking their heads into the hut, waiting to see if it would be safe for them to ask for autographs as well. Ann Lou swallowed a big bite of Polskin and smiled at them. "Sure thing, Teddi." She felt embarrassed that young Teddi had heard her angry exchange with Hayden the night before.

"I'd come to the match, but I'm afraid of the dark," she said, handing Ann Lou the book she had been reading the day before and a pen. "But I think I want to join the youth league!"

Ann Lou signed the book on a random page. She noticed how strange it felt to sign her name 'Henrietta McHubbard' but quickly handed the book back to Teddi. "Maybe I can give you a few tips sometime. How's that sound?"

Teddi beamed. She wished Ann Lou a sweet "Good luck!" and then said to the other kids, "It's okay, guys!" A line of children jumped down into the hut and shuffled up to her, and she gave each of them her autograph. Once her fans were attended to, Ann Lou grabbed her Pyroll stick and packed her rucksack for the journey. She wasn't sure how long she'd be there, but she couldn't bear the idea of leaving her siblings' souvenirs and her mother's note behind.

Once Ann Lou heaved herself out of the hut and onto the mainland, she saw that the Jalopy—the same one they had used for the original human transfer—was being filled up with human and Epitonian Pyroll fans and the Epiton Pyroll team. Ann Lou stared at the boat in front of her with a pit in her stomach. It would be her first time in over seven years leaving Epiton. The thought of intergalactic travel began to stir some emotions inside her, which she promptly bottled up.

Ann Lou watched Hayden and Jung-hoon board the Jalopy together in a big crowd. The human Epiton fans wore red hats, scarves, and mittens over their suits to show their loyalty.

Apollo walked up to Ann Lou and presented her with a uniform.

"You won't need the suit on Cipto, so here's a team uniform for you," he smiled, handing her the uniform of a red jersey and joggers. They had McHUBBARD stitched onto them. She couldn't help but notice that Apollo's muscles were bursting through his own uniform.

"Ready?" he said.

She blushed and nodded.

Ann Lou and Apollo boarded the Jalopy together. She never thought she would be going back on the boat after all these years. It was just as dusty as the last time she was on it, and most of the seats had cobwebs between them. They took their seats at the bow once everyone else had filled in the remainder of the boat. Egan, Fintan, and some others on the team were tossing a Pyroll back and forth at starboard.

Once everyone was on board, the Jalopy flashed its neon green colour internally and accelerated upward. They reached the depths of space within seconds. Many of the children were surrounding the edge of the boat trying to get a good look at the whizzing stars, a sight they had been too young on the first voyage to remember.

Ann Lou started stripping her suit off and slipping the uniform on to prepare herself for the game. She felt the nerves rising with each passing second.

"So, can I ask about Hayden?" asked Apollo abruptly.

Ann Lou froze as she fitted her right arm through the jersey. She turned her head to show him a puzzled look.

"Why?" she asked.

"He always stares at you. Including right now." Apollo pointed a claw toward Hayden, who was subtly glancing in their direction every so often.

Ann Lou whipped her head around to glare at Hayden, who was a few rows behind them. He immediately jumped into conversation with Jung-hoon once he noticed he was being watched.

"Why the sudden interest?" asked Ann Lou, annoyed to even think about Hayden after their fight the previous evening.

"Well, you've never really mentioned him much to me. Seems like he was a big part of your life previously . . . and it seems like maybe he likes you quite a bit more than on a friendly level." Apollo didn't seem bothered from this observation. His chest was puffed out and his chin held high. Ann Lou tittered at his confidence.

"We were pretty close. We were . . . best friends," said Ann Lou with a great sigh. "I think he liked me on Earth, but . . . there's no real reason for him to like me anymore."

"Well, maybe your past speaks differently from what you believe to be true." Then Apollo huffed and looked her straight in the eyes. "I was wondering if you want to be my mate. And not in the 'friend' way you Earthlings use the word."

Ann Lou laughed out loud at the bluntness of his question. "You're mad, Apollo!"

Apollo looked confused, and his silence shut down Ann Lou's laughter. "No, I don't think I am. This is how it works here. I've found someone I care deeply about, and I want to marry you."

Ann Lou's eyes bugged out at the word *marry*. She contemplated the societal differences his proposal presented to her. It was very sweet, but she was terrified at the thought of being married to someone who wasn't a human and, for that matter, someone she hadn't even dated yet. She had never even thought about dating anyone in general. She had also never seen any of the other humans on Epiton dating an Epitonian. Would she be the first? Butterflies were forming in her stomach. She realised that she may have been harbouring feelings for Apollo for many years now, but those feelings had been pushed down along with the other emotions she'd been neglecting to experience over the years.

"But, why me? Why not the thousands of other Epitonians who are madly in love with you?" Ann Lou felt slightly self-conscious, a foreign feeling for her.

"Because you're my favourite creature in the whole universe," he replied kindly. "And you're almost as good at Pyroll as I am," he winked.

The butterflies in Ann Lou's stomach made her feel as if she were beginning to float. She almost felt nauseous and needed to bring him to a pace she was comfortable with.

"Can we . . . try dating? That's what we do on Earth. You date someone for a while, you fall in love, and then you decide if you want to be with them forever if you are compatible."

"Why wouldn't you want to be with someone forever from the start?" he asked.

"Because . . . they might cheat on you or hurt you in some way. Or one of you might fall in love with someone else. There's loads of reasons."

Apollo was puzzled. "I don't understand why someone who loves you would ever hurt you. On Epiton, once we meet our match, we're bonded forever." He noticed the worry in her face and added, "But I'll give this 'dating' thing a try if that would make you feel better."

Ann Lou actually felt happy at that moment. She rested her head on

Apollo's shoulder for the rest of the trip to Cipto, experiencing the bubbling feelings of fiery passion for someone for the first time in her life.

Most of the journey consisted of the Epitonians reciting Pyroll chants to hype the team and the fans up for the game. As Ann Lou giggled at Apollo's raspy voice attempting to follow along with the chants, she also caught Hayden looking at the pair of them with a scowl.

As they neared the end of the flightpath between Epiton and Cipto, the outside view suddenly went very dark. Many of the children, both Epiton and human, were pressing their faces against the glass barrier of the Jalopy to try and see Cipto in the distance, but it was only getting darker and darker. There were fewer and fewer stars nearby to provide light, and the very distant stars were becoming mere pinholes of light, useless for seeing anything close by. Ann Lou gripped Apollo's claw for comfort in the now pitch-black surroundings. Grunting noises were heard around the Jalopy since they had all started tripping over each another and stepping on each other's toes.

"Would everyone just sit down until we land?" sighed Fintan, exasperated.

"My strange visitors, you have already arrived!" announced a happy, squeaky voice.

Everyone's heads turned every which way, looking in vain for the source of the voice.

"Who and where are you?" shouted Fintan in the same exasperated tone.

"I'm Lucy, a resident of Cipto!" said the sweet, bouncy voice. Heads continued whirling around as the Epitonians tried to see if the Jalopy was still in motion or not.

"You might want to take this," said Egan, tossing the Pyroll in a random direction on the Jalopy.

Lucy heard the Pyroll land somewhere near the port side of the boat and wiggled her way over to where she had felt the vibrations coming from. Everyone's eyes watched the Pyroll land. They waited for something to pick it up, but instead they saw a colourless, jelly-like blob approach it, open its mouth, and swallow it. Lucy was now a glowing, translucent blob. She was rotund and droopy, with a slithery bottom like a snail. She didn't have any eyes, only a mouth that looked like a little more than a slight dent in the blobby structure.

"Can you see me now?" asked Lucy.

Everyone stared at her. She seemed quite ugly to them, but she had a very sweet tone. It was almost scary to hear a voice coming from a glowing, protoplasmic blob, but at least they had a point of reference now.

"Uhhh, yes," answered Egan on behalf of the group.

"Excellent!" Lucy cheered, hopping off the ground with a noise like a suction cup, then touching back down with a *plop*. "Please follow me to the arena!"

The Epitonians and humans carefully waited until Lucy had exited the Jalopy. No one said a word. Normally the fans would be singing and cheering before an event such as this, but everyone instead decided to grab each other's hands and claws for dear life. A few of the children whimpered as they all slowly followed Lucy along the stone path, the Pyroll glowing in the depths of her stomach. Ann Lou felt strange. She quickly realised it was due to the chilly temperature on Cipto, a complete turnaround from the environment on Epiton. She wasn't used to the goosebumps forming on her arms, especially when she was about to play Pyroll. Ann Lou squeezed Apollo's claw tightly with her right hand and held her Pyroll stick in her left.

"You might want to loosen your grip, or I won't be able to play with both claws today," he whispered to her. He could feel her trembling in fear.

"Aren't you scared?" she whispered back, not taking her eyes off Lucy.

"Not at all," he answered. "Ciptons are the kindest beings in the universe. You should be way more scared of me!"

As Lucy led everyone through the darkness, there was a faint roar of cheers in the distance. Ann Lou envisioned an arena full of blobs hopping in their seats, cheering on their team. There were even some cheers that sounded human-like. Could Luna be in the crowd? She had never been much of a sport-lover from what Ann Lou could remember, but maybe she had developed new interests since arriving on Cipto. The cheers were getting gradually louder and louder, until it sounded like they were right next to a large crowd. Lucy stopped her slithering at once.

"We've reached the arena!" said Lucy, turning around and facing them. "Fans, please find a seat to your left. Please join us after the match for one of our storytelling ceremonies as a gesture of thanks for travelling to Cipto. We are truly happy to have you here. Now, Pyroll team, follow me to meet the Cipto team and to prepare for the start of the match!"

Lucy continued forward, leaving the Epitonian and human fans to find their way to their seats in the dark. Ann Lou and Apollo were happy they didn't have to leave the glow of the Pyroll. They laughed quietly at all the *ouches, arghs,* and *oofs* coming from fan seats. A few times, they heard a wet *squish* followed by profuse apologies from an Epitonian or human who had accidentally sat on a Cipto fan.

Lucy guided the Epiton team around a large bend. They could see dots of light bouncing in the distance. It looked as if the Cipto team were practicing their Pyroll throwing. They'd see a Pyroll exit the mouth of one blob, fly through the air, and then land in the mouth of a different blob. Ann Lou grimaced in disgust, hoping that wouldn't be the Pyroll they would be using in the match.

"Myope, they're here!" Lucy said in a chipper voice. She seemed to have an extra bounce in her slither.

"Ah! Welcome, welcome!" chirped Myope, who came into view as she slithered near the glow emitting from Lucy. Myope looked exactly the same as Lucy, from what they could all tell: blobbish and translucent.

"I am the captain of the Cipto Pyroll team," Myope said. "I'd love it if you would make yourselves comfortable. We should be starting soon. Feel free to warm up!"

None of the team even knew where to start warming up. They all stood awkwardly in a bunch.

"Uhh," started Egan, awkwardly. "Can we get our Pyroll back?"

"Oops!" laughed Lucy. She spat the light source from her stomach straight toward Egan. Luckily, he caught it just before it hit his face.

None of them could see Lucy anymore. The team turned and stared at Egan, the Pyroll now glowing in front of his face.

"Team huddle, I guess," he muttered.

"This game is all about communication, everyone," said Fintan, grabbing the Pyroll out of Egan's hands, his face now visible in the Pyroll's glow.

"Fintaaan," whined Egan.

"We must listen to each other. Don't be afraid to step on those jellies. We are not losing this game." Fintan sounded even more serious than usual about winning, and the intensity of his menacing expression behind the Pyroll confirmed it.

Ann Lou snuck away from the huddle without anyone noticing. Gently tapping her Pyroll stick in front of her, she walked back to where she had last seen Lucy and Myope. It was so dark that the colour black almost didn't look like a colour anymore. It was more an overwhelming sense of disorientation. She almost couldn't tell if she was standing straight up or not.

"Lucy? Myope?" she whispered.

"Yes!" squeaked Myope and Lucy in unison. They were somewhere to her left. "How can we help you, Earthling?"

"Erm," Ann Lou whispered, "I was wondering if you know many of the humans who live here."

"Oh sure," said Lucy, enthusiastically. "We love our Earthlings. We have frequent storytelling ceremonies where they all share their tales from the Milky Way. Life on Earth must have been so fascinating!"

"Do you happen to know a human, erm, Earthling named Luna, by any chance? She's tall, has reddish hair and glasses . . ." At once she realised that the description she had just given was useless to the eyeless Ciptons. "Erm, she likes to read," continued Ann Lou.

"Did she live in a place called England? And have a crazy grand-mother?" asked Myope.

Ann Lou's heart dropped. "Yes," she answered breathlessly. "Can you take me to her?" She had forgotten that she had a championship game to play.

"Oh, not now, dear, but after the game for sure! She will be at the storytelling ceremony," piped Lucy. "Luna is one of our favourite story-tellers! She always reads to us and tells us stories of her family."

So it was going to happen. Ann Lou was going to see her oldest sister again after seven years of being apart. She was filled with both joy and terror, and the combination was so overwhelming she wasn't sure if she'd be able to play Pyroll. Lucy must have been able to sense Ann Lou's emotion, because Ann Lou felt a jelly-like hand around her own.

"She's doing just fine," added Lucy.

CHAPTER 9

THE PYROLL CHAMPIONSHIP

"E veryone in position!" yelled one of the Cipto Pyroll players in the distance.

"Henrietta!" shouted Apollo from off to her right.

Ann Lou shook her head a few times to clear her head, then walked back to her team, wobbling from a mixture of disorientation and anticipation. She bumped straight into Apollo, who guided her over to the rest of the team.

"You okay, *girlfriend*?" he asked her, putting his arm around her shoulders.

"I'm really good," she laughed with a smile.

Apollo gave her a tight hug. "Stand here. You're positioned right at the start of the downward slope. I'm going to start on the other side. You'll be great." She heard the thump of his feet on the stones as he ran away.

"Ready?" shouted a Cipton. The crowd cheered wildly. Ann Lou could see nothing except the Pyroll tied to the rope that presumably was dangling from the bottom of an arch. She looked down, but there was no lava pool in sight. Who knew how deep this hole was? There was no point of reference. The team's last blindfolded practice on Epiton was nothing compared to this.

She reached her Pyroll stick down to feel for the path where she needed to start. The stick touched nothing, and now she knew that the drop was right in front of her. She moved the stick to the right and felt a gravel-like path sloping slightly downward. She'd have the start there. Carefully.

"Pyroll!" shouted the Cipton voice. The Pyroll fell from the rope, illuminating the walls of the drop in cross-sections, like a scanner moving downward.

The Epitonian team jumped into the drop before the Pyroll had even hit the bottom of the drop—Ann Lou could tell because she could hear their menacing roars echoing downward. She started treading gingerly down the spiral, keeping her right hand against the gravel wall and the Pyroll stick grazing on the edge of the coiled slope so she wouldn't fall. She stopped every so often to look downward in order to locate the Pyroll. The ball of fire was a mere pinpoint of light at this point, so far down that the players' voices could barely be heard. The Pyroll appeared to be bouncing around. She assumed that it was being tossed back and forth, or stolen and recovered, at a constant rate. She continued down the spiral at the steady pace she started with. Then something slithery rolled over her toes.

"Argh!" she shrieked, kicking it away.

"Sorry!" something called back at her. Ann Lou realised a Cipto player must have slithered over her on its way down the spiral. She clutched her heart and stopped to catch her breath. This game was going to be even more difficult than she had anticipated.

Ann Lou decided to sprint a little faster down the spiral now that she had a system for making sure she was stable with keeping one hand on the wall and using the stick to identify the drop. The shouting toward the bottom was getting slightly louder. She couldn't tell if players were coming up toward her or if she was getting close to the bottom of the drop. She was nearing a jog's pace, confident at this point that she could reach her team to help them.

WHAM! She ran into something hard, like a brick wall except it had been coming toward her.

"Hey!" shouted Aithne, who was also clearly disoriented. Aithne's first instinct was to push away the presumed attacker. Ann Lou felt a tremendous shove as her body was tossed over the edge of the spiral.

She screamed at the top of her lungs, unsure of how far she would fall or how hard she would hit. The firelight from the burning rope from above was getting smaller and smaller until she hit something soft that gently broke her fall.

"Ooh! Got me back! Nice play," chuckled the Cipton who had rolled over her toes earlier. Ann Lou was now at the bottom of the drop, having been saved by a fortunately placed Cipton. The Pyroll was several levels up, so Ann Lou sprang up from her landing spot and felt around the wall. Once she found the upward spiral again, she held out her stick in front of her to avoid getting thrown off the ledge again.

The firelight from the Pyroll was quickly moving upward, as if it were nestled under a runner's arm. She watched it flip forward and bounce on the ground, only to be engulfed by one of the Cipto players. The now-glowing blob slowly slithered upward, then catapulted the Pyroll across the diameter of the drop, right into the mouth of another Cipton, who slowly continued slithering upward. This tactic was repeated several times in a row. Even though the Ciptons weren't quick and didn't have much in the way of offence, they certainly could pass the Pyroll in a manner that was tricky for the Epitonians to intercept.

As the Pyroll was yet again being passed across the diameter of the drop, it suddenly made a right-angle turn. Ann Lou heard a grunt from just above her. It sounded like Egan had leapt across the diameter to intercept the Pyroll midair. Impressed with his save, Ann Lou continued upward.

"Fintan?" shouted Egan. "Where are you?"

"Here!" shouted Fintan. He could have been anywhere. Egan threw the Pyroll in the direction he thought Fintan's voice had come from.

"Not there, you *idiot!*" shouted Fintan, who was not the recipient of the Pyroll. It had, however, hit the wall just beside Ann Lou, whose heart nearly leapt out of her chest. She began to dribble the Pyroll up the ledge.

"Who's got the Pyroll?" shouted Fintan, who sounded ready to attack anyone and everyone at this point.

"Henrietta!" shouted Ann Lou. She had no idea where she was in the drop, nor any idea where the top was. She held out her elbow far enough to graze the wall of the drop, hoping she would be able to feel if she were to emerge at the top. Looking up, she saw that the burning rope was getting brighter. She hoped they could make it in time.

In the glow of the Pyroll, she saw a Cipto player slithering toward her. She swiped her stick right through the Cipton, knowing it wouldn't be hurt. The stick's blade hit the Pyroll squarely and propelled it forward. The Pyroll landed exactly where she wanted it to, and she continued dribbling upward.

"Henrietta, I am directly across and up!" shouted Aithne. Ann Lou scowled, not wanting to pass the Pyroll to the teammate who had nearly pushed her to her death. She slap-shotted the Pyroll toward Aithne's voice anyway, hoping she'd targeted the correct spot. Aithne shouted, "Got it!" and continued running upward.

There were a few more pushbacks from Cipto. Aithne tripped over one of them, and the Pyroll went flying down a few levels. Ann Lou decided to station herself toward the top so she could have a chance of igniting the torch. Eventually, she reached the end of the wall and knew she was on the top level. There were many different cheers, distorting her focus. Cheers of *"EP-I-TON"* were blurred against *"CIP-TO"* and other indistinguishable chants sounding from the audience. The crowd was bursting with excitement, their shouts and cheers only increasing in volume with each moment.

The rope was still burning, but Ann Lou had no idea how close it was to the torch. She eyed the Pyroll on its race up the spiral, unsure of who was in possession.

"Anyone up there?" bellowed Apollo, who seemed to be getting close to the level Ann Lou was on.

"Me, Henrietta! Throw upward and forward!" she yelled to him.

The Pyroll came flying in her direction. She backed up, hoping she wouldn't trip over anything, and caught the Pyroll in her stick.

She brought her arms backward and aimed directly at the burning part of the rope. It was as if her vision was targeted to that spot only. There were no other visible distractions. The muscles in her right arm pulled the stick downward in a perfect arc. The stick smashed against the Pyroll, catapulting it closer and closer to the rope. Just as Ann Lou blinked, the crowd erupted in joyous cheers.

CHAPTER 10

Stories and Sisters

"T eam Epiton wins!" shouted a Cipton somewhere in the distance, and the crowd continued their fanatical cheers. Even the Ciptons were celebrating and emitting suction sounds as they happily bounced in their seats.

Ann Lou couldn't believe it. She had just won Epiton their universal championship. This was usually the time the team would surround and embrace her for lighting the torch, but she knew most of her teammates were lost in the drop somewhere.

"Congratulations, Epiton!" squealed Myope, whom Ann Lou could hear slithering up toward her. There were several other cheers of "Congratulations" surrounding Myope's, and she assumed the Cipto team was with her.

"Would you please join us for the storytelling ceremony?" asked one enthusiastic Cipton. "Since you lit the torch, we would love to feature you as the guest of honour at our Main Circle." Ann Lou could hear the Cipton's teammates bouncing in agreement.

"Yes," she started. "As long as you take me to Luna McHubbard."

"Well, of course!" exclaimed Myope. "We must get going immediately! It should be starting any minute!"

Ann Lou could feel her heart beating even faster than it had during the game. The Epiton Pyroll team were now emerging from the drop, the last of them grunting and huffing until they were informed that Epiton had won the game. Once they were herded together, they all followed the Cipton team, one of whom was kind enough to guide the way with a Pyroll to the area where the storytelling ceremony would be held.

Apollo managed to find Ann Lou in the small trail of light that the Pyroll shone from inside the Cipton. He embraced her tightly, full of excitement. "You did it!" he said, swinging her around in his arms. "Girlfriend won us the championship!"

Ann Lou burst out laughing as she held her arms tightly around his strong torso muscles.

When he set her down, she grasped his claw tightly, and the two stayed latched to one another all the way to the storytelling ceremony. Dull murmurs became louder as they approached the area where everyone—Epitonians, Ciptons, and humans—had gathered to start the ceremonies. It sounded like they were at a concert in the moments when everyone was filing in. There were no distinct conversations, but the summation of the noises was a low roar. There must have been tens of thousands of beings together in that area, way more than the number who had attended the Pyroll Championship.

"This way to the Main Circle!" sang Lucy. Lucy grabbed hold of Ann Lou's prosthetic hand with her jelly hand, and they slithered and walked toward the Main Circle together. Ann Lou could feel Lucy bouncing more and more energetically as they approached the circle.

Some of the crowd cheered loudly as Ann Lou walked by them. It must have been the Ciptons, since the humans in the crowd couldn't see her. Her microchip translation was picking up various pieces of conversations, such as "That's the Pyroll legend of the universe!" and "She's my idol!"

Lucy guided Ann Lou up what felt like a long set of stone stairs, then positioned her such that she was facing the crowd in front of her. The cheers and excitement enveloped her. She almost felt that she could see the crowd in front of her just from the sounds that reached her from the distance. Someone patted her sharply on the back, and she recognised the touch as Egan's. The whole Epitonian team must have been standing directly behind her. She felt a sense of pride similar to how she had felt back in school after her hockey team won a game. They'd all skate to the middle of the roller rink and jump into a pile on one another. Her family would give her extra dessert after dinner and let her pick the channel to watch on television. She then thought of how Luna used to sigh at her choice of channel, a memory that made her chuckle. Elbina and her mother would usually sit quietly and enjoy whatever was on. Then Ann Lou, Riff, and Knitsy would arm-wrestle or get into some sort of debate.

She sniffled. It had been a long time since she had thought about her family, especially the specific moments that made her miss them the most. But now Luna was around here somewhere, perhaps just within arm's reach. Ann Lou was shaking at the thought of being able to give her sister a hug again.

Just then, Lucy emitted a bellow that sounded as if her vocal cords had suddenly turned into an amplifier that echoed around the entire area. It was so loud that Ann Lou reflexively pressed her hands against her ears hard in order to block out the explosive sound. She was astounded that such a small creature could emit such a deafening noise. The crowd must have been large indeed if Lucy had to speak that loudly. They cooperated immediately by falling silent.

"Welcome, everyone!" said Lucy. "Cipto is honoured to host Epiton and their fellow humans at today's exciting Pyroll Championship! We are delighted to announce that the result of the exhilarating final game between Cipto and Epiton resulted in a win for Epiton, who continue their reign as the Universal Pyroll Champions!"

The crowd erupted in more cheers and suction-cup noises.

"I now present Team Epiton and Team Cipto, directly beside me. I would also like to present the torch-lighter of the historic game, Earthling and Epiton team member Henrietta McHubbard!" The cheers grew even louder. Ann Lou continued to press against her ears. Lucy's voice was still uncomfortably loud, but Ann Lou felt incredibly happy to feel so important as a team member.

"I invited Team Epiton to sit at the Main Circle for the first two stories, which the entire audience will listen to. From there, everyone can feel free to move around to their own story circles and tell any tales, fictional or real, near or far, old or new, that your heart desires. We cannot wait to share this special Cipto tradition with our beloved guests."

The crowd's volume was at an all-time high. The excitement, although deafening, was empowering, and Ann Lou was basking in the loving vibrations flooding into her senses. Lucy grabbed her hand again and guided her a short distance to the right.

"We want you to sit in the guest of honour's seat," beamed Lucy, gently urging Ann Lou to climb onto a strange seat. She had to heave herself up to reach the top. As she climbed and sat, she felt around to grasp a mental image of the shape. There was no back to it. It had a stony top and bottom which were flat and round, and the middle felt like it was made of two glass cones cinched together at their apexes. As she mentally put together the shapes, she realised it resembled something like an hourglass.

When she felt Apollo's claw gently touch her back, she sat up, completely forgetting about the shape of the seat she was in. He then placed his claw onto her left knee, reaching from below her. He was sitting on the small stone next to her high-up seat. Ann Lou felt more butterflies fluttering in her stomach just from his light touches.

"Everyone please quiet down for our first speaker this evening," continued Lucy, her voice still bellowing. "Our speaker for today's storytelling ceremony is Avaira, who will be reciting one of Cipto's favourite fables, 'The Tale of How Cipto Lost its Light.'"

Excited whispers issued from the crowd. Ann Lou heard another Cipton slithering forward to the centre of the Main Circle. Avaira stopped moving and began to bellow, softer than Lucy but still loud enough for the crowd to hear. She sounded older and wiser than the other Ciptons Ann Lou had encountered thus far. Avaira's voice was creaky but swooning and powerful.

"Maaany supernovas ago on this veeery cosy planet lived a sweet and small being named Connie. She was the most beauuutiful being to eeever live on Cipto. Perhaps even the uuuniverse. Her skin was entiiirely translucent. Her eyes shooone in the suns above. Her voice grasped eeevery creature in a radius of twelve thouuusand moons. Connie would bounce happily eeeverywhere she went, telling stories that made eeeveryone, big, small, old, and young, cry teeears of joy. Her smile brought a beauuuty to Cipto that nooo other creature could replicate.

"One day, Connie fell ill. Her skin was becoming haaazy. Her eeeyes were nearly closed. Her voice fell near siiilent, and everyone was wondering what had happened to their deeear, sparkling Connie. She had lost her bounce, and instead saaagged into the stony ground, where the rest of the town would mistake her for a piiile of mud.

"Her father, Rodney, decided he wanted to bring the shiiine back into his daughter, for the town was suffering without her gliiistening charm. He went to the best and brightest doctor in aaall of Cipto, begging for a cuuure for Connie. The doctor, a wiiise being, said that Connie required a very speeecial kind of cure, a cure that existed in only ooone place in the known universe.

"The doctor went on to explain that she needed to be taken past the Tiiime Belt, a place so far in the universe that time was actually reveeersed. Only then would she have a chance at survival by reversing the daaark illness laid upon her beautiful self. Rodney thaaanked the doctor and hurried home, afraid of wasting any more tiiime. The ooonly way he could get past the Time Belt was with a Jalopy, which Cipto had ooonly one of. It was a pecuuuliar object, but still large enough to fit both Connie and Rodney in for their journey. The Jalopy was, indeeed, an hourglass, adequately representing their need to tuuurn back time.

"The town was deliiighted to allow Rodney to take the Jalopy past the Time Belt to saaave Connie. Cipto was feeling darker and daaarker with each moment of time that passed as Connie grew sicker and siiicker. The two beings boarded the hourglass Jalopy and were jetted off to a place no one had ever daaared to venture. Rodney was frightened as he watched his sweet Connie quickly looosing her life during the journey.

"Maaany moons passed them during their travels. Just when Rodney thought they were getting close to the Time Belt, it turned out to be a shooting star or a friendly neighbouring planet. Sooo much time passed and so much distance was crossed, that Rodney was suuure that the Time Belt couldn't possibly exist.

"After an even longer while, they had reached a point in the universe that looked as if it were the end. A bliiinding light shone in aaall directions and enveloped them both in a peaceful blanket of liiight. They had fiiinally reached the Time Belt.

"No one knows what happened to dear Rodney and Connie in the Time Belt. Some say the hourglass shaaattered. Others say the two were cheated by Father Time. But we dooo know that the two were captured in the Time Belt's griiipping depths. Being lost in the Time Belt erases any traaace of existence. Without a Rodney, there was never a Connie. From that moment forward, Cipto looost its light. Aaall suns went out as if they had been switched off. Newborns were born without eyes, and Cipto would be forever daaark because nothing would eeever be as bright as Cipto's shining star, Connie."

The crowd erupted in cheers once Avaira had finished the story. There were sobs from the audience that sounded fresh and raw as if the Ciptons hadn't already heard the story a million times before.

Ann Lou could hear Apollo snickering below her. She wondered if he thought the story was just too lame for the Epitonians. She enjoyed it, though. It felt nice to listen to something that wasn't menacing or scary. It was peaceful, and she wondered if it had any truth to it. She clapped along with the cheering crowd. A slithering noise sounded in front of her. Lucy had come forward to announce the end of the story.

"Beautiful—just beautifully recalled, Avaira. A classic Cipto story for our guests that holds a dear place in each of us," bellowed Lucy.

Ann Lou could hear Avaira slithering away. The crowd quieted.

"Next, the tradition is for the second story to be recited by the torch-lighter of the Pyroll game. Henrietta?"

The crowd cheered even more wildly than before. Ann Lou froze, completely thrown off guard that she had to recite a story in front of many thousands of beings. She briefly thought about making a run for it, but that wasn't really an option since she couldn't see where she was.

The crowd fell silent in anticipation. At first Ann Lou could only muster several *erms* and *ehms*. Apollo chortled on her left, clearly finding the situation laughable and her embarrassment amusing. She kicked him, and he quickly hushed up.

It was then that Ann Lou remembered Luna's Oxford University English textbook in her rucksack. She hastily dug it out and opened it to a random page.

"Apollo, Pyroll!" she ordered him in a harsh whisper. He pulled out a Pyroll from behind him and tossed it to her, which she easily caught with her right hand.

"Erm," she repeated, clearing her throat.

"Louder, please and thank you!" boomed a Cipton from the far distance.

Ann Lou rolled her eyes, completely frustrated that meeting Luna was taking longer than expected. She stood on her seat and set the Pyroll in the gutter of the book. She opened her mouth ready to speak but her heart sank when she saw all the braille dots on the pages. Her mouth hung open for an awkward moment, but then her microchip translation turned the dots into English text for her to read. Her eyes caught a short poem.

"ERM, AN EXCERPT FROM AN ANTHOLOGY OF POEMS BY E. BOWSER THE THIRD! WRITTEN IN 2090 . . . ERM, THAT'S THE YEAR IT WAS WRITTEN ON EARTH," she said at the top of her voice.

There were many incredulous gasps coming from the crowd. They were already impressed. Ann Lou was glad she didn't have to work too hard to impress these strange beings.

"IT'S CALLED, 'SLICING THE FOURTH DIMENSION.'" She began to read it aloud.

TIME COMES IN ALL SIZES,
A DIMENSION SO THICK AND THIN,
THAT IT PASSES US WITH MANY DISGUISES.
TIME IS ALWAYS MAINTAINED,
YOU CAN LOSE IT, YOU CAN FIND IT,
BUT NONE IS EVER TRULY LOST OR GAINED.
TIME WORKS SO PRECISELY ON ITS CLOCKS,
FOR YOU CANNOT BE BOTH LOST AND FOUND,
ONLY ONE SUITS THE FATHER OF TICKS AND TOCKS.
TIME IS A LASTING GIFT,
IF YOU DECIDE TO CHANGE IT,
BE PREPARED FOR ITS LASTING RIFT.

The crowd roared, bounced with excitement, and shouted with glee. Ann Lou had no idea what the poem meant, but she was relieved that it had been satisfactory for the setting.

"Excellent," said Lucy to the crowd. "What an incredible and exciting story! Thank you, Henrietta McHubbard!"

The crowd cheered louder as her name was repeated.

"You all know what this means," continued Lucy, quieting the crowd. "It's time for the rest of the stories to be told. Anyone may tell a story. Just find a circle of stones amongst yourselves, speak, listen, and enjoy. Now, get storytelling!"

The crowd instantly grew noisy again as everyone started moving around to find a circle of stones to sit at.

Ann Lou stayed in her seat, unsure of where to go next. "Lucy?" she called, looking every which way, as if turning her head would make any difference in the complete darkness.

"I'm right below you, dear!" bounced Lucy. "Would you like me to take you to Luna now?"

"Yes," trailed Ann Lou, shakily dismounting her seat.

"Who's Luna?" asked Apollo.

"She's . . . my sister." It felt foreign even saying the word. She had promised herself not to mention her family, not even to Apollo.

"You have a sister?" asked Apollo.

"This way!" exclaimed Lucy, grabbing Ann Lou's hand again. Lucy guided her away from Apollo and down the stony stairs they had ascended to get to the Main Circle. Ann Lou's heart was racing. She felt dizzy and almost as if she wanted to release Lucy's grip and take off running in fear of facing her sister.

Around them, Ann Lou could hear stories being told in various tongues. She could have sworn she heard Fintan talking about one of the most exciting Pyroll games he'd ever played. A few others sounded like humans speaking in different languages. She even thought she heard Hayden in the distance telling a story about a band he had been in for a short time back in secondary school.

Lucy and Ann Lou approached a circle of stones where a human was telling a story about going to the grocery store back on Earth, which was prompting many *oohs* and *aahs* from the Ciptons.

"Luna, can I borrow you for a second?" whispered Lucy.

"Of course," said the wonderfully familiar voice.

Lucy guided Ann Lou and Luna away from the circle to a quieter spot. "This young Pyroll star requested to see you!" piped Lucy. Ann Lou wanted to reach for Luna but couldn't tell exactly where she was.

"Ann Lou?" Luna extended her hand. When she felt the metal of Ann Lou's prosthetic, she knew instantly that it was her younger sister. Luna lunged forward to embrace her sister. Ann Lou smelled her sister's familiar scent as her face squashed into Luna's shirt. She let out a gleeful laugh and held her tightly around the waist, as she was still shorter than Luna.

"I'll leave you girls to your moment!" said a happy Lucy, flouncing away to find a story circle of her own.

"Wh—what are you doing? I don't understand," started Luna.

"I'll explain everything," said Ann Lou. "We just need a quiet place."

"Let's go to my hut," said Luna without hesitation. She grabbed Ann Lou's hand and led her down the path with a quick intensity. Luna didn't even need a light to guide her. Ann Lou felt incredibly protected to be with her oldest sister. This was her blood family, one of the pieces of her life that had been missing for over seven years. She felt the gaping hole in her heart beginning to repair itself. The sisters strode in silence toward Luna's hut.

Luna pushed open a creaky door, pulled Ann Lou inside, and guided her to a chair. Ann Lou found herself tripping over various objects.

"Take a big step over this pile of books here, and then sit down on your left," said Luna.

As the creaky door closed, Ann Lou sat down and felt something hard under her leg. It sounded like a book as it fell to the floor, its pages crumpling. "Oh, sorry!" she said, bending down and picking it up.

"Don't worry about it. I forget I've strewn my books everywhere around here. Just push it out of your way," responded Luna.

Ann Lou didn't know where exactly was out of her way, so she just gently closed the book and placed it under her chair. "Why do you have things all over the place? Maybe clean up a little?" Ann Lou didn't mean to sound so abrasive, but she couldn't help it in front of her sister. It felt natural.

"It helps me remember where things are. For example, three paces in from the door is a bookcase. Five paces left is your chair. Step over a pile of mugs, and eight more paces is my kitchen."

The logic made sense to Ann Lou. She remembered Luna always feeling around their old house to know where she was going. It had always impressed her.

"I thought you only brought a few books with you, said Ann Lou. "I remember you just had the rucksack full."

Luna laughed as she filled a kettle with water for tea. "I've written most of the books in here." Ann Lou heard teacups clinking together and containers being shuffled around.

"You've *written* books since you've been here?"

"Of course," said Luna. "You told me I could, so I did."

The kettle whistled. Luna poured water and Cipton milk into the cups, then dragged the cups of tea off the countertop and started walking back toward Ann Lou.

Ann Lou remembered the day she'd brought tea to Luna's room and the conversation they'd had about writing books. She couldn't believe her sister had listened to her, considering neither of them ever seemed to listen to each other growing up.

"Tea?" asked Luna, holding out a cup in front of Ann Lou. "Their milk is a bit grainy here but the taste is the same." Ann Lou reached for the cup, missed the handle, and clinked the cup with her prosthetic. Luna took her hand and placed the cup into it.

"I've had nothing but time over the years," started Luna, sitting down opposite her. Her chair made a creaking noise like it was made out of wicker as she sat. "After I lost my chance to go to Oxford, I had to distract myself."

Ann Lou also vividly remembered the day in the kitchen that their family had found out about Luna's acceptance to Oxford. The subsequent events of that day had so overshadowed her sister's great accomplishment that she'd forgotten all about it. She wished so badly that she could see Luna's face, but hearing her voice was just enough of a relief for now.

"I sometimes will read my books at storytelling ceremony nights like these. The Ciptons will enjoy anything you tell them. They're not very good critics. Which is why I need someone like you to critique me." She smiled as she finished her sentence, but Ann Lou couldn't see.

"How do you navigate through this place?" asked Ann Lou. She took a sip of Luna's tea, and the taste reminded her of how their mother used to make it, without the granular milk, of course.

Luna shrugged. "I was used to navigating with all my senses. It's no different here. I've built up muscle memories for places I often go."

"Have you made many friends on Cipto?" asked Ann Lou, taking in a large gulp of the tea and munching on the milk.

"No," said Luna, unfazed. "I have my books and my writing. I enjoy telling the stories to the Ciptons. I don't need any other socialisation. I'm happy with my hobbies." Luna also gulped her tea. "How about yourself? I bet you've made loads of friends, like usual."

Ann Lou swallowed hard. "I kind of alienated myself from the humans." She traced the rim of the mug with her finger. "I quite like my Pyroll team. My best friend is this Epitonian named Apollo. He's . . . well . . . my boyfriend." She hadn't had the chance to tell anyone the news about her and Apollo yet. She wondered if her sister would find it revolting.

"You've always fit in no matter where you go, Ann Lou. I'm really glad you've found your passion in Pyroll, too. I hope to meet Apollo. Are you nice to him at least?"

Ann Lou could detect Luna's sarcasm shining through the darkness. She laughed in response.

"And I'm sorry I didn't go to the game," added Luna apologetically. "If I'd known you went to Epiton, I would've only assumed you joined the Pyroll team. Hearing Mum's name announced at the storytelling ceremony tonight made me question Epiton's Pyroll reputation for a minute there!"

Ann Lou laughed. "You never know, Mum could've had a secret football career for all we know!"

"I'm pretty sure your left arm has a better chance of growing back than that happening!" The girls laughed and laughed until there was a lull in the conversation. "So, what happened, Ann Lou? How did you get off Earth? Mum must have been absolutely thrilled when you showed up on Epiton."

Ann Lou feared Luna would be disappointed. Luna had believed that their mother was alive these past seven years and Ann Lou was about to shatter that belief. But she knew that her sister deserved answers. "Mum gave me her microchip just before the Epiton bus came to pick her up. She—she stayed behind on Earth. I had no choice but to take her place." Ann Lou's voice shook with her words.

Ann Lou heard Luna's teacup fall to the ground and shatter into pieces. She heard Luna breathing heavily and the wicker chair creaked from underneath Luna's trembling body. After a few moments, Luna spoke.

"She's dead. Mum is gone. I was so horrible to her."

Ann Lou reached her prosthetic to pat Luna's knee. "We all were a complete nuisance, sis. At least you don't have the guilt for being the reason she's gone."

Luna emitted a small chuckle. "Sounds like Mum to give up her life so easily. Couldn't kick a ball for the life of her but would sacrifice herself in a heartbeat for any of us. Do Nan or Elbs or Riff know?"

Ann Lou gulped. "I haven't heard from anyone. I don't know how to contact anyone. I wish I could message them, but I don't think the signal is great this far from Earth." Luna let out a somber laugh.

"You heard anything?" Ann Lou added.

"No. I hope they're all right," Luna sighed.

Ann Lou started to cry, softly at first but then hyperventilating and gasping louder with each breath. Luna rushed to her and held her tightly in her arms, propping her on her lap. Ann Lou sobbed in her shoulder, soaking her flannel shirt with tears. Even though Ann Lou was almost out of her teen years now, it still felt comforting being held by her older sister. Luna started to rock her sister back and forth. Her sister's touch was warm and familiar. She continued to hyperventilate, gripping Luna tighter to her face. Tears were streaming, and Ann Lou was nearly screaming.

"I'm s-s-s-sorry I w-was s-s-so mean to y-you!"

"Oh, come on now," Luna said softly. She was rather awkward in these types of situations but was filling the role of comforter better than usual. "You were and always will be my little sister. You're supposed to be a pain in the arse. Besides, my job as the eldest was to be a sarcastic know-it-all."

Ann Lou let out a laugh through her cries. She was able to take deeper, more concentrated breaths the longer Luna held her.

Once Ann Lou was able to breathe again, she said softly, "Why do I feel like this? Why have I been so closed off?"

"You feel an unnecessary guilt, Ann Lou. Mum's not with us anymore. You feel responsible."

Ann Lou could only nod in agreement. Her chin started to tremble, and she dug her head back into Luna's chest. Her blonde hair covered her face and stuck to her wet cheeks.

"You've done nothing wrong, Ann Lou. Mum wouldn't have had it any other way. Look at how much you've accomplished! You won Epiton the Universal Pyroll Championship. You have friends. You're still loved by me and all of our family."

"I've been so mean to Hayden," whispered Ann Lou, her voice choked by sorrow. "I haven't been able to talk to him about anything. I've basically forgotten about life on Earth. I've pushed it down so many times that it's gone. Mum would hate me," she cried.

Luna sighed, draping her head on her sister's shoulder. "We sometimes cope best by not coping at all."

CHAPTER 11

Return of the GeoLapse

L una eventually got up to make the two some more tea. The sisters talked and talked. Ann Lou's spirit felt lighter, as if the weight of guilt was slowly being chipped away after building up into a fortress for seven years.

"Want to head back to the storytelling ceremony? I could read a chapter out of my newest book if you'd like to hear it." Luna placed a book on Ann Lou's lap that was thick and heavy. Ann Lou's heart felt a surge of love.

"I'd love to!" she said, fingering through the pages. Although she couldn't see anything, she could feel the braille that her sister always read back at home. She couldn't wait to hear the words come straight from her sister, the author. "But isn't the ceremony over by now? I probably have to get back to Epiton . . ." Her heart sank as quickly as it had been raised up. Soon she would be stripped of her family yet again.

"Oh, these ceremonies go all night long. You won't be leaving for a little while," called Luna from the kitchen, who was washing the cups in the sink.

Ann Lou turned around and blurted, "Can I live with you?"

The water turned off. Luna didn't move. Ann Lou heard a sigh.

"You know I'd love nothing more, Ann Lou. But we could get into trouble if you don't go back. Besides, do you want to live in complete darkness, listening to me write all the time? You have a life on Epiton. You are a champion Pyroll player. Whenever Cipto and Epiton play each other in the future, you'd better believe I'll be in the crowd for that game."

Luna had a point. Ann Lou had no place here. She was better off on Epiton, but she had to make things right with Hayden in order for her truly to enjoy life moving forward. And now she was ready, thanks to Luna.

"Don't leave my side until I go," said Ann Lou, still looking in her sister's general direction.

"I'd never," smiled Luna.

The two walked five paces forward from Ann Lou's chair, then three paces to the right and out the door of the hut. They walked arm in arm in silence toward the big field where everyone was telling stories. As they got closer, they noticed new and alarming sounds in the distance. Instead of the dull roar of the crowd, there were screams and bangs that only grew louder as they drew nearer.

"Is . . . this normal?" asked Ann Lou.

"Depending on the stories told, sometimes there can be quite a bit of emotion, but . . . it does sound quite odd," replied Luna, her voice keeping low. "Stay close to me."

Ann Lou wasn't planning on letting go of her sister. They cautiously walked toward the loud noises, unsure of what they'd be walking into. The sounds grew more violent and terrifying, and someone slithered toward them, fast.

"Lucy!" called Luna. "Is that you?"

Lucy's slithering stopped. "Luna! Henrietta! Oh, my dears, please take cover and protect yourselves!"

"What's happening?" asked Luna. Ann Lou could hear the terror rising in her sister's voice. Even Lucy sounded more scared than jovial for once.

"You know that group that killed off all the Earthlings all that time ago?" The sisters' hearts dropped. They instantly knew she was referring to the GeoLapse. Lucy squirmed. "They're back. They're trying to take over Cipto."

Luna and Ann Lou felt helpless. How were they supposed to protect themselves from the GeoLapse terrorists who had already taken their home planet and their mother's life? The girls heard Lucy start slithering away again.

"Wait!" cried Ann Lou. Lucy stopped. "What are they doing to everyone?"

Lucy gulped. "Most of the Epitonians and Earthlings have been captured. Even some of my community." Lucy started to sob.

"How did this happen? How did they even get here or know we were all together?" asked Ann Lou.

"I—I—" Lucy started, but it was too much to explain.

"Lucy, go! Get to safety!" said Luna, patting her on her blobbish head.

"Th—thank you, s-sweet Luna! Good luck to you b-both!" Her slithering picked up pace and she was out of hearing range within seconds.

"We'd better go back and take cover, Ann Lou!" shrieked Luna, pulling her sister in the opposite direction back toward her hut.

"No!" screamed Ann Lou. Luna stopped tugging.

"What? Why? We're going to get killed!"

"I have to find Hayden and Apollo and make sure they're safe!" Ann Lou started tugging Luna toward the distant screams. She had no idea where she was running. She heard various slithers in her periphery and assumed other Ciptons had managed to escape and were fleeing to safety. She felt terrible for dragging her sister toward the danger ahead, but that feeling couldn't stop the overwhelming impulse to save her friends.

"Wait, wait!" cried Luna, trying to tug Ann Lou toward her, but she was not nearly as strong as Ann Lou and was still being dragged forward. "You don't know where you're going! You need to let me lead." Ann Lou stopped dead in her tracks, causing Luna to run straight into her back. Luna was right. Ann Lou could be leading them off a cliff for all she knew.

"Sorry," whimpered Ann Lou. "I definitely heard Hayden toward the middle of the field earlier on. And I left Apollo on the steps to the stage."

"We need to start somewhere," said Luna, trying to orient herself. "If my memory is correct, based on how far you—ahem—*dragged* me, we should be just southwest of the ceremony entrance."

Luna directed Ann Lou slowly but purposefully. Ann Lou obediently followed, knowing that her sister was truly their only chance at survival at this point.

"There!" Luna declared as she reached out her free hand and felt a stony wall in front of her. "We're at the entrance to the ceremony field."

They heard more bangs just ahead of them, along with muffled screams.

"Ann Lou," whispered Luna, "I have no idea what is going on in there. Let's go around and get to the stage from the other end. Maybe Apollo is still there."

Ann Lou nodded in agreement even though Luna couldn't see it. She followed as Luna pulled her to the left, away from the stone entrance. Incendiary explosives strobed the field of the ceremony. Flashes of the GeoLapse tying up and beating their victims etched in Ann Lou's brain and she instead focused on the darkness in front of her as they skirted the edge of the field. They treaded as lightly as possible, but in Ann Lou's mind their footsteps sounded like clashing pots and pans. They were perhaps halfway around when they heard familiar voices amid the deafening bangs and screams.

"Get off me, you loathsome Earthling!" shouted a voice that sounded horrifyingly similar to Egan's.

"How dare you touch me? Get your disgusting Earthling hands off me at once!" bellowed the familiar voice of Fintan. They sounded like they were together in the middle of the field, surrounded by a group of GeoLapse who were making a ruckus with them. Then Ann Lou heard a scuffle followed by muffled groans from Fintan and Egan. The GeoLapse had silenced two of the strongest and most intimidating beings she'd ever met in her life. What could they do to Apollo—to Hayden?

Many other screams and cries filled her ears, and she hoped none of them belonged to any more of her friends. Then Ann Lou felt Luna tug her hand harder. Luna redirected them to the right. She must've gauged how big the field was and knew they were approaching the proximity of the stage for the Main Circle. She tugged Ann Lou a bit farther until they got to a set of stairs.

"Okay," whispered Luna into Ann Lou's ear. "Twenty-two steps up, and you'll be on the stage. I'm not hearing anything coming from up there, so let's go see if Apollo is hiding."

Ann Lou took the lead. "One, two, three, four, five . . ." she mentally counted as she climbed the stairs at a swift pace. "Nineteen, twenty, twenty-one, twenty-two." Luna was right behind her with a firm grip on Ann Lou's right arm.

Attempting to be quiet, Ann Lou crouched down and reached her left arm forward with her Pyroll stick, hoping she'd feel for any obstacles or hidden Epitonians on the stage. She felt like she was going in circles. The screams echoing from the field below and the intermittent flashes of explosions in her periphery were not helping her focus on the task at hand. She couldn't shake the feeling that something had gone horribly wrong. She continued feeling around and bumping into the stones that were sitting around the Main Circle during Avaira's story. She was getting frustrated; the stage seemed empty. Then her stick grazed something softer than one of the stones.

"Apollo?" whispered Ann Lou. "Is that you?"

"Henrietta?" he answered.

Ann Lou ripped her arm from Luna's grip and hugged Apollo around the neck.

"Are you okay? We need to get you out of here!" she whispered hoarsely.

"I'm so glad you're alive! I've just been hiding up here the whole time," he replied. "I had no interest in listening to boring stories when everyone left so I was practicing my Pyroll catching when this crowd came in."

"We have to get out of here!" warned Luna, her tone sounding stern.

"Wait," said Ann Lou. "Where's Hayden?"

"He was captured," said Apollo, not sounding bothered at all. "I think that pipsqueak old Pyroll player was part of this whole plan. He restrained Hayden. That's at least what I gathered from all the screaming."

Ann Lou's face turned cold. "Jung-hoon? Jung-hoon is in the GeoLapse? How is that possible?"

"He certainly had me fooled."

"Do you know where they're taking the prisoners? We have to save them!"

Apollo took a deep breath before continuing. "I think I heard one GeoLapse say something about heading to the next planet for invasion. It had a weird name. Oaflander? Antfeeder?"

"Olfinder?" interrupted Luna.

"That's the one."

"How are we supposed to get to Olfinder?" said Luna.

Ann Lou thought a moment. "We could sneak onto the GeoLapse Jalopy."

Apollo snapped, "Do you have a death wish?"

"Hang on," said Luna softly.

Ann Lou perked up. If anyone could solve this problem, it would be Luna.

"Avaira's story."

"I don't follow," said Ann Lou. "Cut to the chase."

"It mentioned the Jalopy that was used to take Rodney and Connie to the Time Belt. The hourglass."

Ann Lou bolted upright at the word *hourglass*. "That's what I was sitting on at the Main Circle. That's where the guest of honour sits!"

"Shhh!" hushed Luna. "So, it's real?"

Ann Lou wasn't sure. "Could it be just a statue of some sort? As a symbol of the story?"

"Only one way to find out," said Luna. "Feel around for it. Apollo, take my hand."

Ann Lou led the way again, feeling around for the hourglass she had sat on just hours before. She knew it would be somewhere in the circumference of the Main Circle. She felt a stone, then made her way around the arc of the circle, feeling each stone as they passed. Eventually, where a stone should have been, she felt a much larger structure.

"This is it!"

The three of them huddled around the structure, feeling every curve for a hole or some sort of button. There was nothing except for solid glass, and top and bottom layers that felt like stone. The stone layer was poking out farther than the glass. Ann Lou and Luna tried lifting the top stone, but it would not budge.

Apollo pushed up on the top part of the glass with all of his strength. The entire hourglass seemed to tilt. Ann Lou crouched and felt underneath it. The hourglass was in fact hinged to its base, and tipping the glass had presented a way to get inside.

"Luna, down here!" whispered Ann Lou.

"You two crawl in," said Apollo with a strained voice as he held the glass steady. "I should be able to fit in the top if it opens." Ann Lou quickly hugged him, and the sisters crawled onto the bottom stone and huddled close.

Apollo emitted a groan as he slowly lowered the heavy structure until the glass securely surrounded the sisters. They both reached out and felt the smooth glass around them. The space was only big enough for them to sit cross-legged next to each other without standing up. They heard Apollo lifting the top stone with more groans. He heaved himself into the top part of the hourglass, then gently lowered the top stone downward to rest on the top of the glass, closing himself in.

None of them said a word for the next few moments. The sounds from outside were somewhat muted, but they could still hear horrific screams and grunts coming from the field, just metres away from them.

The Jalopy awoke and illuminated the inside of the hourglass with a neon green light. Ann Lou immediately looked at Luna. Her face looked the same as it had seven years ago, except she looked slightly older, with just a few newly formed age lines, and she wasn't wearing her glasses. Her pupils were dilated to almost the entirety of her irises, and a grey haze filled her eyes, as if there were a wall of clouds floating around in them. Ann Lou grabbed her sister and hugged her tightly.

Luna looked confused. "Are you okay?"

Ann Lou pulled away. "I can see you!"

Luna gasped, and Ann Lou realised that so much time had gone by that Luna's vision was now completely degraded. She was blind. Luna shed a tear, something she never would have done at home, and muttered, "I don't even remember what you look like."

Ann Lou continued to hug her. They suddenly heard a soft synthesised voice inside the hourglass.

"Hello, Apollo of the House of Aithne, Luna McHubbard, and Ann Lou McHubbard. The Jalopy is ready to depart. Please state your destination."

"Ann Lou McHubbard? Who is that?" asked Apollo from above.

Ann Lou looked up and saw Apollo sitting as comfortably as he could, scrunched up in the upper half of the hourglass.

"It's my real name," replied Ann Lou, softly. "I guess the Jalopy is smart enough to know my dingy Earth microchip doesn't actually belong to me."

A series of louder shouts from outside the hourglass caused the three of them to look in the direction of the cacophony. Ann Lou and Apollo could see several members of the GeoLapse in their classic black clothing and golden GL badges, running toward them with all sorts of ropes, knives, and other weaponry. They had murder erupting in their eyes, and they were prepared to break open the Jalopy.

"Please state your destination." repeated the voice, politely.

"Olfinder! Olfinder! Olfinder!" screamed Ann Lou. The group of GeoLapse had surrounded them. Their faces were terrifying as they swung their weapons and beat the glass with all their might.

"Enjoy your trip," said the voice. As the Jalopy slowly rose from the ground, one of the GeoLapse hung onto its base with his fingertips. The hourglass accelerated into the atmosphere, and the clinging GeoLapse flew off into the darkness.

They flew into the stars, trying not to hit their heads on the glass as the Jalopy clumsily manoeuvred its way through space. As Ann Lou bumped her head against Luna's, she started to appreciate how much smoother the boat Jalopy flew. Once the flying had smoothed out, Ann Lou and Apollo pressed their faces against the glass, taking in the beautiful views of the cosmic structures that stretched for infinity. They couldn't even make out the planet of Cipto anymore, as it was engulfed into what seemed like the darkest part of the universe.

"So, tell me about this name of yours," said Apollo, looking down at Ann Lou through the glass. He didn't seem bothered at all that her name had suddenly changed, which she admired him for. She peeled her eyes off a passing comet and began to tell him her whole story: her family, roller hockey, Hayden, her mother giving up her identity to save her. Apollo listened intently as she talked. He pressed his claw against the glass once she finished. She mirrored him and pressed her prosthetic hand against the glass above her.

"Do you think we'll find Nan?" asked Luna, whose head was resting on the cool glass.

"I sure hope so," answered Ann Lou, still looking into Apollo's eyes.

CHAPTER 12

Olfinder

The Jalopy zoomed through space as the three of them lightly slept. Every time the Jalopy rerouted, they would be hurtled in a new direction, forcing them awake until they could get comfortable again. Mid-dream, Ann Lou thought of something and started rapidly tapping Luna on the shoulder. Luna awoke from her light slumber with a groan.

"Luna, isn't Olfinder the one with the atmosphere you can't breathe in? How will we get around there?"

"It'll be all right," murmured Luna sleepily. "We just have to quickly make our way to the mainland, and maybe someone can give us a mask or something."

The Jalopy began to approach a small planet that was surrounded by a hazy atmosphere. The three of them fell silent as the Jalopy sank into thick grey clouds. Even as they neared the ground, a haze remained; clearly Olfinder's atmospheric composition was different from that of Earth. As a town centre came into view, tiny dots sprinkled throughout the city resolved into Olfinderians, some of them trotting along and some of them running. Ann Lou remembered the television example of an Olfinderian looking like a small, noseless dog with a weirdly shaped mouth and springs for its legs and tail.

The Jalopy neared the ground, and Ann Lou realised that it wasn't going to be a slow and gentle landing. Ann Lou grabbed Luna and held her legs out to brace for the impact. Apollo seemed unfazed, used to this kind of vigorous play. The Jalopy hovered a few inches from the ground and then slammed down hard on its bottom, bounced slightly, slid forward, and stopped.

The Olfinderians trotting along the road stopped to see what the fuss was about. Some had ears raised or eyes widened. When they figured out that the interruption didn't concern them, they continued on with their trotting. Ann Lou couldn't see very far down the road since the fog was still so thick but she could identify that they landed in the middle of a large intersection of three roads. Olfinderians ran all around the Jalopy to continue to their road of interest. Apollo pushed open the stone top of the hourglass and hopped out. He pressed his chest into the hourglass and tipped it up from its base so that Ann Lou and Luna could crawl out.

The ground was soft but firm, like a taut sponge. There was a bit of a bounce to their step as they stood up. They each took a few seconds to get their footing on the springy ground. A few of the Olfinderians stopped to watch Apollo as he hopped in place; they had probably never seen an Epitonian before.

Luna began to cough. She remembered this feeling from the Planetary Diagnostic Test. She knew she would lose consciousness within minutes. "We have to find the mainland quickly!" she wheezed.

Ann Lou noticed that her lungs were also beginning to feel strained.

"Wait, am I missing something?" asked Apollo, looking between

Luna and Ann Lou with an extremely puzzled look on his face.

"You probably don't have the same lung structure as we do," said Luna with airy breaths. "You might have to carry us if we black out."

Apollo looked frantic, unable to help them as they gasped for air.

"Mainland! Ask for the mainland!" Ann Lou tried to scream, but it only came out as a whisper.

Apollo looked down at the fuzzy dog-like Olfinderians, who were just staring directly up at him as he towered above them.

"Uhh . . . mainland?"

More empty stares.

"Like . . . now."

One of the Olfinderians broke the awkward silence and popped forward on its legs.

"Follow me!" it yelped through its foghorn-shaped mouth, then bounded down the road.

Apollo heaved Luna and Ann Lou over his shoulders with ease and ran after the Olfinderian. Even with both girls on his shoulders, he quickly outran the small beast.

"Can you pick up the pace, please?" shouted Apollo over his shoulder.

They made it to the mainland within a few minutes. To Apollo's dismay, the mainland didn't have solid ground between the various huts. The huts were sprinkled among small islands that looked like lily pads sprouting from water—except instead of water, it was a void that seemed bottomless, or certainly way deeper than any volcanic crater he'd ever played Pyroll in.

The Olfinderian pointed its paw at a small island about thirty metres away.

"How am I supposed to get over there?" said Apollo curtly.

"You bounce!" squeaked his guide.

The Olfinderian took a running start, pounced on its springy legs and tail, and bounced high up and over the void in a perfect arc, landing easily on the first island.

Apollo's jaw dropped but he puffed out his chest and grunted, "Sorry if this goes wrong, Ann Lou," to which she couldn't consciously respond.

Apollo mimicked the Olfinderian by taking a running start toward the cliff edge, then jumping down hard on his two legs to bounce across the gap.

"Arghhhhh!" he hollered as he leaped, holding the sisters as tightly as he could. He landed just barely on the ledge of the first island, catching himself before he fell backward. Apollo ran to the door of the first hut and kicked the door repeatedly.

"Let me in! Hello? I have two dying Earthlings here who need help!"

His Olfinderian guide bounced away in fear, prompting Apollo to huff and attempt to break the door down. A human man appeared on the other side of the door with a giant helmet on his head, quivering and holding up his arms in surrender to the terrifying beast. Apollo gave him a menacing look until he gestured for Apollo to come in.

The humans in the room, who also had helmets, just stood there, mouths agape, while some Olfinderians shuddered in the corner. "Help!" shouted Apollo.

The man began performing CPR on Luna while a woman placed a weighty helmet on Ann Lou. Apollo, exhausted, slid down the nearest wall, wrapped his arms around his knees, and watched as the humans attempted to resuscitate the girls.

Luna took a deep breath in after a few seconds and clutched her heart. The woman placed a helmet on her, the breathing contraption, and she lay there with her eyes closed, savouring breaths of sweet air from the device. Ann Lou was starting to turn blue despite her breathing contraption, so the man started chest compressions on her. As he pumped her heart rhythmically, her body moved with each compression. Apollo closed his eyes and gripped his legs tighter, hoping he would see her beautiful smile again.

After several minutes of resuscitation, Ann Lou lurched up in a fit of coughing, and Apollo breathed a deep sigh of relief.

The humans who saved them helped them sit up comfortably against some pillows. The man brought them some food from the kitchen. The food was even less exciting than the Epitonian food. It actually looked like dog kibble. The food first had to be inserted and secured into small compartments within the girls' helmets. Levers then moved discreetly back and forth, automatically bringing the food to their mouths. Apollo, on the other hand, refused to eat anything other than Polskin and Fava cakes.

"Why didn't you two have your helmets on?" asked the man, who sat across from the sisters as they ate. "You're lucky your lungs didn't disintegrate."

"We don't live here," Ann Lou replied between bites. "I'm from Epiton, and she's from Cipto."

"Well, then what on Earth are you doing here?"

Ann Lou and Luna stopped chewing at once. They didn't exactly know what to say. Something like, "Oh, the GeoLapse is currently invading Cipto, and they are heading here to invade this planet next?" It seemed like too much to dump on them all at once. All Ann Lou could muster was, "It's complicated."

The man took a deep breath before getting up. As he walked toward the door of the hut, Luna called after him, "Do you know a woman named Knitsy?"

He froze and looked back at her.

"Knitsy McHubbard." Luna added.

He ignored the question and left the hut. The girls didn't know what kind of response that was. They watched and listened for the door to open just in case he might return, but he didn't.

Apollo and the sisters regrouped to consider the possible reasons for the events occurring on Cipto.

"How were the GeoLapse able to find their way around Cipto so easily?" asked Ann Lou.

Luna thought for a few seconds. "Maybe they've been living amongst us. They could have come with us seven years ago, living undercover."

"But that wouldn't make sense," said Ann Lou. "Most of them don't have microchips for identification. They wouldn't have been able to take the placement test to get here."

Luna pressed her palms into her forehead. "Wasn't the ERA taken over by the GeoLapse? I bet the GeoLapse forced the ERA to test each of them so they could have undercover resources on each planet. They all must have had microchips. They would have known the Pyroll Championship was taking place on Cipto, and that Epiton was the visiting team. It was the perfect time to take down Epitonians, Ciptons, and humans all in one go."

The idea made sense to Ann Lou. "Do you think Jung-hoon was part of the ERA back in Korea? He told me once that he did something with recycling of materials." Ann Lou looked at Apollo. He shook his head.

"Don't ask me," he said. "Epitonians may seem scary to you Earthlings, but we'd never intentionally hurt one another."

"Oh, but you'll push each other into the lava pool to win a game of Pyroll?" Ann Lou snapped.

"There are no rules in Pyroll," he answered.

Ann Lou rolled her eyes. She recalled the conversation they'd had about dating, when he said he didn't understand why someone would ever hurt the ones they love. Despite Pyroll, she had built up a lot of respect for Epitonians.

"I think that the ERA are being treated as the GeoLapse's pawns," said Luna. "They're not the ones hurting people. They're the brains behind the whole operation that the GeoLapse must be incentivising." Luna stopped to think. "It would make sense that Jung-hoon worked in materials recycling. That's what the ERA was meant to be doing, right? He must've not had a choice after they were taken over."

"But what's the incentive?" asked Ann Lou in an annoyed tone. "Jung-hoon was ripped away from everyone he loved. What was so tremendously appealing that it was worth being separated from family and friends? Money? Recognition? What's that gonna do?"

"That's the mystery," concluded Luna. "If we find that out, maybe we have a shot at putting an end to this whole operation. But for now, let's start by finding Hayden."

Ann Lou noticed Apollo's face wrinkle up in confusion. He was staring at the door. The girls watched as it opened slowly and a small head poked around.

"It can't be . . ." said a familiar voice.

Ann Lou hopped up, screamed, and ran to the door. She leaped into Knitsy's arms. Luna recognised the voice too, and she made her way over to join her sister and grandmother in an emotional embrace.

"What in the bloody hell are you two doing here?" Knitsy cursed. "I'd nearly given up hope of ever seeing you two again, for heaven's sake!"

Knitsy stood back to get a better look at the two of them. She looked considerably older than the last time Ann Lou had seen her. Her voice was wearier, her hair was completely white, and she wobbled despite the cane she was clutching. But, even though she was eighty-two now, she still had the same youthful fire in her eyes. Knitsy eyed them both up as she smiled from ear to ear. She didn't need to wear a contraption quite as hefty as the ones the other humans wore; her breathing patch and mask provided her with all the breathable elements she needed.

"My dear Luna, you look just as beautiful as the last time I saw you. And Ann Lou, you're a woman now. What are you, nearly twenty? You are just a stunning young lady," she said. Her expression went solemn. "I didn't even know you were alive." Her eyes quickly shifted to Apollo, and her eyebrows scrunched, just as he had when he saw her.

"And who the hell are you?" she said in a menacing tone to rival that of any Epitonian.

"Nan, we need to talk," said Ann Lou, looping her arm through Knitsy's to lead her to a seat by the group of pillows.

The girls filled Knitsy in on everything: their experiences on Epiton and Cipto, Apollo (to whom Knitsy continued to give menacing stares), how Ann Lou reunited with Luna after the Pyroll

Championship, witnessing the GeoLapse invasion on Cipto, and even the news that Henrietta never made it to Epiton. They watched as Knitsy went through a second cycle of grief. She had only just recently accepted that her youngest grandchild was dead, but instead it was now her only daughter.

"We're so sorry, Nan," said Luna, grabbing Knitsy's hand.

"It's not your fault, any of you. I'm not surprised that your mother did something so noble. I only wish I could have done it instead." She hung her head low.

"We wouldn't have let you do that, Nan. Mum cornered me when we were the last two in the house. If I would've had more time . . ." Ann Lou trailed off. She didn't exactly know what she would have done with more time. Would she still have let her mother stay behind? She didn't want to think through that answer.

Knitsy wiped her eyes. "No point in stressing about the past now. We need to warn the others that the GeoLapse are coming—and save Ann Lou's boyfriend."

"Hayden's not my boyfriend, Nan. Apollo—"

"Don't even finish that sentence, girl. I won't hear of you and this beast being together." Knitsy stuck out her tongue in disgust.

"So, how do we warn everyone?" interjected Luna, who so desperately wanted to change the subject of Ann Lou's love life. "As we discussed before, there must be ERA sprinkled on every planet. If we warn the wrong person, they'll know we're up to something and take us down too."

"We'll just have to wait until the GeoLapse come," said Apollo from behind the girls. They all looked at him. He was right. They had to wait.

Luna, Ann Lou, and Apollo spent the next several days on Olfinder awaiting the news of the impending GeoLapse invasion. The girls assisted Knitsy in her own hut with various tasks such as changing her clothes and combing her hair, while Apollo freely roamed the Olfinder streets trying to listen out for any helpful information. Knitsy wouldn't allow him to come inside her hut anyway, so he had plenty of time to gain familiarity with the area.

One morning, as the McHubbards were all waking up in the hut, the man who had resuscitated Luna and Ann Lou came running through their door, shouting.

"They're back! They're back! The GeoLapse are back!"

"What do you mean they're back, you moron?" groaned one of Knitsy's human hutmates, who was speaking with the covers over her helmet in her bunk.

"The news just said that Cipto has fallen to the GeoLapse! Earth is gone, now Cipto! We could be next!" the man continued to shout, flailing his arms and legs. "I'm trying to warn everyone!"

"There are probably a billion planets in the universe. What are the odds they'd come here next?"

The man stood still, considering the statistics. "You're right," he said calmly. "No, you're right." He walked out of the hut without another word. The rest of the humans continued on with their morning as if nothing had happened.

"It's go time!" whispered Knitsy to her grandchildren, waving her cane in the air as Luna tied her shoes.

Apollo walked into the hut shortly after they were all dressed and cleaned up.

"What did I say about you coming in here, beast!" Knitsy hollered, brandishing her cane at him.

"Nan, you need to calm down," said Ann Lou as she lightly pushed Knitsy's cane down to the ground. "So, where in town should we head?" Ann Lou asked, switching her glance to Apollo.

"I'd say our best bet is the Olfinder Town Pentagon. I've heard street-goers talking about the monthly Olfinder Chorale concert taking place there later today. Perfect place for an invasion."

"Excellent," said Ann Lou. "Let's head out."

CHAPTER 13

The Olfinder Chorale

Apollo, Ann Lou, Luna, and Knitsy left the mainland ahead of the scheduled Olfinder Chorale concert to find a covert location to position themselves for an impending attack. Along the way, they frolicked on the cushiony ground, following Apollo and Knitsy, who knew their way around best. Knitsy refused to follow Apollo's instructions for finding the Town Pentagon. She instead took them there on a circuitous path, just so he wouldn't know where they were.

There was already a crowd forming at the Town Pentagon. Ann Lou was surprised to see that the centre of town was, in fact, pentagonal-shaped. The springy ground formed a pentagonal walkway, which enclosed an area of what looked like grass. The audience appeared to be crowding themselves there. Hundreds of Olfinderians outlined the perimeter of the pentagon. All of them bounced blissfully on their springy tails as they watched the crowd grow denser. The four of them huddled outside the periphery of the pentagon so that they were still in earshot of the chorale and the crowd but hidden enough for them not to be seen through the thick fog. They could just barely make out the outline of most of the individuals in the chorale.

"They do sing quite beautifully," said Knitsy, falling backward. She bounced into a seated position, keen to listen to the Olfinderians' beautiful music.

"Nan, we have a job to do, remember?" barked Ann Lou.

"Oh, just listen to them for five minutes or else you'll never learn to enjoy the beautiful things in this universe," said Knitsy, waving off the criticism.

They all took a seat around Knitsy, knowing that she could win any argument. The crowd immediately hushed as an Olfinderian on one of the vertices of the pentagon raised its tail high and stood very still. Its head was held up with its conical mouth raised high to the sky. The crowd waited in perfect silence, quivering with anticipation.

The Olfinderian then dropped its head and tail in one swift motion, and a low hum began to sound over the entire area. Its head and tail moved again, this time in a pattern of light beating motions. As the Olfinderian continued to move its tail in repetitive and rhythmic motions of increasing and decreasing intensities, the chorale echoed more frequencies out of their conical mouths. They were like small amplifiers with all their heads raised to the skies. The sounds were enchanting and unlike anything Apollo or the humans had ever heard. The Olfinderians in the chorale compressed their four springy limbs as they sang sounds of lower frequencies and hopped high on their hind legs when they sang high frequencies. Each Olfinderian in the chorale had a different part to sing; no two were the same. There were no words, just entrancing tonal pitches that made all who heard them feel almost as if they were floating.

"Riff would love this," said Knitsy dreamily, her eyes closing. She lay back and put her arms behind her head. Luna and Ann Lou nodded and did the same. Apollo scooted next to Ann Lou and watched her close her eyes. He gently took her hand and smiled.

"I'm going to get a closer look," he whispered into her ear and then let go of her hand. She lay there still, listening to the mystical sounds flowing into her ears.

Ann Lou felt as if she were dreaming. She was the only human standing in the centre of the pentagon. The Olfinder Chorale surrounded her, as if they were singing directly to her. Their song was so enchanting that she began to float off the ground. She slowly rose higher and watched the chorale become smaller. In her hazy periphery, she saw Apollo running to the centre of the pentagon where she had previously stood. She smiled at the sight. He looked so strong and intimidating as he ran at full speed. He extended his arms up to her, but her feet were just out of reach. Ann Lou waved to him, a smile broadening on her face. She could see him saying something. His mouth was moving, but she couldn't hear him over the loud chorale. He looked concerned and frightened. He was vigorously pointing to his horns. But she rose higher and higher, still feeling the euphoria of the sounds encapsulating her. Apollo eventually disappeared out of her foggy view.

When the song finished, Ann Lou opened her eyes. The crowd erupted in cheers. The Olfinder Chorale were excited to see their music receive such a positive response, and they all wagged their springy tails with delight. Everyone looked happy. Ann Lou wondered if the warning about the invasion had been a false alarm after all.

"Did anything happen?" asked Luna in a very confused tone. "I feel dizzy."

"That's what you always feel like after listening to them!" exclaimed Knitsy, sitting up and clapping her hands in recognition of the performance. "Absolutely mesmerising every time."

Ann Lou turned to look into the crowd for Apollo, but she couldn't make out much of the crowd from where they were seated.

"I'll be right back. I need to find Apollo," said Ann Lou, also feeling dizzy from the enchanting sounds.

"Don't hurry back!" answered Knitsy.

Ann Lou stood up quickly and began running toward the crowd, who were still dizzily getting up. She scanned the crowd for Apollo. He should not have been difficult to find since he was the tallest and most menacing-looking beast of anyone on the planet. But she couldn't spot him anywhere. All she could see amid the fog were flashes of people in black suits running around and dragging humans and Olfinderians away. Those being dragged away were still in a dazed trance.

Suddenly the crowd began to realise what was happening. Olfinderian families began worriedly looking around for their own. Panic set in as cries rose in a wave from the crowd. The GeoLapse were tying up their prisoners and dragging them to the boat Jalopy. Horrified and needing to stay hidden, Ann Lou ran back to her family.

"They invaded during the song," she said in a hoarse whisper, her voice trembling. "I think they took Apollo. They've got a bunch of other people from the crowd. We have to go now!"

Luna's and Knitsy's faces blanched.

"What about *now* do you not get? Come on!" Ann Lou grabbed both of their arms and pulled them away from their hiding spot, almost instantly realising that she had forgotten her way back to the Jalopy. "Nan, which way back to the large intersection near the mainland?"

"Go up that street!" said Knitsy, pointing. "It's faster, and less busy."

Knitsy tried to get her cane to move faster, to no avail. Ann Lou crouched down so Knitsy could hop onto her back and point out directions. Ann Lou held Luna's hand tightly in her right hand, and they took off quietly, the springy ground propelling them forward and upward with each step. Shouts, screams, and the sounds of humans and Olfinderians being shoved onto the boat Jalopy faded as they distanced themselves from the Town Pentagon.

Once they reached the intersection, Ann Lou found the hourglass

Jalopy in the same spot they left it. Upon approaching the vehicle, they realised that Apollo must have made some preparations in case they needed a quick exit. The Jalopy was resting on its side with both its stone caps on the ground. There were ropes attached to the stones so they could climb in and seal themselves in from the inside.

"What in the world is this thing?" asked Knitsy, eyeing the Jalopy like it was a piece of rubbish.

"Our ride to wherever we need to go next," responded Ann Lou. "Let's get in quickly!"

Luna and Ann Lou helped Knitsy inside one of the halves of the hourglass. Luna and Knitsy pulled the rope from the inside of the hourglass while Ann Lou pushed the stone from the outside until it was sealed. Ann Lou then ran around and got in the other side of the hourglass and pulled the rope on her side until the stone met the glass. The girls took off their helmets.

The neon green light illuminated the inside of the glass. "Hello, Knitsy McHubbard, Luna McHubbard, and Ann Lou McHubbard," said the familiar voice. "The Jalopy is ready to depart. Please state your destination."

"Where do you think they are taking the prisoners? Somewhere else on Olfinder, maybe?" asked Knitsy, trying her best to be helpful.

"Doubt it," said Luna, trying to find a comfortable position. "They'll be heading off to another planet by the time they capture everyone they can. But which one, that's the mystery." Luna squeezed her eyes shut, thinking about any possible leads. "What did you two see during the song? I bet there was some sort of subconscious awareness."

"I usually feel like I'm in a dream. I see lots of different things when they sing," announced Knitsy.

Luna turned her head quickly toward Knitsy. "That's perfect! So, what did you see this time?"

Knitsy squirmed uncomfortably. "Erm," she started. "Mine might be too explicit for young ears."

"Okay, no need to expand on that one, Nan," said Luna, hoping to hear nothing more come out of Knitsy's mouth. "How about you, sis? I only really saw flashes of light and shapes since I've lost most of my visual memory at this point. Did you see anything?"

Ann Lou told them about her dream in stark detail. The thought of Apollo looking so frightened caused her to feel a tightness in her neck.

"You said he pointed to his horns?" Luna asked.

Ann Lou nodded. "Yes."

"Interesting," Luna said.

"What do you make of it?" said Knitsy.

"Well, they're probably going to Antympanica," continued Luna. "There's no sound there. That was Apollo's clue for you. I'm assuming he hears out of his horns?"

Ann Lou's mouth dropped. Luna had, yet again, figured it out.

"We get to see Riff?" asked Knitsy from behind them. She did a little dance in her seated position, kicking out her foot and cane with excitement from within the small enclosure.

"Nan, are sure you are well enough to travel?" asked Luna.

Knitsy's face fell. "You just want to leave me here all alone for another seven years? Get rid of old Nan, yeah?" Her expression was full of anger. Luckily, Luna couldn't see it.

"No, I'm just asking because, well, we were all placed on our planets for our longevity. I don't want to haul you all over the place and have you risk shortening the time that you have left."

Knitsy's face relaxed. "If I get to hug my grandson one more time, I could die tomorrow, happily."

"Take us to Antympanica," said Ann Lou to the Jalopy.

"Enjoy your trip," replied the voice.

"Here we come, Riff!" shouted Knitsy, who resumed her dance within the hourglass.

The Jalopy accelerated into the sky. They could just make out the panicked crowd at the Town Pentagon, all in disarray, and the incredible amount of destruction the GeoLapse had done in just the few minutes since the enchanting chorale concert. As soon as they passed through the next layer of fog, the land of Olfinder was out of sight. Ann Lou imagined how the planet would look in a day, even an hour into the invasion.

Luna could hear Knitsy starting to take off her breathing device and quickly blocked her from removing the patch from her arm.

"Nan, you can't take this off. You never know if you need it in an emergency," said Luna.

"My dear, let me live a little," answered Knitsy.

Once again, they soared through the stars. It never became a boring sight to the McHubbards. Each of them was glued to the glass, looking outward, even Luna.

"So, Antympanica," started Luna. "How do we navigate a completely silent planet?"

"We all used to use sign language with Riff back at home. Do you both remember how to sign?" replied Knitsy.

"That's not going to be any help for me, Nan," sighed Luna.

"We just have to stay alert and stick together," said Ann Lou trying to suppress her worried thoughts of Apollo. "I can't lose either of you this time around."

CHAPTER 14

ANTYMPANICA

The Jalopy approached a green planet. As they descended to the surface, they could see the tops of trees in dense forests. Scanning the horizon, Ann Lou noted that the entire planet seemed to be one large forest.

Every few seconds, they could see little dots jumping in and out of the treetops. The Antympanicans were little fuzzy beasts with a sort of wing that ringed the circumference of their round bodies. They were hopping up from the tops of the trees and spreading out their ringed wings once they reached the peak of their arc. As they floated back down, they resembled sunny-side-up eggs.

The Jalopy was approaching an unidentifiable section of dense forest faster and faster. Branches crashed into the glass as the Jalopy smashed through the treetops. It rolled on its side down one of the massive conical tree trunks. They felt like they were in a hamster wheel, pinned to the glass of their respective sides of the Jalopy by the increasing centrifugal forces. The Jalopy finally rolled off the end of the tree trunk and onto the muddy ground, where friction brought it to a gradual stop.

"Are we still in space or am I seeing stars?" asked Knitsy.

"I'm seeing them, too," joked Luna, picking herself up off the glass.

Knitsy put her hands on the stone base and began to give it a push.

"Wait!" shouted Ann Lou, pressing her face up against the glass between her and them. "Once you open that, we won't be able to hear anymore. Are you ready for that?"

Knitsy and Luna nodded in unison. "I need to see my Riff," said Knitsy.

Knitsy and Luna resumed pushing against the stone, trying to push just enough for it to fall down, since the hourglass was still lying on its side. They mustered enough force to overpower the weight of the stone, and it began to fall. When the heavy stone hit the muddy ground, there was no thud. There was nothing—as if life were on mute. The McHubbards were immediately washed over with the overwhelming silence, which caught them each off guard as they all stumbled out of the Jalopy and attempted to regain their balance. It was only natural for them to call out to each other to make sure they were all right. But each time one of them opened their mouths to say something, the lack of volume from their vocal cords took them by surprise. Ann Lou held her neck as she called out for Luna and Knitsy and no sound came out. She looked over at Luna and imagined how difficult it must be to neither hear nor see anything—to be stuck in a world you can only interact with using taste, smell, and touch.

The McHubbards grasped hands and went in search of mainland Antympanica. Ann Lou traced the letters "H-U-T" on the palm of Luna's hand so she knew where they were headed. It was strange to be sloshing through mud and snapping twigs off bushes, yet making no sound. The realisation popped into their heads that sound creates a balanced structure in daily life, in which it ties together the other senses. Their experience felt somewhat incomplete with the lack of sound. It was so silent that they couldn't even hear their own heartbeats. It was like being on the top of a mountain and trying to listen to someone thousands of leagues under the sea. It was impossible.

As they followed the path toward the mainland, each McHubbard would squeeze another's hand or jerk to the side whenever an Antympanican would bounce into their field of view. Luna was alarmed when one landed in her hair and quickly flew away. The trees' trunks were thick at the base and ramped up until they were just the width of a needle, but the thick forest canopy let in only small pinholes of light. Knitsy looked all around, remembering her torturous time on Antympanica during the Planetary Diagnostic Test, and squeezed her cane harder as she picked her way along the path.

Through the spaces between the trees ahead, they saw what looked like a lake. The lake was completely purple with a sparkle of glittery tint throughout its contents. It extended for what looked like miles into the distance, and thick trees were poking out of the water, making it difficult to see if there was anything in the distance to travel to. They came across a dock, where there were several small, empty boats just waiting to be used. A sign next to the dock had an unreadable language inscribed. When Knitsy and Ann Lou focused on it, the words rearranged into their English translation.

Left: Footpath to Mainland Huts. Right: Boats to The Cabbaged Egg Inn and Bar.

Following the footpath, they eventually reached an area where they could just make out the outline of a group of trees with structures of some sort running upward along their trunks. As they got closer, they could see that huts were stacked one on top of the other from the ground to the tops of the tallest trees. Many of the huts were connected laterally by vines that resembled ziplines. They could see humans zipping along to their neighbours' huts every so often. This forest of tree-huts went on for miles.

Knitsy was having a difficult time treading through the mud, wobbling and frequently getting stuck. Ann Lou cocked her head toward the mainland so that Knitsy would know that they were getting close.

From a distance, Ann Lou could see a pack of human girls walking toward one of the huts on the bottom level. They were smiling at one another and signing to communicate. Ann Lou pointed to the girls and guided Luna and Knitsy toward them. The McHubbards walked up behind the girls as they approached their hut and watched them through the open window as the girls walked in. The family was still hiding just outside the hut, even though they didn't necessarily have to be quiet. Ann Lou could see a hologram in the middle of their hut. It looked as if it was a news station since it had a flashing headline scrolling across it. The English translation read: "CIPTO FALLEN. OLFINDER ATTACKED. WHERE NEXT?"

Knitsy tapped Ann Lou on her shoulder. "Where do we even begin?" she signed, looking concerned.

Ann Lou and Luna jumped as they heard a translation of Knitsy's sign language from inside their heads.

"You can hear this?" tested Ann Lou, also signing to them.

"How is this working?" Knitsy inquired.

"It makes sense. The microchip translates all languages, which apparently includes sign. I can feel the sound almost vibrating around my skull. The skull is close to the bones in the ear so it must be vibrating them as well," signed Luna, matter-of-factly.

"This is bloody wicked," signed Knitsy.

"Let's get on with finding Riff," signed Ann Lou.

The girls in the hut got cups of something that looked like coffee, but it smelled like a mixture of flowers and dirt through the window. Then they sat together at a table and continued smiling and signing to each other.

"Riff probably knows them," signed Ann Lou. "They all look like they're about his age."

"You think your brother has the bollocks to talk to those girls?" signed Knitsy with an eyebrow raised.

"Come on," urged Ann Lou. They awkwardly walked into the hut and up to the table.

"Hey girls," signed Ann Lou.

The girls immediately stopped their conversation and stared at the McHubbards with extreme disdain.

"Sorry to interrupt, but we were looking for our brother," she continued, gesturing to herself and Luna. "We saw him this morning but can't seem to find him." She had to lie not to blow their cover.

The girls continued to stare at her blankly.

"Griffin McHubbard. Goes by Riff." Ann Lou was starting to sweat. The girls clearly did not want to be bothered.

"What does he look like?" signed one of the girls, who looked very annoyed by the interruption.

"Kind of awkward," signed Knitsy in response. "Moppy red hair, bit round in the middle, swears like a sailor."

One girl rolled her eyes. "Sorry, never heard of him."

"Sorry to waste your time," chimed in Luna, who seemed just as uncomfortable as Ann Lou.

The three of them walked swiftly out of the hut and toward a tree about fifty metres away to get out of the girls' visual field.

"Told you so," signed Knitsy.

"We have to find someone who knows him," signed Luna. "Think about it. There's only about ten thousand humans on each planet, and they've been together for over seven years. There's got to be someone who knows him."

They stood in silence for a few minutes, trying to work up the courage to communicate to someone else. Ann Lou watched for opportunities as humans entered and exited their huts and zipped past them on vines overhead. Two boys walked in their direction and started scaling a tree next to them. They appeared to be slightly older than she. Her eyes were mysteriously drawn to the boys. There was something about them that was familiar. Then, she remembered.

"There! That's, that's . . ." Ann Lou was pointing and signing but couldn't quite remember his name.

"Who are you looking at?" signed Luna.

Knitsy wheeled around and saw where Ann Lou was pointing. "Ooh, he's cute," she signed, pretending to swoon. "He looks a lot like your boyfriend, Hayden."

"That's it! It's Matt Murphy," signed Ann Lou. Matt was Hayden's older brother, who played with Riff in their old band, the GeoLads.

Ann Lou ran over to them, but they were already climbing the tree and no longer had the McHubbards in their visual fields. She had to get their attention somehow. So she took a running start and hopped onto the sloped tree, scaling as hard as she could to reach Matt. Just as she decelerated to a stop from the increased slope, she managed to grab a hold of Matt's trousers. As she fell backward onto the ground, she pulled him down with her, and they landed in a heap. The other boy with him felt the vibration of the fall and turned around to slide down and help his friend.

"Matt!" Ann Lou signed, pushing him off of her. "Remember me? It's Ann Lou!"

Matt stared at her, first with fear and then with a look of awe on his face. He jumped up and embraced Ann Lou tightly. He had the same dark skin, curly black hair, and toothy smile, just like Hayden. His face was unshaven, enhancing his punky band image.

"Ann Lou, what on Earth are you doing here?" he signed. "You remember our other bandmate, Joe?" Joe didn't seem to appreciate her presence, which was just the way she remembered him. She nodded to acknowledge him.

"Matt, we need to talk to you," she signed. "We can explain why we're here. But you need to bring us to Riff."

Matt's eyes suddenly got very large. He quickly glanced toward Joe and back to Ann Lou. "Riff's not here."

Ann Lou's heart stopped. She stared deeply in his eyes. "What do you mean he's not here? This is where he was assigned. I saw him get on the bus—"

Matt held his hand up to stop her. "He disappeared a few days ago. We don't know where he went."

Ann Lou wasn't sure what to say. How could Riff be missing? The GeoLapse hadn't even invaded Antympanica yet. Was he with Hayden and Apollo? She continued to stare at Matt, knowing that he was most likely unaware that his little brother was missing as well.

"Can you bring us to his things?" asked Ann Lou, wondering if there would be any hint of where he had gone. Matt and a reluctant Joe directed the McHubbards up the tree that they had started climbing.

Matt generously volunteered to let Knitsy hold onto him as he climbed. He followed Joe, and Ann Lou struggled with Luna as she helped her up the slope that was getting steeper with each step. They had to grab branches to stabilise themselves on the way up. Luna wasn't much for any type of dynamic movement, let alone climbing, so Ann Lou essentially held most of her dead weight on her back as she climbed. She balanced herself with her right arm while holding her Pyroll stick under her left armpit. She was sweating and panting from the extreme load.

About three-quarters of the way up the tree, Matt ushered them to stop and pointed to a vine that extended laterally and slightly downward into an unknown part of the forest. Joe stepped forward to demonstrate what they needed to do. He took out a contraption from his back pocket that looked like a small hook. He looped it over the vine and hopped forward, zipping along. Eventually, he disappeared from view into a sea of other tree huts and vines.

"I'll take Knitsy with my hook. We'll meet you at our hut at the end of this vine." Matt hopped on with Knitsy, who looked back at her grandchildren with a wink as she wrapped her arms around him tightly.

She clutched Matt's shirt and whizzed away from the sisters with great speed. Soon, she and Matt joined Joe in the sea of forest.

"What do we do?" signed Luna. She was trembling and causing Ann Lou to wince from gripping her shoulders so tightly.

Ann Lou thought for a moment. Then she laid her Pyroll stick sideways atop the vine and positioned Luna's hands so she was grasping the stick at either end. "Take this. Hold on tight and jump." She watched as Luna fell forward and slid along the vine.

Ann Lou was next. There had to be something she could use to slide down the vine. She rummaged through her rucksack and pulled out Elbina's ripped jumper. She remembered the last time she used the arm to wrap Egan's horn after the GeoLapse attack seven years ago. She could use the remainder of the jumper as her transportation to the hut.

Ann Lou tossed the jumper over the vine so it hung down on both sides. She clasped either side in her hands and heaved herself off the sloped tree trunk and into the darkness. Her stomach fluttered from the free fall and regained normalcy once she was sliding down the vine at a steady pace. She swung from side to side, watching the maze of huts, humans, and vines above and below her as she passed by. Everything looked as if it were intertwined and connected as she flew through the Antympanican forest. Above her, she could see Antympanicans diving in and out of the treetops. They bounced with grace into upward arcs and parachuted down around her. She couldn't help but smile at how beautiful it was. A beautiful silence. She whirred with glee, her voice lost in the dense atmosphere.

She noticed as she rode along the vine that she was quickly approaching a small hut with lights on. Matt waved as she drew nearer and he caught her in his arms when she reached the end of the vine. Luna, Knitsy, and Joe were already inside waiting for her.

Luna and Knitsy caught Matt and Joe up on recent events, including Hayden's disappearance. Ann Lou searched Riff's belongings at his bunk. It was strange how she could still pick up his scent and remember his face as if she'd seen him just a day before. She thought about the times he would play hockey with her in their upstairs hallway and she'd tackle him when he wouldn't pass her the puck. She'd throw herself into his large teddy-bear frame and catch a whiff of his cologne that never smelled good to her then, but today, it smelled like home.

One of Riff's Death Brigade posters was placed on his bed. The sight worried her, because she knew that Riff loved his music more than anything. Leaving even a poster behind could mean something bad had happened to him. She picked up the poster and inspected it. There were no mysterious markings. Upon turning it over, there was a note written on it with Riff's handwriting. She read it, confused.

"Did you find something?" signed Matt, who looked even more worried now than he had upon learning about Hayden's disappearance.

Ann Lou cocked her head while reading the note to herself. "I did. But I have no idea what it means." She handed Matt the note, who held it next to Joe so he could read it as well.

"Sign it for us," demanded Luna, who was helping Knitsy sit down on Riff's bunk to rest. Knitsy was coughing and trying to catch her breath.

"Nan, please put this on," urged Luna, holding out the breathing patch. Knitsy reluctantly took it and put it back on while Matt signed the contents of Riff's note:

Take Flight - Five Nought Three
Merciless Souls - Nought Four Nine
Please Stay Alive - One One Five
Please Stay Alive - One One Five
Merciless Souls - Nought Four Nine
Dance on Mars - Two Two Four
The End of My Emotions - Three Nought One
Restless - Four Three Six
The End of My Emotions - Three Nought One
Dance on Mars - Two Two Four

Dance on Mars - Two Two Four
Malleus

"Well, they're obviously names of Death Brigade songs," signed Luna, without hesitation. "I've probably heard all of those through Riff's wall at least four hundred times each. But I'm not sure what the numbers mean."

"They could be time marks," said Joe, tapping at his left wrist. "We can still listen to the music stored on ChipMusic. Let me find the first one on the list." Joe's left forearm illuminated with a picture of The Death Brigade and a list of their songs that he had stored. He selected "Take Flight" and skipped to five minutes and three seconds in. Joe was the only one who could hear the song and the family, and Matt watched him tap his toes and nod his head to the beats. "See if you can tell what word they're singing at that exact time," added Matt, still scrutinising the note.

Joe rewound the track several times to focus on the correct word. "Okay, the word at that time is 'you,'" Joe signed.

Matt pulled a pen from Joe's shirt pocket and wrote the word on the note.

"Bro, ask first," signed Joe.

"Shut up," replied Matt. "Get a move on with 'Merciless Souls' at forty-nine seconds."

"I don't have that one on ChipMusic," signed Joe. "I hate that song."

Luna then excitedly held out her arm toward them.

"Riff gave me the album with 'Merciless Souls'!" signed Luna. "Can someone play it for me?"

Ann Lou navigated Luna's ChipMusic with several taps and skipped to the appropriate time on the track. Luna listened intently for a moment and signed, "Heads."

"Got it. 'Please Stay Alive'?" Matt replied.

Ann Lou found the song in her mother's ChipMusic. They repeated the process until they reached the "Restless" track.

"I hate that song too," signed Joe.

"I don't think I have that one," added Luna.

"Me neither," Matt noted.

"Why didn't Riff give me music?" asked Knitsy, feeling left out of the mystery solving.

"I don't have that one either," signed Ann Lou, getting increasingly frustrated.

"Elbina must have it," suggested Luna. "Just skip that one and go to the next song."

At the end of the exercise, they had the following result: "You heads death death heads Mars scream ? scream Mars Mars."

"Great. Riff couldn't even solve his own riddle," signed Joe, rolling his eyes.

"I just think we're approaching it incorrectly," signed Luna, sticking her nose up in Joe's direction. "How else could the time stamps be interpreted?"

Matt looked up. "Riff has perfect pitch. Did you guys know that?"

"What's that?" asked Ann Lou, even more confused than before. "None of our family is particularly musically inclined except for him."

"It means he's able to identify a note without the use of a tuner or an instrument or something to reference what it is. He can just hear a pitch and instantly know what the note is." Matt started pacing back and forth around the bunk area. "That's it," he continued. "Let's check the natural chords at those times."

"Mate," signed Joe, "we don't have perfect pitch."

"We don't need it," answered Matt, his voice getting more excited. "We have our guitars."

Joe nodded, following Matt's logic.

"Can someone fill us in?" signed Ann Lou hastily.

Matt held up his guitar. "Sympathetic resonance. Sound waves still travel here. When a frequency from a note sends out a sound wave, it can cause vibrations to things that resonate at the same frequency."

The boys were met with blank stares from the McHubbards.

"Okay, I'll demonstrate," continued Matt. He looked around for a few seconds and picked up one of Riff's drumsticks. "Watch the two outer strings on the guitar when I tap on the bed rail."

Matt tapped the metallic bed rail a few times. Even though there was no sound, Ann Lou noticed the two outer strings on the guitar vibrating.

"So, the sound from the bed rail and the strings on the guitar have the same note?" she tried to reason.

"Exactly. Music is all around us, even when we can't hear it," smiled Matt. "The vibrations in our heads still come out of our ears. If we turn the volume high enough, we might be able to see the string vibrate with the correct note or chord."

"Brilliant," replied Luna.

"Wicked," agreed Ann Lou.

Joe was already tapping his wrist to find "Take Flight" again. He cranked the volume to the highest setting. They all watched the guitar with extreme scrutiny while Joe scrunched up his face from the blaring music in his head.

"The E and G strings are both vibrating fairly equally," signed Matt, looking at Joe.

"Must be C," Joe answered.

Matt scribbled out their old work and replaced it with the new findings. The rest of them took their turns with playing the songs from ChipMusic and then promptly watching the guitar. The McHubbards passed impressed glances to one another as the musicians worked through the riddle.

 Eventually, their new result was "C-A-B-B-A-G-E-?-E-G-G."

"The Cabbaged Egg Inn and Bar!" signed Ann Lou with excitement. "We saw boats that led there on our way here. He must be there. Let's go!"

"Wait, but what's the 'Malleus' part of the note?" asked Luna as Ann Lou started helping Knitsy up.

"We'll worry about it later. We have a lead. We have to go now and make sure he's all right!"

"We'll come with you!" added Matt, gesturing to himself and Joe. Joe glared at him but didn't refute the statement.

The three McHubbards and the remaining members of the GeoLads made their way to the exit of the hut. It was nighttime, so they huddled close to one another and strode into the silent world. In their haste, they had managed to overlook the words scrolling across the hologram in their hut: "ANTYMPANICA NEXT VICTIM OF GEOLAPSE ATTACKS."

CHAPTER 15

THE CABBAGED EGG INN AND BAR

Knitsy, Luna, Ann Lou, Matt, and Joe all carefully followed the footpath through the gloomy darkness and made their way to the dock with the boats that would hopefully take them to Riff. The lake they had seen earlier glowed purple in the night, with glittery specks floating beneath the surface. The roots of the towering trees that sprouted from the lake looked like a mystical labyrinth.

Upon reaching the dock, they assessed the six boats. They were small and could only fit about two or three passengers each. They also lacked oars. Ann Lou tapped Matt on the shoulder and made a rowing gesture, and Matt held up one finger. He grabbed Joe, and they boarded one of the boats. Joe lifted what looked like a silver disk up from the bottom of the boat. The boat shook slightly, and a propeller began to spin below the surface, sending out silent splashes of the lake liquid behind the boat. Joe then turned the silver disk clockwise, and the boat nosed to the right. Joe let go of the disk, and it floated in midair.

Ann Lou led Luna and Knitsy onto one of the other boats and helped them get comfortably situated. Joe again held up one finger. Ann Lou watched as he untied his bow line, pulled it in, and moved his boat's control disk slightly backward. His boat backed smoothly away from the dock. Then Joe pointed to Ann Lou. She repeated the steps: freeing her bow line from the dock, lifting up her boat's control disk, and pulling it back. Her boat lunged backward a bit but still moved away from the dock in a straight line. She and Joe circled around until their boats were pointed toward the open lake. Ann Lou pushed her control forward slightly to signal that she was ready to go, but Matt just pointed and mimed some sort of tug-of-war. Ann Lou looked where he was pointing and saw that her bow line was still in the water. She pulled it in, then signaled "ready" with her thumb. Matt nodded, and Joe took off ahead of them, leading the way.

They started off on a slow ride, zigzagging through the trees. The trees' roots spread out below the surface, and the boat struck them occasionally when Ann Lou didn't steer widely enough around a tree. Every time they would hit a trunk, the boat would rock to one side at a wide angle and Knitsy would smack Ann Lou's leg with her cane. After they had hit about ten roots in a row, Luna was clutching her stomach. Joe was piloting his boat as if he were a regular at the inn, swerving around each tree with grace and in a perfect path. The ride became tranquil once Ann Lou got the hang of steering. She had only the light of the lake, the boat ahead of them riding smoothly, and the feeling of being with family to calm her nerves. The lack of sound was becoming less scary and more comforting with each second of travel.

Ann Lou kept her hands firm on the wheel and watched Matt and Joe's boat intently to avoid hitting more roots that could send Luna over the edge. Meanwhile, Knitsy was looking around, watching the reflection of the glittery specks on the sprouting trees that they passed.

One particular tree in the shore of the lake caught her eye because the reflections upon its trunk were not purple, but golden.

Before Knitsy had time to call the golden-glinting tree to Ann Lou's attention, dark-clothed GeoLapse revealed themselves from behind trees all around them. They were surrounded—even from below the surface of the lake. GeoLapse in rubber suits surfaced, grabbed their boat, and rocked it violently. They all screamed for Matt and Joe to turn around, but to no avail in the soundless environment of Antympanica. Matt and Joe continued their mellow boat ride, oblivious.

Several GeoLapse carrying batons and ropes were perched on sloped tree trunks, poised to jump onto the McHubbards' boat as they passed. Luna, without fully understanding the situation in front of her, grabbed the control disk in front of her and pushed it as hard as she could, rocketing the boat forward. They skimmed the side of a tree trunk, then hit a root that shot them straight into the air for a few seconds before they crashed down hard, directly alongside Matt and Joe's boat. The disturbance got their attention. They immediately saw the GeoLapse hanging onto the rudder on the back of the McHubbards' boat and poking out from every tree in the distance, in front of and behind them. Joe whipped around to see the remaining four boats full of GeoLapse coming straight toward them at full speed. He met Ann Lou's eyes, cocked his head forward and zoomed off at full throttle as Matt kicked a GeoLapse away from their boat. Ann Lou followed suit and tried to steer within Joe's wake, terrified because she couldn't hear if anyone was around her ready to attack. She saw the glints of gold-like lights strung along the trees on shore as they zoomed past.

Ann Lou pointed to the boats behind them and tapped Knitsy's shoulder for her to keep watch. Knitsy positioned herself to face backward as they sped forward. Her white hair would not stay tucked behind her ears; it was flowing straight past her cheeks, making it difficult for her to see. But, from between strands of hair, she could tell that the GeoLapse were gaining on them rapidly. Ann Lou swerved the boat every other second, barely avoiding full-on collisions with the trees in the lake. Their hearts pumped violently, but they could not hear the pulsating sounds; they could only feel their hearts beating against their rib cages.

When Matt and Joe's boat made a quick left turn into a narrow corridor of trees, Ann Lou panicked. She knew she wouldn't be able to turn nearly as precisely as Joe, so instead she took a right turn into a less densely packed area of trees. There was no sight of Matt and Joe at this point, but they had to keep driving.

Knitsy tapped Ann Lou's shoulder, and she looked back to see the four GeoLapse boats in a diamond formation, about to surround them. Ann Lou pressed her full body weight on the control disk, hoping it would shift into some sort of turbo mode, but it didn't. Ann Lou and Knitsy could see the GeoLapse's evil smiles as they waved their batons. Ann Lou closed her eyes as the boat to their left drew to within a foot of their boat.

She opened her eyes after a few seconds of inactivity and looked back to see that Joe had driven directly into the side of the nearest GeoLapse boat. The other GeoLapse boats rerouted to focus their attack on Matt and Joe, closing in on them from all sides. Ann Lou wheeled her boat around to see if she could use the same tactic they had. Her eyes met Matt's, but he held up his hand and waved her off. She wouldn't leave them. She couldn't. She saw him mouth what looked like a solemn "Please." Knitsy pointed frantically, begging Ann Lou to keep going. But Ann Lou just watched in horror as the GeoLapse dragged the boys from their boat, knocked them unconscious with their batons, and tied them up.

Knitsy whacked Ann Lou with her cane, and Ann Lou snapped out of the horrible trance and turned the boat around. She looked back one last time and saw a GeoLapse boat speeding back toward the dock with Joe and Matt as their captives. The three remaining GeoLapse boats were farther behind but still on their tail. Ann Lou, full of anger, hung hard rights and lefts at full speed. Then she saw an extremely large tree in front of them and aimed straight for it. Luna was crouched down on the floor of the boat and Knitsy decided to join her, knowing Ann Lou surely had a plan, and that no matter how many times she whacked her with the cane, she wouldn't give up on it.

As they closed in on the giant tree, their boat skidded onto the slope of the trunk at full speed and rocketed them into the air. Each McHubbard held onto a side of the boat as it flew through the air, narrowly avoiding intertwining vines that crisscrossed its path. Their arc brought them crashing down into a cluster of vegetation. Ann Lou halted the boat and crouched down. She peered up from her crouching position and saw the GeoLapse boats slowly approaching the brush they were currently stuck in. Luckily, the McHubbards' boat was well camouflaged. As long as they didn't make a visual disturbance, they might be safe.

The GeoLapse boats passed by, craning their necks in every direction looking for the soaring boat. They continued forward and out of sight. When Knitsy popped her head up, her hair was plastered all over the front of her face. She looked like she had just gotten off a rollercoaster. Luna was lying flat on her back and refused to get up.

Ann Lou tried propelling the boat in any direction to get them out of the dense thicket, but the rudder appeared to be stuck on branches below the surface, and there seemed no chance of getting unstuck. Knitsy tapped Ann Lou on her shoulder, and she whipped around to see Knitsy pointing farther into the dense thicket of trees. Ann Lou followed her finger and saw a faint light coming through the trunks and branches. It was so faint that it could almost have been confused for a reflection from the lake, but the more she focused on it, the more she could see that it had to be something else.

Knitsy helped herself out of the boat and onto a patch of brush that they had crashed into. Ann Lou gently took Luna's hand and helped her up.

"We're safe," she signed to Luna. Luna nodded in response.

Knitsy took a hold of Ann Lou's left forearm, and the three McHubbards manoeuvred through patchy weeds and sharp plants, following the faint light just ahead of them through the trees. They came to an opening where a path lay in front of them. Just down the path, they saw the sign for The Cabbaged Egg Inn and Bar. Knitsy kicked her leg out in triumph. Ann Lou smiled. She could even feel Luna's grip loosen as relief washed over her.

They walked up to the main door together. There was light glowing through cracks in the large wooden door. They weren't sure if they should knock or not. Almost instantly, as if something had detected their arrival, a shadow appeared behind the door. The door opened a tiny sliver, and the shadow began to hop around.

"Password?" came through in each of their heads as a translation.

The McHubbards stood there for a few seconds, confused. Luna then raised her right hand in front of her face and finger-spelled "malleus."

The door swung open, revealing a small Antympanican. It continued bouncing around.

"Please come inside quickly."

The McHubbards scuttled inside to find a cosy bar area. Several Antympanicans sat on high stools in a semicircle around the bar, each holding a mug of something that resembled wet dirt. Slender small antennae would protrude from the Antympanicans' heads every so often to touch the dirt. The bartender was busy, passing out drinks quickly with its antenna at one end of the bar, then soaring to the other to tend to other customers. The McHubbards could hear murmurings translating in their heads as the Antympanicans moved about on their stools.

"They must be here already. Look at the shape of this lot that just came in."

"Another one over here, kind barman."

"Did ya hear Tony caught Celia in someone else's nest again?"

The McHubbards stood and stared at the strange little creatures in awe. Their voices didn't match their physiques. They were quite cute little creatures, but their voices came out husky and gruff when translated. One of them caught sight of the McHubbards with the cluster of eyes on the top of its head. It jumped down off its stool and hopped over to them excitedly.

"Can I help you to a room? Or are you interested in any of our food?"

"Any cabbaged eggs?" signed Knitsy, half-joking.

"Ignore her," signed Ann Lou, shooting an annoyed look at her grandmother. "Can you help us find someone? Griffin McHubbard?"

"Ah," bounced the Antympanican. "I'll show you to his room. Follow me. I'll also get started on making you a plate of our finest cabbaged eggs." The Antympanican bounced off and Ann Lou could see Knitsy snickering from behind her as they followed.

They approached a set of narrow stairs, which the Antympanican easily bounced up, one by one. Knitsy was having a difficult time ascending, her cane wobbling with each step. Ann Lou stabilised her from the back and watched as she fell into a silent fit of coughs. Ann Lou waited for Knitsy to catch her breath, then supported most of her weight as they climbed the stairs slowly. Once they reached the top landing, they found the Antympanican next to a closed door. The family let Knitsy open the door, which she did excitedly.

She dropped her cane when she saw Riff lying down in the bed. Riff looked just as he had when they all last said goodbye, except he had a scruff of facial hair. He had lost most of the baby fat from his face and was at least a foot taller than he had been seven years before at the age of sixteen. He still had the same round middle and the same backward hat with floppy red hair poking out from underneath it. His eyes bugged out when he saw Knitsy, and he jumped up from the bed. He stood up cautiously at first, and then embraced her. She promptly thwacked him with her cane for the mess he had just put them through. As he hugged her, he caught a glimpse of Luna and Ann Lou poking their heads in the door. He scooped up Knitsy and embraced her and his sisters in one group. He towered above them. Ann Lou smelled his cologne and smiled. It was the same, horrible cologne smell that she had grown up hating, but she loved it now.

Riff withdrew from the embrace, staring at them all. He was in complete disbelief that they were all in the same room.

"Come sit," he signed, helping Knitsy to a seat on the bed. "What are you all doing here?"

"We should ask you the same thing," signed Luna. "That was some clue you left."

Riff looked down at his feet and then continued to sign. "I've had this weird hunch. Can't seem to shake it. I've been seeing the news saying the GeoLapse first attacked at the Cipto and Epiton Pyroll tournament. Then Olfinder. So, I assumed they were coming here next." He paused. "I just wanted to go into hiding for safety and I thought I could leave a clue for Matt and Joe to join me, but they never found me."

"Why didn't you just tell them to come with you?" asked Luna.

Riff pinned his gaze on her. "I'm at least smart enough to have figured out that there are humans on each planet who are loyal to the GeoLapse. You have to be careful what you say around here. Plus, Antympanicans are known to gossip. You're not the only smart one in the family."

Luna raised her nose into the air and looked away. Riff then looked at Ann Lou. "So how did you get here? When I heard the GeoLapse took over Earth, I thought you were . . . well, I thought I'd never see you again."

The McHubbard women spent the next few hours catching Riff up on their past seven years, from leaving home to reuniting with one another. Riff was sad to learn of their mother's passing but was not surprised that she had given her life to save Ann Lou's. When Ann Lou told him about Matt and Joe's capture back on the lake, he looked as if he might cry.

"We wouldn't be alive if it weren't for them," signed Ann Lou, trying to comfort her brother. Riff continued to look down at his trainers.

"So, what next?" signed Knitsy. "Where do we all go from here?"

Riff looked at his grandmother and put his heavy arm around her bony shoulders.

"Let's get something to eat downstairs and listen in on the Antympanicans' gossip. There's sure to be a clue in there somewhere."

"You and your clues," signed Luna, still looking away.

"How are we hearing them speak?" asked Ann Lou as they got up from their seated positions.

"The Antympanicans communicate through movement. That's why you'll hear their translations when they bounce or jump."

"So can you hear the translations as well?" signed Ann Lou.

Riff's expression grew sad again. "I'm completely deaf now. Over the first few years, I was able to learn their language with the remainder of my hearing. And then a couple years ago I became fully dependent on sign language and lip reading."

Ann Lou felt bad for Riff. He could no longer hear his music. She wondered how it affected him, since music had been his only solace back on Earth.

"So, no more drums?" signed Ann Lou.

"Oh please, nothing could stop me from playing my music. The rhythm never goes away. Vibrations are my best friend," he replied with a sweet smile.

The four McHubbards made their way downstairs and took a seat on the couches while the Antympanican who had brought them to Riff came soaring from behind the bar with a heaping plate of cabbaged eggs balanced on its head. The family dug into them, not caring that the dish smelled vile and nauseating.

"I've literally never been this hungry in my life," signed Ann Lou, as she shovelled three eggs into her mouth. Bits of yolk dripped down her chin.

"I had almost forgotten that bad smells existed," signed Knitsy, wrinkling her nose in disgust but filling her mouth with an entire cabbaged egg. "Having only smelled a breathing mask for seven years, at least this is something new."

They were completely filled up with food and nearly asleep on the couches when one of the Antympanicans from the bar soared over and bounced in front of Riff.

"Griffin McHubbard, good to see ya."

Riff patted it on the head and signed back, "Good to see you, Tony. How's Celia?"

Knitsy, Ann Lou, and Luna glanced sidelong at one another.

Tony continued to bounce. "Don't even get me started on that piece of—"

"Drink, Tony?" called the bartender, bouncing up and down from behind the bar, its eyes just managing to peek over the ledge as it hopped.

Tony jumped about a foot in the air. "Keep 'em comin'!"

The bartender soared over with five mugs so they could each indulge in whatever was in them.

"So, what's the word in the forest, Tony?" signed Riff, taking a sip of the drink. The other McHubbards were afraid to taste it after their experience with the cabbaged eggs. At least now they weren't as desperate to ingest anything.

Tony bounced and hobbled. "Did ya hear about Ole Man Anvil? Do I have a story for you—"

"That sounds riveting, Tony," started Riff. "But anything on the GeoLapse front?"

Tony leaned in close to Riff and did a small hop. "Did ya hear that they're here?" Tony's voice translated as a whisper. Knitsy couldn't help but let out a silent laugh.

"You know, I have heard that through the canopy," began Riff, glancing at his family. "Do you know where they might go next?"

"Word around the lake is that they have enough extraterrestrial beasts to officially take over the Universal Union. Heard they wanna set up camp in Harvinth. But they'll have a helluva hard time getting there." Tony's hearty chuckle filled their ears as he rolled in his seat.

"Why is it so hard to get to Harvinth?" signed Luna.

Tony looked at her, his three eyes focusing intently on her. "Ya have to go through the Time Belt. Things never go smoothly through the Time Belt."

"That exists?" asked Ann Lou, remembering the story she had listened to on Cipto.

Tony hobbled back into a normal sitting position. "It exists just as sure as my Celia is unfaithful!" He continued to laugh and all the McHubbards shared uncomfortable looks with one another.

"How do you get through the Time Belt?" signed Luna, avoiding the subject of Celia.

Tony dimmed his laughter. "I've heard rumours. But the rumours never match up when I hear somethin' new. All I know is one wrong move, and you'll be lost in time forever. A right move, and ya can turn it all back." Tony flipped out his antenna and sucked up his entire drink in one slurp. "Ya gonna finish that?" he asked, his three eyes focused on Knitsy, Luna, and Ann Lou respectively.

"All yours," responded Ann Lou to a now excited Tony.

"Looks like we have to go to Harvinth," signed Luna to her family. The rest of the McHubbards shot her a loathing look.

"Are you nuts?" replied Riff, signing with a vigor that Ann Lou's microchip translated into an angry tone. "Why would we ever go there?"

"First of all," started Luna, "our little sister is there and in terrible danger. Secondly, do you want the GeoLapse to take over the universe?"

Riff didn't know how to respond. He'd felt safe in hiding. Now he had to venture back into the dangerous depths of Antympanica and endure a potentially horrifying trip through the Time Belt.

"She's right," added Ann Lou. "It's us or no one."

Riff visibly sighed. "At least let me get my poster from my room."

"I'll draw you a new one on the ride there," signed Luna, jokingly.

"Enough from you both," signed Knitsy with a threatening frown on her face. "The Jalopy is close to the mainland. How do we get there without being seen by the GeoLapse?"

Knitsy had raised a good point. Her three grandchildren could not answer that question and considered their predicament for a few moments.

"Ya need to go somewhere?" hopped Tony. "I've had enough of these to be bonkers enough to help ya lot out." His antenna was now pointing to an empty mug. Tony sat up and soared to the bar. A few minutes later, he returned with three barmates.

"I don't think this is a good idea," stumbled one of the Antympanican recruits. The McHubbards couldn't tell if the stumbling was from the drinking or if it was actually communicating completely coherently.

"Relax, I'll buy ya lot a drink when we get back," bobbed Tony.

"*If* we get back," hobbled another skeptical Antympanican.

The four Antympanicans huddled at the front door. Each was going to carry one of the McHubbards on their backs as they soared through the treetops, remaining unseen by the grounded GeoLapse. None of the McHubbards knew how the small creatures could possibly carry one of them since they didn't even reach the height of their knees. Even still, the McHubbards each chose an Antympanican and grabbed on to their fuzzy, round bodies.

"On my ready," shuffled Tony. He stood still for a few moments.

"Oh, just go already," pranced one of the recruits, clearly annoyed it was being plucked from the bar.

"Gooooo!" sprung Tony, and each of the Antympanican-human duos leapt into the night. The wingspan of each Antympanican was marvelously huge compared to the size of their bodies. The round wing surrounding their main body unfolded into the size of a small, flattened parachute, allowing them to zoom through the night sky with aerodynamically impressive speed. The McHubbards each gripped their Antympanican partner for dear life as they raced toward the stars and accelerated downward into the treetops, only to quickly be propelled back into the night sky.

It was a beautifully nauseating flight, as each pair was following a sinusoidal flightpath every minute or so. When they emerged from the treetops, they could see hundreds of other Antympanicans doing the same thing as far as they could see in the distance. It was difficult to tell where they were, since the treetops of Antympanica spread throughout the entire planet, and once they flew back downward within the dense forest, they were brushing away exotic-looking leaves and branches from their faces.

After hundreds of leaps and dives, the four duos all descended toward the same target: the hourglass Jalopy. They landed softly, each Antympanican extending its parachute wing to land like a feather drifting down to the ground. The McHubbards worked quickly to prepare the Jalopy.

Just as Ann Lou had signed to Riff how to close the final stone that would seal them in, he took one last look at his friends. The four Antympanicans stood in front of him, sagging their wings in a manner that suggested they were going to miss their human friend.

"Thank you all so much," signed Riff, smiling brightly. "I don't know how I would've survived these years without you. Especially you, Tony."

"The pleasure is all ours, Griffin McHubbard. Go save the universe," danced Tony. The others bobbed in agreement.

"And you lot go have a drink for me," laughed Riff.

With that, the Antympanicans were off into the night, propelling themselves back toward The Cabbaged Egg Inn and Bar in beautiful arcs of soundless flight.

CHAPTER 16

THROUGH THE TIME BELT

Riff fit the stone top onto the hourglass once the rest of his family were secured inside. Ann Lou and Luna were situated in the bottom half, and Riff had to squeeze in with Knitsy in the top half. He was almost too large to fit in the Jalopy at all, but his sisters insisted that someone should be with Knitsy to stabilise her both mentally and physically. The Jalopy illuminated with its usual neon green light. The sound was officially back to fill their now popping ears.

"Hello, Knitsy McHubbard, Luna McHubbard, Griffin McHubbard, and Ann Lou McHubbard. The Jalopy is ready to depart. Please state your destination," recited the usual script of the Jalopy.

"Harvinth," whispered a breathless Ann Lou.

"Enjoy your trip."

The Jalopy rose off the ground and accelerated into the night sky. Riff peered out his window, trying to get a close look at the mainland before it was lost in the treetops. He could see humans being dragged out of their huts and hauled into a large boat. The GeoLapse's golden badges glinted in his eyes, angering him enough that he pounded his fists into the glass. They had taken his best friends. He had to stop them. Knitsy patted Riff's arm as he hid his face in his large hands.

The land of Antympanica vanished from their view. No one was sure how long it would take to get to Harvinth. They vaguely remembered its distance from Earth being considerably longer than that of the other host planets.

"Wasn't Harvinth, like, a billion light years away from Earth or something like that?" asked Ann Lou, watching the stars zoom past.

"Thirteen point two six, to be exact," said Luna in a monotonous tone. She was resting her head on the glass.

"Right."

The family rode in silence for hours, maybe even days. They would think they were approaching something in the universe—a planet, an asteroid, perhaps another travelling Jalopy—only to look back at it hours later and have it appear the same size as it was before. The family felt cramped and restless in the Jalopy, and they secretly wished that they had stuffed some extra cabbaged eggs into their pockets since they were famished from the long ride. Ann Lou and Luna got into a fight about personal space.

"You literally just elbowed me in the stomach. Can you please stop touching me?" snarled Luna, sounding dangerously close to elbowing Ann Lou back.

"I literally didn't touch you, Luna," whined Ann Lou, rolling her eyes.

"Who could've done it then? Nan? You think it was her?" said Luna, facing Ann Lou with her hands thrown upward.

"Would you two just shut the hell up down there?" signed Riff from above. He could feel their disturbance from the top half of the Jalopy.

Knitsy proceeded to whack him with her cane. "Language!"

"Ann Lou, I'd give you my left arm to switch places right now," Riff signed.

Tensions ran high as they continued into the depths of the universe. They had to have flown past a few billion stars at this point, and the view no longer constituted an interesting sight. Each McHubbard was sitting with arms folded, scowling and trying to avoid each other in the claustrophobic area, when they all saw a pinhole of bright light in the distance. A warming sensation developed within the Jalopy as the pinhole of light exponentially began to expand until it seemed to shine on them from all directions, as if they were entrapped in a bubble. The feeling of warmth was comforting and peace-inducing.

"What's going on?" signed Riff. "Have we died?"

"No, you idiot," responded Luna. "It's the Time Belt. We've made it."

The family all held their breath in anticipation for the rumoured arduous journey ahead. Soon, they were blinded by white light; even Luna could sense it. They felt as if they suddenly were in an entirely new place, if that's what one could call it. They were each floating in free space, no longer within the Jalopy, staring at one another as the blinding white light enveloped them all in its peaceful blanket. Was it a whole new dimension? Could they have actually died, as Riff guessed?

All around them, thousands, perhaps millions of moving images flashed as if on a panoramic wall within the light blanket. They rec-ognised these pictures as themselves, all of them, from their births to their most recent experiences. The family watched in silence as their ears were filled with an orchestral score of symphonic music. The mood of the music changed to suit whichever image they focused on, from sad to jovial. Similarly, they could smell and taste the memories they relived. As Ann Lou watched herself taking a bite of her first birthday cake, the smell of the cake warmed her nose, and the taste swarmed her taste buds. They could also feel a strong wind blowing over them from all directions, perhaps keeping them floating within the Time Belt's enlightening grasp.

"Longest friend of time . . ." boomed an omnipresent voice. "You are requested to change one event in your experience of time."

The McHubbard children watched as their grandmother rose higher than the three of them and was slowly being rotated in the free space. Knitsy watched her life unfold through the images that came and went like a camera reel, speeding through her eighty-two years of life. None of the McHubbards felt scared. The voice was almost comforting, and it filled their bodies with a freeing vibration. Luna, Riff, and Ann Lou could not speak or move in any particular direction; they could only watch their grandmother from below.

Knitsy blissfully watched her summary of life flashing before her eyes. She enjoyed re-watching her grandchildren grow up, speaking their first words, tying their shoes, opening presents under the Christmas tree, and skipping down the tunnel to the school bus. She also watched the horrifying moments: her husband dying, Ann Lou lying in the hospital without her left forearm. But the hardest moments of all for Knitsy to bear again were the ones involving Henrietta. Knitsy bawled as pictures of her daughter flashed before her. She watched the moment where she said goodbye to her daughter for the last time.

"Choose now, oldest friend," boomed the voice. "Choose one event to change. Do not waste what time you have remaining."

The voice was stern, but Knitsy nodded. She knew how to respond to the task at hand.

"I would stay back on Earth instead of my Henrietta," she cried. "So that my grandchildren would still have their mother."

The Time Belt rumbled, sending a deep thrumming tremor through their bodies. "The dead cannot be recalled from their final resting place," thundered the voice. "The dead are at peace and your selfish choice would only disturb that peace. You will be punished for your heedlessness."

A black speck appeared above them and grew conically downward toward Knitsy's head. The children watched their grandmother rise higher and higher as the rumbling voice's last sentence echoed through the free space that went on for infinity. Knitsy's arms were spread out wide, and her hair was blowing in all different directions. She looked down at her grandchildren in terror as she rose closer to the black hole. As soon as Knitsy was enveloped by the black hole, it disappeared as quickly as it had appeared, along with the entirety of the Time Belt.

Luna, Riff, and Ann Lou felt like they were falling into nothingness. The happiness they each had felt from the blanket of light dissolved instantly and was replaced with fear. They landed back into the Jalopy, en route to Harvinth once again, as if nothing had happened.

"What was that?" shouted Ann Lou. "What's going on?" She looked up and saw Riff alone in the upper half of the hourglass.

"Nan's gone," said Luna quietly, her voice shaking. "She's dead."

CHAPTER 17

HARVINTH

The Jalopy zoomed toward what appeared to be Harvinth, a small planet that looked entirely sandy from the view from space. None of the McHubbards spoke after Knitsy's untimely departure within the Time Belt. They couldn't even cry. They were all locked in a state of disbelief.

As they approached Harvinth, there was only one structure to be seen: a dingy-looking rectangular building that they were quickly nearing. The Jalopy did its usual crash landing, smashing the McHubbards' faces into the glass. Not one of them uttered any grunts of pain; they only exited the vehicle in the usual fashion.

The three of them dusted the sand from their clothing and faced the building. Someone in a green lab coat was standing outside the doors, waiting for them. It was Jung-hoon. Ann Lou hesitated, fearful that her suspicions about him might be true. Ann Lou was already tugging Luna to get back into the Jalopy when he called out: "Wait!"

Jung-hoon began to run toward them as quickly as he could. As he approached them, he grew a relieved smile.

"The three of you have done beautifully," he said, extending his arms out and hugging them all in one group. The siblings just stood there, confused.

"Come with me," he continued. Jung-hoon began to walk into the building, but when he didn't hear footsteps behind him, he turned back. "You're all right," he said, looking back at them. "You're safe. Let me grab you all a cup of tea and I can explain everything."

Each of the McHubbards' stomachs started to growl. They took each other's hands and reluctantly followed him into the old building, their fear outweighed by their extreme hunger and thirst from Harvinth's hunger inducing atmosphere and also after travelling through space for hours, or perhaps days, or maybe even weeks. Jung-hoon sat them down at a cafeteria table and brought over a teapot and rock-hard biscuits, which they consumed ravenously. The food and drink could have been poisoned and they would not have cared.

"This building is designed to counteract the hunger from the outside, so you should be comfortable in here," said Jung-hoon.

None of the siblings acknowledged him as they cleared the biscuits and swallowed the contents of the teapot with great speed.

Jung-hoon resumed speaking once they had finished inhaling their food and drink. "Let me take you down to the ERA headquarters—"

"What do you want from us?" croaked Luna in a bitter tone. She hadn't spoken since they left the Time Belt. Ann Lou was speechless at the sight of her disloyal acquaintance. Luna must have sensed Ann Lou's hesitation to call him out.

"I understand that you are confused right now, Luna. But let us straighten everything out at headquarters." Then Jung-hoon looked at them and gasped. "Where's Knitsy? I thought you collected her from Olfinder."

"She died when we were passing through the Time Belt," said Luna, her voice trembling but remaining strong in tone.

"Oh dear . . ." he said. "We need to get you down to headquarters immediately." He stood and ushered them out of their seats. Ann Lou and Riff stood up, but Luna remained seated.

"I'm not going with you," announced Luna. "I don't trust you."

Jung-hoon looked offended. "This was to be expected. How about if Elbina explains everything to you instead?"

The McHubbards' faces all lost colour at the same time.

"Where is she?" demanded Luna.

"If you'll just follow me—"

"Bring her to us."

Jung-hoon sighed and walked away. Riff and Ann Lou sat back down and stared at Luna. She could sense their unease.

"I'm not giving in this easily without knowing the story," said Luna. "For all we know, they could be planning to take us prisoner as soon as we walk into their headquarters." She gave off an air of power and authority. Ann Lou and Riff silently agreed with her.

Moments later, they heard clinking heels approaching their table. They all looked in the direction of a young, thin, beautiful woman wearing a green lab coat. It was Elbina. She wore her usual large jumper underneath the lab coat. Her bony hands poked out of the sleeves and covered her mouth in disbelief at the sight of all her siblings sitting right in front of her. Now twenty-one years old, Elbina carried herself with a newfound confidence that the siblings were surprised to see. She wore patterned trousers, high heels, a light coat of makeup, and flashy jewelry. Her thin, wispy hair was held up in a high, tight ponytail, emphasising her bright eyes and bony cheeks.

Ann Lou stepped forward toward her with her Pyroll stick tightly gripped in her right hand. She was fuming. How could her sister betray them all like this? She was almost prepared to strike her sister, but Elbina held up a hand to stop her.

"To save time, I just wanted to let you all know that I know everything, and I am not the bad guy."

Her siblings looked at her, confused.

"Let me see if I can explain everything I know. There's a lot, so you'd better make yourselves comfortable," started Elbina. She cleared her throat. "If you don't mind, I'm a bit hungry, so I'm going to turn on the Gasser." As they all sat at the table, she pulled out the old contraption they all knew so well. She looped the tubing around her nose and turned it on. It began to buzz and shake Elbina's body as she spoke.

"Right, so here's what's going on," continued Elbina, clasping her hands in front of her, which were trembling from the vibration of the Gasser. "I'll start with the basics. Harvinth was established as ERA headquarters after we were all moved over seven years ago. As you probably have guessed, the ERA members who were placed on the other host planets have been secretly reporting in to the headquarters here."

"Yeah, and helping the GeoLapse. We know," said Luna, still maintaining her rude tone.

Elbina shot her a glare. "Luna, this will be much quicker if you listen to me." Riff and Ann Lou shared surprised looks with one another and laughed out of their view and earshot. Never in a million years would they have expected Elbina to stand up to Luna, of all people.

Elbina continued. "When we left Earth, the GeoLapse membership was increasing exponentially. The ERA were wildly outnumbered, so they pretended to form an alliance with the GeoLapse to help them take over the Universal Union. The ERA have been playing along this whole time, gaining the GeoLapse's trust. It was the ERA who gave them the idea to take prisoners on the host planets and bring them to Harvinth. The GeoLapse think the prisoners are being gathered on Harvinth so the ERA can brainwash them and conscript them into the GeoLapse. But the ERA are actually building an army that will help fight back against the GeoLapse."

"How did the GeoLapse get to Cipto in the first place?" asked Ann Lou. "We thought they were stuck on Earth."

"Each planet in the Universal Union is equipped with something called a Jalopy Cabin. The ERA has a few on Earth at its headquarters at the White House in the United States. When the time was right, they granted the GeoLapse access to the Jalopy Cabins so they could get to Cipto in time for the Pyroll championship. Once the GeoLapse reached Cipto, they collected prisoners on that large boat Jalopy. But since then, the GeoLapse have been using both Jalopies to get to other planets."

Ann Lou's face went white again, and she shuddered as she recalled the terrors of the GeoLapse attacks.

"If it makes you feel any better," Elbina said, putting her hand on Ann Lou's arm, "the GeoLapse were instructed by the ERA to capture as many beings as they could and specifically not to harm them."

Riff's blood was starting to boil. He signed, "Ann Lou saw my friends get beaten!"

Elbina looked at him and smiled. "Matt and Joe are alive and doing just fine, I promise. They're downstairs."

Riff and Ann Lou jumped out of their seats. "And Apollo and Hayden? Fintan and Egan?" shouted Ann Lou.

"All downstairs," responded Elbina, calmly. "But first you have to let me explain the rest." Ann Lou and Riff took their seats again, their hearts racing.

Luna chimed in. "Weren't the ERA feeding lies to all the country leaders? I'm not sure I believe this whole 'playing along' story."

"They had to gain the trust of the GeoLapse somehow," Elbina replied. The GeoLapse was too strong. The ERA needed additional resources."

"So . . . many . . . people . . . died, Elbina," said Luna slowly.

Elbina nodded. "I know, Luna. I'm not saying I agree with their tactics. I've only just recently joined the ERA. I'm just telling you what I've learned since agreeing to be on the team," said Elbina. She sounded annoyed.

"I can't believe you joined them. I had faith in you," spat Luna.

"Keep going," interjected Ann Lou, looking back at Elbina, who looked saddened by the blow from Luna. "So, why Harvinth?"

"This is where it gets interesting," said Elbina, pulling her chair forward and not looking at Luna. "So, as you know, Harvinth is located outside of the Time Belt—"

"Oh, we know," snarled Luna.

"And everything past the Time Belt, including Harvinth, experiences linear time in reverse."

The siblings looked at one another. "Uh, what exactly does that mean?" asked Riff.

"As soon as the humans colonised Harvinth over seven years ago, that event started the clock for the reversal of time. So, for example, if we were to go back to Earth from here right now, where it's the year 2227, we would land on Earth seven years in the past from when we first landed on Harvinth, which was in 2220, so we would actually land in 2213. You basically go back in time double the number of years that Harvinth has been colonised."

Ann Lou and Riff were completely lost.

Luna sat up straight in her chair. "So you're saying the ERA wanted to colonise Harvinth so that we could go back in time on Earth . . ."

Elbina nodded.

". . . so that they could stop the GeoLapse before they grew too big?"

"You've got it," said Elbina, clapping her hands together.

"Brilliant," said Luna airily. "Whose plan was that?"

"Mum's," replied Elbina softly.

Luna stood up. "Have you gone bloody mad in your time here, Elbs?"

"Let me go over the timeline with you. It'll explain more. Please, no more interruptions until I finish," asked Elbina in an unusually confident tone. The rest of her siblings nodded. Luna still stood where she was.

Elbina proceeded. "So, in a previous linear time on Earth, before this one, we lived our normal lives almost exactly as we remember having lived them this time around. Mum was secretly the head of the ERA. She couldn't tell anyone, not even us or Knitsy, because there were so many secrets that she couldn't let loose. At that time, Earth's delegate to the Universal Union was secretly a member of the GeoLapse. Being the important person Mum was, she was aware of the happenings at the Universal Union meetings. She had heard that they just admitted a new planet, Harvinth, into the Union. It was the only planet in the Universal Union that was located outside the Time Belt, and Mum figured out colonising it would reverse linear time. She bargained with one of the delegates of the Universal Union to take out the traitorous Earth delegate, and at the next meeting he was squashed by one of the other delegates by 'accident.'" Elbina put finger quotes around the word *accident*.

"Mum became the interim Earth delegate of the Universal Union and helped the humans move to the various host planets, which included Harvinth. The colonisation of Harvinth was the event that started the clock for the reversal of time.

"Her first plan was to wait as many years as the GeoLapse had been around, then travel back to Earth so that we could take the GeoLapse down right when they started forming. But after years of waiting, the universe was in shambles from the GeoLapse takeovers. She knew that a new plan had to begin immediately, and this time it had to include the ERA pretending that they were in an alliance with the GeoLapse so that the ERA could have a strong influence on the GeoLapse's actions to steer them away from complete universal control.

"So, before reversing the time back on Earth, she wanted to find someone she trusted to be the next Earth delegate of the Universal Union, but they had to be in a position of political power to even be considered for the job. Elections were conveniently being held for the President of the United States at the time when they were going to head back to Earth, so Mum went to someone she knew—someone in our family—who was trustworthy enough to be elected President and who could then be elected Earth's delegate to the Universal Union.

"Since Ann Lou and Hayden were happily married on Epiton, Mum approached Hayden to run for president since he was extremely easy to get along with and he could be easily influenced by his mother-in-law. He also spoke in a convincing American accent. She flew all of our family to Harvinth and prepared Hayden to be sent back.

"That was the first time Earth was sent back into the past. Once Hayden was sent back, that event began the current linear time that we all remember now. Again, since Harvinth was colonised by humans for eight or so years, Hayden was placed on Earth that many years before the colonisation, and just in time for the presidential election, which he won. Hayden maintained his adult status when he traveled back, meaning that there were two Hayden Murphys on Earth at the same time.

"President Hayden began to crumble under the pressure, so the ERA had to isolate him and take him under their complete control by tampering with his food with a special remedy. He was still able to move forward with the plan because his hunches about moving the humans were coming from the ERA's tampering, even though the ERA still had to put up a fake front for the GeoLapse. The ERA also sent President Hayden little Easter eggs, if you will, to reassure him of the plan. For instance, one time when Hayden was doubting the plan, I apparently acted as—" here, Elbina affected a French accent "—'Dr. Blair Watson, ERA chief scientist of the French division.' I had to pressure him to work with the Universal Union secretly so that the ERA as a whole wouldn't blow their cover with the GeoLapse.

"President Hayden even forgot who he was married to after he was sent back, but he still had faint memories that he didn't understand. When he eventually found you, Ann Lou, after he had escaped the GeoLapse attack on the White House, you stepped up and presented the results of the Planetary Diagnostic Test to all the families on Earth. But you were in your older form. Our younger selves didn't have anything to do with our older selves coming back, so that's why we don't remember anything.

"So, in summary, Mum's new plan to turn back time on Earth for a second time was to 'ally' with the GeoLapse to gather a universal army for the ERA to then send them back to Earth to take down the GeoLapse once and for all. If the plan can be completed, the ERA can then focus on finally rehabilitating the Earth according to their actual plans for saving the environment, and no one will have to be moved to host planets. Earth can stay inhabited by humans."

When Elbina finished, the siblings all stayed silent for a few moments, trying to piece together everything she had just told them. Finally, Riff broke the silence.

"Mum is ace. But why was she freaking out when we were all doing the test and being placed if she knew what was going to happen?"

"It's hard anytime a mother has to be ripped from her children or see them in pain," Elbina said. "Also, going back in time naturally changes events, which adds a slew of unexpected challenges. One such event resulted in the GeoLapse attack on Ann Lou's primary school when she lost her arm, which didn't happen in the previous linear time. Because Ann Lou couldn't take the test this time around and wouldn't be placed on Epiton, Mum decided to give her own microchip to Ann Lou, since she knew Ann Lou was previously placed on Epiton and flourished there. Mum knew the plan could still be executed without her being in charge of the ERA."

Luna sat down at the table again, her aggression having softened. "If we're going back in time, why can't we just save Mum?"

"It's really dangerous to mingle with people who have died in a previous linear time. Changing such a large-scale event like that could set a whole other set of changes in motion for this upcoming linear time."

"Hayden and I were married?" asked Ann Lou, changing the subject, and pressing her fingers into the sides of her forehead. "What happened to President Hayden?"

"He and all the doubles—so me, Luna, Riff, Ann Lou, Mum, and Nan—were ordered to stay under supervision of the ERA at the White

House. Eventually they destroyed the doubles because they weren't needed anymore and having two of the same person could get tricky."

"Where are the GeoLapse now?" asked Luna.

"Invading more planets," replied Elbina, grinding her teeth. "They send their prisoners here after an invasion, then continue on to new planets. But that just means we will have more of an army in the end."

"That's just . . . a lot to take in," signed Riff. He put his hands over his face.

"It is," answered Elbina. "Let me take you to your friends and I'll make you all some dinner from our rations, okay? We can take the next several weeks to go over the plan and prepare. We need to travel back a little bit after President Hayden is sworn in as president for the first time, just to ensure that we don't change anything about the elections. So we have a few weeks to get ready."

Elbina led her siblings down into the dormitories, where they saw humans, Epitonians, Ciptons, Olfinderians, and Antympanicans, bruised but resting comfortably on hundreds of bunks lining the dormitory floor. Ann Lou raced down the rickety stairs in search of her friends. She instantly recognised the towering Epitonians in one row and caught a glimpse of Egan, Fintan, and Apollo passing the Pyroll to each other. Ann Lou sprinted toward them and jumped into Apollo's arms. She kissed him all over his face and he excitedly embraced her and swung her around in circles. Egan and Fintan joined their embrace.

"We never got to congratulate you on winning us the Pyroll championship, Henrietta!" cheered Egan, clapping Ann Lou on her back. "Well done!"

"Yes, well done, Henrietta!" added Fintan.

"Mind if I have a few moments with my girlfriend, boys?" said Apollo, puffing out his chest.

"Oh, don't be doing anything I wouldn't do," joked Egan, making kissing noises toward Ann Lou and Apollo. Fintan grabbed Egan's shoulder and pulled him away.

Apollo looked into Ann Lou's eyes and smiled. He grabbed her hand in his claw, very gently this time. "You figured it all out. I'm so proud of you."

Ann Lou shook her head. "We wouldn't be here if it weren't for you, Apollo." She saw that one of his horns was missing and his left arm had a huge gash in it, probably from his capture back on Antympanica.

"You're hurt. Elbina said they weren't supposed to hurt you!" she cried, gently prodding his wounds with her hand.

He laughed, shaking a bit since his body was still weak. "I wouldn't have lost as much eelich as I did if I hadn't put up such a fight. I'll be better by the time we need to go back to Earth, though."

Ann Lou hugged him around his waist tightly and said, "I love you."

Apollo huffed in pride, excited to hear those words coming from her. "I loved you the moment we first played Pyroll together," he replied sweetly, hugging her back.

"I'll be your mate," she added.

He pulled her back from her hug and stared at her shining blue eyes. "What?"

She smiled. "You've shown me greater love than anyone I've met in the universe. I am so in love with you. I know you'd never hurt me, and I certainly would never hurt you."

Apollo smiled the widest she had ever seen him smile, showing all his razor-sharp teeth. "So, do we like, keep dating?"

"Let's get married. But let's do it the way you'd do it on Epiton *and* the way I'd do it on Earth. We need to do it here, though. Before we get sent back on our mission." All she knew is that she wanted to be with him now.

"I need to go tell the boys!" Apollo went running off after Fintan and Egan. Ann Lou laughed as he ran off. He reminded her of a small child running to tell his mother something.

"Hey, you," said a familiar voice.

Ann Lou whipped around and smiled broadly, just as she had so many times at the roller rink. Hayden stood there with his hands in his pockets, unsure if she'd be happy to see him. He had two black eyes and a swollen lip.

"Hayden . . . You're all right!" She leaped into his arms and gripped him tightly. He hugged her back with the same tenacity. "I should have never treated you so poorly," she whispered in his ear as they embraced. "You didn't deserve that."

"You're my best friend always, Ann Lou. In forward and reverse time," he whispered back.

They broke their embrace, and Ann Lou started to laugh. "You know, we were married at one point in time."

"I'm sure it was wonderful," he answered. Ann Lou looked down at her feet in embarrassment. "But I overheard you and Apollo. I'm happy for you. I'll just have to try harder the next time around." He laughed and smiled.

"You're perfect the way you are, Hayden."

"Maybe you dig the American accent instead of the British one? I'll use that in front of you from now on," he smiled as he spoke in his classic accent.

Ann Lou laughed as she always had. "Why don't you try it on Elbina sometime? I think you'll find it easy to grab her attention." She winked at him.

The two found an empty bunk to sit on and talked for hours, catching up. Elbina eventually came around with hot bowls of strew that she had concocted using items from the humans' rations. She had been planning the recipe in her cooking journal for a while, and it was one of the most delicious dinners that she had ever made. She cooked enough to feed the whole army of humans, Epitonians, Ciptons, Antympanicans, and Olfinderians. Elbina's dish received universal praise from everyone who tasted her meal, making her feel as excited as she had when her family praised her on Earth.

"This is totally radical, Elbina," said Hayden in his American accent as Elbina passed out the food to him and Ann Lou.

Elbina giggled and blushed. "I told you I'd make you a stew better than your mum's."

Hayden's eyes widened. "Does it have the corn stuff in it?"

"*Jus de cornichon*, and yes," Elbina corrected him with a smile.

Hayden stared at her with a smoky look in his eyes. Ann Lou just rolled hers.

As the evening progressed, Ann Lou couldn't help but look around the dormitory and smile. Riff was sharing pints with Matt, Joe, and their Antympanican friends. Luna was reading her newest book to a circle of Ciptons and Olfinderians, and Elbina was confidently passing around her culinary creation and speaking in fluent French as her ERA comrades came in to plan tactics with her. Ann Lou couldn't help but think how extraordinary her family was. Their differences had created hardships for them on Earth, yet they all had managed to turn those around and use them as strengths on their host planets. An overwhelming feeling of love erupted in her heart, and she thought of Henrietta and Knitsy. They would be so proud of them all. The feelings of guilt that Ann Lou had built up over the seven years were now just a faint memory. She was proud to have shared her mother's name.

CHAPTER 18

An Epiton and Earth Wedding

Several weeks later, everyone awoke in the dormitories, full of excitement. Today was the day that Ann Lou and Apollo would marry. Ann Lou had no idea what the Epitonian traditions were, so she was exhilarated at the thought of a mashup wedding.

Hoping to maintain a sense of Earth tradition, Ann Lou wanted to make sure she dressed in white. She remembered watching Knitsy's memories in the Time Belt and seeing images of both her and her mother on their wedding days. She wanted to capture that same essence for her own day. Elbina gave Ann Lou some of her jewelry to wear and did her makeup, something she had never worn in her life. Elbina also fashioned a dress out of some white sheets from the dormitory supply room and embellished it with lacy paper flowers made from the pages of one of Luna's books. Ann Lou looked and felt like a princess, something she had never experienced before.

Her siblings walked her to the exit of the old building in which they had been staying. The wedding ceremony was to be held outside. They were quite nervous to brave the outdoors on Harvinth, knowing how hungry and thirsty they would get. Elbina sensed their hesitation and assured them.

"This is why I forced you all to have such a big breakfast. It should hold you over for as long as the ceremony lasts, but you are to march straight back here once it's over, understood?" The rest of the siblings nodded in confirmation.

"Good," continued Elbina. "Now, I've collected flowers for you to hold while walking into the ceremony." She handed out exotic-looking flowers with purple stems and the strangest leaves—some square-shaped and yellow, some triangular and blue, and others with pentagonal green leaves that glowed pink.

"Do not, I repeat, do *not* eat these," Elbina warned sternly. "Right, Riff? Right, Luna?"

"Pretty sure I will avoid them at all costs," signed Riff, holding his stomach at the mere thought of their Planetary Diagnostic Test. He waved a hand so she wouldn't give him any flowers to hold.

"Don't worry, I learned my lesson," said Luna.

Music began to play outside, composed by the GeoLads and a small group of Olfinderians. Riff peeked out of the main doors to see Matt and Joe strumming on guitars that they had fashioned during their brief time on Harvinth and three Olfinderians humming around them. Matt and Joe were trying their best not to fall asleep as they strummed along with the hypnotic sounds of the Olfinderians until they figured out the solution was to play louder and drown out the enchanting tones. Riff could also see a crowd of intergalactic beasts seated outside and ready for the wedding to begin.

"That's our cue," said Elbina, giving Luna her elbow. "We're off now, Ann Lou. You look stunning. Mum and Nan would be so thrilled for you." The sisters smiled and hugged one another, and Ann Lou's brides-maids headed out the door, walking to the rhythm of the song.

"Ready?" whispered Riff, holding his arm around her waist while her right hand held the poisonous flowers.

Ann Lou smiled at her brother and signed back, "Ready as Knitsy is to kick me in the arse." Riff laughed. Ann Lou noted how neatly he had cleaned up for her wedding. He had taken off his cap and formed his matted red hair so that it was neatly curled behind his ears and coiffed over on top. He had fashioned a bowtie out of the remaining pages of Luna's book. Ann Lou rested her head on his shoulder, and he led her out of the building and into the environment of Harvinth.

The music and singing grew louder as they walked outside. All the wonderful intergalactic beasts that had been recruited for the ERA army stood up and smiled as she walked down the aisle with Riff. Her translation picked up a few of the Ciptons saying, "That's the Pyroll legend!" and a small crowd of Epitonians muttering, "Who'd have thought Apollo could land an Earthling like her?" Ann Lou laughed as she walked down the aisle. Hayden smiled his bright, flashy smile at her from the front row, and her sisters beamed at the end of the aisle.

Ann Lou nearly teared up when she saw Apollo, Fintan, and Egan, who had donned bowties exactly like the one Riff was wearing. She was sure that Knitsy was having a coughing fit from somewhere in the universe at the sight of this and that her mother would be telling her to hush up and look at how beautiful and lucky she is to have family, friends, and a loved one from her great adventure.

Riff hugged Ann Lou tightly at the end of the aisle and blew his nose in a handkerchief as he took his seat next to Hayden. Avaira slithered forward between Ann Lou and Apollo. She cleared her croaky old throat.

"We are gathered here todaaay," she boomed, "to witness the union of Apooollo of the House of Aithne and Ann Looou McHubbard." Ann Lou could see Fintan and Egan whispering to each other, pointing at her as they realised that her name was not actually Henrietta. The ears of everyone in the audience were plugged from Avaira's booming voice, except for those of the Antympanicans.

"Love is laaarger than the limits of how you speak, live, and look. Aaall of us here come from different places, near and far, frightening and peaceful, ancient and neeew. One of the few similarities that we share as a group is that we aaall have beating hearts. Hearts that caaare and looove. We are lucky to have a couple in front of us today who test the boundaries of looove and prove that it still reigns strooong, regardless of our diiifferences. Apooollo and Ann Looou, may the love in your hearts be as fiiiery as the Pyroll that brought your two souls together."

A few sniffles sounded from the audience.

"And nooow the rings, please."

Jung-hoon stepped forward from the audience, handing Apollo and Ann Lou gold-banded rings, each with a small bubble of fire set where a diamond would normally be.

"Made these myself," whispered Jung-hoon to Ann Lou. His eyes shone with a thin, glassy wall of tears. He then blinked toward Apollo. "Don't drop this in the lava pool."

The couple proceeded to place the rings on one another's fingers. Ann Lou had to stuff Apollo's ring around his claw.

"Now before you kiss one another and officially become maaarried, I was told that a sort of teeest needs to be paaassed?" piped Avaira.

"Yes, it does!" chimed Egan, grabbing Fintan as they both stepped forward. They stepped in front of Avaira to explain the rules. Ann Lou hoped this would be quick since her stomach was starting to growl for something to eat.

"They have to play Pyroll together," started Egan.

Ann Lou's eyes gleamed with fierce competitiveness as she shot a broad smile at Apollo.

"But blindfolded."

Ann Lou's face fell immediately. Egan continued. "The happy couple must prove that they can successfully retrieve the Pyroll and light the torch while blinded and also while an opposing team plays against them—me and Fintan," he gestured. "This test of marriage proves whether or not the couple is ready to tackle all of life's challenges. If they fail, they cannot get married. Ready?"

Ann Lou glared at Apollo and punched him in his good arm. "You didn't tell me it was gonna be a test!"

Apollo laughed. "Relax, it'll be fun."

Just ahead of the ceremony, Ann Lou spotted the Pyroll arch with the torch and rope. Everyone quickly hustled to the arch, which was, indeed, towering above a massive drop, leading straight into a fire that the Epitonians had started at the bottom. Egan handed Ann Lou and Apollo each a blindfold.

"Where are your blindfolds?" she snarled at Egan.

"Why would we be wearing blindfolds? Fintan and I aren't getting married again," he responded in his usual menacing tone. He pranced away with a stupid smirk on his face.

Jung-hoon marched up to Ann Lou. "Don't forget this," he said with a smile, handing her the Pyroll stick.

"Thanks, Jung-hoon," she said, taking it from him and thinking of the first time he had given her the stick back on Epiton. She was happy to have her old friend back.

Apollo and Ann Lou positioned themselves around the circumference of the crater with everyone else in the ceremony audience crammed alongside them. The Ciptons were already vibrantly bouncing in place in anticipation of watching the best Pyroll players in the universe battle it out.

"So, how are we going to do this?" whispered Ann Lou to Apollo as they both applied their blindfolds.

"We just did it on Cipto a little while ago. Plus, we're way more agile than those two old blokes anyways," he answered.

"But we could at least see the Pyroll that time. And Egan and Fintan can see everything!"

"Trust me," said Apollo warmly, taking her left forearm in his claw.

"Ready?" shouted Fintan from across the crater. The audience fell silent. Ann Lou felt around with her stick for the start of the downward slope. She could feel Apollo's hand tighten around her forearm.

"Pyroll!" shouted an overly enthusiastic Cipton, which looked as though it was so excited it might just bounce right into the crater itself.

Ann Lou tried shaking off Apollo's hand so she could start making her way down the slope. Instead, she heard him grunt into a jump, then instantly felt herself being pulled straight down into the drop.

"Arghhh!" she screamed, flailing her limbs and Pyroll stick around in a desperate attempt to catch on something. She could feel some of the paper flowers flying off her dress as they fell into the depths of the hole. Apollo pulled Ann Lou around his shoulders and she gripped his neck so tightly that she was afraid she might choke him. He landed on the bottom of the drop, his knees bending to absorb the impact. Ann Lou was pulling his head backward to catch her fall, yet his landing was perfect. The crowd above went wild.

"Never . . . do that . . . again . . . or else . . . I want . . . a divorce," she wheezed while climbing off him.

Ann Lou took a step away from Apollo and tripped over something hot and round. It was the Pyroll. She began to dribble it with her stick, but the farther she went, the closer she was approaching to a searing heat directly ahead.

"Not there," she muttered, knowing that was where the fire was located. As she backed up and skirted to the right, she heard loud footsteps charging from behind her.

"Up here!" shouted Apollo. She batted the Pyroll toward the sound of his voice.

"Got it!" Apollo shouted. More screams of excitement erupted from the crowd.

Ann Lou began to feel around for the slope and finally found it after a head-butt with the wall. She raced upward, unsure where in the drop the three Epitonians were. Something started burning her right leg, and she reached down and ripped from her dress several paper flowers that had caught fire. She wished that Apollo had told her not to wear anything flammable for their wedding. Her stomach was also hurting from the hunger that seemed to increase exponentially with each second of exposure to the outside.

She heard grunts coming from the levels above and boos from the crowd. Apollo must have dropped the Pyroll. She continued racing upward, pushing herself so hard that her lungs felt as if they were on fire. She bumped into someone's back and slid under their legs in case they wouldn't move for her. Reflexively, she stuck her stick out over the ledge and felt the Pyroll meet the blade. It must have been passed to whomever she had just slid under. Guiding the Pyroll ahead of her, she dribbled as quickly as she could, hearing the footsteps gaining on her from behind.

"Apollo, where are you?" she screamed.

"Here!" He sounded directly across from her and slightly above. She smashed her stick into the Pyroll, and he seemed to catch it, judging from the cheers in the crowd. The couple raced out of the crater, Apollo holding the Pyroll tightly.

The crowd moved back in a wider circle concentric with the crater's circumference to allow the players more room. With his blindfold on, Apollo had no idea where to throw the Pyroll. He took a guess and threw it as high as he could. The Pyroll missed the torch by mere inches.

"Nooo!" shouted the overenthusiastic Cipton, who was nearly melting on the spot.

"Hurry so we can eat! I'm starving here!" Riff shouted, to the surprise of his sisters. He held his stomach in pain and eyed Elbina's flowers. Elbina tossed the flowers into the drop so he wouldn't be tempted.

The Pyroll arced back down into the drop and directly into Fintan's hands, and he came racing out of the crater and began to target the torch with his unblindfolded eyes. Ann Lou dove toward the sound of his footsteps and reached her stick out to trip him. The Pyroll flew out of his hands and rolled near Apollo and Egan. Egan dove for it and Apollo listened for his footsteps and jumped on his back before he could grab it. Apollo ripped the Pyroll out of Egan's hands.

"Apollo, throw it to me!" shouted Ann Lou, her stick ready to strike and her stomach ready to explode. The crowd fell quiet again.

"Coming for you now!" answered Apollo, following her voice.

Ann Lou took her chance at a swing in case the Pyroll hit in the exact place she was hoping for. She felt the ball of fire meet her stick as she followed through with her most powerful swing to date. Fintan jumped on her a millisecond too late. He managed to bring her crashing to the ground, but not before the Pyroll had separated from the stick. No one from the crowd made a single noise, not even a breath, until they saw the Pyroll land.

The cheers from the crowd indicated that Ann Lou and Apollo had beaten Fintan and Egan and were officially eligible to be married. They both ripped their blindfolds off and ran into an embrace. The crowd couldn't settle down from the excitement. Even Egan and Fintan were cheering along. Ann Lou's family raced to congratulate her. Avaira slithered forward and used her booming voice to recapture everyone's attention.

"Congraaatulaaations, Ann Looou and Apooollo! You may kiss your neeew spouse. I now pronounce you . . . maaarried!" she cried.

The crowd continued to scream for joy as the married couple kissed one another passionately. Antympanicans soared above them like doves.

Ann Lou was ripped away from the kiss by Riff, who grabbed her and the rest of their siblings to sprint inside the building to eat and drink something, anything, before they all began to slowly die untimely deaths on Harvinth.

Once inside, the celebration continued with more serenades from the Olfinderians and the GeoLads, joined now by Riff on the drums. Elbina had also prepared the wedding food by assembling dishes that looked and tasted exactly like the favourites from each planet. Once she was done with her culinary duties, Elbina and Hayden danced the entire night together, laughing and reminiscing about their childhoods. Ann Lou even managed to pull Luna up for a dance.

The rest of the evening was full of song, dance, family, friends, and a lot of love.

CHAPTER 19

A Glitch in Time

The next day, the recruited army was to report to Harvinth's ERA headquarters within the old building. Everyone shuffled down the stairs to a basement the size of an auditorium. Live video feeds from all the host planets displayed on gigantic screens within the auditorium.

A panel of ERA officials in green lab coats sat at the front of the auditorium. Within a few minutes, the auditorium was filled with beings from all the host planets, Earth, and some other planets that had recently been invaded by the GeoLapse. The mood in the auditorium was tense. No one knew exactly what was going to be asked of them. Ann Lou and Apollo sat quietly next to one another holding hands, their matching rings gleaming in the dimly lit room. Then Riff, who sat to her right, scowled at her.

"What is your problem?" Ann Lou barked at him.

"You've been married twice before twenty and I still can't get a girl to talk to me at twenty-three." He shook his head and put on a fake, moping face. Ann Lou smiled and punched him in the shoulder.

"Attention all," announced Jung-hoon, raising a hand to quiet the crowd. "Thank you for being here. I understand all of you were involuntarily recruited to be in our army to fight the GeoLapse, so I sincerely apologise for the agony that your families must be feeling and the pain you have been caused. But you all will go down in history as the heroes of Universal War 480,394,899,306."

The McHubbards raised their eyebrows. A universal war was apparently a common occurrence.

Jung-hoon continued. "We'd like to give you an overview of the plan to be executed, which will be going into effect tomorrow morning."

Ann Lou and Apollo looked at one another in fear. They had been so busy thinking about the wedding that they hadn't realised that their time together on Harvinth was nearly at its end.

"We now present the video, made for us by our fallen leader, that explains the plan of action." Jung-hoon sat down with his panel and a screen behind him began to play a video. It was Henrietta, sitting in the McHubbard family kitchen back on Earth. Her eyes were reddened but dry. The McHubbards all gasped in unison, trying to hold back tears.

"Hello, all—Epitonians, Ciptons, Olfinderians, Antympanicans, my fellow humans, and most importantly, my family. I'm filming this for you today, July second, 2220, on Earth. My children have just left on their buses to go to their new host planets. I have had to stay back because of unforeseen consequences of our previous plan.

"So, I'm sure it is now over seven years into the future on Harvinth, right before we are to send the army back to take down the GeoLapse. Everyone currently on Harvinth will board a Jalopy and travel to Earth together so there is only one pass-through at the Time Belt. The Jalopy will then travel to the various deployment locations, ending at the White

House in Washington, D.C. on January twenty-first, 2213, which is President Murphy's swearing-in date. Remember, this date is about seven and a half years since the colonisation of Harvinth in early July 2220.

"Hayden Murphy, you will once again take your place as the President of the United States of America. Ensure that the other President Murphy returns to ERA headquarters in the White House immediately after he is sworn in so that you can step in and take his place. When you attend the first Universal Union meeting, you will alert them of the plan in place.

"GeoLapse are situated on every continent that is inhabited at the time I speak: North America, Africa, Asia, and Europe. Therefore, you have been divided into four battalions, each with equal proportions of the various populations. Each battalion will be taken to the secret GeoLapse headquarters on its assigned continent. The number of GeoLapse at these locations will be very small compared to what they are today, when I speak to you, but we still need a universal effort in order to succeed.

"The GeoLapse have a history of exposing humans to the outside environment as a means of killing them. So, humans, you will require special uniforms to allow you to withstand the environmental conditions. I am hoping the ERA on Harvinth will have finished development of suits for the human army to use. If my understanding of the environments of the other host planets are correct, the rest of you all can safely manoeuvre Earth's outside environment without special protection.

"I wish you all the best on this heroic effort. If we do not succeed, the plan will be iterated until we do, but that will be under the rule of a different head of ERA, I am afraid. Thank you all for your efforts and your loyalty to the Earth. We are forever in your debt. Oh, and if my children and mum are there, I love you all so much."

The camera flashed to a blank screen. The crowd remained quiet and the McHubbards' mouths were all agape. Luna signed to Riff, "Mum basically said that—" but Riff waved her off and signed back, "Remember, I can lip read."

Luna nodded her head, her eyes quickly averting from Riff back to the now blank screen. None of the siblings had expected to see old footage of their mother.

"So now," started Jung-hoon, standing up again, "you will each come up here, and we will inform you of which continent you've been placed on. Pack your things tonight and we will all leave via Jalopy in the morning."

Jung-hoon sat back down, and the crowd began to form a line.

Later that evening, the McHubbards and Hayden sat together on adjacent bunks to discuss where they'd been assigned for deployment.

"Of course we've all been separated again. What're the odds?" sighed Elbina, falling back on the bed with her arms extended.

"At least we're all with some familiar faces we've been living with for seven years," said Ann Lou, trying to remain hopeful.

"Not me!" whined Elbina, flailing her arms. "My hosts were single-celled organisms! But at least I can keep Hayden in his place before he goes all power hungry from the election results." She smiled at him, and he smiled back.

"I'll vote for you, man," signed Riff, clapping Hayden on the back. Ann Lou translated for him.

"You can't. Besides, I'll already be sworn in by the time we arrive," Hayden responded.

"Well, he certainly wasn't voted in for his sense of humour," signed Riff, looking at his sisters. Ann Lou decided against translating that one.

Luna sat on her bunk with her palms covering her face.

"What's wrong, Luna?" asked Ann Lou, patting her leg.

"Nothing," she responded curtly. "I'm just . . . erm . . . nervous is all."

Luna wasn't generally one to showcase her nerves, but Ann Lou decided not to probe. She had a feeling there was something else on Luna's mind.

"Where's Apollo going?" asked Hayden, trying not to sound too interested in the answer.

"He'll be coming with me to Mount Cameroon in Africa," answered Ann Lou, embarrassed to look directly at Hayden.

"Ann Lou, you are one lucky duck!" signed Riff, clapping Hayden on the back again.

"You need to get married so you can get placed with your person," she bantered with a shrug.

"I thought family came first over scary husbands," he jested back. Ann Lou threw a pillow at him with a laugh.

The next morning, the ERA and their recruited army boarded the boat Jalopy. Everyone eagerly watched the view as the Jalopy rose above the barren desert of Harvinth and sped off. Elbina clung to the glass longer than anyone else, watching her home of seven years disappear into a cluster of stars in the galaxy. The mood in the Jalopy was jovial despite the looming events. Pyrolls were being tossed around, and laughter, singing, dancing, and conversations in many different tongues could be heard. No one really noticed the lengthy journey that they had endured by the time a familiar light came into view.

Most of the passengers felt the Time Belt's warm, peaceful light before they saw it. The blanket of light enveloped them, its warmth producing a strong tranquility in their midst. Each of them remembered the sensation from their trip to Harvinth and instantly knew what was happening. White light from all directions filled the space of the Jalopy until they all were, again, floating in free space, not one of them feeling even a twinge of nerves thanks to the support of the light blanket. The entire army faced one another in one large circle while the images of their lives surrounded them like film reels going through hundreds of images per second. Their senses were activated as they relived memories.

"Shortest friend of time . . ." boomed the omnipresent voice. "You are requested to choose one event in your experience of time to experience again in your future."

A baby Cipton rose higher from the group, still rotating in free space. No one could see what the Cipton could see, since there were no visual memories, but the baby was squealing with joy from its recollection of its few memories. The blinding light shone through the baby, making it nearly invisible. The baby smiled happily, clearly having chosen a memory from its inventory.

"More stories from Avaira!" it squeaked giddily.

"Your event will be granted in due time," rumbled the voice, filling everyone's ears and bodies with a shiver.

The black hole didn't appear this time. Instead, the baby Cipton and the rest of the army began to fall as if the light blanket had been torn from beneath them. There was nothing except darkness around them now, nothing to grab onto to save themselves. Fear reverberated into their bodies. Then, as quickly as they had entered the Time Belt, they exited and crashed into the floor of the Jalopy. The McHubbards looked around to see the baby from Cipto being held by its mother.

"That was a great memory to choose, darling," said the mother, squashing her baby with a hug. Avaira even slithered over to thank the baby for thinking of her.

"I wish Nan had just chosen to swap out those cabbaged eggs for some chips," remarked Riff.

The joviality resumed and continued the entire rest of the way to Earth. Once the McHubbards saw their home planet, they felt a sense of bittersweet excitement. As they drew closer to the planet, they were looking into the past. Somewhere on the planet existed younger versions of themselves.

The humans started suiting up as the Jalopy hurtled toward land. The first stop was Dikson, Russia. Luna, all geared up, said goodbye to her siblings. She looked as if she were about to cry, but it could have just been the haze in her eyes.

"Luna, you'll do great there," said Elbina. "It's nearly dark here all winter, so this will be just like Cipto. You'll be amazing."

"I never got to show you the books I wrote about us," said Luna solemnly. "I wrote you stories."

Elbina hugged her sister. "I'll read them someday. This is just a 'see you later,' sis."

Luna sighed, not wanting to say anymore. She embraced the rest of her siblings and walked to the exit of the Jalopy to join her battalion. Her siblings watched as she secured her green bodysuit and shielded face mask and adjusted her aluminum gloves and shoes to fit snugly. With one last wave, she walked down the ramp of the Jalopy and was out of sight into winter's darkness.

DIKSON, RUSSIA

Luna could have spent the entirety of her time in Dikson without realising it was dark. Everywhere she went was a nighttime of sorts, although she couldn't imagine life any other way. She still had to navigate the same way she'd navigate anywhere.

She could feel the rough and stony ground under the flimsy soles of her aluminum shoes. The fact that she was actually back on Earth kept popping into her head, filling her with a mix of hope for Earth's future and fear that the plan might fail. The addition of sneaking around hiding from a powerful universal terrorist group didn't settle her mind any. She decided to stay close to some Ciptons that she heard slithering in front of her.

She could hear the squeal of feedback coming into her head from her microchip translation. The entire battalion could talk and listen to one another even if they weren't in direct earshot. The leader of their battalion was a Cipton, and its sweet and squeaky voice was starting to come in behind a layer of white noise.

"Hello, Team Dikson! I am your battalion leader, Iris. I have word from the ERA that the Asian GeoLapse headquarters are located in one of the abandoned ships at the port that is northwest of the city. Please carefully make your way to that area. I'm told it's dark outside, so as long as we keep quiet, the GeoLapse won't be aware of our arrival. Now, here is the plan of action."

As Iris quietly squawked away reviewing the plan, Luna maintained her focus on the slithering sounds in front of her and continued to follow them. The battalion was very quiet as they approached the GeoLapse headquarters. Luna could only hear faint footsteps and the sounds of wings expanding into parachutes, but she was sure it wasn't quite loud enough for the GeoLapse to recognise anything coming their way.

Once they arrived, she felt the ground beneath her change into what felt like sand. Her feet no longer had sharp stones pushing up on them, and the surface felt much more comfortable. Iris rang in her ears again.

"Olfinderians, please begin!"

Luna knew she had to stand quite far back from the Olfinderians in order to not be in the trance zone. Even the time she had listened to the chorale from a safe distance back on Olfinder, she had still been affected by the musical enchantment. Though the Olfinderians' tiny paw-steps were nearly muted by the sand, she could hear them running quite far ahead so that they could surround the beached ship. She stepped backward about fifty steps and heard them start to sing with a low humming frequency. The GeoLapse on the ship would start to feel dizzy from the music, but since there weren't nearly as many Olfinderians in this battalion as there had been in the chorale, they wouldn't be put into a complete trance.

In the distance, Luna could hear the sounds of footsteps clanging on metal. She imagined GeoLapse running onto the deck of the ship trying to find where the disturbance was coming from. Her hypothesis was confirmed when she heard a gruff voice say in a language she had never heard, "What is that noise?"

"Keep it up, Olfinderians!" whispered Iris, "but make sure they don't see you. Ciptons, Antympanicans, and humans, move in!"

Luna heard the Olfinderians' paws retreating to the port side of the ship so that the GeoLapse at the bow wouldn't see them. She followed the slithers up to the side of the ship, which the Ciptons easily scaled. The idea was for them to sneak around the ship's small spaces to take out unarmed GeoLapse. Luna placed her hand against the rusty hull of the ship and waited for someone from Antympanica to locate her. One came soaring up to her, offering her its back, which she timidly mounted. It leaped high into the air at an incredible speed and extended its wings. She could hear other sets of wings extending into parachutes around her.

"Landing you starboard stern," fluttered the Antympanican as they slowly descended.

When Luna's feet were firmly in contact with the deck, she quickly found a wall and flattened her back against it in case anyone was looking. She heard a slithering coming from directly behind her and felt her arm around for an opening. An open porthole was directly to her left, and she climbed in and found herself bumping into something squishy.

"Luna!" Lucy the Cipton shrieked with excitement. "I'm so glad you're here!"

"Shh!" Luna hushed. "Let me help you. Where are you going?"

"There's a pipe over here that I'm going to use to get into the lower deck. You should fit. Come with me."

Lucy entered the pipe first. Then Luna manoeuvred her long, thin body in. She held onto what she could grasp on Lucy's body, and Lucy pulled her through. After several twists and turns, they reached the end of the pipe, where Luna was able to clumsily pull herself out and onto solid ground.

"Intruder!" shouted a deep voice across the echoing room in Russian.

They had been caught. Luna instinctively put up her fists, which were only slightly more threatening than Lucy's squishy body. She braced herself against a wall but had no idea where to punch or kick. Lucy fell into a slimy puddle in front of her, causing the attacking GeoLapse to trip over her and fall flat on his face. Lucy proceeded to burrow out from beneath their would-be attacker and form the shape of a blanket over his head to keep him disoriented.

"Epitonians, move in, please!" ordered Iris nicely.

Luna hopped onto the fallen GeoLapse and restrained his legs. She could hear other GeoLapse running in for backup. Still holding down the GeoLapse, she kicked a leg out behind her, hitting one of the other GeoLapse directly in the nose and another in the head. They fell over and did not get up. Luna stood up to feel around for an object to use as a weapon. The GeoLapse on the floor next to her had a baton, which she swiped and held out in front of her. As she felt her way out of the room, she bumped headfirst into one of the Epitonians.

"Sorry!" she exclaimed, moving out of its way as it growled at her.

Iris spoke again. The static noise was increasing. "Humans, head to the bow. We need backup, please."

Luna followed the now chaotic cacophony that was sounding from the bow area. She heard wings flapping about and the receding screams of GeoLapse who were probably being flown away to be dropped off some high cliff. There were Epitonians huffing as they grabbed one GeoLapse with each claw, cracked their heads together, and hurled them off the ship. Luna had no idea where to go but was immediately struck in the shoulder, forcing her to the ground. She rolled to the side and swung her legs around, tripping the attacking GeoLapse and whacking him with the stolen baton to keep him down. Luna was then thrown to the side and pinned up against the rails of the ship. There were many hands on her, and she couldn't move any of her limbs, let alone the baton she was still squeezing in her right hand. The GeoLapse ripped the baton out of her hands and punched her in the face, right against her mask. The blow impacted her nose, and she could taste the blood dripping down into her mouth. Her attackers then lifted her up and heaved her over the railing.

She fell without screaming. It felt as if she was falling in slow motion. Her arms and legs floated upward. She was hyperaware of what was happening to her body; her head was throbbing, her stomach ached, and the iron from the blood in her mouth dried her throat.

She was caught by a soaring Antympanican, who parachuted her to the sand and then quickly soared away. She slowly sat to a seated position and touched her face mask, noticing that her face didn't feel bruised. It was as if the pain had magically dissipated midair. Confused, she stood up and called for Iris.

"Iris, this is Luna. Are you there?"

No response. The feedback was all noise. Then she heard a loose GeoLapse run past, followed by the quick footsteps of an approaching Epitonian.

"Hey!" she screamed in its direction. "Can you help me? I've lost signal!"

But the Epitonian continued running as if he hadn't heard her. She continued screaming for help, even hopping within the field of view of another GeoLapse, who also didn't acknowledge her presence.

Luna shakily lifted her hands to her face and carefully slipped off her mask, exposing her to Earth's deadly atmosphere. But nothing happened. She had anticipated this happening and hoped she wasn't right but of course, she was. Her fears had come true.

No one could see her.

PRAGUE, CZECH REPUBLIC

Riff, Matt, and Joe exited the Jalopy with their battalion at the European GeoLapse headquarters. Riff couldn't hear anything coming through the translation, so he decided to stay on Matt and Joe's heels.

Riff trailed his friends around the empty city, wondering what life there had been like in its prime. Back in school, he'd read that Prague was well known for its music. Concerts used to be held in castles, and chamber ensembles would dress in Mozart's classical garb. He wished he could have experienced it firsthand. They passed gargantuan castles and walked up and down many steep steps. There was even a wall of one building with beautiful graffiti poking out from behind a thick layer of dust. They arrived at the Old Town city centre, which was quite compact with tall buildings. Riff saw an old clock on one side of a building and walked over to it. It had many strange dials and faded colours. He also noticed that the hands of the clock were missing. It was strange but a beautiful paradox, looking as if it were frozen in time.

Suddenly Riff felt himself being pulled backward by Matt, followed by an explosion several metres away from the clock. Riff saw many dark-clothed individuals popping out from behind buildings and running toward their battalion. The Epitonians in the group immediately began to fight back. The smaller creatures darted to a safer location. Antympanicans offered their backs to the slow-running humans and Ciptons. Riff, Matt, and Joe each propelled themselves midrun onto the back of an Antympanican and soared into the air, hopping over the tops of the tallest structures in Prague. Riff could see dots of GeoLapse emerging from their hiding places around the city. The Antympanican–human duos lunged into the tight spaces between buildings, only to soar immediately back into the sky. They landed on the grounds of a castle, and Riff felt the ground start to rumble.

"Run!" he shouted. A few moments later, the GeoLapse filled the grounds with their own army. Riff sought safety by running to the edge of the grounds and seeking out a flight of stairs that would take him to the top of one of the castles. His heart pounded as he raced up flight after flight, the blood rushing out of his head and his vision becoming blurry. He saw a window up the next flight of stairs that was pouring light in the corridor. He decided to stop and rest to see what was transpiring outside.

What he saw was a bloodbath. Epitonians bashed through crowds of GeoLapse, taking out three or more at a time. Antympanicans soared in and out of the grounds to perform dive attacks. There were even Olfinderians stationed along the castle walls singing their enchanting song to put the GeoLapse in a dizzy trance.

Then Riff caught sight of Matt and Joe being cornered by a crowd of GeoLapse. Several Ciptons stood in their way to bounce off any attacks, but they were quickly outnumbered with the number of GeoLapse closing in on them all.

Riff puffed out his chest and released a deep exhalation. He continued to the top of the castle, emerging from the topmost ledge. Out of the periphery of his vision, he noticed that something was behind him, and he swerved. A GeoLapse had followed him up the castle steps and was swinging a baton toward his face. Riff heaved himself toward the GeoLapse but was struck in the face with the baton. The mask he had on protected him from the environment, but it wasn't of much use as a defence accessory. Riff was knocked off his feet and over the ledge. His fingertips caught the ledge and he peered around to the sides of him to see if anyone or anything could catch him. He grimaced from the pain in his skull and the weight of his entire body pulling downward on his fingers.

Riff looked up to see the GeoLapse poised to strike him with a baton. Just before the baton would have cracked against his head, he let go of the ledge, falling along the fortress wall. Tony caught him and soared up into the air.

"Go to that corner, now!" Riff signed to his saviour.

"I got ya, Griffin McHubbard!" replied Tony by quivering his wing midair.

The duo began to streamline into a dive to save his friends. They accelerated closer to the attacking GeoLapse, who now had pinned Matt and Joe up against the castle wall. As Tony swooped within a few feet of the wall, Riff jumped directly onto the GeoLapse's backs, distracting them and unpinning his friends. Riff threw as many punches and kicks as he could at the attackers, but he was not prepared for the explosion. Riff flew feet into the air, yet somehow he managed to land softly on his back. When he sat up and looked around, he saw that he was surrounded by a flurry of Antympanicans who had perished in the explosion. Their wings were still extended into parachutes. They had saved Riff at the last moment before the explosion and flown him to safety.

"No!" he screamed, first scooping up Tony and holding him close to his chest, and then gathering the rest of them up in his arms. Riff began to run in a random direction. He didn't know where to go; he just wanted to get their bodies away from the clutches of the GeoLapse. He ran as fast as he could, blood pumping so hard that his eyes bulged with each pulsation. He could only feel his heart thudding. Finally, he found a building to crouch behind. The Antympanicans in his arms each had their three eyes peacefully closed. Riff wrapped them each in their own wings so they could stay comfortable, wherever Antympanicans go after they die. Still carrying them, he ran around another corner and found a much taller and thinner castle, which he began running toward.

Soon he noticed someone chasing him. Glancing back over his shoulder, he was relieved to see Matt and Joe sprinting toward him.

"You okay, man?" asked Matt.

Riff didn't even know he was crying. He was trembling as he held Tony and his hosts in his arms. Matt and Joe looked at one another, then took some of the comfortably wrapped Antympanicans from Riff's arms.

"Come on," ordered Joe, leading the way.

They made their way into the tall castle and up the steps to the topmost landing. There, they knelt and gently placed the fallen Antympanicans next to one another.

"They'll feel like they're always ready to soar," said Matt sweetly, tears also filling his eyes. Joe nodded in agreement.

The GeoLads embraced in a huddle and had a moment of silence in front of their fallen friends.

After a few moments, Riff gestured back toward the castle where the main battle was still unfolding.

Matt and Joe didn't look at him, only at each other.

"Shall we go?" Matt asked Joe. Joe nodded, and the two stood up and silently left the landing.

Riff followed them out, unsure why they were ignoring him. He shouted their names, but they continued to ignore him. He even ran in front of them and waved his arms, but they still walked on as if he were a ghost. Riff screamed as loud as he could, knowing he could be drawing attention to the GeoLapse in the neighbouring grounds, but no one emerged to attack him or his friends who were sprinting away from him.

No one could hear him.

MOUNT CAMEROON, CAMEROON

The Jalopy flew to the west coast of Africa to drop off the third battalion. Apollo was elected to lead this battalion into the attack on the African GeoLapse headquarters.

When the Epitonians noticed that Mount Cameroon was an active volcano, they seemed excited and appeared to forget that there was a task at hand. Ann Lou even had to remind their leader.

"Excuse me," she snapped her fingers in front of his face. "We need to focus."

Apollo shook his head and came back to his senses. "Everyone get in your positions, immediately!" His voice sounded menacing and stern, just like a true Epitonian.

The Epitonians took the lead, running ahead to scale the volcano. Ann Lou wondered if they thought this was just going to be like a game of Pyroll. Antympanicans soared overhead, gathering an overhead view of what was awaiting them. The reports from the Antympanicans started swarming into Ann Lou's head.

"They're everywhere outside the perimeter of the volcano," said a gruff voice. "There's no downward spiral like the volcanoes in Pyroll, though. Just goes straight down into the lava pool. The GeoLapse are all just at the top."

"Easy," huffed Apollo, still running across the barren ground. "Antympanicans, I want you to fly the Olfinderians around the top of the volcano so they can sing as close as possible. Try not to get too close for the GeoLapse to attack."

"On our way," replied the Antympanican.

Straight away, the Antympanicans zoomed from their positions above the volcano back to the running battalion, snatching the Olfinderians as they galloped. Ann Lou could see their springy tails wagging in anticipation for their time to sing. It was enchanting to watch, even from so far below. The Olfinderians' frequencies reached the ears of everyone on the ground, putting them slightly in a daze, but not tranquilising them.

The Ciptons slithered up the volcano with ease, although much slower than the Epiton climbers, who hopped up the volcano with great speed and agility. It had been a while since Ann Lou had scaled a volcano, so she struggled to grip her first few rock holds while also holding her Pyroll stick. She took a few deep breaths and tried again, this time holding her stick between her teeth and focusing on more sturdy rocks to grab.

Once at the top, after taking a few seconds to catch her breath, Ann Lou saw many GeoLapse running around trying to fight the singing dogs in the sky, but they were so dizzy that they ended up falling over themselves. The Ciptons helped trip the ones who needed a little extra push by flattening just in front of their next footsteps.

Ann Lou also saw Fintan and Egan each dangling two GeoLapse above the lava pool at the top of the crater. She looked away so she wouldn't have to see the result. Apollo was running around shouting orders such as "Louder, Olfinderians!" "Closer, Antympanicans!" and "Ciptons, keep tripping!" Ann Lou was impressed with how well the operation was being handled.

She noticed an Olfinderian that had been snagged in midair by a GeoLapse. It was being stretched between the pull of both the GeoLapse and the Antympanican holding it, and the Olfinderian's song had turned into a desperate cry. She sped over and thwacked the GeoLapse on the head with her stick, knocking him completely unconscious.

"Tell everyone to fly higher! We need to keep you all safe!" Ann Lou ordered the Antympanican who had regained possession of the relieved Olfinderian. It nodded to her and flew higher.

Ann Lou heard pounding footsteps and whipped around to see GeoLapse running toward her from multiple angles. She backed up, holding her stick out in front of her for defence. They approached as a wall-like unit that only became denser the closer they came. She stumbled on something behind her and noticed it was the rim of the crater. She had nowhere to go but down into the fiery pit.

The GeoLapse had their arms outstretched to push her, and they were just inches away when something large grabbed two of the attackers and tossed them down into the pit. Apollo was now trying to take on the rest of her attackers. She swung her stick at one that was coming at Apollo from behind. Working as a team, they cleared what they thought was the entire attacking group, but Ann Lou was almost immediately whacked on the head by yet another GeoLapse and found herself falling down into the depths of the lava pool. Apollo didn't even notice as he was too busy fending off more GeoLapse. As Ann Lou fell, she closed her eyes and accepted that this would be her end.

When she opened her eyes for one last look at the light above, she saw something diving at her full speed. Fintan grasped her as they both continued to fall. He shouted, "Save her!" and pushed her with all his might toward the light above, slowing the speed of her fall just enough for a soaring Antympanican to catch her. She was rocketed back up toward the crater but watched in horror as her dear friend Fintan fell to his death in the depths of the lava pool below.

"Nooo!" she screamed, reaching out as if she could grab him. "No no no!" She watched, sobbing, as other members of the battalion were tossed over the edge by the GeoLapse and plummeted to their deaths.

She couldn't continue. There was no energy left in her body. Her head was throbbing, and her teammate had just sacrificed himself to save her life. Precious lives were being lost everywhere she looked. All she wanted was her mother.

The Antympanican held her and flew around gently for a while, noticing how unstable she was. Part of her just wanted to jump off, but she knew she'd be immediately saved again.

When Ann Lou dared to look down, she noticed that there were fewer GeoLapse at the top of the volcano. The battalion was winning, and her mother's plan was working. She thought of her other siblings and hoped that they were okay.

Once it was safe to do so, the Antympanican flew her to Apollo, who was barking final orders to some Ciptons as they finished off the last GeoLapse at the headquarters.

She thanked her saviour and ran up to Apollo to jump into an emotional embrace. He knelt down to her level to ask if she was all right. Her eyes were puffy from crying, her head was aching from where she had gotten hit by the GeoLapse, and she was trembling so violently that she could barely stand up straight. He held her hands, telling her that everything was almost over, and that she had battled heroically.

"B—but Fintan," she sobbed. "He's gone."

"We lost a lot of heroes today. He, especially, will not be forgotten," Apollo said solemnly. "I owe him everything for saving you."

Ann Lou sobbed as she noticed Egan sitting alone on the edge of the crater, his head dangling low.

When Ann Lou reached to embrace Apollo again, her arm went straight through him.

"What?" she cried, waving her arm, trying to touch him.

But Apollo just looked as if he had forgotten something. He walked over to the Ciptons to praise them. Ann Lou followed him, trying to grasp his shoulder or hand, or anything she could grip as he swaggered toward them in celebration.

"Apollo . . . Apollo!" she screamed. But he didn't address her.

She leapt toward him, hoping to grab his stomach, but she landed on the ground face first, not having even felt him as she fell onto the hot and rocky ground. He continued walking away.

No one could touch her.

WASHINGTON, D.C., UNITED STATES OF AMERICA

On January 21, 2213, the Jalopy's final stop was at the White House to drop off Hayden, Elbina, and the rest of the ERA. Once safely inside, the ERA made their way to the recently inaugurated President Murphy's dormitory to allow the new President Murphy to step in. They walked in the dormitory to find him pouring some orange goo into a cup of coffee at his desk.

"Hello!" he said enthusiastically upon seeing the ERA barging in. He locked eyes with the other Hayden Murphy standing amongst the ERA. "Oh?" he added. "Is—is there a new plan?" he asked with a half-smile.

"Yes," responded Elbina. "You've done wonderfully. Come with us and this President Murphy will now step in."

The old President Murphy stood up as if he knew the drill, grabbed his coffee, and obediently strolled out with the ERA. New President Murphy stepped into his new living quarters.

Hayden thought it was funny that he had supposedly spent so much time in this dormitory yet remembered nothing at all about it. It scared him that he had such a great responsibility on his shoulders, but it comforted him to know he had already succeeded once before.

Hayden sat at his desk and noticed a piece of paper lying on a silver tray. It read:

Thursday 21 January 2213
5:00 p.m. Inauguration Ceremony
7:00 p.m. Dinner with the Universal Union in Danforth Commons

It was a light schedule, and luckily, the Inauguration Ceremony had already been completed by the old President Murphy. All Hayden needed to do for today was meet with the Universal Union and review the new plan. He practiced reciting what he was supposed to tell them.

"A future universal army is in a war with the GeoLapse at this very moment. We need your help to eradicate the past GeoLapse, which is actually the current GeoLapse." He decided to run through his speech a few more times.

* * *

Elbina and the remainder of the ERA relocated to the ERA headquarters within the White House to reveal themselves to the old ERA and let them know that the new plan was officially in action. After a few stares from members seeing their own doubles, the old ERA obliged and allowed use of the cameras to verify the status of the battles against the GeoLapse taking place around the world.

"Camera one on Dikson, two on Prague, and three on Mount Cameroon, please," ordered Elbina sweetly but sternly. Once the cameras had settled on the scenes, she and other members of the ERA inspected what was happening.

"The Mount Cameroon battalion has nearly defeated the GeoLapse headquarters in Africa!" shouted Elbina, excited to see that her mother's plan was working.

"It appears that Dikson and Prague may need some backup," remarked Jung-hoon from over her shoulder. "I need someone to take the Jalopy to Mount Cameroon to bring some extra resources in for the two remaining battalions in action."

"On it, sir, we'll go," replied one mousy man, who was followed out by his double and a horde of other ERA to assist him on the journey.

"Excellent. Now we just have to deal with the D.C. area," continued Jung-hoon.

He walked away to discuss ERA tactics with some other members across the room. Elbina took this opportunity to look at her siblings' locations in more detail. She zoomed in and out of different parts of the battles to find them. She located Luna hopping through a porthole, Riff running up the stairs of a castle, and Ann Lou using her Pyroll stick to save an Olfinderian. She sighed with relief and smiled broadly, proud of their heroism. Her smile quickly faded, though, when she saw each of her siblings glitching on the video. They would disappear for a few seconds and then reappear. Maybe it was just electrical interference.

"Elbina, come look at this," called Jung-hoon. Elbina quickly forgot about the glitches and went over to where she was beckoned.

Jung-hoon was studying a live video feed of the outside of the White House. When Elbina looked closely at it, she saw a dark mass moving toward the White House. It almost looked like a wave was slowly approaching from all directions, about to crash into it.

"What is that?" she asked Jung-hoon.

"GeoLapse. They're coming now. Their largest headquarters are in this city. I'm afraid we don't stand a chance." The dread in his voice was severe. Jung-hoon slid down to the floor in defeat.

"I have an idea. I think we have a chance," Elbina said softly. She began to run out of ERA headquarters when Jung-hoon called after her again.

"Elbina!" he shouted, extending an arm.

Elbina wheeled around on her heel. "Yes, Jung-hoon?"

"I—I . . . I'm really proud of you," he said, smiling gently.

Elbina wore a confused look on her face but accepted the compliment and continued out of ERA headquarters, headed straight for Hayden's dormitory. She hurled the door open as Hayden was buttoning his jacket for the Universal Union meeting. She instantly blushed upon seeing him and was at a loss for words.

"Elbs!" Hayden cried happily, jogging up to her and planting a kiss on her lips.

Elbina soaked in this moment that she had dreamed of since she was a young teenager. She kissed him back passionately. After losing herself for a few seconds, she pulled back and tried to focus on the urgent business that had brought her there.

"We need the Universal Union. The GeoLapse are coming right now to destroy the ERA headquarters," she said, taking large breaths.

Hayden paused, his hands still around her waist. He slowly digested this piece of information. "Come to the meeting with me," he said.

The two walked to the Universal Union meeting together, hand in hand, and reached the outside of Danforth Commons. They paused before a set of doors with D-shaped brass handles. Elbina heard Hayden take a deep breath and pull both doors open. He flashed a bright smile and flicked his black curly locks away from his face.

Ahead of them was a room full of the most peculiar beasts either of them had ever seen. They had thought that the beasts they had come to know from the host planets were strange looking, but they looked nothing like the ones before them. There was a giant rock with one eye, a squirrely looking purple bean with three legs, and even a hairy giant that was shoving cakes into its mouth at a rapid pace. Many more beasts were arriving through the Jalopy Cabins on the side of the room.

Hayden and Elbina walked forward to a table with empty seats. The rock delegate began to speak.

"Welcome to the Universal Union, new delegate of Earth. I am your leader and the delegate from Rhothgo. I gather there are some issues about the state of the Earth that need to be addressed?"

Hayden froze, gripping his chair until his knuckles turned white. Suddenly the speech he had been practicing in his dormitory was nowhere to be found in his memory. He could only stare in fear. Elbina knew this was her moment to speak up.

"Hello. I am also a resident of Earth. I have come bearing a request from both President Murphy and the Earth Rehabilitation Association."

Rhothgo tightened his fists and furrowed his brow over his eye. "Go on," he said darkly.

Elbina gulped. "Long story short, we are currently at war with the GeoLapse, a terrorist group that is growing exponentially on Earth.

Their ultimate plan is to take over the Universal Union, and, well . . . they succeeded."

"What do you mean they succeeded?" asked the Minag delegate, sitting forward in its chair.

"We just crossed the Time Belt on our way back from Harvinth. We've seen the destruction in the universe that the GeoLapse has caused. We came back to attack them with an army—a stronger army. Essentially, we have an army made up of citizens of some of your own planets helping us."

There were gasps from the crowd and even screams from some of the delegates.

"What do you need from us now?" demanded the Rhothgan.

"The last of the GeoLapse are surrounding the White House as we speak," piped up Hayden, his hands still gripping the arms of his chair. "We need your resources. There are more than we anticipated."

The entire Universal Union turned their attention toward the Rhothgan, who sighed deeply and rolled his eye.

"We are here to serve the communities within the Universal Union. Tell us what you want us to do."

The ERA spent the next hour devising a plan with the Universal Union about how to attack the GeoLapse. The delegates from nearly one hundred planets positioned themselves around the White House. Many members of the ERA, including Elbina, and all the doubles from the previous linear time volunteered themselves for the final battle as well. The humans in the battalion suited up appropriately for exposure to the outside. Hayden grabbed a suit and began putting his legs into the green bodysuit.

"What are you doing?" shrieked Elbina. "You can't be in this. You know the plan. You need to stay hidden!"

"How can I just sit here doing nothing? And you know the plan too! What makes you any less important?"

"Because you're in power. People are looking up to you to save the Earth. No one knows who I am," she responded softly.

Hayden grew a solemn look on his face. "But . . . I do."

But Hayden knew she was right. He would've sounded hot-headed if he were to agree that he was better off hidden. Instead, he took off the suit, kissed Elbina deeply, and sought the safety of his dormitory before turning to Elbina one last time.

"Come find me as soon as it's done."

She smiled at him and held her hands to her heart.

The Washington, D.C., battalion quietly waited in their positions. They could hear a mass of thousands approaching from the outside. They just needed to wait until their attackers were close enough.

BOOM! Explosions came blasting through the front doors. The GeoLapse barreled through the doors yelling at the tops of their lungs, swinging batons, and holding grenades in their hands. In a matter of seconds, the White House was in utter chaos. The GeoLapse didn't expect to have an army fighting back, especially not an army full of intergalactic beasts, some of which were fifty times their size. But the GeoLapse continued running through the halls, beating and thrashing anything that came in their paths.

Elbina was being chased by a GeoLapse holding a grenade in his hand. She wished that she could run as quickly as Ann Lou. The GeoLapse threw the grenade, but the Rhothgan rolled himself down the hallway, shielded Elbina, blocked the grenade's path, and splattered the GeoLapse with one simple movement.

The Kilo-209 delegate luckily hadn't had enough cakes at the Universal Union dinner, and it began shovelling other GeoLapse into its mouth. Other Universal Union delegates were daintier with their attacks, including the photon of Vignet who buzzed into some of the GeoLapse's eyes, distracting their visual path for a few seconds, and the math genius of Casper, who sat in silence in the corner trying to calculate the approximate length of time the battle would last.

Elbina continued to run around the halls of the White House attempting to keep the GeoLapse from entering the ERA headquarters or Hayden's room. She even managed to nab a grenade off a GeoLapse who had just been taken down by a joint effort of the delegates of Minag and Pangica. She decided to shift to a defensive strategy and patrol the hallway leading to Hayden's room to keep him safe. Upon turning the corner into the hallway, she saw several GeoLapse headed in her direction. She turned to run back but realised that she was now cornered by two more GeoLapse running toward her from the opposite direction. She was just in front of Hayden's door, which completely gave away his hiding place. Elbina knelt down to brace herself, then pulled the pin out of the grenade. The grenade exploded in her hands, yet she wasn't dead. She felt no pain and wasn't maimed. The explosion hadn't even startled her. She looked up and saw dead GeoLapse lying all around her.

Elbina jumped up, her heart racing. She turned and reached for the handle on Hayden's door. Instead of interfacing with the now bloodied metal handle, her hand went straight through the door, as if she were a ghost. Elbina nearly fell through the door and was staring straight at Hayden, who was hiding under his desk. She knew at once that he didn't sense her presence at all. She understood now why the ERA had been so nervous upon hearing that Knitsy had died within the Time Belt and why Luna had been so upset when they said goodbye at Dikson.

But Hayden was safe, and that's all that mattered. She ventured down to the lower floors of the White House to see how the battle was evolving. The Universal Union had massacred the biggest GeoLapse army with ease. She even went to the ERA cameras to check on the other locations. All the battalions had defeated the GeoLapse.

Henrietta's plan was a success.

ANOTHER STORYTELLING CEREMONY

T he Cipton crowd boomed in whooping cheers as Avaira finished her story. The baby Cipton that was seated in the hour-
glass-shaped seat bounced up and down with excitement,
emitting small suction-cup noises.

"What an incredible story, Avaira!" announced Lucy from atop the
Main Circle. "Did everyone enjoy 'How the McHubbard Family Saved
the Universe'?"

The crowd erupted in shouts of glee. Suction-cup noises filled the
storytelling ceremony area.

"Where did this story come from again, Avaira?" Lucy asked.

"It is said to be a lost story from plaaanet Earth," croaked Avaira.

"But I don't understand!" squealed the baby Cipton. "Where are the
McHubbards now?"

All the Ciptons fell silent, eager to hear the answer.

Avaira cleared her throat. "It is saaaid that the McHubbard family met the same fate as our dear Connie and Rodney from our planet's faaavourite story, 'The Taaale of How Cipto Lost Its Liiight.'"

The crowd considered this for a moment, murmuring amongst one another and hoping for a further explanation.

Avaira continued. "Like Rodney, the matriarch of the McHubbard family vaaanished within the grips of the Tiiime Belt. To be lost in the Time Belt erases any trace of further exiiistence once one passes back through the Time Belt in reveeerse. Without a Knitsy, younger generations of McHubbards simply would not exiiist. When the remaining members of the family retuuurned to Earth, they slooowly disappeared, becoming looost in tiiime."

"How is the Earth now?" continued the baby Cipton, stretching forward as far as possible from its seat.

"Starting the moooment the murderers were destroyed and the scientists could focus on the environmental affairs of their planet, the Earth was slooowly rehabilitated to its priiime. Earth today shelters a growing population of huuumans, graaassy lands, abundant fresh water, a plethora of aaanimals, and breathable air for the humans to surviiive and thriiive in the outside world," explained Avaira.

"Are the McHubbards still alive?" squeaked the baby Cipton.

"Heeere's what I belieeeve," croaked Avaira. "I believe that those lost in time still exist in a diiifferent land. The ooonly thing we know for certain is that whereeever the McHubbard family now exists, they are lost in time together as a faaamily. They just need to figure out how to escape the cluuutches of the Time Belt."

ACKNOWLEDGEMENTS

The non-British readers might notice that the spellings of some words are a bit wonky and I wanted to point out that I used the British spelling convention to not only give myself some practice while I still live in the U.K., but to also put myself fully in the McHubbard family's shoes as they conversed with one another.

I would first like to thank the girls in my junior year AP English Language and Composition class at Nardin Academy for laughing along as I recited my assignment for the "Tuesday Morning Monologue". I had written the monologue from the perspective of a dog, and it was the first time I realised that people could actually enjoy my writing.

Thank you to the team at DartFrog Books for taking me on and answering my every question, especially Gordon and Suanne for managing me, Mark for this wicked cover design, Amy for sharing incredible writing tips with me and for her meticulous editing, Andrew for the fantastically thorough final proofread, Evan for getting me set up with a beautiful website, and Simona for putting it all together.

A gargantuan thank you goes out to my incredibly talented and artistic cousin Claire, who so diligently drew every chapter illustration to perfection and gave the story a true visual component. She did this while also being a full-time high school student and I couldn't be more excited to have her on this project with me.

Thanks to my biggest motivator, my mom, who not only read the beginning drafts multiple times but took a picture of every punctuation error she could find and texted them to me, predominantly because she couldn't figure out how to comment on a document. It made me laugh every time. I am overwhelmed by your support for everything I do, and I am certain that this project would have never come to fruition without you.

A massive thank you goes out to my friends and family, especially those who were the first draft readers of the manuscript and were not afraid to tell me when something was truly awful, as well as those who inspired many of the characters in the book.

To my readers - thanks a million! I hope you enjoyed the first instalment of *The Jalopy Chronicles* and look forward to future (or past) adventures of the McHubbard family.

About the Author

C aeli Ennis crafted the story of the McHubbard Family in her flat in Southampton, England during the COVID-19 pandemic. She is originally from snowy Buffalo, New York, where she enjoys nothing more than spending the summertime at the cottage in Hanford Bay with her family and friends. Caeli sought to build characters with physical disabilities to prove to readers that anyone and everyone can help save the universe. She works as a development engineer and in her free time takes the train to new cities, jams on the cello and piano, and plays with every dog that trots by.

Printed in Great Britain
by Amazon

77369630R00182